the normals

the normals

a novel

David Gilbert

BLOOMSBURY

Published by Bloomsbury Publishing, New York and London
Distributed to the trade by Holtzbrinck Publishers

All papers used by Bloomsbury Publishing are natural, recyclable products made from wood grown in well-managed forests. The manufacturing processes conform to the environmental regulations of the country of origin.

Library of Congress Cataloging-in-Publication Data

Gilbert, David, 1967–
The normals : a novel / David Gilbert.
p. cm.
ISBN 1–58234–456–6 (hc)
1. Young men—Fiction. 2. Human experimentation in medicine—Fiction. 3. Collecting of accounts—Fiction. 4. Antipsychotic drugs—Fiction. I. Title.

PS3557.I3383N66 2004
813'.54—dc22
2004002499

First U.S. Edition 2004

1 3 5 7 9 10 8 6 4 2

Typeset by Hewer Text Ltd, Edinburgh
Printed in the United States of America by Quebecor World Fairfield

For Susan Leness Gilbert

His mind is engaged in a rapt contemplation
    Of the thought, of the thought, of the thought of his name:
        His ineffable effable
        Effanineffable
Deep and inscrutable singular Name.

                                     —T. S. Eliot

1

T HE THIN sentiment never changes. *Sally . . . I'm leaving . . . Billy.*
No real surprise. No drama. No heartbreak. After all, Sally is leaving
next week, for Cambridge no less, business school and the annoyingly
acronymed HBS. Billy is simply sneaking away, well, sooner. She'll likely
forgive the lack of ceremony and forwarding address and only bemoan the
loss of his packing ability. *So good-bye.* But his handwriting is driving him
nuts, wavering between print and cursive, drooling across the page and
compressing near the bottom as if penmanship has suffered a grand mal
seizure. Billy wants calligraphy, not this remedial scrawl. Out comes a new
sheet of paper. Then another. *Dear* seems wrong, too loopy, too formal.
Sorry looks askew. He switches pens. Felt. Ballpoint. Maybe a pencil. But
nothing helps. If only he had a fountain pen. Defeated, the various
attempts are surrendered in a neat little pile flagged by a Post-it—*I'm
so pitiful*—which is rewritten twice.

Ridiculous, Billy thinks.

But done.

A glance around the kitchen–living room–dining room–library–guest
room–media center, four hundred square feet of hyphenated space and
wasted time. Most of his belongings have already been bagged and tagged
and mailed yesterday to his parents in Ohio. The entire shipment stood
seven boxes tall, Frankenstein's monster as fashioned from cardboard. No
doubt it will be a surprise delivery. Years without visiting and suddenly
the beast comes crawling home in laundry form. *Hi Dad, how's Mom?*
Seven boxes, no note. The essential Billy Schine. The rest of the apartment,
furniture, dishes, TV, and stereo, belong to his girlfriend, Sally Hu, a
securities analyst from Brooklyn. Billy has known her since college, their

relationship evolving from casual acquaintances during junior year not abroad, to decent pals upon graduation, to neighbors in New York, to pretty good friends following a painful breakup (hers), to roommates after a rent hike, to what-should-we-do-for-dinner companions, to bored back-rub buddies, to one-night stand-ins, to habitual offenders, to a couple by romantic default. They've been fucking dutch for almost a year. In Sally's parlance, pleasure is a body-fluid exchange, intercourse a corporal merger, orgasms a pooled mutual fund. Head is always split fifty-fifty, sixty-nine the preferred delivery system. Assisted masturbation is the minimum investment. Kinky deviations, silly fantasies, supplementary devices are hedges against sexual inflation when love and marriage and children turn such commerce into safe thirty-year bonds. "It's like we're insider trading," she once told him, all too obsessed with her banking jargon.

"Please," Billy replied from between her legs.

"Like we're outsourcing sex."

"Okay, enough."

"Price-fixing penetration."

"I'm trying to eat pussy here, not rally the Asian markets."

"You pig."

This is how they often talked.

Or was.

Billy heads toward the window, checks the street for trench coats despite the heat. But the minglers below are just the normal Lower East Side crowd. Ragnar is nowhere to be seen. Truth be told, Billy has never actually seen Ragnar, though he has an idea of the man, if, perhaps, a tad clichéd: Ragnar the relentless pursuer, Billy the offender on the run, Javert and Jean Valjean without the catchy tunes. Billy enjoys this image and squints his eyes dramatically as if the window is a movie still. Glimpsing him from the street, you might wonder if he's an actor. He's attractive enough, as tall as most diminutive stars, and has a smile that could roil foreign lands into anti-American protest. But there's something about his complexion—no scars, no pockmarks, no moles, no pores, you'd swear—that resembles a forensic facial reconstruction where clay is molded around a skull in hopes of a re-creating a long-missing person. Under fluorescence he can appear frighteningly anonymous. Years of uncertainty have sculpted a deep rumple in his brow, lending him an expression often mistaken for sarcastic scorn, and when spied in conjunction with that already mentioned smile, can be suspected as profound bafflement. Without uttering a word, his lips can launch a thousand fists. Socially, he fights against this first impression—*I'm better than this, nicer, smarter, really*—and winces through introductions as if cramping. In flip moments of weakness, he'll blame astrology. Or the typecasting of astrology. Billy is a Cancer, a crab, a sign that insinuates not only a horrific disease but also a public louse. His birth seems to fall on the high and low of human suffering. No wonder Cancers are notoriously oversensitive. Maybe that's why Billy habitually stays home under the guise of sickness, treating sniffles as the flu, headaches as migraines. Some might consider this hypochondria, but far more *philo* is involved. Billy loves being sick, relishes the notion of rest and rehabilitation. Imagine a car accident and broken bones and months of recuperation, and if for a moment you're intrigued by the care and attention, the character arc of recovery, then you share something with Billy and chances are you've never been seriously injured or ill. Oh, but you could be brave. Yes, a survivor. Victims interviewed on television always seem thankful for their misery, telling misty-eyed reporters they have no regrets. None. *This is who I am, Barbara, Stone, Diane.* A higher purpose is often mentioned in the next artificially respired breath. Yes, a blessing. Billy envies their inspiration.

Awful, he knows.

He should be thankful for his health.

After all, health is all he has.

And health might save his life.

The phone rings its typical cardiac of fear and trepidation. Caller ID has no clue. Not Ragnar. Not Sally. Not the temp agency asking where the hell is he. So Billy answers, uneasily, expecting bad news, maybe from a pay phone in a hospital, his father stuttering on the other end.

"Hello."

"May-I-please-speak-to"—pause—"William A. Schine?"

The voice unfamiliar, Billy relaxes his grip. "Who's calling please?"

"Hargrove Anderson Medical."

"This is William Schine."

"Mr. Schine, I'm calling to remind you that your shuttle for the research center leaves today from the Port Authority at three-thirty."

"I know. I have all the information."

"Three-thirty sharp."

"Yeah, I know."

"You have no idea how many of our volunteers forget."

"Well I'll be there."

"Three-thirty. Port Authority."

"Got it."

"Just making sure."

"Thank you."

Billy hangs up. He has five hours to shower and pack, plenty of time.

He uses Sally's soaps and shampoos for the last time. As usual, voices mutter in the ruin between nozzle and drain, of his mother, his father calling for him—*Billy!*—or worse, the sound of an intruder jamming open the lock, of Ragnar kicking in the door. Billy has highly suggestible ears. Electric razors, airplane engines, air conditioners, all carry a ghostly charge. Twice he shuts off the water and pokes his head through the plastic shower curtain (a tacky ocean scene smelling of a first condom) and listens.

Nothing. Of course nothing. And the voices begin again.

He gets dressed. On goes the recently purchased disguise: acid-washed blue jeans; *Cats* T-shirt (feline eyes glowing from the nipple region, NOW AND FOREVER written on the back); I♥NY baseball cap; cheap mirrored sunglasses. Billy inspects himself through streaks of rubbed-away steam. Not bad. He could be a Times Square tourist composing postcards in his head. An old familiar fantasy, that he's a spy, bubbles up from the wellspring of memory when as a child he would sneak around his house and search for evidence, nothing specific, just random traces of something in the sleepless night, once planting a tape recorder under his parents' bed so he could catch their whispers after goodnight. (Doris: "Is he asleep yet?" Abe: "I don't know." Doris: "I think he's awake." Abe: "I really don't know.'') Plots soothed the boy. And as an adult he can still fall under this spell, especially when his shoes make a certain patter on the pavement and strangers offer him their glance for an extra beat—Billy will start feeling as if he's on a mission even if the mission is buying a loaf of bread. It's almost meditative, his version of yoga where he stretches into the person he wishes he were, all slick and sly. But the balance is tricky. The smallest miscue— pushing instead of pulling on doors, hailing an already taken taxi, pressing and pressing the elevator Close button—can throw him on his back.

With care, Billy makes the bed. Sally's numerous lace pillows are arranged in a conciliatory gesture, and then rearranged, as if bedding has a language in which an apology might be spelled. He folds his towel the way she likes and tissue-wipes the toilet rim clean. He relinquishes his disposable razors as well as his really good hairbrush, hoping they might be considered a gift instead of a few forgotten things.

11:16 A.M. Little more than four hours left. Still loads of time.

Out from under the bed comes the hard-shell suitcase, bright red. Billy clicks open its satisfying, semiprofessional latches and puts in the remainder of his clothes: boxers not briefs, khakis and blue jeans, pocket tees and button-front shirts in any color but black, a sartorial existence that has stayed the same since college despite his near-constant lament for a new style. All he needs now is a book. He scans the shelves for the right book, the perfect book, the book he would want if he were stranded on a desert island. But which book is the right book? Which book represents him? Which author? Which cover should ride the front of his nose, the standard bearer to the taste of William A. Schine? Stanley Elkin? Robert Musil? Nathaneal West? Kafka? Virgil in the original? Horace? Too pretentious? Too hip? Too obscure? Too sensitive? Thick or thin, *Magic Mountain* or *Death in Venice*? Just one book, that's his decree. Billy, being a big reader—wait, that's not true. Billy loves books more than he loves reading, loves the physicality of books, the effort contained within books, all that potential trapped inside. The collected Philip Larkin or the selected Emily Dickinson? Maybe Nabokov? He buys cheap secondhand paperbacks almost every day, knowing full well they'll remain forever in progress, receipt slips marking the page where attention wandered toward

5

the television or a magazine or a nap. (*Moby-Dick* is by far his favorite unfinished book, *Don Quixote* a close second.) He's the master of the first line, the first paragraph, maybe the first chapter, then focus fades and the book migrates from couch to bed to couch again to under the coffee table to the corner of the room and the tower of other unread books capped every few days by another book, the tower growing higher and higher, leaning, until finally this Babel is disassembled and stuffed into the already overstuffed bookshelf, a mosaic of fraudulent desire.

Sally once asked him why he bought more books when so many went unread.

"But I want to read them," he told her.

"Then read," she said.

"I will, at some point," he said, more to himself than her.

"You already have enough books to last a lifetime," she said.

"Point taken, okay." And for the rest of the day Billy sulked, a conversation about clutter turning into an unintended death sentence.

On the third shelf he spots and pulls down *The Oxford Dictionary of Quotations,* fourth paperback edition. Nice and hefty, the book hasn't been touched since college days, when its genius on demand was used to pad many a paper (Byron in the epigraph, Shelley in the epilogue, bullshit in between). A handy key word index allows instant recall of the world's greatest words, a best of language, from Abelard to Zola. This is the soul of literature, Billy thinks, figuring whatever he needs will be in this book— as Keats said, "Give me books, fruit, French wine and fine weather and a little music out of doors, played by somebody I do not know." Billy smiles. He really should read more Keats. He tosses the dictionary into the suitcase, the book resting up high on a mound of clothes, too high for the latches to snap without the groaning pressure of an ass.

Now he should go.

The apartment is given a final once-over. Unarticulated boxes cramp the floor like a bivouac for the at-home homeless. This weekend he and Sally were to tackle the majority of the packing. She won't be pleased, especially about these abandoned books. But the coffeepot has been cleaned, and the cereal bowl has been washed, dried, and restacked, and the *New York Times* has been folded so that her hands might feel like the first that have touched this day, Friday, August 20, 1999.

The note on the coffee table shouts ten recriminations against a shoddy existence.

Jerk, asshole, how can you leave like this?

Billy slips back on the sunglasses, the I♥NY baseball cap.

He closes the front door and double locks. As usual, the stairs seem near collapse. In the vestibule he opens the mailbox—*S. Hu*—and nestles the keys inside. His name was never needed here. Inside for the most part are her postcards, her letters, her magazines and catalogs, her attention on all the bills, on the lease, on the security intercom.

B. Schine is nowhere to be seen.

2

T H E *C A T S* T-shirt might've been a mistake in this weather. The black color absorbs the already overburdened air, the never-before-washed fabric itchy on the skin, the whole touristy intent turning into a glib hair shirt woven with humidity. The yellow titty eyes weep with the beginnings of sweat.

He must look absurd. Like one of those hipsters who wear irony on their sleeve. Hopefully his deodorant will hold.

The subway is eight blocks away. There's still no sign of a potential Ragnar hiding among the Judy Garlands and Mickey Rooneys of the Lower East Side, a locale where everybody under thirty puts on a show. The crucible for the melting pot has been covered with a dross in the arts. Echoes of a better life, of opportunity, have been refined into blatant ambition for fame, as second- and third-generation Americans bankroll their sons and daughters who return to these tenements and pursue their dreams fresh from college. They're the nouveau poor—if not actors, artists, writers, musicians, filmmakers, then obsessed with actors, artists, writers, musicians, filmmakers. They applaud art with a series of self-reflective sighs.

Billy is glad to be leaving.

Why did he ever arrive?

Maybe because his mother and father have roots here, a nineteenth-century famine and a twentieth-century pogrom bringing their respective families through Beekman pier and into this neighborhood. But today's Ludlow Street holds saloons with velvet ropes, and the synagogue, the oldest in the city, has been converted into a private party space where cantors have a techno beat. Mirages from earlier times—bakeries and butchers mostly—float between handbag boutiques and restaurants. Apartments in old settlement houses now sell for half a million dollars, their doorways bearing holes instead of mezuzahs. Long forgotten are the Moskowitzes and the Smiths of the Fourth Ward. Tammany Hall has been renovated into a megastore.

On Delancey, on Rivington, on Stanton, Billy pictures himself in the crosshairs as Ragnar trains his scope on the levanter Schine, right in the cheesy pictographic ♥ of his cap. Billy is ready for the bullet, definitely hollow-tipped. Each step seems maintained by a metronome of trigger squeeze and exploding brain—*Boom!-Splat! Boom!-Splat! Boom!-Splat!*—a dirge from a one-man marching band. Before finding purchase, the laser sight will ideally cross his vision and give him the clarity reserved for the soon-to-be fucked. The *Oh,* ———— moment. Then slug will slam into skull, rip through memory and function, and leave behind only tissue. A champagne celebration of blood will geyser into the air. *You're dead!* Eternal darkness, his only concept of the afterlife, will close in around him, like the bath emptying while Billy stays sprawled in the tub, and slowly nothingness will tingle every pore until finally he can breathe. But nothing happens, over and over again, nothing—wait—nope, nothing, which leaves Billy with the weird inverse of relief.

He exhales noisily (never sighing, no way, not for him). You could say Billy suffers from survivor guilt along with pre-traumatic strees coupled with the Stockholm syndrome where this city acts as his captor. Seasonal affective disorder might be an issue as well. Billy hates the summer—fall, winter, spring, fine, but summer, sorry, summer sucks. Summer is for people with no imagination who think deep tans can make all the difference in the world.

You could also say Billy suffers from an unhealthy sense of drama.

You see, he owes some money, sixty thousand dollars to be exact. Nothing like gambling or drugs or a double cross gone wrong. His problems are far from dark and brooding, almost the opposite, in fact: student loans. Billy is in the hole for a Harvard education (minus the dubious praise of a partial scholarship). For three years after graduation he was diligent. He wrote thirty-six checks, smallish sums, but the consistency was appreciated and the path ahead was clear. Soon he would be nearing his full earning potential, the promise of his future collateral enough. But around the time he learned that his mother was sick, Billy missed a month. Missed another month. Then another. If he was a morning late on the due date he might as well have been a month late, the postage launch window becoming as tight as a rendezvous in space. He'd claim forgetfulness—*Oops, slipped my mind again*—but like many world-class procrastinators, Billy has a great memory. Almost every hour—*Shit!*—a flash of willful disregard squeezed his diaphragm, a bit of physiology he mistook for his heart, and he'd mutter to himself, *I really should pay.* Not paying was more of a bother. But Billy continued forgetting. What would happen? he wondered. What were the consequences? Debtors prison? Would anybody even care?

First came the letters, faux personalized, with their feeble threat of a poor credit rating. "You'll never be able to secure a home mortgage." *Aw shucks,* Billy thought. These notices always seemed to arrive in the mail with offers from Visa or American Express or Discover, like Macbeth's witches promising him the kingdom. Soon enough, phone calls followed these letters. The representatives on the other side were from financial support services based in the Dakotas, in Nebraska, these teledunners crossing time zones and catching the East Coast during its dinner hour (Billy once temped for accounts unpaid).

"Ah, Mr. Schine," they'd start, "I'm calling on behalf of—"

Billy would interrupt with, "Excuse me, I'm having dinner."

"Ah, this is not a solicitation, sir."

"I don't care, my food is getting cold. Have the decency to call during normal business hours. This is my private time."

"But—"

"Have some shame," Billy would tell them half-naked on the couch, TV muted.

And the nice folks from Bismarck or Salem always did.

This back-and-forth went on for two years.

But in July a different variety of letter appeared. Typewritten on an old manual typewriter, the words carried an intimate hunt-and-peck quality. Wite-Out had been used. *Wite-Out!* Billy could practically hear the slow slap of the keys, the curse on a typo, the twist of the crusted cap, the delicate strokes of liquid paper and the blowing dry of the wet pearl. There were twelve corrections in all, including an entire sentence swept under in what seemed a frightening whisper of style and frugality.

Dear Mr. Schine,

For your information Ragnar & Sons has been contracted by your lending institution to help collect on your delinquent obligation toward Nellie Mae, which our records show as a chronic nonremittal. Ragnar & Sons specializes in the serial evader and we pride ourselves in creating the necessary environment for repayment. As a legitimate organization, we have three years of experience in the restitution field and over thirty years of practical training. Our track record is excellent. Our word is to be taken seriously. If you care for any references, we can dig some up. From now on Ragnar & Sons will be handling your account for the duration of the agreed-upon terms signed and dated July 11, 1989. Unlike many large institutions, Ragnar & Sons can provide close personal attention for our clients, as such, we demand respect, Mr. Schine, in the form of installments, a minimum five hundred dollars a month until full amortization, beginning this August. Please be prompt so we can be ensured of your new era of fiscal responsibility. Ragnar & Sons will do all we can to facilitate a productive relationship. We're a hands-on, old-fashioned, proactive company. You should know, Mr. Schine, we run a sensible operation, our dun well within SOP and in accordance with the bylaws of the FRS. We highly recommend you employ your expensive education before you slip behind any further. Satisfy us with a reply in no less than three weeks using the enclosed envelope.

Assuredly,
Ragnar & Sons

The return address was somewhere in Queens—Billy reckoned the professional restitution trade commuted from the outer boroughs. But within this threat was an element of care. The stationery was rich in rag, the letterhead engraved. No wonder Wite-Out had been used. Billy placed

11

the paper against a lampshade and saw the X-ray of broken words, in particular, the fractured sentence: "Understand, Mr. Schine, you fuck, we will hurt you, we will Merrill Lynch you to the highest tree in Central Park if you're even a day late on delivery." Hmm. Their legal department must've recommended softer language. *How about saying we're a sensible operation.* Or perhaps this was the primary message, the subliminal advertising, the tits in ice cubes, the pricks in ultraslim cigarettes. Either way, Billy was impressed.

He filed the letter in a folder marked Fucked.

And on the first day of August the phone call came.

"May I speak with William Schine?" The voice was local and unsettingly calm.

"May I ask who's calling?" Billy asked.

"No, actually, you may not."

"No?"

"That's right, I'm not going to tell you, I refuse."

"Well—"

"Until I know whom I'm speaking with." The proper use of the interrogative was unsettling, like a grammarian diagramming your last words.

Billy sat there, frozen. He was going to lie about his name, but his mouth only thawed with the truth. "Uhm, this is him," he said. "Or is it 'he'?"

"Well, Mr. Schine, this is your account rep from Ragnar & Sons."

"I'm having dinner right now. Can I call you back?"

"I don't know, can you? I'm having my doubts."

"Mr. Ragnar, my food—"

"I'm not Ragnar. Get that straight. Lucky for you I share none of his blood."

"I'm in the middle of eating and it's rude—"

"You want rude, Mr. Schine? I sent you a letter that went without reply. Now that is rude and not the best way to start a relationship. Ragnar & Sons expects common courtesy in these matters."

"Or what?" Billy said. "You'll repossess my education?"

12

"You're sounding rude again," the voice replied without pique. "But you do raise the fundamental dilemma of this line of work, and that is the lack of actual property to repossess. What do we collect on, your transcript, your degree? Not like a car or a house. Nothing concrete. This is where Ragnar & Sons has truly revolutionized the college loan collection industry. If our hand is forced, we will go after the repository of all that education. Guaranteed. Your sponge has soaked up someone else's money. If that money isn't forthcoming, then Ragnar & Sons will squeeze it dry."

"Oh please," Billy said, knowing bluster.

"We call it a King Tut."

"A King Tut?"

"We break your nose and remove your brain through the nasal cavity."

Billy oohed false fear.

"It's an Egyptian embalming technique," this man from Ragnar continued. "When done correctly, the face is perfectly preserved. The old man is a sucker for open caskets."

"What a softy," Billy said.

"You think I'm kidding."

"Honestly," Billy told him, "I have no idea. It works either way in my book."

"Just pay us the money, okay. Our terms are reasonable, ridiculously reasonable, if you ask me, but now we're a ridiculously reasonable organization. But no matter what, unrequited earnest is a punishable offense. And yes, your brain is on the table."

"Your letter was great, by the way," Billy said.

"My letter?"

" 'Unrequited earnest' reminded me of it."

"You liked my letter?"

"Very much."

The voice on the phone worked a small bit of enthusiasm, like a toothpick. "That was my first written notice of nonremittal. I didn't really know what I was doing, I just sort of winged it."

"Well, it was a home run," Billy said.

"I thought maybe I went—Mr. Schine, please, let's get back to your business."

"But my business is so boring."

"Well, your business is my business now."

"But I have no business doing business with you guys."

"Is this how you always talk? Because you should really think about getting serious, Mr. Schine. You're in a serious situation. We'll get our money. We will be satisfied one way or another."

"Trust me, I'm not very satisfying."

"Shut up and listen," Mr. Ragnar man shot back. "You owe us money. Period. How you get this money, by borrowing it, kiting it, scamming it, conning it, using credit cards and mirrors, I don't care as long as you get us our monthly due. Try Wall Street. The Internet. You should be a millionaire by now. I mean you have to be a real asshole to be struggling in this economy, especially with Harvard in your sail. It's a lousy six grand a year. So get us our money."

"And if I don't?"

"You will."

"But if I don't?"

"How are your parents doing?" he asked with sleepy care. "They all right? I know Alzheimer's can be rough on a family. I sent your mother a bouquet of flowers on your behalf. Give the Whispering Pines Assisted Living Center a call and see."

"You'd go after my parents?" A curve of outrage pricked Billy's throat, like a barbless hook easily removed, quickly forgotten, his filial thoughts catch and release in a pond full of sucker trout. "That's nice. Rough up my already battered folks."

The man from Ragnar retreated. "All I'm saying is that I know you, know your whereabouts, your Asian skirt girlfriend, your possible escape routes. With computers it's virtually impossible to disappear."

Billy was unable to stop himself. "That's a pun," he said.

"You're an ass," the man muttered.

"You've got that right."

"I'm giving you two weeks and then bang, I'm in your near future and

I'll put your nose to the grindstone and cut your teeth on payment schedules and, what's that other expression, oh yeah, pop your fucking kneecap with a hammer and screwdriver. Have a swell day."

On that, the line went dead.

For the next few days Billy considered getting a real job, a job with stock options and health insurance, a job with a sense of promotion. This whole temp thing was becoming a bit silly anyway. Since graduation, he's been a migrant keystroker for People Person Services—"We judge our temps by your needs"—which shills Billy as an information processor—in other words, he can read and touch type. For fifteen dollars an hour he samples potential careers without making a series of misguided commitments, without feeling stuck because he's climbed the first crappy rung and suddenly this job is his only qualification. *This is who I am.* But like many experiments where the investigator is also the subject (think of Spallanzani studying digestion by tying string around his food, or van Leeuwenhoek exploiting the early microscope by focusing on his own ejaculate), there's a danger of self-absorption where experience becomes an excuse for indulgence. Of late, Billy has grown all too fascinated by his own lack of purpose.

But now he has a nemesis. An enemy. A villain in the flesh.

Maybe that makes Billy a hero.

He pictures Ragnar as a family man from Flushing, his kids calling him Daddy, his wife kissing him on the cheek as he climbs into his car for another pressure-filled day. There he is, driving into the city by way of the Midtown Tunnel, riding above the necropolis of Queens, seeing all those cemeteries crowded with the borrowers of life, the tombstones reflecting the skyline in a lifeless gray lake. Of course the traffic for the tollbooths will frustrate him—*C'mon! C'mon!*—but he'll be pleased with the order and the required charge, the specific relationship between coin and passage when the gate salutes compensation.

You may proceed, good American.

But where is Ragnar now?

Billy looks around the street. A chase might be nice.

His suitcase is heavy and is shifted from hand to hand every few

15

minutes, strain's short-term memory loss growing shorter with each swing. Billy pauses near the entrance for the F train, puts the suitcase down. He imagines a flower arrangement wilting by his mother's bedside, daisies probably, the love-me, love-me-not petals littering the table. *XXOO, Billy.* So sweet, the nurses might say, while Abe asks, "Why now?" A drop of water plinks the visor of Billy's baseball cap. Spit from a bitterly bored teenager? No, an air conditioner from the building above. Plink, plink, plink. Instead of condensation, Billy conjures up sweat from a hesitant jumper who stares down and wonders if the fall will finish him, if things are really so bad. Walking the streets of Manhattan, Billy is often afflicted with a peculiar form of vertigo: he fears a body landing on him and killing him, suicide as inadvertent murder. The combination of tall buildings and depression seems as deadly as booze and pills. The sidewalks, he thinks, should be a bloody mess.

Down into the subway he goes.

For most people, Ragnar & Sons would be enough to dispel any flip doomsdaying about an early death—the random crime, the failure of machines, the heart attack in a bacon cheeseburger with fries—and prove the case that, yes, you want more time, just a bit more, please, in the prayers you say and the sins you leverage in the hopes of another day. But Billy is sick and tired of the same old day. He wants something more, even if that something might be worse.

3

T HROUGH A CONFUSED series of trains, Billy transfers himself below Manhattan, jumping in and out of sliding doors and sprinting through stations and slipping from downtown express to uptown local to crosstown shuttle until he's positive—or fairly positive—all traces of Ragnar, even if illusory, have been lost. Wall Street. Morningside Heights. City Hall. Astor Place. Hunter College. On platforms, as the third rail snaps and headlights prick the tunnel, the gore on the track takes on a creepy quality—a sock, a pacifier, mysterious green puddles—and once inside trains, under the commercial strip of molding, where Dr. Z promises to eliminate your acne, and Ramon and Dolores learn the hard cartoon truth about AIDS, and Tide calls attention to the bacteria on the pole you're gripping, Billy can hardly believe that anyone is healthy, let alone himself.

But he's FDA approved.

On paper at least.

Then again he's always tested well.

Two weeks ago, while seated in the waiting room of the HAM recruitment office, Billy completed the medical history form without incident. *No* to allergies, drug or otherwise, though he's never been stung by a bee, so who knows. *No* to current medications. *No* to hospital admissions. *No* to operations. Not even a tonsillectomy or an appendectomy in his past. *No* to fractures. Nary a sprain or dislocation, a tear or rupture. On headaches and shortness of breath, chest pain, fainting, Billy hesitated before deciding he's free of these afflictions unless he's been exercising inadvertently. He pitied those who checked *Yes* on tarry stool, the same with incontinence and hemorrhoids and bowel irregularity. *No*, thank you. Along the margin of sexual dysfunction he almost wrote *Define*. Asthma brought back memories of friends with those wonderful inhalers and his lame imitation with a Pez dispenser. Measles and mumps, diphtheria and rubella, were all but rumors growing up, some poor kid down the block taking the brunt of those infections, the class absentee with lice and impetigo and conjunctivitis. Chicken pox? *No*, not even after his mother forced him into the company of his next-door neighbor—a lovely girl with chicken pox—for help in corrupting the flesh. But the virus was never consummated. "Sooner would be so much better," his mother informed him. "Because later will be so much worse." Nervousness and moodiness and depression were rounded down to *No* with a rationalization on the human condition. Besides, a *Yes* was followed by a *Please explain* and an explanation would sound so pathetic. *Sometimes I get sad for no reason.* There was a brief debate on memory loss and his early years, the amnesia between zero and five, the long blackouts between six and ten, the various gaps since then. Childhood seems to him like a series of small head traumas. Perhaps one day he'll recover a vital chunk, and the false screen will lift, and molestation or abuse or an awful accident will be revealed, some smoking gun that murdered hope and replaced it with puppet scorn. But after all these years, nothing has surfaced, and Billy is left with hollow blame. But he assumed this question addressed recent memory loss so he replied accordingly and moved on. Polio and scarlet fever and tuberculosis caught him by surprise—oldies but goodies—and he was curious whether smallpox or bubonic plague or leprosy would follow, but medical history ended with *Other*.

Billy marked his only *Yes*.

He thought he might have *Other*.

Other was a distinct possibility.

The next section of the form—Habits—he fared just as well.

Smoking? *No*, never smoked. But he wishes he smoked, chain-smoked, had brand loyalty, a collection of ashtrays, could unwrap the cellophane and pinch away the nicotine heat shield and tweeze away the first victim, could light a match with style, better yet, a Zippo, could blow smoke rings, could bum butts and dispense butts in the warm karma of cigarettes, could bitch about no smoking in the office, could escape outside and join the instant brethren on the streets, could tamp, flick, stomp filters, could quit and fail and quit again.

Too bad Billy always coughs and tears up and becomes terribly dizzy.

Drinking? *Occasionally,* but he drinks mostly beer and wine, a few glasses a week with a sporadic bender thrown in every month. But he's expected more from his drinking self, whiskeys and martinis ordered wet and dry, shots, doubles, straight up and clean, the knowledge of the perfect Bloody Mary, maybe even a problem drinker, a nasty drunk, an alcoholic pouring all his promise down a glass, hitting rock bottom, needing help, recovering with Betty Ford, telling stories about his boozy self, the memoir of mash, cataloging the liters of this, the pints of that, and the quarts in between, harking back onto old times as he orders a soft drink with rue and maybe a twist of gin-soaked lime.

Too bad Billy hates hard liquor and hangovers can crush him for a week.

Controlled substances? *Long ago,* experimented in college, marijuana, cocaine, mushrooms, but never near an addiction, and upon graduation forgot those things like he forgot so many a required course (LSD on par with Chaucer: enjoyable, perhaps even important, but once was enough). Still, he's fascinated by the downfall of drugs, the obsessive cutting of lines on a mirror, the ravings in a nightclub, the dealers and various seedy characters in your circle, the scoring of a bag, the jones, the raising of stakes, speedballs and scag, the argot of junkies, holing up and cooking spoons and withering away until friends stage an intervention and enroll you in a treatment program where you withdraw with your demons and are reborn, and invariably a few months later you OD and are found in your apartment with a syringe exclaiming the end of your sorry life.

Too bad whenever the rare joint is passed his way Billy is reminded— *Ah, shit*—the second after inhaling why he should stay away from the stuff.

The next section—Family History—consisted of matching the disease with the appropriate blood relative. Billy has no siblings. He is an only child (in his youth misheard as *lonely*). Grandparents on either side are total mysteries, never met, never even seen in photographs, rarely discussed except as traditional blocking characters against his parents' true love.

Statistically speaking, they're probably dead, either from heart disease or cancer, the exact cause as obscure as the whereabouts of their graves. Uncles, aunts, cousins are also unknowns, part of the New York life Abe and Doris fled, a landscape they hang in a *musée imaginaire* of high romantic art.

All Billy has are his parents.

He checked *Mental Illness* for the both of them.

Then he signed on the dotted line confirming the above information was true.

The form completed, the interview followed. "Right off the bat," the HAM recruiter asked him, "how'd you learn about our clinical pharmacological unit? Or CPU, as we say in the trade." The woman leaned into the letters with the instinctive semaphore of a cheerleader. She would've been the cornerstone of the pyramid, Billy thought, the catapult for the more delicate girls. Her name was Florence Baker-Blau and she frightened him.

"On the radio," he answered.

Which was true. He had been lazing in bed, on his third snooze bar and second Ragnar regret, when a voice screamed in his ear: "Hargrove Anderson Medical is looking for volunteers to participate in a Phase I drug study. No disease or disorder necessary. No previous experience required. No skills needed. No labor involved. Room and board is free, and you will be paid a generous stipend. If you're interested, please call 1–800 HAM STUDY. You must be over eighteen years of age and in good physical health. That's 1–800 HAM STUDY. Earn money while benefiting medical research. Our quest is to bring people better treatments and greater options. Join us. That's 1–800 HAM STUDY. A job you can be proud of. 1–800 HAM STUDY. Call now for more information." For the rest of the day the advertisement looped in Billy's head like an infectious chorus. *HAM STUDY. HAM STUDY. HAM STUDY.* By late afternoon he weakened and called and made an appointment with a secretary. "No food or coffee after midnight, just water," she told him. And here he was, tired and hungry, hoping he might resemble a decent male specimen.

20

Florence, Ms. Baker-Blau (Billy uncertain of their social standing) beamed. "The radio, that's great," she said. "Really great. Super. Which station?"

"Uhm, ninety-two point three, I think, FM."

"Oh, K-ROCK."

Billy had hoped to avoid those embarrassing call letters.

"Well, that makes my day and it's only nine o'clock." She wrote a note on her clipboard, her cursive like soap bubbles blown from a pen. "Hargrove Anderson usually focuses their recruiting dollars in the classifieds of alternative weeklies and college newspapers and neighborhood giveaways. It's cheaper, of course, but I pushed hard for moving into the radio market, in particular, the contemporary rock, hip-hop, speed metal, alternative types of format. Young people are really suited for this line of work. The twenty-somethings"—she raised her hands in surrender—"guilty as charged. So I'm pleased."

Her office was small and windowless. Billy thought he recognized the faint odor of toner and the soul-crushing spirit of a former copier room where ambition is murdered by a thousand cuts of light. As Ms. Baker-Blau talked, Billy tried to look interested, nodding and smiling, flexing his face into nonverbal interjections, but his chair, this fucking chair, a high-tech Swedish contraption designed to enforce comfort, reacted to his every gesture with either a swivel or a recline. It was like a bronco trained in dressage. Just breathing threatened his balance. And there was Florence, Ms. Baker-Blau, this Amazon well within accidental footsy range. A sneeze could be grounds for sexual harassment. Propped on her desk was a photo of Mr. Baker or Mr. Blau (who got top billing?) glaring at Billy as if ready for a fumble. And her computer screen saver, the dream life of software, had exotic fish swimming around an aquarium, the sound effects reminding him he had passed on his morning piss, knowing a urine sample was required and hoping he might wow them with his bladder command. Christ, Billy needed to go, which made him fidget, which spurred the chair, which threatened his professional relationship with the Baker-Blaus, which collectively provoked his sweat glands and slowly turned his shirt into a Rorschach of what could only be interpreted as a disturbed young man.

"I love K-ROCK," Billy said.

"Yeah, K-ROCK's great," Ms. Baker-Blau agreed. She was not unattractive, not unattractive at all. The teased blond hair and gold jewelry and athletic build were set against a wide nose and large hands and a lip-heavy smile. She was two turns from pretty, three turns from homely, a combination that cultivated excessive personality and enthusiastic fellatio. She had the mien of a Norse debutante who could swing a bludgeon with devastating pep. Leif Eriksson's trophy wife.

"So William—do you go by 'William'?" she asked

"Mostly 'Billy,'" he answered with his usual defeat: After college he had attempted the adult permutations—Bill and Will—but those versions of himself seemed tough and sturdy and entirely unbelievable. A Bill is comfortable in a foxhole; a Will is dependable and steadfast. Bill and Will are buddies. Bill would pounce on a grenade to save Will, and Will would give the most beautiful eulogy about brave, brave Bill. So how about William instead? No chance there. William personifies a massive checking account and a well-dressed manner and charitable donations in the thousands. William is a trustee; William earns respect. Now Liam is a pleasant graft, a nice word in the mouth, full of soul and depth and human appetite, but try implanting Liam onto Schine with a straight face. He might as well be Moisha McGahern or Shamus Glickstein, Paddy Hebe the limey shegetz from County Kibbutz. Multiplying his mother's Irish Catholic side by his father's German Jewish side is like multiplying by zero. In the end, Billy is the product of nothing. But at least he isn't a Willy.

"It means helmet," he told Florence Baker-Blau for no reason.

"Really."

"And yours means flowery. Florence. It's Latin for 'flowery.'"

"And I thought it was just a city in Italy."

"Well, that too."

"Flowery, I like that." She smiled, the desired effect. "Names are so fascinating. I mean, to name a child, what a responsibility." Her eyebrows were like well-plucked diacritical marks emphasizing the warmth and compassion of her baby blues, pupils spying the future of swollen bellies. "What a thing to do."

22

Billy agreed. Wholeheartedly. His bobbing head, if cleaved, would reveal a name-your-baby book cuddled in his parents' bookshelf, the pages marked with checks by *Robert, Tess, Emma, Charles,* the paper holding possible traces of Doris's fingers as she tested the names aloud while Abe checked the meanings for an appropriate message. Would *Gideon* have given Billy a different life? But there was *William,* circled extra thick. What prenatal enthusiasm in that pen. "I've always hated my name," he told the recruiter.

"I think most of us hate our names," she said.

"Oh." *Even you, Florence?*

"Your application says you went to Harvard."

"Yep."

"That's impressive."

"Not really. I majored in sociology and minored in classics. I had what you could call a passive-aggressive education." This was his stock response to Harvard, an old line he handed over as spontaneous wit, and though the joke was often well received, Billy could smell the staleness of the material.

She asked if he was an artist.

"Me? No. Not at all."

Ms. Baker-Blau appeared disappointed. "Because a lot of our more educated volunteers tend to be artistic types. You can earn good money and support your, well, your craft, I guess. People will sketch or write or do whatever they do while they're engaged in a study. A few have had success since. We also get graduate students who are doing their research while we're doing our research, which I think is a hoot."

Billy had no idea how to respond. Should he claim an ulterior motive, a dream he was financing, a project in the works instead of the unglamorous truth of temporary escape? He wanted to give her the right answer, but his right answers were always lies, so he just sat there and grinned.

"You're twenty-eight?" Ms. Baker-Blau asked.

"Yes, but recently," he said.

"And you're currently a temp worker?"

"Yes. Full time."

"Right right right." Ms. Baker-Blau shifted in her chair to signify the official beginning of the interview. "Billy, this is a prescreening interview, more informative than anything else. We'll go over your application and answer any questions you might have before your physical."

Billy shifted—more like jerked—to signify he was ready.

"Have you ever done anything like this before?"

"No. Never."

"Well, we do love our educated volunteers. They're always civil and mature and considerate. It's also much easier on the explanation process. A lot of difficult words are thrown around, technical words. For example, 'pharmacokinetics.' Hello! Pharmacokinetics anyone? You say 'pharmacokinetics,' 'pharmacodynamics,' 'pharmacogenetics,' and you see eyes glaze over and you know you've lost them."

Billy expressed, *Those ignorant fools,* nonverbally.

"You see, Phase I testing focuses primarily on the absorption, distribution, elimination, and metabolism of the substance in question. ADEM for short and easy. ADEM is our main concern in these first-in-man trials. It's all about safety. Efficacy comes later, in the Phase II, Phase III, Phase IV testing when we start using people actually afflicted by the disease or disorder under study, but during this early stage, we just want the ADEM on normal healthy individuals like yourself. Plus a detailed record of any adverse events."

"Adverse events?"

"Yes. Or AEs."

Adverse events. Those two words pulsed in Billy's head, a siren accompanied by a flashing crimson light. Adverse event. It seemed more suited to a meteor hurling toward earth. A tidal wave. A pestilence. A thousand natural disasters beyond one's control. An adverse event was a promotion into big-time catastrophe while Ragnar & Sons offered a smaller, more everyday phenomenon.

Ms. Baker-Blau assumed his pause carried a qualm. "Be confident," she told him. "We take extreme precautions."

"Oh, I'm sure you do."

"We have rigorous guidelines. Super rigorous. Before a NiCE—that's a New Chemical Entity—is given to our normal, healthy volunteers, it's gone through a slew of range-finding studies. We use nonhuman lab domesticators who receive doses much higher than the doses you'll receive. I mean, much higher. To-the-moon higher. So we already know the LD-fifty."

"LD-fifty?"

"Well, technically, that's the lethal dose in half of the NoHoLDs."

"Oh."

"Which sounds more dangerous than the truth of the matter."

"Doesn't sound unreasonable to me," Billy assured her.

But Ms. Baker-Blau kept on explaining. "You have to understand, Billy, these are absurd doses. HAH-hahs we call them. Hugely abnormal hits. But when we enter Phase I, we already know the gist of the drug, all the expected hazards, and the FDA has approved the protocol, and a local institutional review board has been convened to monitor the prudence. I can say without hesitation, without any hesitation whatsoever, none at all, your safety is our main consideration. You should know nobody has ever died as a direct result of Phase I testing. Never ever ever. Never directly." Ms. Baker-Blau, Florence, Flo, rested her buoyant head on her shoulder as if mourning even the possibility. "But are there risks involved?" The rhetorical question lingered before landing on the God's honest truth. "Yes. There are. No ands, ifs, or buts. Risk is part of the job. But without risk, without that entrepreneurial spirit, where would this country be?" Patriotism lifted her head. "These are experimental products, Billy, perhaps important discoveries with a real benefit to society. HAM invests hundreds of millions of dollars in developing these new products, and from the lab to your corner pharmacy, a product will go through years of investigation, years of trials, years of FDA bureaucracy, and after all those years, Billy, all those grueling years, the product more often than not will never get to market. The chances are so slim. Still, no matter the expense and the effort, you press on because you never know, you just never know. Pick a disease, a disorder, a defect, from cancer to the common cold, and HAM is there."

Billy told her to sign him up.

"On the molecular level. Biotech compounds. Genetic engineering."

"I'm in," he said.

But the woman was on a roll. "So are AEs worth the risk-to-benefit ratio? Absolutely. Otherwise we wouldn't continue with their development. Are they super dangerous? Not likely. Not if you're one hundred percent honest with us." She waved his medical history form like a pom-pom. "And you might think AEs must mean intensive care. No no no. They're generally small discomforts." Ms. Baker-Blau began listing them as though they were the sickly reindeer on Santa's sleigh. "There's asthenia, a fancy word for weakness, there's diarrhea, xerostomia, nausea, there's pyrexia, meaning fever, dyspepsia, i.e., upset tummy, urticaria, tachycardia, insomnolence and somnolence, hypopraxia, pharyngitis, diaphoresis, which just means excessive perspiration."

Billy squeegeed his brow. "I might already be a guinea pig."

Florence frowned the way a beauty queen protests world hunger.

"I mean because I'm sweating so much," he explained.

Ms. Baker-Blau lowered her eyes. "Billy, this is important, so listen. We consider our normals an essential part of the HAM team, and we treat them as such. A guinea pig, a human guinea pig, conveys the wrong message. Way too, quite frankly, Mengele."

"Mengele?" Billy said. The Angel of Death sounded like a cocktail party faux pas.

She nodded. "It does have that connotation." From her desk she pushed forward a brochure with the deference of an illuminated manuscript. "I want you to see this. We just got these in. Same people who do the Canyon Ranch Spa."

On the cover was a photograph of a large building with wings embracing a courtyard, the architectural style institutional pragmaticism, part dorm, part corporate headquarters. A sans serif U. There were no curves, no pitch to the roof, no roof really, only a maximum usage of space. The camera's exposure must have been minutes, for the sky had a tidal sheen and the building seemed smeared in medicinal jelly.

"This is the Animal Human Research Center," Florence told him. "What we call the AHRC." This woman certainly loved her acronyms.

"Very nice," Billy said.

She—"No!"—quickly corrected him. "It's the nicest. It's located in

26

upstate New York, near Albany, right on the Hudson. We provide a shuttle service to and from the center, absolutely free, which is rare in our business. Usually transportation is out of your own pocket. The shame is the picture doesn't do justice to the place. Imagine all around you acres of woods and shoreline, bird life galore, the most amazing light. The land was once owned by a Rockefeller."

"Oh."

"And HAM has created a state-of-the-art facility."

The brochure cleverly matched the building, designed like a glossy triptych with front panels opening upon the dollhouse interior of the AHRC. Inside was the typical room, with three beds and a color television and a semiprivate bathroom; the common room with board games and a big-screen TV and a video library; the cafeteria-style dining room; the kitchen with fruits and snacks, a steaming plate of spaghetti Bolognese, the chef a graduate from the nearby Culinary Institute of America; the lab with rows of microscopes; the technicians, the researchers, the nurses, care their middle name; the healthy normal volunteers watching a brilliant sunrise or sunset from a window; the inventory of famous drugs developed by Hargrove Anderson Medical.

Ms. Baker-Blau proudly told him that this center put other CPUs to shame. "Maybe other companies would consider you a guinea pig." Her fingers gave the term evil bunny-ear quotes. "Some of them have been known to use homeless drunks under the guise of charity. Disgusting. But Hargrove Anderson has respect for the work you do. We value our normals. We want our normals to have a good experience. We want return business. That's why we pay so well."

Billy asked about the stipend.

"Depends on the study. Anywhere from a hundred and fifty to two hundred and fifty dollars a day."

"The longer the better," he told her. "And the sooner the better."

"That's good to know because we have a two-week in-patient study we're still trying to fill. Back-to-school season kills us. It's a parallel design. One hundred seventy-five dollars a day."

"Sounds perfect," Billy said.

"You should know that the pay can bump up nicely if there's any minor unanticipated duress. MUDs they're called. Maybe an extra fifty dollars a day. Sometimes higher. And you should also know that there's a clause about improper behavior, controlled substances, drinking, smoking, being aggressive with the nurses or other volunteers, if that's the case, we'll send you packing without pay. Fines are served for lateness. And if you're having a particularly bad reaction to the drug, just you alone, we'll pull you from the study and figure in the difference. But we're very fair. Often we'll give you full value."

"How quickly would I get paid?"

"A check upon completion. But this isn't easy work. No no no." Florence shook her blond grindstone of a head. "This is tougher than it seems. You're up early. You're poked and prodded. Endurance is involved, maybe a different kind of endurance, but endurance nonetheless. All those particulars will be spelled out"—the phone rang and she finished her sentence on a lesser note—"further along in the process. Excuse me for a few."

Ms. Baker-Blau huddled for privacy. Billy was feeling better, though he regretted the whole guinea pig comment and cringed over flowery, and did he really say "Nice office" when he first walked in here? Sadly enough he was trying for a compliment, but his lips gave the sentence a sarcastic spin. Still, he was feeling better. The Swedish stallion of a chair had been broken. His bladder had passed the bursting point and like a marathoner had settled into the long haul. The fish in the screen saver aquarium seemed downright adorable, bumping noses with affection. Even Mr. Baker or Mr. Blau softened, his glare becoming soulful around the edges, as if he feared someday his wife would leave him and he was already begging her to stay.

Ms. Baker-Blau hung up the phone.

"Is that your husband?" Billy asked of the photo.

"Yeah. His first-year wedding anniversary present to me—you know, paper. I gave him Knicks playoff tickets, so expensive, you can't believe. Fourth row."

Billy said, "That's nice," with just the right tone, he thought.

"The frame's not even silver. Anyway." Ms. Baker-Blau clapped her hands and clicked her teeth. "Unless you have any more questions, we're all set for your physical."

"I'm good to go."

She led him down the hall, into examination room #2. The table inside was covered in what seemed to be butcher paper prepared for the choicest Billy Schine cuts. "Undress to your underwear," Ms. Baker-Blau said, her head tilting to the left, as if this request had kicked free a buttress. "Someone will be in shortly." With that, she said good-bye, Billy smiling and nodding until the door closed.

And that was the last he saw of her.

But today, the day of AHRC induction, the subway seems packed with Baker-Blau types who wear effort-filled outfits neither stylish nor hip, who read books bought in paperback carousels, who fold the newspaper to the sports or gossip section, people you might discount because maybe you've read better books or seen better movies, as you spot the person across the aisle thumbing the *New Yorker,* or better yet, the *New York Review of Books,* or who's halfway finished with a certain kind of novel, you wishing he or she would glance up so you could wink without winking and convey *I am with you, we are alike, trust me,* while the Baker-Blaus around you are those you simply humor, smiling and nodding, the mass populace who, once pitted against your own shallow sense of worth, become a nagging reminder of what you've become.

Billy finally surfaces in Grand Central. A recent restoration has rediscovered the stars in the vaulted ceiling, the aquamarine sky once again alive with constellations. The zodiac shines down on the polished brass and marble, on the upgraded stores and restaurants, on the oh-so-forties feel. Shoes tattoo their reflections as if soled in metal, and voices recirculate the air into a general hullabaloo. Evening rush hour starts early on an August Friday. Hundreds of commuters speed through the main terminal toward their summer portals where the sun has some meaning beyond sweat. Billy wonders how many have an undiagnosed disease, a genetic time bomb, a fast-spreading malignancy, a nearly blocked artery, a death certificate on the verge of being served? How many are feeling as good as they'll ever feel again? There are indisputable percentages and nasty statistics to consider, cold actuary tables sluiced for blood. (Billy once temped for an insurance firm.)

But Billy himself is 100 percent healthy. The team of HAM doctors and nurses weighed and measured him, adducted and abducted him, ausculated and palpated him, percussed and probed him, squeezed and fingered him, electrocardiographed him, blood and urine sampled him, and two days later he was notified of his peak physical condition. They offered him a fourteen-day in-patient Phase I study for an experimental atypical antipsychotic. It paid twenty-five hundred dollars and started in a week.

Interested?

Billy hits the street and heads west.

4

TIME TURNS into debt on the Avenue of the Americas.
It happens in lights, the wattage by no means impressive when compared with the candy-colored neon and the billboards of models, actors, athletes, musicians, celebrities. The buildings around Times Square could've been decorated by teenagers in desperate need of Ritalin. *Me, me, me,* they scream. But this sign is more of a whisper, a *psst* from a dark alley. *Hey you.* And peering down like the loan shark version of Big Ben is the national debt clock. Its dun races in the five trillions, its vig compounding more than ten grand a second, while another dun—Your Family Share— ticks in the forty thousand dollar range. The precise number is as fleeting as the precise nth on Billy's wristwatch (now being checked) but either way, in twenty-two minutes and God knows how many more millions, he'll be vamoosed. Billy gauges the worth of his upward stare. Maybe he does this self-consciously, pursing his lips and wiping his chin, performing worry, but the image seems made for him and carries the same sort of weight as love songs for the recently split or beer ads for the barely sober: brief morbid flashes where time and space converge on your sad story.

Hands down, he thinks, this would be the ideal locale for his death.

Billy searches faces for Ragnar.

Everybody is a potential assassin.

Ragnar?

All these pedestrians would become bystanders, the final player in the trinity of murder. "I was there! I saw it happen!" they'd tell reporters while behind them kids would wave and jump in the piñata burst of the live feed.

Billy tilts his chin back, offers up his throat for a switchblade.

But cell phones are the only weapons drawn. The electronic ring of famous symphonies, Beethoven in pockets and purses, in theaters and restaurants, drives Billy—no, drives everybody, even people with cell phones—nuts. It's like a telecommunicative form of self-loathing. And the denial, the cell phone denial, like cell phones are the bane of your on-the-move existence, like you have no choice, like your shit-eating grin is somehow sheepish. As fears of radiation and brain tumors creep in and more and more people use headsets, the lunatics are getting harder to spot. Someone yelling "motherfucker" could be talking to his broker.

Ragnar?

Unsatisfied, Billy checks back with the national debt.

All this thinking has cost the country another quarter million.

He should go while he's still early.

But the trip north requires some brainless reading material.

He stops in a cavelike kiosk where magazines peer from racks. The people on the covers are mostly beautiful unless politicians or murderers or unfortunates caught up in the day's events. Their faces mark the weeks and months, like a Gregorian calendar with a publicist, all the issues postdated as if milk has been mixed with ink. Change only happens to these people here, Billy thinks, while the rest of us just have the weather. And how often does his own calendar depend on Sally's subscriptions for a sense of where he is in the week: Monday, the *New Yorker;* Tuesday, *Newsweek;* Wednesday, the *Village Voice,* etc. Monthly glossies remind him he's another *Vogue* older. All these magazines are the visible version of the ever-sloughing layers of skin, dust mingling with insert slips.

Browsing the racks, Billy thinks he sees somebody he knows—yes, near the financial section, with *Fortune* in hand, Winston Feller, his first-year roommate from Harvard. Ever the teaser, small and quick, a champion high school wrestler, Winston, then known as Winnie, taunted football players until they chased him around the cafeteria or quad. Seven years later he seems uncomfortably wedged within his featherweight body, like a child athlete who has pumped muscle over hormones. He could be a late-blooming dwarf.

Billy glances away. Did Winnie spot him? Did Winnie have the same rush of recognition? Billy figures if Winnie says hi, then he'll say hi; otherwise, he'll pretend ignorance. Winnie lives in Westchester, with Charlotte, his gorgeous wife, pregnant and due in late December, near the big day, their own millennium bug—*Ha ha!*—in the oven. Billy knows this because Billy is a compulsive reader of class notes. With every issue of *Harvard Magazine,* he ticks up the century, from 1923 to 1999, and instinctively mocks those fools who bother writing in with their latest update, as if anybody cares about their new job or most recent accomplishment. In particular Billy eats up the crap of 1993, most of the people unfamiliar yet all of them successful, like Winnie here. What an asshole. Billy can picture him in his upscale suburban yard fooling his Labrador retriever with false tennis ball throws then coming inside and shadowboxing his wife's punching bag stomach.

Winnie must've recognized Billy. I mean Billy has hardly changed since college. Maybe it's the hat and dark glasses, which Billy now removes. Winnie steps up to the cashier. Billy edges toward the newspapers nearby. Funny how you'll humor an old acquaintance despite your low opinion, how you'll tap him or her on the shoulder with a *hey, remember me, please.* Winnie, now leaving, passes Billy as he holds the *New York Post,* the headline all but screaming CLASSMATE BUMPED INTO, PLEASANT IF INNOCUOUS WORDS EXCHANGED. But Winnie says nothing. He's gone.

Billy feels slighted, then—*oh, fuck him and his kind*—reconsiders.

Back outside, the national debt clock is given another glance, once again, overly dramatic, the way Billy tilts his head and grimaces, like his face is being projected, but how often do you find a symbol written across the sky. Here he is, on the vanguard of ruin, the point man for when this clock will stop and the billing period will end and everyone will have to pay an unforgiving sum. The great seal will break. Mass liquidation will flood the land. God will no longer favor our undertakings. Billy could turn this corner into a pulpit and sermonize on the conversion of flesh: "We are all collateral, all compounded by interest, all pursued by a higher lender. Remit now!"

But who will listen? Nobody needs saving nowadays. Things are going well. Manifest destiny has gone virtual. Somewhere in the decade,

Generation X discovered six other letters: NASDAQ. Besides, most of the people milling around Times Square are tourists more worried about pickpockets and exchange rates. Billy does spot a boy, six or seven or eight, who seems transfixed by this unholy arithmetic. Or maybe it's the flashing numbers. The boy sways on his mother's arm while she scans a map, she a tree to his monkey. Billy watches them, downright stares behind the safety of sunglasses. Such easy affection, he thinks, such natural love, and neither notices the trade.

In general, children spook Billy. Dogs too. Every time he considers a possible life with a child or a dog, he sees the child tucked in a tiny coffin, the dog mashed up by the side of a road. When children or dogs pass him on the street, their eyes seem to stick onto him as if they're glimpsing his hidden soul. They're his judge and jury and his case is never strong. Pigeons know better, he thinks, avoiding both children and dogs alike, the avatars of W. C. Fields. But the unfortunate undeniable truth is that Billy wants every child and dog to love him, often resorting to silly faces and goofy prattle. The mother closes the guidebook on her thumb and with son in hand walks toward Billy. "Excuse me," she says. "I'm lost." Her accent is German but her English is impeccable.

"Where do you need to go?" asks Billy.

"Times Square."

"You're basically there." He points west. "A block in that direction and you'll be in the thick of it."

"Thank you."

"Right in the heart of the action."

"Thanks again."

"No problem, ma'am." *Ma'am?* Where did that come from? He's far from Southern. Weird how giving directions can make you feel like a minor superhero—Mapman—like all those nothing good deeds where you lend a hand or give up a seat or tell a blind person the light has changed, these things proving yourself—what?—vaguely human. Weird and sad how the slightest drop of your own kindness can fill you up.

Mother and son move on their way, the son skipping while the mother tries reigning in his exuberance. For them, this is a small moment not

34

worth remembering. New York, August 1999, will certainly land in the scrapbook, the sights captured on film, but this jaunt down Forty-third Street, mother tugging son closer, son twirling under her arm, the two of them now dancing, will quickly be forgotten.

Billy watches them, a face captured in the background of a family snapshot.

3:27 P.M. Millions of dollars have been lost.

Now he really has to go.

Times Square will have other clocks, clocks counting down until the New Year. Maybe for the first time in history, time itself is overexposed, the millennium profiled on all the networks, in all the papers and magazines, and this is only August. Y2K (the year formerly known as 2000) has sold out. In no time Dick Clark will be emceeing from high atop the festivities, his face, like this country, a miracle of wealth and surgery. Greenwich mean means diddly and screw those islands in the middle of the Pacific, this is the place to be, this is the crossroads of the world, this is where the ball will drop and the blast wave will begin.

Eastern standard rules.

With all the fears of computer malfunction and civil chaos and a possible apocalypse from those doing complicated biblical math, the real dread will be the day after, the week after, the month after, when a new batch of beauties grace the newsstand racks and checkbooks are dated double zero with barely a second thought, when what seems to have been a period is just a fleck of dust brushed away.

What happens—Billy starts running—when nothing happens at all?

5

FTER BEING early for so long, Billy is now typically late. He runs
across Forty-second Street, running with his suitcase awkward on his
leg—*Shit!*—running running—*Oh Jesus!*—the crosstown block endless,
running running, winded, walking now, okay, walking, but walking
quickly through Times Square, bumping into the heavy afternoon
crowd—*Sorry, sorry*—crossing Seventh Avenue, below that jumbotron,
the envy of home media centers everywhere, the network anchor straddling
the intersection like a modern colossus of Rhodes, Helios extinguished by the
twenty-four-hour news cycle, waiting for the light on Broadway, on the heel
print of Times Square, where his mother and father first met—at the Winter
Garden theater—where his father once worked—Forty-seventh Street, the
diamond district—where nearly thirty-eight years to the day they themselves
sprinted west for the Port Authority and their lovers' escape from New York,
Billy running again on the green, running as though he's being chased by a
villain more frightening than Ragnar & Sons, passing the electronic tickers
for various stock exchanges, running, uh-oh cramping—*Shit!*—cramping
cramping, slowing down, thinking he really should exercise more, walking
and still cramping, a stitch in his kidneys, a stitch and a cramp and now
throbbing in his head, behind the left eye, surely a bad sign, an embolism, an
aneurysm, shifting the suitcase to the other hand, should run, just run
through the pain, but still walking, in five steps pledging speed, in five steps
promising a hard kick for the finish, first step, second step, third step, fourth
step, and noticing the traffic light on Eighth blinking Don't Walk, no point
in running for the red, fifth step becoming a resignation toward the curb,
swearing he's a fat man trapped in a thin man's body, his metabolism falsely
advertised as athleticism.

As promised, the HAM van is parked in front of the Port Authority. It's as glorious a sight as any multiple-occupancy vehicle can possibly be. Relief washes over Billy as well as sweat, uncontrollable sweat, delayed, like his glands have finally caught up from behind. The *New York Post* wilts under his arm. His sunglasses steam. His *Cats* T-shirt is alive with angrily sardonic claws. But no worry. There's the bright blue HAM van with a logo of a sun either setting or rising over the plains. But relief quickly turns to *Fuck!*—the hood is up—*Fuck!*—a person is slumped over the engine—*Fuck!*—a group of people, perhaps his fellow normals, are scattered around the van as if they're playing a childhood game and this is jail and they're waiting for their last remaining teammate who might set them free. All this planning, all this serpentine, and his getaway is fucked. Billy, deflated, crosses the street.

As usual, a taxi bullies the crosswalk, nudging its fender with impunity and passing a few inches from his toes. Of course an immigrant is behind the wheel seeking the brutal dream one fare at a time, thirty-five cents a quarter mile, whatever tyranny they've escaped manifested on the road.

Billy cuts toward the front of the van.

"You William Schine?" asks the person tinkering with the engine.

"Sorry I'm late, but I guess we're going nowhere soon."

"No, you're late, my man, you're just lucky I'm patient."

"Well, thanks."

"Damn right thanks," says the head under the hood. "Now you can do me a favor and take a look here."

"I'm sorry," Billy confesses. "But I know nothing about cars." Not that he doesn't wish he knew something about cars, cars and the piano and the French language and tap dancing and painting in watercolor.

"Just take a look."

"But I'm worthless."

"All I need is an extra hand."

Billy approaches the man. Upon closer inspection, he's lounging more than repairing. A magazine is open across the radiator, a can of soda balanced nearby. "I'm Corker," he says.

"I'm Billy."

"Well, Billy, what do you see?"

"Like I said, I'm not mechanically inclined."

Corker points towards the filter. "What you see is a traffic cop on your—don't look—right. He's over there and he's under the impression we're stalled because there's no standing around here, just pickups and drop-offs, so we're having engine trouble. He even tried to give me a jump but I disconnected the starter."

"Clever," Billy tells him.

"Nah, he's a dumbshit," Corker scoffs. "Right in front of his face, this loose line, and he goes for his cables like he knows what he's doing. Must be the battery, he says. Idiot."

That would've been Billy's only guess.

"So I told him I'd call a mechanic friend of mine. And here you are." Corker eyeballs Billy's outfit.

"I'm the mechanic friend?"

"No, you're the idiot who's ten minutes late." Corker either smiles or yawns or depressurizes his ears. He has a large muscular neck. Billy imagines his chin bench-pressing a couple hundred pounds. He looks the type who can shoot, clean, dress wild animals; build a shelter; fashion sticks into spears; survive in the wilderness for months; consequently, he also looks the type who is itching for the end of the civilized world. You might want his company on a deserted island, but he'd butcher you if things ever went bad.

"So I should what?" Billy asks.

"Just fiddle around, put on a show and tell me to give her a start." Corker grabs his soda and magazine (*People* of all things) and heads for the driver's seat.

Okay. So what would a mechanic do? Billy taps the battery and checks its terminals. Uh-huh. He measures the oil with dipstick expertise. No problems there. He unscrews the radiator cap, peers inside. A-OK. He plucks the fan belt. Nice and tight. He rubs the distributor or carburetor or alternator, whatever that thing is, and finds nothing wrong. He inspects hoses and pipes. Hmm, baffling. Then he notices the washer fluid container—Aha!—and peels off the lid. "Here's your trouble," he says, showing Corker the lid. "The manifold was, um, elastically deformed."

Corker, his eyes rolling, smiles and nods from behind the wheel.

"Now give her a try," Billy shouts.

The van, of course, starts.

An absurd sense of resourcefulness comes over Billy, the same sense he has when he changes a lightbulb or plunges a toilet or hammers a nail, as if he briefly understands wiring and plumbing and carpentry. Before dropping the hood, he stares into the mystery of internal combustion. Though he's done nothing useful, his fingers are smudged with the evidence of hard honest labor, oil like dirt or paint or blood. The engine idles. It seems unnaturally exposed, a cracked sternum. Temptation floats a dare: reach deep inside one of those dark-churning cavities.

Billy closes the hood. He wipes the grime on his pants, marking them a job well done. Per instruction, he tosses his suitcase in the back and goes around to the sliding door.

Not including Corker, there are seven people inside, six men and one woman. They sit two by two in three rows, the lucky remainder in the front passenger seat. Only middle seats are free and they're discouraged by a tangle of elbows and ankles and carry-on bags. Nothing personal, but no one wants his company. Billy shuts the door and says, "Hello," with apology. Everybody avoids eye contact with him like he's the teacher asking a difficult question and they might be called upon for the answer. *Please not here, please not here, please not here* is the communal vibe. Billy stays crouched near the doorwell until he realizes he's simply heightening the tension.

He goes toward the way back.

There's a domino effect of relief ending in two defeated sags.

"Sorry," he says as space is made.

6

DRIVING ALONG the West Side Highway or Joe DiMaggio Expressway or Henry Hudson Parkway—every few miles the name changes—Billy is relieved to be leaving. Yes, finally gone. As always he finds the sight of the river a surprise. The gray water resembles an extra swath of blacktop, a superloop around Manhattan inexplicably undeveloped. The fact that the Atlantic is nearby seems dubious. Any whiff of salt air on the street is more often mistaken for something tawdry. And from this vantage the skyline has a different spirit: the buildings are familiar yet vaguely foreign, like Canadian architecture. Farther north, the city turns Gothic. Old apartment buildings loom like castles over bluffs.

This flipside holds no strains of Gershwin, no postcard panoramas.

Billy watches the city disappear and takes stock, an annoying expression but traveling always puts him in a pensive mood. Maybe movies are to blame, movies where the main character can be seen gazing from the window as the landscape is reflected against glass. It seems, when in motion, introspection is preprogrammed. It could be a new take on Newton: every onward action has an equally sappy reaction, especially when music is involved. The radio plays the latest teen sensation, the sexed-up granddaughter of a crooner who tells boys her *pa-pa-pa-parameters.* Perhaps not the best song, but regardless, a prickle of absence strikes Billy, as if he's leaving himself behind, the himself of his normal routine, the coffee cart, the diner, the bar, the movie theater, the bum on the corner, the record shop, the bookstore, the deli, the fixed portions of his day, the subway, the soda and hot dog for lunch, the old woman on the stoop passed every evening, and while there are variations in this schedule, momentary blips, the rare memorable event, they are by far the exception.

His day is as spontaneous as *TV Guide*. Manhattan passing behind glass, Billy drifts away from the van and haunts the himself he's departed, a ghost going, "Ho hum."

There he is, jammed in the alcove of the Signet Corp, the full-timers with their arrogant medical benefits and 401(k) stares bumping into his chair. All summer long he's been doing data entry for this market research firm. He punches in product warranty forms inlaid with valuable consumer information: marital status, income, education, hobbies. Mornings start with a stack on his left, afternoons end with a stack on his right. Somewhere in between the computer shuffles the deck into curves and profiles and distributions.

No one will notice him missing.

No doubt People Person Services has already filled his slot with one of their patented artistic types. The temp profession attracts an unsavory creative element who constantly remind Billy that this is just a job, nothing more, a paycheck. They're cultural fundamentalists: their career path is the only possible career path. Some conceal tattoos with the seriousness of sneaking freedom into a repressed country. Many become upset by Oscar snubs. Most only shop in independent stores. A handful praise vinyl, a few debate craft, a couple pass leaflets for their next show. Numerous use the term *partner* in a heterosexual context. Half have creative advanced degrees and the other have plans for creative advanced degrees. Nobody is in the least bit insincere. All discuss portfolios and manuscripts and screenplays and canvases and short films and tryouts with the allure of a dream described by a narcoleptic ten-year-old. And none of them like Billy. They're suspicious of anyone who follows a different bliss (their word), and as far as they can tell, Billy has no identifiable bliss. Twice he's been accused of blisslessness. But if they tied him down and tortured him to talk, they'd hear him squeal on beauty and rat out truth until he's bearing witness against himself. Because he wants to care, he just doesn't have the strength.

Thoughts cruising over Midtown, Billy drops down on Sally, crunching her numbers and doing her due diligence, never suspecting how her day will end. She might leave work early, summer Fridays always slow, and run a few errands, maybe stop in the gym for a yoga class. Regardless, she'll call him and leave a message, telling him when she'll be home and asking what they should do for dinner. In her time-space, Billy still exists. She has no idea that their life is uncoupling by the minute, that waiting for her back home is a poorly written apparition. Strange, Billy thinks, how clocks can divide and run so differently, how in the meanwhile all assumptions can be rendered false without your knowledge. *Tick tick tick.* You're a walking talking anachronism waiting for the impact of a long thrown switch.

So good-bye.

Every few minutes he envisions Sally reading his note. Billy gives her arms a bag of groceries, the prop for domestic bad news, a carton of eggs, farm fresh, dropped on the floor. *Oh God, gone!* Billy cringes. How could he? Is he really this kind of person? Months, years from now, he'll probably still wonder, still weigh the evidence, like he still remembers hitting poor Jasper Moss in the face with a baseball, Jasper distracted by an airplane, "An L 10–11," he oohed right before the ball smacked his nose, unleashing blood, Jasper crying and Billy—*Huh?*—laughing—*Huh!*—though he quickly covered his smile and ran over and apologized like a fiend. No matter how lax his morals, such memories never leave Billy. Almost daily they pop into his head like random firings of synaptic shame. The note to Sally will remain in psychological place like a bookmark in one of the novels he should've finished. So many bookmarks. His mother and father are constantly dog-eared. His friends are always losing their page, the same chapter reread, until Billy shelves them by no longer returning calls or e-mails, whereupon he bemoans his lack of close friends. But Billy knows this about himself. Indeed, he knows himself too well, knows he knows himself too well. Etc.

The van crosses the Henry Hudson Bridge and leaves Manhattan behind.

Clouds hang in the sky like blooms of artillery flak.

Only Ragnar will miss him, Billy thinks.

He turns around and checks the back windshield for any tailing fenders.

7

FOR MUCH of the trip, the van is silent. Everybody hangs under banners of distraction—magazines, Walkmans, computer games, sleep—interspersed with bored glances at the landscape. City and suburbs are gone, farms and hills in their place. Towns are evident by exit alone. The weekend traffic moves well considering the volume. Corker stays primarily in the middle lane, a good enough driver, Billy supposes, except for his annoying habit of staring into passing cars as if he's searching for an ex-girlfriend. He'll match speeds, the lateral version of tailgating, and peer over for a few seconds longer than safe. He'll sneak into blind spots and hide there, stalking, the heel of his hand ready on the horn. "Caught you," he accuses when the car tries changing lanes. Conflicted emotions seem to arise concerning flashy sports cars driven too slow: They're effeminate matadors in jewel-encrusted outfits, their wasted aerodynamics as ostentatious as red capes. They incite in Corker a bullish road rage. All of a sudden he'll crouch forward and stamp hard on the gas and try to tarnish their pace and expose their purchase as a fraud.

"Oh yeah, Mr. Porsche," he'll mutter, nearing seventy-five, eighty, miles per hour. "Passed by a van, what a joke. You should be lapping the field in that sweet rig. Proves money cannot buy balls."

Corker drives a tale of jealousy and intrigue.

Nobody in the van minds these outbursts except for Peter Swain. No introductions have been made, only roll call, which put a "Here" or "Yep" on the faces. Peter Swain is the "Yo" in the front seat who chain-smokes conscientiously, always asking if you mind, really, honestly, keeping his cigarette in the three inches of open-window jet stream. His brand of choice is Virginia Slims, though he used to smoke Silk Cuts, but these he finds more humorous. The back of the van despises his secondhand sarcasm as well as his legroom, bucket seating, and first pass with the air-conditioning. Whenever a convertible crosses their path and Corker insists on a romantic duel, Billy feels a small thrill of justice as Swain nervously retightens his seat belt.

Brad Lannigan and Sameer Sirdesh sit behind Peter Swain. Lannigan reads *Hamlet* while Sirdesh snoozes against the window. Lannigan is somewhere in his mid thirties. His looks are pure trompe l'oeil, interesting only because he fools you into believing he's handsome when he's simply tan and in good shape and has nice hair. He's constantly glancing around, nodding like he's heard your thoughts and fully agrees and hey, I don't need *Hamlet,* wanna talk. But Lannigan has no takers. Certainly not Sirdesh, who's been sound asleep since the first mile. What with the sad pillow of two hands and the van's mattress of shitty shocks, he must be unspeakably tired.

Behind them sit Bruce Ossap and Val Dullick. Billy guesses they're friends from before, buddies on an adventure together. They bump shoulders and share magazines—*Playboy, Guns and Ammo, Penthouse, Soldier of Fortune*—and elbow inside jokes about tits and Uzis. Their body types seem inspired by comedic effect: Ossap, squat, Dullick, lanky. Between them lurks the physiology of a rolling pin. They both sport the same high and tight haircut, the same outfit of white T-shirt tucked into blue camo pants, the same fist-pumping attitude of me and you, pal. They could be commandos ready to hide themselves in a hot tub.

And in the way back, on either side of Billy, sit Gretchen Warwick and Rodney Letts. Knees dangerously close, incidental contact threatened with every sharp curve, feet stay planted on the floor and eyes shun even the idea of company. Gretchen looks left, on the median strip, Rodney looks right, on the shoulder. They could be Janus in the backseat.

Billy stealthily sizes up Gretchen. She plays computer solitaire, and as her thumbs deal the virtual deck, her tongue peeks between lips like the horror movie Blob oozing through a seam. She's neither fat nor thin, tall nor short, young nor old, though the less charitable might think otherwise. Three pockmarks are grouped in the center of her forehead like bullet holes in a rural Stop sign. Her head is similar in shape. But her face is far from that explicit. She's more of a Yield. From most angles she's ordinary, sometimes ugly, often severe, with her thin suspicious lips, large nose, wide critical eyes, almost Paleolithic brow, and square chin. Her skin is so pale you imagine her sweating skim milk. (DNA testing might place her genes in the foothills of the Caucasus.) Yet every turn of her head carries a single degree that refracts a strange beauty, her awkward features catching the light and suddenly becoming exotic, like a diamond with a single facet. Right there, right now, she shimmers. Then it's gone. Ninety-nine percent of the male population would probably pass her by, but the remaining one percent would be devastated. Billy, it seems, falls into the latter.

Maybe she intrigues him because she's the only woman in the van. Being in transit always makes Billy mindful of love. Planes, buses, trains have an aphrodisiacal effect on him, terminals and stations like singles bars. There's nothing seedy about this, nothing cheap like getting laid in a wheelchair-friendly bathroom. Nope. Maybe the occasional fantasy, but in general, his leanings are far more romantic. With every trip, he imagines meeting his future wife. He might pooh-pooh fate but he's a fool for the chance encounter. He'll check left hands for wedding bands, scope gates for possible brides, treat ticket agents like desk-bound cupids. Foolish, he realizes, especially when he recalls the people he's normally stuck with, but he always wonders if behind him or ahead of him or across from him is the woman of his dreams, the woman he's just missing, who might make everything all right.

On the other side of Billy is a different story.

Rodney Letts is miserable from all angles. Haggardness hangs over him as well as an improvised hygiene, like he licked himself clean this morning and stuffed perfume inserts into his pockets so he might overwhelm the obvious, that he's a mess. His skin has the quality of an old dried sponge with bits torn away, particularly around the nose, which bears a black stain on its tip. Billy assumes drops of water, if mixed with booze, might expand his presence tenfold. His eyes have the punch-shy manner of a man who's clawed through a variety of bad temperaments until finally settling on harmless coot.

45

An hour into the trip he asks Billy if he knows the time.

"Four-thirty-eight."

"Exactly?"

"According to me."

"Good enough." Rodney digs inside the grocery bag he's been hugging from the start and rustles free a Ziploc pillowed with raw spinach and raisins. He breaks the seal, sniffs the atmosphere. He nods for his own encouragement then pinches a leafy wad, pauses, commits. Chewing is the minimum, swallowing the goal. He could be eating aluminum foil. But he's determined, his fingers already preparing the next mouthful. Sensing his companion's interest, he asks Billy if he wants a bite.

"Uhm, no thanks."

"Why would you, unless you were—" Rodney stops talking and peers at Billy like he's just recognized a childhood enemy and he's ready to Popeye the Sailor Man his ass. "Jesus," he asks. "Do I really look this bad, or are your sunglasses fun house mirrors?"

"You look fine," Billy lies.

"No, I think I look like shit." Rodney bobs and weaves his reflection. "Grade A. Obvious, so obvious. And I was worried about my liver count. Idiot. One look at me and they'll stamp sayonara on my forehead. And I bothered shaving."

"Shaving" is a stretch, unless he used a ripped can for a razor. "You look fine," Billy promises. He removes his sunglasses, hoping this will end the man's self-observation. "These are maybe the worst sunglasses in the world. Really cheap. Trust me, you look fine." In natural light, Rodney looks even worse. His raw eyes could've transmitted salmonella.

"I'm doomed," Rodney mutters. "Reason why I'm eating this crap." He picks a raisin from his molar and inspects the black pulp like it's the most innocent thing he's ever scraped from his teeth. "All this crap because I'm an asshole." He inventories the contents of the grocery bag. "Dried apricots, Herbal Clean tea, goldenseal—a buddy of mine recommended—iron supplements. Before this trip's over I got to drink this entire bottle of vinegar."

"What, are you anemic or something?"

"Nah, I'm bit of a drinker," Rodney says with obvious modesty.

"Oh."

"Two days I've been eating this junk, praying for an acceptable liver count, all because on Wednesday, fucking hump day, I said my good-byes and got carried away and pricks ran me a tab knowing I'd be flush in two weeks. Okay, maybe I insisted, but still, they were undermining their investment. My own stupid fault. Usually I stay dry the week before and I'm fine, but me and my good-byes. Even yesterday I said a small see ya with scotch."

"So you've done this before?"

Rodney smiles. "Get loaded?"

"No, I mean the drug-study type of thing."

"Christ, I've got my Ph.D. in guinea pig. Six years I've been doing this, all over the country, all the big companies, three, four, five times a year, lending them my"—he spreads his arms—"only asset. Even have some aliases so I can load up on studies and improve the old cash flow without them bitching about overextending the system."

"So who are you?" Billy asks.

"Like the man said, Rodney Letts. How about you?"

Billy gives him his name.

"Well, I bet your liver is nice and clean. No dehydrogenase in your piss. You'll be golden." Rodney unscrews the cap to the vinegar and tests its smelling-salt bouquet. "But me, I'm fucked, which is too bad because I need the money. And this job, man, it's the easiest job in the world. All you do is sleep, soak in the tub, eat decent food, watch TV. In return all you've got to do is bleed, piss, and swallow whatever they give you. If you're on placebo you're laughing all the way to the bank."

"What if you're not?"

"Still not too bad. You can count on flulike symptoms; those are standard. Then there are always a few add-ons. Depends on the drug. Like what we're pigging, this atypical antipsychotic, you can expect your head being messed with mightily. A two-week stupor. But however you're feeling, really lousy, say, just keep your mouth shut. Don't tell them anything, especially if you're feeling fucked. That's a rookie mistake.

Because then they get all nervous and they'll send you home early and pay you less than full. Best to keep the major side effects quiet and let the blood do the talking. They just care about your blood anyway. Oh, they'll pretend to be interested in your head but all they want is right here." Rodney taps the inner crook of his elbow. "Let them pop your cherry without fuss and you'll both be happy. That's my only advice. But look at me. I'm about to drink vinegar, for fuck's sake."

"You're really going to drink that?" Billy asks.

"Got to," Rodney says. "Hopefully this'll bring my count down to acceptable levels. It's an old-fashioned remedy. This shit will overwhelm everything in your system." Rodney prepares his chaser: a two-liter bottle of water. "I'm thinking chug, right. One fell swoop." He pauses. "Hope I can keep it down."

"Me too," Billy says.

"Not that bad, right? Just red wine gone bad." Rodney sniffs. "Okay, really, really bad." He raises the bottle. "Well, Billy Schine, nice meeting you. To our health, mine in particular." He sucks down about a quarter of the vinegar before the taste hits him and crumples his throat. Gags take over. Eyes squeezed tight, lips pained, he's a bullfrog perched on a pile of rags, tongue wrapped around a hornet. Tearing, drooling, sweating, Rodney bends over and repels a thick rope of saliva down to the floor. Billy thinks about rubbing his back. Then reconsiders. Rocking back and forth, the man is going through his own version of Elisabeth Kübler-Ross until his stomach reaches—*chaa*—acceptance. He wipes his face, smiles. His breath smells like salad. The van notices the commotion, heads snapping around like Billy's slugged Rodney in the stomach. Ossap and Dullick glare, twins with different parents. Lannigan asks if everybody's all right back there, hungering for more than just the *yep* he gets. Sameer Sirdesh still sleeps. Swain tells Corker a Dodge Viper is hardly a sports car. Gretchen registers none of the drama, just her computer solitaire.

Billy decides this might be the time to unfold the *New York Post* and escape any further encounters with Rodney Letts and his vulnerable liver count. The headline screams THE SHROUD OF CHUCK in typical *Post* fashion. Billy loves the big bold print, the puns, loves how every day is a day of

48

infamy. Below the headline is a photograph of an MRI with an uncanny resemblance to that face so celebrated in Turin. The brain's magnetic gray tones are smudged and swirled in perfect likeness of beard and eyes and long hair, the gaunt beatific expression. It could have been a charcoal sketch from the original. The photo caption explains that this is the MRI of Charles Savitch, from Menomonee Falls, Wisconsin, a plumber who has a tumor with mystifying implications, full story, page four.

After all the front-page fuss, the article is shorter than expected. It's accompanied by another photograph of Chuck Savitch, this one from his 1984 high school yearbook. Never the most flattering time in your life, Billy thinks, and wonders why are these the preferred headshots for killers and victims alike? His own senior year photo would've been criminal enough—William Adamas Schine, features half-cooked between adolescence and adulthood, hair positively cubist, clothes seemingly pieced together from the lost and found. And don't forget his senior quote: "Demand me nothing. What you know, you know. From this time forth I never will speak word." Iago. Oh, please. But at least it isn't being reproduced nationwide, like Chuck Savitch here, his chin gnawed by pimples, his shoulders stuck in mid *Huh?* Inside his smile, buckteeth lean forward like obnoxious sightseers straining for a view. That sweeping middle part is consistent with hockey hairdos immemorial, and that sport coat and tie flirt with the flare from the previous decade. But his eyes are undaunted. They will never guess that in fourteen years he'll be living with his mother, terminally ill with what was if anything a nativity of cancer cells. Billy decides this is the prime reason for high school yearbook pictures: they're naïve portraits of forthcoming anguish.

The hospital is scant with the details, citing privacy issues, but they've released a statement claiming that the MRI was stolen from the radiology department (a recently born-again technician suspected) and that they're in the process of conducting an internal investigation. "This image is the sole diagnostic property of Mercy Hospital and Mr. Savitch and any unauthorized reproduction without permission is illegal," the spokesperson claimed. But the image is already floating around the Internet. A Christian Web site was the first to post it, followed by supermarket tabloids, and now mainstream media. Rumors of fraud, of forgery, are debunked by the Savitch family who promise further neurological exams if need be. "I'll leave the religion stuff alone but my Charlie is not dying from some hoax," his mother is quoted as saying. The *Post,* in a sidebar, interviews an oncologist from Memorial Sloan-Kettering. He hazards that in all likelihood this is a late-stage glioblastoma multiforme. "The configuration of the neoplasm is symptomatic with that type of cancer, albeit unique," the doctor says. "All tumors spread in different patterns, but I can assure you any resemblance with Jesus Christ is purely coincidental and not in any way the intention of the cancer. The only truth in this story is that Mr. Savitch is an extremely sick man." So sick, he's been discharged from the hospital for the hospice of his own home. Treatment options are limited considering tumor size and location. Pain management is the most reasonable course of action. This pleases the evangelicals who regard even the hint of surgery or radiation or che- motherapy as desecration. People are starting to converge on Menomonee Falls, "miracle chasers," the *Post* calls them. The millennium is of course mentioned. And there have been whispers within the pilgrim community of cures, the sick and infirm canceling trips to Lourdes and Fatima and rushing here instead. Time is short, everyone agrees.

Billy feels the beginnings of a headache.

This sort of nonstory is nothing new. Yet here it is, again, and Billy knows, yet again, he'll eat up every unsavory bite and participate in the event despite himself, feeding the insatiable media mouth with his eyes and eagerly awaiting the next morsel, like a rat on that worn-out sinking ship who mocks the tastes of man while gnawing through its cargo.

Billy stops reading, gazes out the window.

Not much to see except the median strip and the southbound traffic. The occasional deer lies shattered on the side of the road, and while sad, it seems exotic, as if swiped by a cougar instead of a fender. In the distance, Billy catches sight of a shape, doggish in nature, a dead-doggish shape. His stomach tightens and he begins mourning the death, his insides tingling with life-affirming sadness, more abstract than tears, and he keeps this vigil until the poor corpse passes—just a shredded tire. Lassie is

50

nothing but litter. But within the median strip actual live rabbits frolic, trapped between the northbound and southbound lanes. Billy finds the setting depressing, like Flopsy and Mopsy in a crack den. Not that he has an overwhelming affection for rabbits. Please. They're basically rodents. Semiprofessional prey. The only time they're featured in wildlife programs is when they're pursued by more glamorous claws. So why—*why!*—does he lean toward Gretchen and say something about them?

"Excuse me?" she asks.

"Nothing," he backtracks. "Forget it."

"No, you said something about rabbits."

"Stupid," he says.

"No," she says, all glint. "Tell me about the rabbits."

"I must sound like George. Or is it Lennie? Lennie or George? You know, from *Of Mice and Men.* I always confuse the two. I think it's Lennie. Not that I'm trying for some literary reference here."

"Actually, I made the reference, and I'm pretty sure it's Lennie," she says.

Billy nods, petrified. "Yeah, sounds right. Lennie loved the rabbits. *Tell me about the rabbits, George.* Yeah." Pretending that this has settled the conversation, Billy jumps back into the newspaper, headache or not.

"Wait, tell me about the rabbits, _____?" She leaves a blank for a name.

"Billy, I'm Billy."

"I'm Gretchen."

"It's so stupid, but I was feeling sorry for them. You see them? They're all over the place, hopping in and out of the bushes, and I was thinking they must spend their entire life, generation after generation, in that median strip, living with speeding cars on either side. It seemed, well, depressing until I said it out loud."

"Maybe it's like a moat. Maybe it protects them."

"The constant noise. The exhaust."

Gretchen gestures her chin at his chest. "Maybe it stops the cats."

"Do you think cats are a—oh." Billy pinches his *Cats* T-shirt. "A joke. Well, you see, I'm wearing this shirt ironically. I swear I know nothing about Old Deuteronomy or Macavity or Grisabella. In fact, I don't know why I'm wearing it." The idea of Ragnar seems so far away. "And this silly hat. I guess it was a mood."

She smiles, a crook somewhere between intrigue and wariness, Billy's not sure, but he settles on interested unease and he smiles in return— comfortably embarrassed—and says, "We now return to our regularly scheduled silence, already in progress."

He's asleep, or pretending to be asleep, hoping he might fool himself and actually fall asleep—eyes closed, mouth open, breathing ZZzzs, thinking dreamy thoughts, e.g. Gretchen watching him snooze and taking in his face and allowing his lazing cheek to slip on her shoulder as they ride the bumps of the thruway, until Billy actually does fall asleep and dreams, or remembers his dream when the van turns for the exit and pops him awake from a nightmare of driving, of him behind the wheel and every hundred yards there's a dead body in the middle of the road, and Billy speeds no big deal over these bodies like this is the way of the world, tires rolling flesh and bone into macadam.

"We're here," Rodney Letts tells him. "Roughly."

Fast-food restaurants and gas stations and various national chains are clustered in a line, herding animals sipping at the oasis of the main strip. Billy, still half-asleep, imagines a predator bursting forth in a flash of impossible speed and pouncing on this dim-witted prey, tearing through stucco and drop siding and ripping out the warm innards of adolescents in paper hats.

Corker says to no one in particular that two hours and twenty minutes is pretty decent though last week he had made the trip in two. The van takes a left, another left, and heads down a street that dead-ends on a gatehouse and a chain-link fence warning of private property ahead. Corker waves at the guard who peers from his air-conditioned booth. The gate lifts. Corker shouts, "You fucking lazy prick," through his closed window. The guard shouts something in return, his window also closed.

Ossap and Dullick are suddenly excited. They perk up like eight-year-olds entering the magic kingdom. The guard could've been a beloved character living inside a toadstool, a host to an animatronic world of wonder where, if you keep your eyes peeled, you might spot a unicorn somewhere along the route.

Ossap flips open his cell phone, dials. "Hey," he says. "Tell Father we've arrived and we'll be talking soon."

Lannigan, *Hamlet* in hand, turns around. "You guys brothers or something?"

Dullick stares long and hard before answering. "Why do you care?"

"I don't."

Ossap palms shut his phone. "We're cousins."

"Not related by blood," Dullick clarifies.

Ossap refines. "My father is very sick and he needs money for a trip back to his homeland. That's why we're here." His tone is similar to a soldier providing name, rank, serial number.

"Where?" Lannigan asks.

"Hungary. He's Hungarian, Hungarian-American."

"What's he have, your father?" Lannigan asks.

"I'm sorry but I really don't want to talk to you," Ossap says.

Billy finds the bluntness stunning, almost awe-inspiring.

A clearing appears up ahead.

"Welcome to the AHRC," Corker shouts.

8

FREE FROM the van, everybody stretches and reconnects with joints. Unlike the city, where humidity can seem overly intimate, as if expressed in percentages of public sweat, the heat here feels removed from human concern. Whatever burns in the sun. Woods of pine border the property. They carry the menace of early American settlements. Witches and Indians could easily roam in their shadows. In the middle of the clearing stands the AHRC: six stories of glass and metal siding, with wings extending from either side. It resembles the sort of building used in science fiction movies where the story needs the creep of the cold distant future. But in this setting, alone in the wilderness, the future appears lost. If cities were born from the sky, say air-dropped like paratroopers, the Chrysler, the Empire State, the Citicorp, *Go! Go! Go!* floating down and landing on Manhattan, then the AHRC would've been the unfortunate soldier who jumped a bit too late and got caught up in a heavy gust and drifted deep within enemy territory.

Corker cracks opens the back of the van.

Suitcases are collected.

Rodney Letts grabs his bag—literally a bag, a blue recycling bag. His belongings press against the plastic; they seem cancerous. Rodney opens up the cinch, shoves in his grocery bag of liver-saving items and slings the load over his shoulder. Billy has seen his type in the city, people who prospect for cans and earn their keep in five-cent increments. Those people always shame him with their small deposits of dignity. They work harder than he does—hell, they even do environmental work. Right now Rodney beams like he's worth his weight in aluminum. "How do I look?" he asks Billy.

"Good," Billy lies.

"Yeah?"

"Yeah. You look good."

"Good, good, good, good," Rodney mutters. "Maybe there's a chance."

Billy reconsiders for the sake of charity. "Take my hat. Your hair's a bit messy." Like oil spills and cormorants, he thinks.

"I've always had impossible hair," Rodney says.

Billy hands over his I♥NY hat. It crowns Rodney the way whipped cream might crown a turd. "Much better," Billy says.

"But I hate New York."

"It loves you. Trust me."

"Fits perfectly. We must have the same sized melon."

"I guess we do."

"Kids called me Bucket."

"They can be cruel."

"I didn't mind."

Billy, infused with goodwill, tells Rodney, "Maybe we could clean up your face as well. You have . . ." Billy touches his own nose, like "Simon says clean the black crud on the tip of your nose."

"That's permanent," Rodney says.

"Oh, God, sorry."

"I don't know how or when but one day it just appeared."

"I'm sorry."

"Might be frostbite."

"I'm sorry."

"Or some weird freckle or sun spot."

"You should probably get it checked by a dermatologist," Billy says, immediately feeling ridiculous for giving this man a skin-care suggestion.

"Yeah, maybe."

"I'm sure it's nothing," Billy says.

"I've had it long enough I'd be dead if it was something."

Suitcases collected, they follow Corker across the courtyard—nearly an acre of limestone. The basic seating order of the van is maintained on foot, people having bonded by proximity. Up ahead, Swain smokes, guided by a trail of last cigarettes, while Corker tucks in his company shirt and rehearses how he should hold his clipboard: officious? casual? somewhere in between? Lannigan saunters with his tan angled for a final taste of sun, his deportment casting Sameer Sirdesh as faithful Gunga Din. Next come Ossap and Dullick. My God, these two travel heavy, each arm pontooned by a duffel bag. They walk buddy-buddy, whispering and nodding like bad boys in church whose jokes will always remain private. Billy starts to hate them. It's unreasonable, unjustified hatred, really the best kind, before any strain of understanding can get in the way. Side by side, Dullick and Ossap are an exclamation point of bully camaraderie. Plus those four duffel bags.

Gretchen wheels her suitcase over toward Billy. "I'm expecting multiple costume changes," she whispers.

Billy—"Huh?"—is baffled.

"From those two," she says.

"You know I was just thinking the same thing. Because that's a lot of luggage."

"Maybe they're traveling on after the study."

"I don't like them," Billy says.

"Because of their luggage?"

"I just don't like them."

In the middle of the courtyard looms a sculpture, a hand, Billy realizes, a huge hand done in bronze, maybe fifteen feet high and pointing skyward, like those foam fingers raised drunkenly in stadiums and arenas, the elephantiasis of *We're #1!* Billy wonders if this is corporate artwork as brag, a *Go HAM!* salute. Because he also sees God in there, what with the scale and the visual line directing your eye toward heaven. *Look up! He's watching you!* Like the famous finger of Adam on the ceiling of the Sistine Chapel. Adam and God. Creation. Life. Then death pops into mind. The less famous but equally thrilling Last Judgment frescoed over the altar. The Resurrection. Now Billy pictures the rest of the statue buried beneath the courtyard, hundreds of tons of decomposing bronze and the AHRC is its headstone. The sculpture could be portraying the first punch of everlasting life, and along with the saved come visions of the damned,

56

of emerging corpses, of flesh-eating zombies, real horror movie stuff—
Night of the Living Dead and *Dawn of the Dead* and *Day of the Dead*—and
with dusk of the dead fast approaching, the finger's shadow stretches
toward Billy with creepy solicitation, like Nosferatu gesturing for—

Oh.

Billy notices where the shadow is falling.

The black inlay within the limestone is not decorative but functional,
arranged in gradations of degrees and numerals—Billy, you idiot, the
courtyard is the face for a clock, a giant sundial, the finger the gnomon—
even worse, a bad pun: a digital sundial.

Billy kicks the ground, executed in a single joyless skip.

"What is it?" Gretchen asks.

"I just noticed that this is a sundial."

"What'd you think it was?"

"I don't know. A hand. A finger."

"It's good luck," Rodney informs them. "Before you go inside, you're
meant to punch the clock. Same as when you leave. Guys up there must be
rookies," he says of the rest of the group who have unknowingly breezed by
this charm. Rodney steps on the base and taps the heel; the touched bronze
suffers from the vitiligo of who knows how many hands wishing for a
break.

"I'm not going near that," Billy says.

"You've got to."

"No I don't."

"Why not?"

"I'm just not."

"Oh, come on," Gretchen says. Her tone is already familiar and
flirtatious, spreading a thin layer of pucker all over Billy. She reaches
up and pats the surface. The hollow insides sing. "I feel like Fay Wray,"
she says. But Billy is thinking of Louise Brooks, not so much in appearance
but in attitude, improvising a scene from *Pandora's Box* (a movie he's seen
in poster alone). "Just touch it," she tells him.

"No thank you."

"Scared?"

"Not scared," he says. "Just not tempted."

He has to admit, the sculpture is impressive. Rendered muscularly, all flex and strain, it transforms the act of pointing into heavy lifting. No detail is lost. Every line, every wrinkle is represented, hangnails, calluses, the cross-hatching of lived-in skin. The sun seems to radiate from the bronze in a hot clap.

"No good luck for you," Gretchen says, hopping down.

"You know, the time's not even right. It's three hours slow."

Gretchen squints. "Maybe it's using the wrong finger," she tells him, and Billy swears she's squinting the space around his chest and leaving his lungs short. Her whole imperfect face seems to rally around that squint.

Up ahead, the group has come to a stop within the building's embrace, and when Billy and Gretchen catch up, they hear the reason for the pause: a rap-rap-rap of fists against the windows of the north wing where faces peer down, pressed hard against the top five floors like slide specimens holding small samples of insanity. Mouths and eyes contort, writhe, and buckle, like air is acid; lips kiss glass, tongues frenching with eroticism gone wrong; fingers claw skin and hair; foreheads slam a numbing rhythm; voices scream, the words unintelligible but the message clear: *run away while you can!*

Billy watches this Grand Guignol, dumbfounded.

"Your welcoming party," Corker says.

Billy is struck in particular by a window on the fourth floor. Within it a person shakes as if in seizure, his features convulsing, his mouth drooling, now spurting, water spraying down his chin and chest, spraying against the window, spraying a finale of death. Billy recognizes this modest special effect from his boyhood days when he would stand in front of the bathroom mirror and make believe some violence against him: a fist, a bullet, a knife, rabies if he were brushing his teeth. He'd gush and gurgle as if tap water were life-slipping fluid. He could die like that for hours.

"Every new group gets this show," Corker tells them. "And guess what, tomorrow you'll probably be doing the same."

Behind them, they hear barking, howling really, like an honest echo of pain.

58

"And those are the goddamn beagles who never shut up."

"Animals are in that wing?" Ossap asks, intrigued. "Monkeys and stuff?"

"Yeah. And the beagles are loud as hell."

"Because of their broad chest and manageable size," Ossap says.

"What's that?"

"That's why they love beagles, right, for research?"

"I really don't know."

Ossap's upper lip curls in what can only be assumed is a smile. "Beagles are the best because you can just crack them open and get to their hearts, and they're small, unlike your other broad-chested breeds. Beagles can fit into a standard-sized cage. They're docile. Obedient. Total suckers. This friend of mine, he thought about breeding them for medical research but got into minks instead."

"At least they're good for something," Dullick says.

Ossap agrees. "I fucking hate beagles."

"Inject their fucking eyes with perfume for all I care," Dullick says.

"Slice and fucking dice them," Ossap says.

"Toss them in the fucking Cuisinart," Dullick says.

"Mutate them." Ossap pauses. "The fuckers."

Ossap and Dullick give phantom high-fives with their chins.

"Snoopy is a beagle," Lannigan says.

Dullick frowns. "Not Snoopy?"

Ossap quickly jumps in with, "Snoopy fucking sucks."

Corker ends this conversation by pulling open the AHRC's large glass door. He waves his passengers inside like they're smoke or some such substance lighter than air and soon destined to fade. As the door closes behind them, Billy swears its pneumatic hinge squeaks "Flight of the Bumblebee."

9

AIR-CONDITIONING is the governing principle inside the lobby. The walls hum sixty-eight degrees, and coolness drops down like confetti, at first thrilling, but then annoying, sticking to Billy's skin and leaving him goose-bumped. Dead ahead is the reception desk—an atoll on a sea of black marble—monitored by a woman on the phone. She glances up, sees Corker, hangs up, takes a deep BTU-infused breath, and smiles. Barely, Billy thinks.

For some reason Corker greets her with a Cockney accent. "Hallo, luv."

"She's on her way."

Corker leans on the desk. "Two hours and five minutes. Not bad for a Friday."

The woman nods. She has the long neck and ellipsoidal head of a Modigliani, her almond eyes embittered by an unpainted life of answering phones.

"We left a little bit late so that's why we're a little bit late," Corker explains.

"Okay."

"Traffic wasn't too bad."

"Okay."

"You know, if you ever need me to get you something, anything, in the city, don't hesitate to ask, because I can, no problemo. I can even give you a lift, maybe on a day off. We could get lunch then grab a new batch of norms and head on back."

The woman tilts her head as if she's just heard a pile of shit fall from a very great height. "You have a pickup at the train station," she says.

Corker flinches. "I know that. Christ, I know that." He hands over the clipboard. "The seven-oh-two from Boston. Thirty-seven minutes from now, twenty minutes from here, so in ten minutes I'll leave and still be early, so don't worry about my end, okay, missy." Missy. He actually called her missy. Billy's shocked, pleased, embarrassed—the sort of reaction he usually has when watching afternoon talk shows. It's the trifecta of guilty pleasure.

"Relax," the woman says. "I was just reminding you."

"Well, I don't need reminding. Or relaxing."

Her "Sorry" has been trained in jujitsu.

Corker is incapacitated. "I was just, maybe, yeah."

There's a pause, the audience of eight wondering what will happen next, where this will lead. Corker can only look away for a few seconds at a time as if he's still driving and she's the road, and she seems to understand this and spreads her lips like the endless unreachable destination, and when Billy sees Corker stare into those flat blue eyes he thinks he can see Corker's whole story: Corker as an infant, a boy, a teenager, a young man, the entire physical evolution of Corker in four progressive steps, and in the gross Corker, Billy glimpses the mitigating circumstances of the person, the insecurities of the reptilian brain surrounded by millenniums of gray. Nothing worse than jerks with sudden souls.

"I'm gone." Corker waves good-bye with his nose.

He's answered with eyebrows.

The receptionist says, "Strange, strange man." Her face loosens. Disdain suits her better. "Anyway, welcome. Your study coordinator will be here—" just then, stage right, a woman scurries in holding a stack of manila envelopes like freshly baked pies. She seems a generation removed from the family orchard, picking Post-its instead of produce.

"Hello," she says. "I'm Carol Longley, your study coordinator."

Billy's tempted to sing back, "Hello, Mrs. Longley," for she reminds him of his favorite grade school teacher: black curly hair, heart-shaped face, pair of glasses practically drawn on with a Magic Marker. She's the dream gal of eight-year-olds before their idea of beauty changes in high school. "Okay, we're in a bit of a rush, so if you'll grab your bags and follow me, we'll get you checked in as quickly as possible and settled before dinner, which, egads, is fast approaching." She even sounds like his teacher—enthusiastically high-pitched and able to shatter the most cynical of glass. "Quick like a bunny," she says.

They follow her into a hallway where a dozen chairs are lined up against the wall, their scooped plastic shell assuming their asses. Mrs. Longley reads names and hands out the corresponding envelopes. "Inside you'll find copies of the informed consent, the drug protocol, the two-week schedule, so refresh your memory while waiting and prepare any questions you might have, because you'll be asked to sign the informed consent in the next few minutes. Those of you who've done this before—Mr. Letts, I think you're the only one who fits that bill—will find their ID necklace inside. The rest will have theirs done in the first station. Now, there are four stations in all. Enter the station, give the person your envelope, and do what they tell you. Once done, wait outside the next door until you're called inside. When you're done with the last station, return to your seat and wait for the rest. Okay." She claps her hands. "Let's go." Billy half expects her to pull out a stopwatch and stretch a yellow ribbon across the finish.

Peter Swain is up.

Brad Lannigan is on deck, stretching.

Billy is last in line. He watches Rodney as he retrieves his ID from the envelope—under laminate, the man is six years younger, which must be like decades in drunk years. His nose was unmarked then. His eyes were clearer, if a bit more sour. Rodney regards the photo like it's an old friend long believed dead. He cups his hands over himself and whispers, "Please pass, please pass, please pass," his eyes closed, his body swaying, breaking your heart if you're the slightest bit pessimistic toward someone who wants something so badly.

In the first station a woman steers Billy against a green backdrop and adjusts the mounted digital camera so his head and shoulders are officially framed. Composition seems to cross her mind briefly before she realizes she's wasting her time and steps toward the computer.

"It's all done digitally?" Billy asks.

"Uh-huh."

"Cool."

The woman might as well be typing *Like I care.*

Billy, nervous, runs his fingers through his hair and wipes the layer of travel from his face. While he pretends to be casual about his looks, no big deal, rarely shaving, letting Sally cut his hair, trumpeting the occasional pimple and taking odd pride in dandruff, the truth is, he's terribly vain. Mirrors are a continual source of fascination—a staring contest follows every piss—and most shiny surfaces catch his attention. Car windows, storefronts, elevator doors, silverware. But often their reflection feels two-way, as if on the other side stands the victim of false impressions who leans against the glass and shouts, *Who the hell do you think you are?* And cameras slay him. Whenever one is pointed in his direction, Billy puts on a jokey face and hams things up. He's rarely caught candid. Afterward he regrets these little displays—they seem so desperate, so phony, even if he's mocking the whole convention of the party pic, the group photo, the tourist snapshot. Still, you'd think he could be himself once in a while. Just smile. Just be. But no. Even worse, when he's presented with a sleeve of photos, he will speed-thumb through the Billyless images and only alight on himself—laughing broadly, gesturing slickly, winking cheesily, beaming bogusly, slouching sadly, gawking insanely—and wince. Focus a lens on him and he turns into an adverb.

Billy stands there, smiles. Guilelessly.

"Don't bother," the woman tells him. "You're already laminating."

"Laminating? No 'smile' or 'on the count of three'?"

"You looked fine. Now come over here." She asks for his left arm and wraps around his wrist a green plastic bracelet, unbreakable, the kind used in clubs to distinguish the legal drinkers from the illegal. A bar code is printed across the front. She shoots it with an optical scanning gun. The computer registers him like a can of beans. "Keep this on for the entire study," she tells him. Then she punches a hole in the upper-right-hand corner of his freshly laminated ID and slips through a cheapo chain. "And wear this at all times, outside your shirt, always in full view. For meals you swipe the magnetic strip before entering the cafeteria. If you lose it, it's a ten-dollar fine for a replacement." She dangles the ID in front of him like car keys for her son.

The laminate is still warm and smells of toxic clean. The Billy Schine it contains is far from flattering; he looks bruised, bloated, drowned. "I think you've captured my corpse."

"It's not that bad."

"A suspected boating accident."

"You look fine."

"It's like I'm wearing my own memento mori."

She's suddenly sensitive to her art. "It's how you look," she says, guiding him to the door and the next station, where, she adds rather cryptically, joy awaits.

Joy comes in the form of a two-hundred-pound black woman. Better yet, sea-glass brown, her skin battered smooth and frosty when dry. She sits on a stool in the middle of the room, not so much inhabiting the space but wearing it like an antebellum hoopskirt.

"Okay, Mr. Schine, have a seat and roll up—are you left- or right-handed?"

"Right, but I throw lefty and play guitar lefty, though I don't play guitar much."

"So, right?"

"Mostly, I'd say. And pool. I don't know why, but I play pool lefty."

Her droopy eyes droop further. "Your left sleeve, up to the shoulder."

The chair Billy plops into resembles a clinical Barcalounger. It's menacingly comfortable, as if TV might be watched intravenously. The slightest squirm unleashes vinyl farts the color of teal.

Joy snaps on surgical gloves. Fingers are wiggled expectantly like the order of the day might be criminal. "So, I'm the phlebotomist for your study, meaning I'll be drawing your blood over the next two weeks. Twice a day. Twenty times next Saturday. That's your PK day, 'PK' for pharmacokinetics, which is the main point of this study. That'll give us the internal life of the drug, a half-hour-by-half-hour analysis for ten hours. It's a long day for the both of us, so feel sorry for me as well. I'll

64

never take too much blood, only a little more than a thimbleful, not enough to have any effect on you. But instead of needle-sticking you all those times and leaving your arm looking like a pincushion, what I'm going to do is insert this cannula"—she picks up a small needle-nosed tube from the instrument tray—"so when we need blood, all we have to do is connect a test tube. What that means is you'll have a medical device in your arm and you should treat it with respect and leave it alone. Don't play with it, don't pull at it, don't pick at it. No joke. Best pretend it isn't even there. You can shower, you can do whatever you normally do. The cannula will be changed every four days, and if there's ever any discomfort, let me know. We can always go to the needle. Clear?"

Billy nods. How old is she? Twenty-five? Thirty-five? Forty-five? Her age seems hidden under a layer of timeless weight. Billy likes her instantly and for no good reason. She seems nice. Sweet. Maybe it's the warm and fuzzy undertones of a large black woman, a nurse, possibly racist in nature, or nurture, at least stereotypical (the Aunt Jemima factor) and totally undeniable. You jerk. Who do you think she is, Butterfly McQueen? Hattie McDaniel? Because guaranteed if she were a large white woman, she'd simply be fat.

Joy ties a rubber cord around his biceps. "Pump your hand."

"So how'd you get the name 'Joy'?"

"How'd you get your name?"

"My parents."

"Imagine that."

"Is it a family name?"

"My mother died in labor so my father tried putting on a happy face."

"Jesus, I'm sorry."

"It was a long time ago." Joy rips open an antiseptic swab and wipes clean the peachy underside of his arm. "You've got good ropes. A five on the phlebometer."

"What's that?"

"Thickness and definition of the vein."

"Oh."

"These are bodybuilder veins."

"Inside weakling arms. Must be my inner Charles Atlas."

"Aren't we quick."

"Huh?"

"Clever."

"You make it sound like a diagnosis."

"Either way, it makes my job easier."

"Cleverness?"

"No, your veins. Nothing worse than chicken veins." Joy leans over Billy; her cleavage is viselike. "Okay, here we go," she says, holding the cannula by the neck like a viscious species of worm. The needle pushes against the skin and the skin bends and briefly withstands before the needle breaks the surface and slips in. Two strips of medical tape secure the parasite to his arm.

Joy reaches for a test tube. "You're a watcher," she says.

"Excuse me?"

"Most people turn away." She marries the test tube to the cannula, and blood begins to flow, its rich red hue flummoxing even the best colorist. "But you're a watcher."

"Yeah, I don't mind."

"Some people faint." Joy unknots the rubber cord. "And the ex-junkies drool."

"Am I drooling?"

"Are you an ex-junkie?"

"No."

"Then you're just salivating."

"I sort of find it relaxing," Billy says, like a vitrine filling with his blood, he imagines, filling and filling and Billy slowly fading as his fluid self drains into glass until every last drop of what lies beneath skin is exposed.

Joy detaches the test tube, shakes it, labels it, racks it with the seven other samples. "You're all set," she says.

Billy asks, "Which one belongs to the woman?"

"Why?"

"I want to see Snow White."

*   *   *

66

In station three Dr. Paul Honeysack wears the prerequisite white lab coat and sits behind a desk. He's in his gaunt thirties, overworked, underpaid, on the threshold of the cynical forties where age will be added to the growing list of disappointments. By the looks of him, Billy figures his twenties were without much humor (only podiatry would've made him laugh). His cheeks are pictographed with acne scars that tell the story of brutal teen years underscored with shy obsessive eyes that remind Billy of a boy who never had a doubt of what he wanted to do in his life. Even as friends played in the dirt, little Paul Honeysack probably dreamed of today—and here it is, you schlub. "You're the last one?" he asks.

Billy nods.

The doctor thumbs through a file. "William A. Schine, date of birth 7/11/72, Cincinnati, Ohio, screened and approved, New York, 8/14/99." His eyes alternate between the papers on his desk and the man in front of him; he could be sketching a portrait in vital statistics. "What year Harvard?"

"Ninety-three."

"So I'm older."

"Harvard?"

"No, Cornell, then Emory, but I had a lot of friends at Harvard."

"Oh."

"Almost went."

"Oh."

"Are you an artist, writer, filmmaker, actor?" he says as if saying blah-blah-blah.

"None of the above."

"We don't get many Ivy Leaguers here unless they're the creative type."

"So I hear."

"Are you working on a Ph.D.?"

"No."

"You a reporter?" he asks warily.

"Nope, I'm nothing."

Honeysack rechecks his paperwork as if somewhere in the documentation, in the height and weight, is the verbal and math of an SAT score, the verification of his intelligence. The goddamn SAT. Reach back and remember that fateful day when Billy received the notice from the ETS. His first piece of official mail—Mr. William A. Schine in the cellophane rearview mirror—he hesitated before discovering his crass cognitive worth. Where would he fall in the world? He used a kitchen knife as a letter opener (the envelope begged for such respect) and sensed he was slicing through skin. Inside was a sixteen hundred combined. *You asshole.* No studying, no preparation. *You fucking asshole.* He simply enjoyed the process: the desk with the ripple grain of wood, the number-two pencils forming a river raft, the eraser barge, the clock moon, the calculator as your only friend—it was like Huck and Jim floating toward Princeton, New Jersey. Then there was the drama of broken seals and multiple-choice ovals, the strange pleasure in shading the answers and creating a design and transforming a blank sheet into a mental punch card. His public school was glad for the statistical bump, though his teachers considered themselves the butt of an inside joke (their beloved wunderkind, Vanessa Freen, totaled a measly twelve sixty) and his classmates treated him like the lucky winner of the standardized lottery. Of course his parents cooed nonstop about what their combined DNA scored. "You're proof of the properness of our choice," his father told him, as if hydrogen had bonded with oxygen and produced a brilliant life-giving sea. *Fucking asshole, who do you think you are?*

Honeysack steeples his fingers down to business. "I'm the doctor-in-residence for your study, the acting physician, a liaison between the nurses and the researchers. I'm a disinterested participant. A neutral party." He smiles like Switzerland. "I have no relationship whatsoever with this particular study, no conflict of interest, so feel free to tell me anything about your day-to-day status. How you're feeling. How you're holding up. Tell me about any adverse events you might be having, big and small, because nothing's too small for us. Think of me as your friend here. Even if you have issues with the politics of the place, the people, the food, let me know and maybe I can help." He quietly claps his fingers. "Okay?"

"Okay."

"How's your health been recently? Any colds, any illness whatsoever?"

"No."

"Have you taken any drugs in the last month? Over-the-counter? Prescription? Um, other, less legal substances?"

"No."

"Drinking heavily?"

"No."

"Allergies?"

"No."

"Would you say, right now, at this particular moment, you're feeling fine."

Billy considers this. "Sure," he says.

"Nervous?"

"A bit."

"Of course. That's perfectly natural. Anxious or nervous?"

"More nervous than anxious, I'd say."

"Okay, okay." Dr. Honeysack ruffles some papers. "Now Mr. Schine— 'Schine,' is that a Jewish name by any chance?"

Billy startles, as if thrown into another unfamiliar time. "My father's Jewish."

"Eastern European?" asks Honeysack.

"German," Billy says.

"Me too. German, that is, not Jewish. 'Honigsack' before we came over."

Billy wonders what the proper response should be, what with the history involved, and decides on a what-do-you-know shrug.

"But that was ages ago," Honeysack says, then he tongues the corner of his mouth as if investigating a hidden canker. "I ask that question because if you were Romanian or Lithuanian and a Jew, we might be concerned. Genetically speaking, there'd be a much higher risk of developing agranulocytosis."

"Is that serious?"

"It can kill you."

"I'm pretty sure German," Billy says, remembering how his father

69

would get teary over *The Sound of Music,* perhaps fancying himself a Baron Von Trapp type, or possibly a Christopher Plummer type. "Maybe Austrian," he says.

"That's fine, too." Dr. Honeysack hands him a ten-page document. "Now let's go over your informed consent. It's very important that you understand everything in this form. Now you've signed a primary consent form, but this is the conclusive form. As you know from the packet we sent you, you'll be testing Allevatrox, an experiment atypical antipsychotic for the treatment of schizophrenia, a severe mental disorder." He glances up from his copy of the form. "Of course you know what schizophrenia is. Sorry. Some of our volunteers are, well, less knowledgeable. Anyway. We'll go over the purpose, the protocol, the research procedure, the risks, the payment to volunteers, the confidentiality, the right to question, the subject's rights, the IRB contact, and the voluntary participation clause for Phase I research." Dr. Honeysack takes a deep, well-deserved breath. "First, the purpose—"

"Can I just sign now?" Billy asks.

"You've read everything, understood everything?"

Billy lies. "Yeah."

"And you have no questions?"

"Just where do I sign?"

"Well, just to be sure, I'd like to go over some of the possible adverse events that you might experience during the study, just so you know what to expect from an atypical antipsychotic. Since this is what we call a load-up bioavailability study and not a long-range treatment program, a lot of these AEs simply won't happen. You'd need the added element of time. Over time, maybe, but in this short period, not likely. That said, there is a chance of having dystonic reactions, which means sudden muscle tightening, normally in the neck and or jaw area. These are more disconcerting than dangerous. Nothing to worry about. There's also a chance of something called an oculogyric crisis where your eyes involuntarily look toward a certain direction, often upwards. The glories, we call it. This generally happens when you're tired or in front of the television or not really engaged in the world, your eyes just sort of roll upwards. Another potential reaction is akinesia, and it's the most common of the extra-pyramidal symptoms. It's characterized by a decrease in spontaneous movement, meaning less flamboyant limb movement and facial expression. You'd get a wooden appearance, a shuffle instead of a trot. Akinesia can also have psychological repercussions such as lack of motivation and spontaneity, a diminished range of affect. On the other side of the extrapyramidal spectrum is akathisia. With akathisia you'd experience motor restlessness, fidgeting, purposeless movements, like obsessive leg crossing or skin rubbing. As you might expect, psychologically it might make you nervous and jittery. Okay, now we come to the bane of neuroleptics, and hopefully something Allevatrox has done away with, and that's tardive dyskinesia. This is the most worrisome adverse event because it can be, potentially, irreversible. Once again, you really need the added element of time for the symptoms to develop. It manifests itself by way of extreme facial behavior, like tongue thrusting, mouth chewing, lip smacking, eye blinking. A disturbed facial appearance. It can also effect your fingers, give them a constant wiggle and snap. It can impinge on your respiratory muscles and cause grunting and odd breathing patterns. It can turn into something called truncal dyskinesia, causing your torso to move in sharp thrusting motions which, to the passerby, can be unsettling." Dr. Honeysack stretches his shoulders in what Billy first assumes is an example but in fact is just a yawn. "That's about it," the doctor tells him.

"That's all," Billy says.

"Sounds worse than it is."

"Sounds just about right. Where do I sign?"

"Last page, above 'human research volunteer.'"

Billy gives his celebrity autograph, large and loopy and entirely illegible. Honeysack hands him the countersigned duplicate; his signature could be razor wire over a Dunkin' Donuts. "Keep this copy for your records," he tells Billy.

Your records almost makes Billy laugh.

Business completed, Honeysack leans back as if reclining into Billy's wavelength. "Do you have any questions before you leave, anything at all?"

Billy thinks for a moment then asks, "What do you do here besides this?" hoping he might ingratiate himself with this man, that afterward Honeysack will say to himself, *Billy Schine, nice guy, a perfect normal.*

"Like my real job? I'm a researcher here, but every year we're put on a random study as medical supervisor. It's our version of jury duty."

"So, what are you working on?"

"What am I working on?" Honeysack hums a sigh then smiles. Billy can see the ten-year-old in that smile, before the onslaught of zits and school, before precociousness went stale. "You're not a spy, are you?" he jokes. "No, I don't think so. I'm working on, um, this fairly radical preservation technique in trauma care. The basic concept is to take a severely injured person, say a car-wreck victim, and slip them into a state of cryobiostasis by flushing the aorta with a saline solution we've developed. We chill this solution to forty degrees, in effect putting the heart rate on the edge of no pulse. This keeps the trauma patient viable for a couple of hours so that the ER can determine the best course of action vis-à-vis the injuries. It's not as crazy as it might sound. It's as crazy as freezing sperm. It's a temporary measure, a few hours of life-saving stasis. The doctor I'm working with, he's a genius in the field. He developed the technique. So far it's worked beautifully, at least on dogs."

"Dogs?"

"Yes, and pigs." Enthusiasm lights Honeysack's face, except for the acne scars; they stay in shadow, a rawboned chiaroscuro.

"How about using humans?" Billy asks.

"Well, they're trickier," Honeysack says. "Not so much physiologically but legally. After eight years we're ready to move up to the next phase but we're still shooting sows in the stomach and miraculously saving their lives. All we need is our Anne Miller."

"The leggy entertainer?"

"No, the first American who received penicillin."

"I had another Ann Miller in mind."

"My Anne Miller developed severe strep after a miscarriage."

"My Ann Miller was a dancer, singer, actress, a triple threat." Billy remembers her from *On the Town.* It was—or is—one of his parents'

72

favorite musicals. It always seemed to play on a Sunday on a channel without sports, and his mother and father would transform the living room couch into a pew, the television into an altar, and they'd sit and gaze upon the famous montage—the sailors on shore leave—and grow giddy with every vista, every landmark, every street and avenue and storefront from 1949, the stained glass of the old days, the old stomping grounds, the old haunts of Times Square, like a life flashing before their exiled-in-Cincinnati eyes. His mother was crazy about Gene Kelly while his father wondered whatever happened to Jules Munshin anyway?

"Must be different Ann Millers," Billy says.

"Must be." Dr. Honeysack gets up for good-bye. Billy mirrors him and starts for the door when Honeysack calls him back. "Oh, who should we contact in case of an emergency?" he asks. "I forgot about that. It's on page five, name, address, phone number, a next-of-kin kind of thing."

Billy thinks about his parents, his mother in Whispering Pines, his father by her side filling her head with memories of how things once were, stroking her left hand and lifting her ring finger into the sunlight, that small diamond breaking shards of light onto plain white walls. The phone would beckon like a telegram. *Your son, William Schine, he's in the hospital.* Billy imagined himself on his back, waiting for his father, waiting and waiting, half of him moaning *don't come,* the other half screaming *please.*

Billy writes down Ragnar.

The fourth and final station is a bathroom where a urine sample is required. Billy arrives to find the door closed. A nurse, unhappy in her chore, waits outside with what can only be described as a urine cart with six cups of pee. Billy grins an awkward hello.

"We still have somebody in there," she says.

"Oh."

"And he's been in there forever."

From behind the door: "I heard that." It's Rodney Letts and he sounds petrified.

"Turn on the faucet or something," the nurse tells him.

"What do you think I've been doing all this time, cleaning the sink?"

"Well, people are getting impatient."

"Pressure does not help. I needed to go. Or I did. I was really ready to go. But I've lost it. It's disappeared. I know my bladder, it's stubborn, and it's not going to give me a single drop." Rodney talks near tears. "Is it really so essential? How about I give you my sample in an hour or two? How about if I take the cup with me?"

"We don't do it to go."

Ms. Longley walks over from down the hall. "You all right in there, Mr. Letts?"

"Who's that?"

"Ms. Longley."

"I'm sorry, Ms. Longley, but I can't go."

"Yes, you can, just relax."

"No, I can't. I can't go. And now all this pressure, this urinalysis. But I want to go, I want fill a bathtub for you people, but I can't. I'm sorry."

"Okay, Mr. Letts," Ms. Longley soothes professionally. "Why don't you come out and regroup and have a glass of water, maybe walk around a bit, and then give it another go? In the meantime, Mr. Schine can scoot in and do his business."

"It's just that I'm"—the door unlocks—"intimidated." Rodney stands in the doorway, I♥NY ridiculously crooked on his head. "Give me an hour," he begs. "Two hours, maybe tomorrow morning. Yeah, tomorrow morning would be great. Tomorrow morning, no problem."

"You have all the time you want. It's just that we can't clear you from admissions until we have a urine sample. It's regulations." Ms. Longley reaches for him though she has no intention of touching the man, only prompting him forward. "You'll have to wait down here until you can tinkle."

"But I can't." A surprising chuckle comes over Rodney. "I'm fucked— sorry," he says. "Language. Poor language. No excuse." He grins. "Tinkle, right, I should just tinkle, just get it over with and"—he humphs—"just let it happen, let it flow, right."

"How about a drink first and then we'll see what happens."

"Yeah, okay, a drink." Rodney, resigned, passes Billy.

"Mr. Schine, all yours."

The urine attendant hands him his cup. "Please, just halfway up."

A small sign hangs near the bathroom sink: PLEASE URINATE OVER TOILET.

Billy prompts his bladder with a soft tickle under the glans helmet and its oh-so-sensitive chinstrap. Here we go. There's something strange about peeing in a cup, he thinks, something oddly circular, something, well, all too potable and self-absorbed, as if you're pouring yourself a warm glass of chardonnay. Cheers. The piss rises in a hurry, a deep yellow. Urinalysis will find five bowls of sugar-encrusted cereal for breakfast. Billy resumes into the bowl but then spots the sad empty cup of Rodney Letts resting on the sink. Inspired, he grabs it and gives it two inches of well-earned relief.

Back in the hallway, he tells Rodney, "All yours."

Hearing this, Rodney crushes his water-cooler cone and steps into the bathroom with a sense of bravery, not of a hero, but of a man who accepts his own demise. Ears strain in the hallway, acoustics wrapped within Rodney's urethra. Finally, the tension is eliminated by the telltale splash of piss on water followed by a triumphant groan behind the door.

Rodney reappears, glorious.

Brad Lannigan is the first to applaud.

10

THEY'RE TAKEN up the stairs to the third floor. The hallway is color-coded for easy identification, a green stripe running along the middle of the wall. "Green is your color," Ms. Longley tells them. "You should always see green. If you see red, blue, yellow, or orange, you're in the wrong area and you should go find green. In your rooms, on your bed, is a green T-shirt. It's important that you always wear that shirt."

"Go green," Lannigan cheers.

They pause by the nurse's station where two women are introduced, Nurse Clifford and Nurse George. They glance up in unison, smile in unison, close their binders in unison, stand in unison. They're conjoined by routine. Their white slacks and loose pink blouses disappoint Billy. He had hopes for the nurses from the past, the nurses in the movies, the Florence Nightingales who gave extreme unction with their tears and acted like salaried nuns with earthly benefits. But alas, no more virginal vestments. No more peaked cap. No more pale hosiery. Only the shoes—white and orthopedic—have stayed the same. Nurses, it seems, have gone through their own version of Vatican II. Nowadays they dress in classic dyke.

"Hello," the nurses greet by rote. Though they look nothing alike, they share a steely firearm stare, front-sighted and methodical, braced for the recoil. Their idea of mercy would be shooting you in the thigh.

Ms. Longley lectures the group about listening to the nurses and doing what they say. "Remember," she tells them. "They're trained professionals, not your maids."

The nurses cross their arms, clench their lips into tight pink fists.

"They're here for your well-being and safety."

The nurses nod.

"So help them do their job and they'll help you do your job."

Billy thinks, *your job.* What is their job? They're stand-ins for the real stars, he thinks, stuntmen who take the cure before the afflicted step in for their close-up. The sick are loved. They're the certifiably unsick. Nothing will save them.

Toward the end of the hall, Ms. Longley points out the lounge area, and halfway down the hall she shows them the only pay phone. "Change is not provided," she clarifies. "And cell phones are forbidden." The white white of the hall, the white walls, the white fluorescent light, the white floor, smell perpetually scrubbed, a sort of antiseptic potpourri with the green stripe unleashing a scratch and sniff pine, which is necessary when you pass the ten dormlike rooms, three beds per room, each door revealing an anarchy of odor: feet versus armpits versus farts versus a dozen other minor smells searching for their rightful claim.

Billy is assigned room 306, along with Brad Lannigan. Thank God neither Ossap nor Dullick were called forward, nor Rodney, who ever since receiving the gift of urine has been nudging Billy with overly grateful eyes. The absurd fantasy of Gretchen was squashed earlier when she was given her own room, being the only woman in this study. Room 302. Two doors down. Just twenty-six steps.

"Dinner is in fifteen minutes," Ms. Longley informs Billy and Lannigan. "So don't bother getting too comfortable."

Too comfortable? This room is not designed for comfort. Part hospital, part motel, part residence for the aesthetically challenged, no loose parts or sharp corners or unnecessary touches threaten to put out taste. The walls are a patronizing yellow—a just-relax shade. The beige carpet could've been woven from concrete. Opposite the door is a large window with thick curtains prepared either for blackout conditions or a small theatrical production of the world outside, starring the courtyard and the HAM sundial's faulty interpretation of time. There's a bureau crafted for three sets of clothes, and a mirror suitable for three sets of expressions. A digital clock has its own niche, the numbers red and ornery. The only extravagance in the entire room is the television, a Zenith Horizon, seventeen inches wide, bolted into the ceiling by a contraption that resembles a halo for spinal cord injuries. Of the three beds, the first two carry a towel, a washcloth, a minibar of soap, and a green shirt. The other roommate is present in luggage alone, an army duffel bag, which claims the bed by the window, arguably the best bed, as Lannigan makes clear when he rests his fists against his hips and mutters, "I suppose Goldilocks found his just right."

"I suppose," Billy says.

"Oh well, first come, first serve. I would've done the same. But I think he tested all the pillows which is beyond the pale even in my book." Lannigan turns toward Billy, his bland face pleading handsome; the man has a shrill form of charisma. "In terms of beds, I have to say I hate the middle. I'm the youngest of three, all boys, and growing up I was always jammed in the middle. That said, I am willing to sleep there, it's just—"

"I don't mind," Billy tells him.

"Really?"

"No problem."

"Because I can take it."

"Really, I don't mind." Which is the honest truth, considering Billy's childhood fears of madmen and monsters, of their sneaking through his house and searching for victims, room by room, bed by bed, murdering in order of appearance. His bedroom would have been the first attacked, and he often considered himself an early warning system for his parents, his dying screams their alarm. With Lannigan nearest the door, Billy figures he stands a fighting chance against whatever might burst in.

"You sure?" Lannigan asks. "Because I can take the middle."

"Positive."

"Please, let me." Lannigan is a martyr in retrospect.

"That's all right."

"Well, okay," Lannigan says, jumping aboard his negotiated bed. He crosses his feet, weaves his hands behind his head, clicks his tongue. This calm lasts maybe ten seconds before he's up again, checking the vista from the window, picking up a comic book—*Superman and the City of Doom*—then a Bible from the mysterious third roommate's bed, inspecting himself in the mirror, peeking into the bathroom, finding the remote control, unfortunately tethered to the wall near the middle bed, and—*click*—turning on the TV.

"I wonder if the channels are all the same this far north," he says. "If channel two is still CBS or if they're different." He flips around; Dan Rather appears. "It's the same," Lannigan confirms, pleased, like he's discovered absolutely nothing new.

There are floods in North Carolina.

Droves of bloated pigs float belly-up.

Submerged rooflines resemble capsized boats.

Billy opens his suitcase, its cache like artifacts from an earlier era. *The Oxford Dictionary of Quotations* goes on the bedside table.

"Some light reading?" Lannigan asks, picking up the book.

"Yeah."

"This has all the biggies?"

"Yep."

Lannigan reads, " 'The world, as we know it, is a place in which great men battle little men and neither are ever right about or certain of their size.' Guess who said that."

"Who?"

Lannigan bows. "Me. Not bad, huh? But I've always been good with quotes. Or imaginary quotes. As Shakespeare said, 'The easiest path toward greatness is through the already wet words of others.' " Lannigan grins, gestures kittenishly. "Me again."

Billy starts unpacking. "I saw you reading *Hamlet* in the van."

"Not reading, memorizing."

"So you're an actor."

"Yep. And let me guess, you're a painter."

"No."

"A writer?"

"No."

"Please, not another actor?"

"No, none of that."

"A mime, a performance artist?"

"I don't really have a specific career."

"A musician?"

"Nothing."

"A juggler?"

"No."

"Well, you have that look," Lannigan says. "What Rilke called 'the desperate contentedness of the poet, like a starving lion surfeited on air.' Okay, enough, I'm sorry."

Billy slips the suitcase under his bed. "So are you going to be in a production of *Hamlet* or something," he asks, hoping he might turn conversation toward Lannigan and slowly slink away into the long grass of an answer.

"Yep. A pretty good production too. Off-Broadway, but that's basically Broadway nowadays. It's sort of my big break. The director is a friend from way back and he's gotten suddenly successful and he's cast me, like we've always discussed, our *Hamlet*. Very exciting. We open in November."

"And you're Hamlet?"

"No, not quite. They've gotten a name for that role."

"Who?"

"I'm not sure yet."

"So what's you're part."

"I play Voltimand, the courtier. Want to hear my big speech?"

"Why not," Billy says.

"Ask me as the King, 'what from our brother Norway?' "

" 'What from our brother Norway?' "

Lannigan launches into:

> "Most fair return of greetings and desires.
> Upon our first, he sent out to suppress
> His nephew's levies, which to him appeared
> To be a preparation 'gainst the Polack . . ."

On and on Lannigan goes, giving Billy the full light of his performance, Billy keeping his expression easily lit despite the discomfort of over-enunciation and extreme gesticulation, Billy instantly reminded why he

80

avoids the theater, where bad acting fills him with the public embarrassment of others, where a missed line or cue, a prop gone wrong, a ringing
cell phone, can rip his heart more than any well-wrought scene, where the
tension of possible mistakes undercuts even an Olivier.

> ". . . That it might please you to give quiet pass
> Through your dominions for this enterprise,
> On such regards of safety and allowance
> As therein are set down."

Lannigan, as Voltimand, gives a small bow, then Lannigan returns with
a *ta-da*.

"That's great," Billy says.

"It's not me," Lannigan explains. "It's the language. Shakespeare gives
you everything on the page. All I have to do is follow along and trust in his
words. I tell you, it's an amazing experience."

"It'll be a Voltimand for the ages," Billy says, hearing the joke too late.

But Lannigan smiles anyway.

The CBS evening news shows footage of Menomonee Falls, Wisconsin.
A large crowd has gathered around the house of Charles Savitch, estimated
to be a thousand strong and growing. Satellite vans have started camping
in nearby driveways. International press is involved. The footage quickly
flashes the now famous MRI, then the high school photo, then the
unconfirmed glimpse of Charles Savitch behind the curtains of his living
room. Dan Rather returns, stern-faced, as if he's the high school principal
and this news is a too popular troublemaker.

The bathroom is a standard, if snug, arrangement of bathtub, sink, and
toilet. Billy slips on the green shirt followed by the ID necklace. He's glad
for the end of *Cats*, particularly his nipples which have been rubbed raw by
the poly-blend. He checks himself in the mirror. He looks mildly official,
like a janitor for the Pentagon. Back in the room, he sees Lannigan
standing by the window. He's shirtless. His chest rubs, humps, slaps the
glass. "A new arrival is coming," he tells Billy.

"Oh."

"Come over and pretend to fuck me in the ass."

"What?"

"As a joke, to freak this guy out."

"I don't think so."

"He's stopping," Lannigan narrates. "He's looking around. He's"—the performance becomes more vigorous—"C'mon, just grind my ass. It'll be great."

"No thanks."

Lannigan stops, dejected. "He's gone."

"Too bad."

"Next time we should rehearse or something, really get something down."

Thanks to the gods of slapstick, the Zeus of poorly timed entrances, the Athena of wacky misunderstandings, for the last minute their other roommate has been standing by the door.

"Hello," he says.

"Hello."

"Hey."

His name is Do. Do as in deer, as in female deer. Rami is his last name. Jay Rami. But everyone calls him Do, he explains. Besides the sol-fa syllables of his last name, there's nothing particularly doeish about the man, except maybe his eyes, narrowly set and dark, deer-in-headlight eyes, surprised and doomed and forever in the way. But really those eyes are more racoonish, Billy thinks, opossumish, night-critter eyes neither wounded nor mournful, devoid of poetry and pause, small black eyes peering from a mass of moonbeam flesh as if formed by two angry thumbs. Tires would not swerve for these eyes. "I know, stupid," Do says about his name. "It started with a teacher, first grade, like the first day of first grade. She took attendance and called Jay Rami, but I was absent, so she called my name again, and this time she sang 'fa sol la ti do.' I've been stuck ever since." He talks like he's leaving a too long message on an answering machine.

"Well, nice to meet you," Lannigan says.

"You guys just got here?"

"Yep."

"Cool. Where you all from?"

"New York City. The both of us," Lannigan says.

"Cool. I'm from around here."

"Cool."

"Not really." Billy guesses the guy is nineteen, twenty years old. His skin is covered with freckles, freckles like foxing on an old sallow print of a bare-knuckled boxer who never won a bout. "Either of you ever done this before?" Do asks.

"What?" Lannigan says rather lasciviously.

"Test drugs."

"Professionally?"

"Yeah."

"No, never professionally." Lannigan squint-stares, and Billy knows Lannigan is casting Do as the rube, and poor Do hasn't a clue.

Around seven o'clock, a female voice drops into their room via a small speaker in the ceiling. "Please stand outside your door for dinner."

Nurses Clifford and George wait for them in the hall. "Okay," Nurse Clifford (or perhaps Nurse George) says. "Soon enough this will become routine, but until then, pay attention. All meals are mandatory, breakfast, lunch, dinner. Diet is an important component to the study. A nurse will always escort you to and from the cafeteria. Always make sure you're wearing your IDs. Okay? All set?" No one dares a question.

Down the hall they go, down the stairs, onto the main floor, Nurse Clifford/George in front and Nurse George/Clifford in back, proper quotation marks around an unpleasant bit of language. Nobody talks much, except for Ossap and Dullick, who whisper and stare down any company, like Billy, who unwittingly enters their orbit and overhears something about security cameras. Billy glances about for a familiar face. Sameer Sirdesh seems to have found himself in the company of other immigrants, two Mexicans, a Colombian, an Algerian, and two Chinese. Rodney Letts sneaks up from behind, buddies himself with Billy, thanking him, once again, for his piss. "Looks like they got a pretty good pack of mules for this study," he says.

"Mules?"

"Yeah, these legal immigrants, who knows, maybe even illegal. Some day they'll open a big old CPU right in Mexico. Fuck balloons of cocaine, here, swallow this beta-blocker." Billy spies Gretchen up ahead. She's being trailed by Peter Swain who is blatantly, offensively, ogling her ass— *Pig!*—which Billy finds neither small nor big but pleasantly muscular, like a figure eight hewed by ice-shattering skates.

Entering the cafeteria requires a swipe from the ID followed by a push through a turnstile, an operation some people have problems with. (See Do, who swipes and swipes and swipes, a bottleneck developing behind him, and still he swipes—*fucking moron*—until Billy comes over and properly aligns the magnetic strip.) The cafeteria is like any other cafeteria except for its abundance of color. Trays come in blue, red, green, yellow, and orange, as do the meals, served from platters flagged blue, red, green, yellow, and orange, as do the tables, arranged in sections of blue, red, green, yellow, and orange. It's like a rainbow segregated.

Billy sits with Rodney, Do, Lannigan, and a couple of already seated greens who nod the newfound company hello. Nearby Billy notices a table of orange normals. They eat with little joy. Their bodies seem to have retained every drop of water. Cheeks are near bursting. Necks distend below jawlines like snakes digesting a pair of tube socks. Hands are hands children might draw. Billy watches these bloated faces float above photo IDs—they could be nasty cartoon balloons proclaiming, "This is not who I normally am."

"Probably some sort of dipine," Rodney says.

"What's that?" Do asks.

"A calcium-channel blocker, pretty cush except for the obvious swelling."

"That's not swelling," Billy says. "That's five words worse."

"It's not that bad," Rodney assures, glad to be the man in the know.

Dumpsters are no longer his métier. That black skid on his nose takes on the qualities of a sagacious birthmark.

"I wonder if it does the same to your cock?" Lannigan cracks.

"Not sure about that."

The table settles into their meal: iceberg lettuce, chicken parmigiana, cherry Jell-O.

Nobody complains.

Billy takes in the other colors. The reds are sweating, sweating into their meatloaf, sweating, sweating—Christ, they're sweating. Their forks might as well weigh a hundred pounds, the main course the second leg of a triathlon. And how about the blues? They're all wearing sunglasses, or rather, protective anti-light shields—massive black bars of privacy against all things illuminated. The yellows, three, four, five of them, are puking. Luckily, they're equipped with vomit bags. Wherever Billy looks, there's a strange burst of color. Three reds start laughing. Two yellows clench their stomachs. An orange swoons. A blue takes off his sunglasses, squints, rubs his eyes as if flashbulbs are popping. A red shoots milk from his nose, either a side effect or giggle reflex. More reds laugh and sweat. A blue has an unnoticed nosebleed. A yellow gets up and rushes toward the bathroom. A red eats his whole dessert—a bowl of chocolate pudding—in a single sweaty slurp. An orange is crying without the luxury of tears. A yellow drips milk into a glass of water, mesmerized by the liquid trail of fat.

After dinner, the greens go through orientation. During this time, as Ms. Longley stands and greets them officially and introduces the staff for their study, the nurses and doctors and phlebotomists rising up under the power of half waves, their smiles brief, their postures still holding the contour of their seats, their asses not escaping the gravity of indifference—*yes, hello*—as Ms. Longley moves onto the business of being employed under care, mentioning the rules and regulations as well as the grounds for expulsion—smoking, drinking, drugging other than the sanctioned drug—plus the fines, fines for lateness, for rudeness, for general misbehavior, all contained under section four of the informed consent, enclosed within the information packet, presented upon arrival, *right, right, right,* whereupon she segues into a discussion of the IRB for any complaints, physical or psychological or monetary, which leads into the daily schedule, so important, knowing the where and when, especially on PK day, so please pay attention and, no matter what, listen to the staff, the staff nodding *if only,* Ms. Longley telling the group this will be routine soon enough, smiling as if milk and cookies are being discussed, a giant two-week recess—during this time, as the meal digests and her words describe the days ahead in the stock language of motivation, the communal spirit of the project, the well-balanced dinner proving too much for some stomachs, hence the farts, smelling of digestive mothballs, most silent though a few squeak free and punctuate Ms. Longley as she mentions the proud history of safety at Hargrove Anderson Medical and the real desire for communication, for dialogue and partnership, the doctors and nurses and phlebotomists checking watches with why-do-I-have-to-be-here brows, the cafeteria crew protesting the holdup by loudly scraping the serving pans into the trash—during this time, Billy surveys his fellow greens.

They number twenty-six: twenty-five men, one woman. All of them listen respectfully, or pretend to listen, nodding their heads even when there's nothing to agree on. Personalities have been shelved for the sake of good first impressions. They look like novices in a monastery, Billy thinks, with their green frock (the particular shade all wrong for their complexion; colorwise, they're winters wearing spring) and their earnest unripe air. Arms wear the stigmata of cannulas, fingered like self-doubting Thomases. IDs dangle from necks with the sanctity of security-clearance crucifixes. They inspect the laminated photographs as if they're wearing their old wicked selves. They seem newly proud. *This used to be me. This asshole.* They hear about the communion of doses and blood draws, transubstantiation in terms of hard cash, and for this earthly promise they'll kneel for days. Sin finances forgiveness. Money will cleanse their soul. For normally they are the uninspired, the unnoticed, the forgotten five minutes from now, scrub people who grow in places with little sun, who fill the landscape with nothing special, the backdrop of bus stations and fast-food restaurants, the folks you deny as your own when you stand in line with them, holding a twenty-four-ounce soda and microwaved burrito supreme, not me, but them, people who fight with loved ones in public, who walk around shirtless and talk too loud, who are forever the injured party. If you made a composite of their faces, you would find a person with wary eyes and suspicious lips and a forehead believing in expedience no matter the price. A victim thumbing through a book of mug shots might pause for a moment and think this person familiar, something in the features, until realizing that the nose is all wrong and the chin is different and no way with those ears. But their innocence is often mistaken for guilt. They are the rarely believed, the easily blamed.

"Any questions?" asks Ms. Longley.

Billy sees Gretchen, two tables away. Not really that attractive, not right now, not from this distance or this angle. She's a wedge of face, more defense than offense. Never graceful but scrappy, her mouth seems formed with a mouth guard in mind.

Hands shoot up.

"Can we get paid in cash?"

Ms. Longley: "No, only checks."

"Check checks or money orders?"

Ms. Longley: "Certified checks."

"Where can we cash them?"

Ms. Longley: "Most any bank."

"Do we have to have photo ID?"

Ms. Longley: "Probably."

"Can you vouch for us?"

Ms. Longley: "No."

"So there's no chance of cash?"

Gretchen, bored, reaches for her empty bowl of Jell-O and runs her finger along the bottom for the last remnants of whipped cream, certainly a sexy gesture, but it's not the licking of her finger that fires Billy, it's a few moments later, when she inspects the bowl again and makes a pout of *nothing more* and then lampoons her own girlishness.

Billy wonders if Gretchen knows he's watching.

"Can we get direct deposit?"

"Can we get some cash up front?"

He wonders if Gretchen even cares.

11

R OOM 306 breathes with sleep and central air. Do's asleep. Lannigan's asleep. The TV has long since cooled from the last bits of news: Chuck Savitch and his anthropomorphic brain tumor seen waving from the bay window of his mother's house, the crowd outside expressing their gratitude in the currency of camera flashes. The before-bed conversation (Do: "I wonder how we're going to feel tomorrow night?" Lannigan: "I hope we'll need those big dark glasses like the blues.") has degraded into snores. Thanks to the heavy curtains, the room is impressively closed-in with darkness. It gives Billy the impression of being trapped, like he's in a cave and every lightless particle is a rock pinning him down, and nobody knows he's missing, dying while they frolic above him, hand in hand, on the warm green grass. Billy moves his legs as proof against paralyzation. Are those dogs barking in the distance?

The digital clock glows red.

12:02 A.M. 12:23 A.M. 12:52 A.M.

Lannigan asleep. Do asleep. And Billy wide awake.

Not dogs, just the suggestion of dogs in the hum of central air.

1:00 A.M. Six hours until the alarm.

1:28 A.M. Five hours and thirty-two minutes until the alarm.

His brain is frantic with the awful math of diminishing sleep.

He counts backward from a hundred; he tenses and relaxes the muscles from his toes to his forehead; he tosses himself into dreams (*I'm flying . . . I'm stuck in molasses);* he rolls around for a comfortable position, stomach, left side, back, right side, repeat.

1:53 A.M. Five hours and seven minutes until the alarm.

Shit. Shit. Shit shit. Fuck.

Billy glances toward Do and Lannigan. Essentially, they're already awake, already greeting tomorrow morning, well rested, while Billy lags behind, knee-deep in yesterday.

Sleep can be a competitive sport.

He's tempted to scream, to make nightmare noises just loud enough to startle.

But there's another option.

Slipping free from the bed, Billy tiptoes toward the bathroom, the floor treated like twigs. He listens for disturbances in nearby sleep, stops, lets the silence resettle before continuing on. There's something calming, peaceful, about sneaking around in the dark, practically a childhood hobby for Billy, getting up in the middle of the night and stealing around the house, into his parents' room where he would watch them sleep, Abe and Doris intertwined like they were in a cold lonely place. He would try willing them awake by yelling *Help!* inside his head. He would crouch down until inches from their lips and smell their nighttime breath. More than once he would take something before leaving, a sock, a hairpin, or he would pop a button from a shirt, snap a shoelace, like a bitter ghost.

Billy reaches the bathroom door, finesses it open, closes it.

On goes the light.

The available real estate is minimal for the chore at hand. Maybe the floor, but the space is tight and a tad unhygienic. Maybe the toilet, but the toilet has no seat cover and maybe he could manage the ass-saddle, but this area seems specifically zoned for defecation, plus sitting on the pot too long can cause hemorrhoids, he was once warned in his too impressible youth. Maybe the shower, often an ideal locale, what with the running water and nozzle massage and soaps and shampoos and easy cleanup, but a shower right now is out of the question.

So Billy jerks off into the sink.

Underwear down, hips leaning forward, testicles pleasantly resting against cool porcelain, Billy begins. The first dozen strokes are uninspired, like a rally before a tennis match. Thoughts of *am-I-really-doing-this?* cross his mind, though only briefly. He's never been the type who imagines models or actresses or girls next door or aloof classmates in eleventh grade who might suddenly be interested in his tongue. He has no fantasy woman, no pinup posters taped inside his eyelids. Instead, he prefers personal history, the physical memoir of women he's touched and explored. In particular, he alights on their small intimate details, the galaxy of moles, the whorl of pubic hair, the veins and scars and tan lines, the knobby knees, the fur creeping around thighs, the belly button, the ridge of vertebrae. He cherishes freckles and collarbones, pilosity in natural light. Tits and ass, while wonderful, are more like product placements, the crass commercialism of propagation, whereas a birthmark the shape of Sicily is something else entirely. And really, when all is said and done, after a few months of physical distance, the random stand and steady fling and all the versions in between occupy just one fuck-byte of memory, whereas the marginalia, the scrawl of the pen, the edits and corrections, can bring you back to that first moment.

Boswell had his Johnson, Billy has his prick.

In all, there are fourteen lovers he can choose from, from Melissa of the walnut mole on the inner thigh, to Wendy of the scar under the chin, to Lily of the dimpled knees, to Diana of the lunar stretch marks on the breasts. But the severe present participial—standing up and snapping a quick one into a sink—distracts Billy from the past. Usually such work is done on his back, in bed, often followed by a nap, though in his youth he could be quite adventurous. Anywhere, anytime, twice in a library bathroom after discovering *Our Bodies, Ourselves,* with its sweet illustration of that pubescent girl. Then there were those special masturbatory techniques, like binding your wrist with a rubber band so your hand would go all numb, or using ordinary household items extraordinarily, e.g., those yellow cleaning gloves turned inside out, or licking your own armpit for virtual cunnilingus, a trick a teenage friend taught him, the closest thing to eating snatch without actually eating snatch, he said.

But Sally Hu, now his fifteenth lover, interrupts the past. Billy sees her reading the note, sees her saying *Asshole,* sees her puckering her lips which causes that single black freckle under her nose to disappear. Already she's slipped into abstraction. Yesterday morning might as well have been last year—Sally toweling the last remnants of her shower, Billy spying her from bed as she dried her legs, her thighs, her pubic wisp, with strange prosaic grace, then wrung her long black hair into one of those terry turbans women seem genetically gifted to engineer. Arms akimbo, she stood in front of the bureau and said, "Like I don't know you're pretending."

Billy gave up nothing.

"To be all asleep, you faker. But I know you're watching me." She spoke with an endearing New York accent. Here she was, as exotic as a specimen from Captain Cook, cheekbones molded by muscular thumbs, eyes pinched tight, nose fashioned from the leftover clay, skin fired eggshell smooth, but if you inspected the hallmark you'd see *Made in Brooklyn* stamped on the underside. Her voice embraced the monoglot of the streets, the raunchy assimilation of stoops. Sometimes she seemed like an Asian actress as dubbed by a bleach-blond moll.

Billy stirred awake.

"You're a lousy fucking actor," she told him. Her family was an American success story, her parents immigrants from China with three disputed corners of the Korean deli trade. They hated Billy. Every week they visited with produce and untranslated pleas of leave him soon.

Billy rubbed his eyes. Look at her. Even her breasts were imported treasures, perfect bowls with nipples unlike any he had ever encountered before: dark and cone shaped and fully realized on all levels of excitation. Pert Buddhas, Billy thought. He reached up for some spiritual enlightenment.

"Way too fucking late," Sally said.

"But it's early."

"It's too late and it's too early."

"Early late."

"None of that now." Sally started browsing her closet. "So what's for breakfast, honey? Eggs and bacon? An omelet? French toast?"

He tugged down the comforter and exposed himself. "Sausage," he said.

Sally clipped on her bra. "What a seducer you are."

Billy stomped his heels against the covers in spoiled protest. Maybe she would smile. Maybe she would humor him one last time. The sun transformed the dust motes and skin chaff into beautiful phosphorescence. We sleep in our own filth, Billy thought. Then he began playing with himself.

"Are you really?" she asked.

"I'm like a mountain climber."

"I wish."

"I mean in answer to the question why." He gestured toward his erection. "And you, you are my Sherpa."

"I'm so flattered."

He mused aloud, "Norgay Hu. Certainly more appropriate than Sally."

"Fuck you," she demurred. "You told me Sally means princess."

"Not 'Sally.' 'Sarah.' 'Sarah' means princess. In Hebrew. 'Sally' might be a form of 'Sarah,' but it's also a sudden outburst, an attack by the besieged."

"I know how that girl feels."

"You sally me. I sally you. We sallied. Please. Let's sully the sheets, Sally?"

"You're already exhausting me." Then she asked as cool revenge, "You working today?"

"Yes," he lied. "I'm working."

"Any plans tonight?"

"Nope," he lied again. "You know, 'Billy,' 'William,' in German means, as you can guess, will, as in force of will, as in purpose and determination and desire, as well as helmet, as will as helmet. Anyway, one of those combined forms, as in armor for the head, as in"—Billy beckoned with his dick—"the will of my helmet or helm my will, please."

"And you haven't even had coffee yet."

". . . !"

"What?"

"Help me out a little."

"You should see your face." Sally went over and sat down on the bed. "Where are you working today?" she asked.

"Signet," he lied.

"Again?"

"Yep. Half a day. A turn-and-burn."

"And you really need a fondle? You're really that desperate?"

"Yes," he answered. "Just so I know I'm not going at it alone."

"You know, this is my second-to-last Friday of work," she said. "I really should've taken the summer off and traveled or something." As Sally talked, she reached down—"At least gone to the West Coast or something"—and cupped his balls. She rubbed them, rolled them, weighed them. She edged her finger toward his perineum. "Silly not to have taken some time off."

Billy closed his eyes around Sally at business school, in class with her hand raised, in a study group, in the library, old Sally Hu, her fingers doing his balls like a frantic commodity trade a minute before the exchange closes. "Could you at least pretend to miss me?" Billy asked. "Maybe think back fondly on me, all those business-school types, young CEOs in the making, and maybe you'll feel nostalgic for a person like me, maybe you might think he was *the* guy or *the* kind of guy." His tone was dismissive though he meant every word.

"I'm rubbing your balls, for Christ's sake."

"Just pretend for a second."

"If you'll pretend to come."

"I'm not trying to be flip, okay, I mean, maybe I'm normally guilty of being flip, I know, of taking nothing seriously, but that can wear you down."

"Billy, you're telling me this while you're jerking off."

"It's just, it's like, at the end of the day I've got no muscle for it, for—"

"Either jerk off or talk."

And Billy, the weakling, decided on the former. He shut up. Soon enough Sally scooted down and began—*Hello!*—licking his balls, knowing this would speed up the process, like a shortcut home. Her tongue mechanically flicked along the seam, and she held her hair away from the action as though dangerous gears were down there. Billy perched on his elbow for the visual thrill. The cooperation between her mouth and his hand resembled genital CPR. A cock code blue.

Sally peered up. "Close your eyes."

"Do I have to?"

"Yes."

Billy leaned back, closed his eyes, though he still watched her through his squint, watched her work the pouch of old man skin, the tip of her tongue twirling, flicking, her lips smack-sucking, her left arm resting against his thigh, her skin hairless and impossibly smooth against his sunless flesh, a nice little contrast, like honey on snow, like she was poured onto him, and he wanted to shout, "I'm leaving this afternoon, I'm disappearing for no reason concerning you," he wanted to come clean, but her tongue was stopping up his mouth and dripping silence into his ear, the pleasure just pleasurable enough to slip him away for a second.

He came—

—Comes. The porcelain is an added perk against his balls. As always, there's an ejaculatory montage where flashes of weirdness temper pleasure. Jerry Lewis? Monkeys in a tree? The Brazilian rain forest burning? Opening his eyes, Billy sees his portrait in the mirror, a sort of Frans Hals, *The Masturbator.* And while he has no feelings of guilt or shame in the act itself—*God no!*—maybe there's something in the spillage, in the mess, in the soiling. Semen can seem like radioactive waste, the unfortunate by-product of heat. His seed, spooge, spunk (no word can salvage the substance) plays as ironic leitmotif under the stamp of American Standard.

There's no "Finally" from Sally; no "You owe me"; no tossing of yesterday's boxers for the mop up; no "You better get moving or you'll be late."

No, "I'm snuggling with myself," from Billy.

No, "You make a cute couple."

No, "Opposites attract."

No, "I'll see you tonight."

No one last lie.

There's nothing but the familiar smell, the brackish backwater of tidal pools drying in the sun. Billy runs the water into the sink and imagines a million versions of himself drowning in the water, like those pigs in North Carolina, bloated Billies running down the drain, shoulder to shoulder, connected by the sticky pull of death.

95

Off goes the light—*Christ, it's dark*—and Billy fumbles back toward bed without any presumptions of stealth. His hands flail about, a zombie jolted awake by autoerotic galvanism.

A voice surprises him. "Can't sleep?" It's Do.

"Not really," Billy answers.

"Me neither."

12

6:56 A.M.

Billy wakes up with *Where am I?* in his lungs. Vision slowly loses its
nocturnal blur. Gray rubs into a lighter wash and the residue of his
bedroom in New York resolves into this room in Albany. He touches the
cannula in his arm like a drunken memento, a piercing, a tattoo, from
somewhere in the night. *Oh yeah, I'm here,* catches his breath. He waits for
the alarm, goes through his normal morning doom and gloom where
awful images flash through his head, often suicidal in form—pistol to
temple, noose around neck, shotgun in mouth—the ultimate in snooze
bar. They comfort him the way a twisted mother might whisper shhh-
shh-sh into a fevered ear. *Don't worry, honey, you can always kill yourself
tomorrow.*

6:57 A.M.

Waking up a few minutes before the alarm is always a pleasant surprise.
Internal rhythms are in sync with the sun and the moon and the forever
expanding universe instead of—*Beep!Beep!Beep!*—white-knuckle-holy-
fucking-shit fear. Walking up before the alarm is like cheating a villain
his due, stopping the bomb's countdown a second before zero. Yes, Billy
feels connected, also a tad complicit. Poor Do and Lannigan. They're
screwed, he thinks. In three minutes their world will blow.

6:58 A.M.

Billy closes his eyes, just an extended blink, a brief good-bye kiss to sleep. No big deal.

6:59 A.M.

He falls straight through the mattress and into a dream. It's his only recurring dream, in which he's sitting by himself in a packed cineplex watching a movie, a great movie, and he's eating popcorn and drinking soda and just loving this movie, glancing over his shoulder, seeing upturned faces flicker with almost ecstasy, we're all loving this movie, he thinks, and this excites him even more than the movie, to the point where he wants to nudge his neighbor and say, *Wow, huh?* wants to stand up and shout, *Can you believe how good this movie is?* their reaction more important than the action on-screen. But of course he says nothing. The movie itself changes with every dream—comedy, tragedy, thriller, musical, farce, sci-fi, horror, documentary—and Billy never remembers the plots in any detail, which is a shame, because they're always so good. No, all he remembers is being spectacularly entertained and feeling terribly alone.

7:00 A.M.

The alarm sounds.

The ceiling speakers beep as if the whole building is reversing, crushing Billy under its wheels. After this revelry, "Good morning" is announced, followed by "Breakfast is in half an hour. Half an hour. Please be ready. Thank you." The third floor stretches with activity: pipes groan, toilets flush, TVs begin to bicker. The walls must be paper-thin. Even yawns slip through the drywall.

7:04 A.M.

Do is the first up. He rises mechanically, like a switched-on robot inhabiting no wasted movement. First thing, he makes the bed. His trowelish hands smooth the sheets with wet-cement respect. Pillows are fluffed, set in place, briefly admired. Then he goes into the bathroom.

7:12 A.M.

Into their room walks either Nurse Clifford or George (Billy can't quite remember who is who, which seems to be their goal, to be a nameless figure known only as Nurse). She draws open the curtains as if ripping Band-Aids from eyeballs. She tells them, "Fifteen minutes until breakfast."

"Eighteen minutes," Lannigan corrects.

"Just be ready."

"My mother used to do that, lie to me so I'd get up sooner for school. It drove me nuts. She'd lowball me by fifteen minutes."

"I was simply rounding down."

"Yeah, right."

The bathroom door opens, revealing Do, half-soaked in his clothes. His hair could be a drowned Pomeranian still struggling for life.

"What were you doing in there, jogging?" Lannigan asks.

"I forgot my towel," Do says, his face pelted by hundreds of microscopic blushes.

7:16 A.M.

Lannigan dismounts from bed with gymnastic flair, as if he's been sleeping on a balance beam. He begins stretching. The presentation resembles yoga though the positions are more theatrical and less disciplined, like ten action-packed poses. Shirtless in boxer-briefs, his body is lean, his left nipple pierced. The routine ends with an arching of the shoulders back back back, until, resembling a figurehead for a flamboyant ship, his sternum cracks. "There we go," he says, going loosey-goosey.

99

Billy wonders if he's gay. Probably. Or maybe. Lannigan certainly gives the impression. Plus he's in great shape, perfectly tan, has hiply cut messy hair and overly hinged joints, and speaks with the sort of articulation of men who enjoy every suprasegment of their own speech, as if eavesdropping on themselves. Yes, Billy figures he's gay, without prejudice, with, in fact, the self-serving acceptance of enlightenment. *My gay roommate.* But Lannigan's effeminacy seems too studied, like a person who only reads reviews and never bothers with the actual book. He steps clear of his underwear, grabs his towel without regard to his exposed penis, a bit of uncomfortable exclamation in what should be a straightforward sentence leading Lannigan into the bathroom. "Towel," he says to Do.

7:19 A.M.

"Ten minutes until breakfast" is announced.

Do, still wet, sits on his bed and thumbs through the informed consent. "Think the side effects are going to be bad?" he asks Billy. But Billy is in the strange part-time employment of consciousness where thoughts play like dreams. Ragnar flies on wings. Sally spits fire. Gretchen licks his cannula. From nowhere his old friend, Charlie Mauck, drops in, Charlie who called two years ago and left a message which Billy never returned. And then there's—"Huh, Billy?"—Do, with that voice, that air-bubble-on-vocal-cord voice, that please-just-swallow voice.

"Not too bad," Billy says.

"But brain stuff."

"Yeah, basically."

"Atypical antipsychotic," Do reads.

"Better than a typical psychotic, right?"

"And you're not nervous at all?"

"Sure, I'm nervous, but not that nervous."

Do looks toward the closed bathroom door. The voice behind it sings a made-up pop song, the lyrics concerning a boy and his hamster. "What do you think of Lannigan?" Do asks.

"Not much, really."

"He's kind of out-there."

"I wouldn't take him seriously."

"Tardive dyskinesia," Do reads. "Sheesh."

Billy watches Do, slumped, his hair slowly drying into a rusty mess. Billy finds himself liking Do—or liking himself for liking Do, the simple country boy, the large man-child, as if liking Do, talking to Do, humoring Do, is somehow magnanimous.

7:27 A.M.

Billy is finally on his feet, in the bathroom, brushing his teeth and peeing. The layer of dried semen splits his piss into two streams, neither hitting the bowl, until Billy power-pees and breaks the barrier and throws down a good solid rope. He washes his hands, dabs water in his hair. He does his best to ignore the sink, an awkward lover turned inanimate at the stroke of midnight.

7:30 A.M.

They line up in the hallway, twenty-six strong, and follow Nurses Clifford and George down the stairs and into the cafeteria. They walk as if shackled by bad dreams. The other colors are already eating: the yellows in collective cringe, the oranges napping on Formica, the blues Hollywood hungover in their giant sunglasses, the reds still sweating up a laughing storm.

Rodney, tray in hand, beelines for Billy and his table. "Hear the news?"

"What?"

"Two yellows washed last night."

"What happened?" Billy asks.

"Bad reaction or they just broke down. It can happen. You snap, you get tired of all the probing, and the money starts meaning nada, and you're all, 'Get me out of here.'" Rodney seems giddily refreshed, like he spent the night in a champagne bubble bath.

101

"What are they on?" Do asks.

"Don't know yet. But I do know that this is their ninth day and the ninth day is always a bitch because the ninth day isn't the tenth day, which is your first glimmer of hope, because damn you're almost done. And it isn't the eighth day, which is the beginning of the next week, and hell, you figure you can last anything for a week. Besides, nine is just a bad fucking number. Upside-down six, square root of three, three threes, three sixes, six six six, a bad number, nine, because it has shit in it without it being obvious. Nothing good ever happens with nine. It's even an ugly word. Nine," Rodney says with Nazi accent.

7:34 A.M.

Breakfast is pancakes with maple syrup. People lean over their stack with the glee of a relic from childhood, a toy unearthed in the attic. *Pancakes!* Forks are held in enthusiastic fists. Gretchen sits two tables down. She's caught Billy staring in her direction more than once, always responding with a conspiratorial brow, as if they're the only normal people amidst all these normals. My God, her eyes are playful. They might as well be little balls of wool waiting for a kitten to pounce. And Billy sees Ossap and Dullick sitting alone. Plates and condiments are spread around them in what Billy swears is a mock-up raid. The saltshaker is surrounded; the saltshaker is doomed.

8:01 A.M.

"Report to the dose room in five minutes" is announced over the speakers. The greens hush. It's like rustling trees suddenly gone still by something more sinister than a breeze.

8:07 A.M.

The dose room borders the cafeteria. The layout is like a futuristic college lecture hall, where students are fed information in new and improved ways.

A hundred medical lounge chairs are divided into ten rows, the chairs color-coded with either a blue, red, yellow, orange, or green headrest cover. Each chair has its own computer station. Up front, where the blackboard would be, a large-screen TV is permanently tuned to CNN.

"The Clintons will arrive today at the fashionable Hamptons in Long Island for the second leg of their vacation and spend two days attending . . ."

The green section is located in the back three rows.

"There was a Concorde scare at JFK yesterday. The mishap seemed to have been caused by operational error possibly . . ."

Windows face the courtyard where the bronze hand hails the yellow taxi sun.

"*Who Wants to Be a Millionaire?* is being called a true . . ."

Billy takes a seat, and Do sits nearby.

"Showtime," Lannigan says, clapping his hands.

8:16 A.M.

Nurses appear, or not nurses per se but dose technicians, informally known as feeders. They wheel carts emblazoned with miniature standard-bearing flags, like a drug regatta, Billy thinks, each boat with its own course, its own aisle, its own batch of buoys to circle.

8:27 A.M.

The feeder in front of Billy is American-heartland attractive, attractive like a familiar fast-food restaurant in a strange land, blond, buxom, big-teethed, her eyes the "*o*" in wow. She brushes an optical-scanning pen over his bar code bracelet. The computer beeps.

"I feel like produce," Billy says.

"Huh?" she says.

"Nothing."

The cart is crowded with two-ounce cups. They come snuggled in slots, slots labeled with bar codes, bar codes arranged in ranks, ranks aligned with letters: A, B, C, D. The setup reminds Billy of an odd game of chance and he's tempted to rub his hands together and venture a guess. Some cups are missing, those numbers already swallowed. The feeder consults her clipboard, sweeps a few more bar codes, then hands Billy a cup from row D.

Two gray pills are nestled inside.

"You need water?" she asks.

"No thanks." Billy jostles the cup, the pills leapfrog. Billy has loved pills ever since he was a boy and popped M&M's like they were life-saving cures, often going into shock and struggling for a few milligrams of candy-coated relief. Tic-Tacs were also excellent because they rattled when dispensed and sat so nicely in your palm. Pills seemed to be a sign of complexity, a need for something else. Billy envied those kids with parents who had full medicine cabinets, the Mrs. Silvermans with headaches, the Mr. Doljacks with bad knees. Billy would stare at Tommy Schuller, known throughout the neighborhood as "that Ritalin boy," and wonder why he was so lucky, so extra cared for.

Billy slams back the cup.

The feeder clicks on a penlight. "I need to check your mouth to make sure you're not cheeking the dose. Tongue up, left, right, all around, all set."

This lack of trust pleases Billy.

"In about ten minutes you'll have your blood drawn. I'll come and get you."

"Okay."

She moves down the line.

8:35 A.M.

Poor Do. He's hacking, drinking cup after cup of water, rubbing his Adam's apple like it's a Gobstopper in need of the Heimlich. His pills did not go down smoothly. He swallowed them individually, first regarding them like they were teardrop diamonds, hard and sharp, then washing them down with frantic gulps of water. His face reddened, and his mouth yucked, and five minutes later he's still yucking. "I think they're trapped in my throat," he says. "Trapped sideways or something."

"They'll work their way down," Billy assures him.

"I can feel them, just there." He presses his thumb into the Windsor knot of soft flesh where clavicle meets sternum, presses his thumb too hard for comfort. He could be holding himself hostage. "Right there, I'm positive. Can feel them every time I swallow."

8:48 A.M.

The bleed room has eight color-coded medical loungers. Phlebologists stand on duty like barbers of old. Blues, reds, yellows, oranges, greens come in, sit down, get scanned and hooked up. They give blood in two-teaspoon increments. The whole process lasts about a minute from hello —

"Joy, right?"

"Yes." She glances at his ID. "Mr. Schine."

"Please, 'Billy.'"

"I'll probably stick with calling you Mr. Schine."

"Okay."

"Arm please."

"Can't wait, can you, to see these perfect veins?"

". . ."

"Have you always worked in the blood field?" Billy asks, seeking conversation during this intimacy, seeking, maybe, a friend. He wants to be the cool normal, the cordial normal, curious about her own well-being, as if Joy is a waitress and Billy is the patron who strives against the cold economic exchange.

". . ." from Joy.

"You're not much of a morning person?"

"Pump your fist, please."

"Am I being annoying?"

"My son kept me awake all night."

"I couldn't sleep either."

"Okay, you're done. Next."

"I'll see you. Thanks."

—to good-bye.

9:23 A.M.

Everybody is dismissed, color by color, the palette never mixing.

9:26 A.M.–12:16 P.M.

Whatever.

Whatever in your room, the lounge, the hall, the pay phone.

True time is only measured in pills and blood.

Otherwise whatever wherever.

Lannigan works out a complicated custody settlement for the remote control. On paper he calendars the days then divides them into viewing periods: morning, afternoon, evening. They draw numbers, he fills in the slots. "Totally fair," Lannigan says. "If you have prime time on Tuesday, on Wednesday you'll have the morning and on Thursday the afternoon and by Friday prime time again." He places the schedule on the bureau. "If there's a certain show you have to see, you can always barter with somebody. Okay?" Lannigan is the only one who truly cares, so he agrees with himself and tells Do he's got the helm.

"Problem," Billy says.

"What?"

Billy lifts the remote that's tethered to the wall near his bed. "The remote only reaches the middle bed, my bed."

"Aw shit, that's right. So maybe we switch beds, maybe the beds can be like the ladder, part of the rotation."

"Sorry, but I'm not switching beds."

"So the person has to stand by your bed? That's not fair."

"Well, I'm not switching beds."

"Then what?"

"How about I change the channel. You tell me and I'll change."

"So you'll be the middleman," Lannigan says. "Our thumb."

106

"I suppose."

"Okay. So Do, you're in charge."

Do, who up till then has been quietly reading his comic book, all huddled in bed, knees by his chin, crash position meets cannonball, rocking slightly—he glances up toward the television where a Saturday morning educational program explains the nature of the universe in kid-friendly terms. Do asks, "What do you guys want to watch?"

"Your call," Lannigan tells him.

Do meekly says, "You can change the channel," then looks toward Billy and Lannigan for tacit approval. After a full circuit through premium cable, he stops Billy on cartoons.

12:34 P.M.

Lunch is sloppy joes with potato chips and lemonade, and Billy thinks of the atypical antipsychotic diet as being childhood based, as if the cafeteria has Mom in the kitchen and the action of Allevatrox is backward, to a time of sweeter voices inside your head. Billy hoped that the empty seats on either side of him might land Gretchen, but no, she eats with Peter Swain. Instead Billy gets Ossap and Dullick. Ossap greets the table with, "Fuckers," and Dullick drops his tray from a loud enough height.

"Guys," Lannigan says. "How're things?"

Dullick answers, "Peachy," with faggot undertones.

"Fuckers tripping yet?" Ossap asks.

"Not yet."

Dullick turns to Billy. "Pass the salt."

"Yeah," Ossap adds, "and pass me some fucking ketchup."

"So, you guys friends?" Do asks.

"Why do you want to know?"

"No reason really."

"We're . . . acquaintances."

"Associates."

"Family."

They tap cheers with lemonade and dig into sloppy joes.

Ossap, "These are the best."

Dullick, "I love my meat."

Ossap, "Oh yeah, love the meat."

Dullick, "Meat meat meat."

Ossap, "And more meat."

Dullick, "But I think the meat needs more spice." He aims his cannula towards his bun and makes a spurting squeeze-bottle sound. "Much better." This inspires Ossap to scoop his finger inside his bun and spread the mess around his cannula. He pretends infection, gangrene— "Aaaaah!"—and then licks the gore away.

They both cackle. High-pitched (Ossap), deep-toned (Dullick), it's an odd counterpoint of *hee-hee-hee-ho-ho-ho,* sort of bogus, sort of genuine, like fools who fake laughter until they fall apart on the floor.

1:11 P.M.–6:13 P.M.

More television via Lannigan's tongue to Billy's thumb.

"Change."

"Change."

"Change."

By chance, a film version of *Hamlet* is on, and Billy assumes Lannigan will want to stay put, but Lannigan quickly—"Please God change!"— barks.

Billy lingers. "Should we wait for Voltimand's appearance?"

"Nah, just change."

"This could be research."

"Look, change the channel, okay."

"Let's at least see who plays Voltimand."

"They cut the part for the movie, okay." Lannigan gets up and grabs the remote. "Now we have rules," he says. "And I'm in charge and when I say 'change,' change." Lannigan changes the channel. His viewing habits lean toward shows heavy with teenagers.

Grilled chicken and mashed potatoes and string beans are served with butterscotch pudding for dessert. More important, Billy sits with Gretchen, having sprinted for the free spot near her chair. Much of their discussion revolves around dinner at this early hour, the well-balanced meals, the reversion into a steady, timely diet.

"I feel like we're in an orphanage," Billy says. "Like we're the unadoptable who've grown up and can't quite leave the place."

The man on the other side of the table rolls his eyes. He has a fine-enough face, if a tad broken, particularly around his oblong chin and mansard forehead, as if they were slammed in youth and the pieces never quite grew right. Whatever accident lay in his past aggravates his orbit, but the damage plays as exotic. His ID reads Luke Sillansky.

"What do you think, Luke?" Gretchen asks.

"I'm not waiting to be adopted, that's for sure."

"You don't want a new mommy?"

"Depends on the mommy."

"No," she tells him. "You're more like Fagin, Fagin by Calvin Klein."

"Now there's a scent," Billy says, eyebrows a go-go.

"I'm not faking," Luke answers. "I'm true to the bone."

"She meant Oliver Twist," Billy nips, hoping he might impress Gretchen and humble Luke. But nobody seems to have heard him.

"I've lived a life, that's for sure," Luke continues.

Billy forms his hands into a bowl. "Some more, please," he says.

Still, nobody is listening, not even Gretchen, who rolls her head toward Luke Sillansky as if her eyes are harder than a windshield, or a lead pipe, or whatever it was that smashed up that face.

Billy thankfully stops himself from singing the opening of "Food, Glorious Food."

6:59 P.M.

Another dose.

7:17 P.M.

Another blood draw.

7:54 P.M.

More television.

10:32 P.M.

The night nurse walks in, draws the curtain like a sail in the horse latitudes. "You have to stay in your room until the morning," she says. "No wandering." From her pocket she produces an electronic thermometer and she goes from bed to bed and sticks the funnel-like nubbin into ears, a fresh nubbin for every ear. Billy is thrilled with the slightly invasive touch, as if this device is a soft whisper of "how do you feel" and somewhere inside his head is the answer.

11:37 P.M.

Lights out and darkness bursts with black firework flare. Billy hopes he'll be able to sleep tonight, hopes he can avoid another tryst with the sink. A flashlight would be handy. Then he could huddle under the sheets and read quotes, a tick growing fat on the perfect words of others.

A voice. "You guys feeling anything yet?" It's Do.

"Not yet," Billy says.

"Like what?" Lannigan asks.

"I don't know, like anything."

"Like an itch you can't scratch, like deep under your skin, like on your bone, a bone itch, and it kind of spreads everywhere so your hair feels carbonated, like every pore is a bubble, like you need to rip your flesh apart to get to that itch because it's driving you nuts and there's no way your fingers can reach that deep without drawing blood, like maggots are under your skin, like that kid you heard about in grade school with the broken leg and the cast and all that itching and when they cut the plaster away there was a squirming mess underneath. Something like that?"

11:48 P.M.–11:51 P.M.

Lannigan puts on a show of dying in bed.

11:58 P.M.

Lannigan dies again.

13

O N   S U N D A Y , after the morning feed and bleed, there's an optional
ecumenical service in the dose room, which Billy skips in favor of a nap
followed by some wandering around the third floor. Routine is already
plowing a path under every footstep. Mundane prescience hangs over time.
Everybody knows what comes next: lunch. Passing rooms, Billy sees bodies
stretched on beds, their eyes staring toward the television's event horizon.
They could be adrift on rafts, the floor filled with atypical antipsychotic
sharks ready for the slightest slip of ankle. In the spaces between these
doorways hang framed posters, not from museum exhibitions or world-
famous destinations. No, they are HAM inspired, advertisements blown up
and proudly displayed like family photographs if the family in question
celebrated medical adversities rather than graduations or weddings. The
people pictured are good average folk, their faces occupying the middle
beauty bracket, their features rubbed from the Rosetta stone of physiog-
nomy. Cut and paste and you could collage anyone. Billy browses them, the
Mr. and Mrs. Cunningham of erectile dysfunction and vaginal dryness, the
Richie and Joanie of attention deficit disorder and social anxiety, the Fonzie
of acid reflux. But these are very special episodes in otherwise happy days.

Maybe it's sunburn, but no, it's winter.
Maybe it's skin irritation, but you're rarely this red.
Maybe it's an allergy, but usually you just stuff up.
Maybe it's acne, but you're forty-six years old.
Maybe it's rosacea, an unsightly epidermal condition that affects over 13 million
Americans. Talk to your dermatologist today about a topical therapy that can
really make a difference.

These are the kind of ads plastered in subway stations and bus stops, in places where literate boredom resides, where you read without intention, you the sucker always deciphering, always linking letters into words. If only you could pause comprehension, Billy thinks, push your temples and become illiterate and revisit that time when billboards carried the mystery of John Donne. *What's that mean?* But it's incurable, this viral comprehension, and it starts with cereal boxes and the fun facts of milk. All this information jammed in front of your face and you're the cornered prey. No matter what, the words have you nailed.

Now men who despair over the frequent nightmare of nighttime urination can sleep snug like a baby. No more endless trips to the bathroom. No more worries of an embarrassing accident. No more time taken away from your important rest. Because benign prostatic hyperplasia, a common noncancerous enlargement of the prostate gland, shouldn't be something to lose sleep over.

The afflications are photographed in gauzy near-death light, in the magic hour when pollen is alive, when liver spots glow like honeydew, when you're no longer as young as you think and you're older than you realize. That ache, that throb, that funny feeling, it's telling you something. Forgetful? Irritable? Uh-oh. Billy absorbs these images as if they are old master canvases painted with patented morbid affection. Of course those afflicted are just actors impersonating discomfort, the fourth estate of performers who inhabit the pits of print advertising. They pretend to search for answers. All they want is a cure.

"Billy?"

He turns and sees Gretchen in the doorway of her room.

"What're you up to?" she asks.

"Just taking in the artwork," he tells her.

"Uplifting, isn't it?"

"Yes." He invests his answer with the sight of her in a silk peach bathrobe. A pair of glasses, nerdy chic, hedges her eyes like a collaboration between warring instincts. "I didn't know you wore glasses," he says.

"Yep."

113

"Not that I know you well enough to know anything."

"Well, glasses can be the first surprise."

Billy smiles, the verb hardly doing justice to the thrill in his lips, the vestibule, the commencement of what might follow, of what is already churning in his lungs.

"I love this one," Gretchen says gamely. She goes over to a glossy young woman laughing among a group of female friends.

A birth control pill proven to better your skin. A fantasy drug, right? Too good to be true? But it is true. Introducing a birth control pill that can help reduce mild to moderate acne and prevent an unwanted pregnancy. Nearly nine out of ten women saw a significant change in their complexion while being 99% certain of contraception when taken correctly. Now a perfect choice for women who have reached menstruation, are seeking contraception, have no known contraindications to birth control pills, and are unresponsive to topical acne medication. Now you can be confident inside and out. So clear your mind as well as your skin. See, miracles can happen.

"You know what Madison Avenue calls this woman," Billy says of the clear-skinned, ovum-independent woman. "She's a Merry Andrews. All these people are Merry Andrews and they populate the piggy spots, which is industry code for the pain-is-good approach. Nice, huh? And fake doctors in lab coats are grinders, and product is kickapoo, and Middle American appeal is called P&G, after Procter & Gamble. Pretty perfect for this country, huh? The puritan and the speculator."

"Thanks, professor," Gretchen says.

"I've done some temp work in the advertising field."

"Lucky you."

Together, if not hand in hand then perhaps with sensibilities entwined, Billy and Gretchen peruse this rogue's gallery of remedy. The drugs themselves come in a variety of forms (creams, sprays, solutions, lotions, inhalers, suppositories, liquids, patches) but by far the preferred method is oral (tablets, capsules, pills), illustrated ten times actual size as if a jewel worthy of Elizabeth Taylor. Shapes and colors compose a digestible

114

geometry: blue triangles, orange circles, pink rectangles, green diamonds. They could have been manufactured in a confectionery lab, consumed in a bowl of milk. Billy and Gretchen struggle in pronouncing their generic names: tretinoin emollient, omeprazole, sumatriptan succinate, azithromycin, trimethodenzamide hydrochloride, doxazosin mesylate, loratadine, raloxifene, pravastatin sodium, finasteride, norgestimate ethinyl estradiol. They sound ethnic in their morphology, immigrants fresh off the boat. But like movie stars—"like Norma Jean Mortenson," Gretchen says; "like Roy Scherer and Issur Danielovitch," Billy says—these drugs have brand names with the sizzle of Marilyn Monroe, the brawn of Rock Hudson and Kirk Douglas. Vigorous exclamation points seem sculpted in their meter, like weight-bearing spears. There's Suprax and Tigan, Orudis and Calan, Ultram and Hyzaar, Procardia and Orap, Rufen and Sansert, Videx and Ziac, Tonocard and Pen-Vee, Cozaar and Imdur, Voltaren and Lasax. Billy hears sacred undertones in the names, pharmaceutical spin-offs from the Bible, the Torah, the Koran, the Vedas, the Pali Canon, the I Ching. An equal-opportunity apothecary. And always there's the HAM corporate logo: the sun either setting or rising on the promised land of choice.

"Hargrove Anderson Medical," Billy intones.

"Tomorrow's Company Today," Gretchen finishes.

Billy turns toward her, her pale hexagon of a face pictured in the lower-left-hand corner of his own unfocused malaise. She's in that tricky age, he thinks, often bemoaned by actresses, when their lives fold into no-great-roles-for-women-except-dutiful-wife-or-mother. There is, in the clothes-line sag of her mouth, a worn sadness.

"How are you feeling?" she asks.

Billy almost mistakes this question for something else. "All right, I suppose."

"Any side effects or anything?"

"No, not yet."

"Me neither."

"I actually feel good," he says, Gretchen dissolving into his bloodstream.

From down the hall a man appears, first in voice—"Gretchen"—then in body, slim and nebbish, though the neb has been honed to a studied point of tousled intellect, like a nib spewing love letters disguised as letters to the editor. "It's starting now," he says, fast approaching.

"Oh yeah, already?"

"Absolutely." The man stops in front of them. Fingers tap against thumb in a continuous four-part beat.

"Billy," Gretchen says. "Do you know Stan Shackler?"

"No."

"Hey," Stan says, his hand far too busy for a handshake.

"Stan here has a Ph.D.," Gretchen informs Billy.

"Not yet," Stan says. "Soon though. Now we really should go."

"Whatever you do don't ask about his dissertation," Gretchen says.

"That fascinating, huh?" Billy says.

Stan Shackler puffs himself up, as if loosening a French cuff. "Actually, it is quite fascinating, and it's already getting attention within certain circles. I just don't want to talk about it. I think about it too much to want to spend a second of my time talking about it, talking about it with people who will have no idea what I'm talking about. I'd be the only person who understands the conversation."

"How long have you been working on it?" Billy asks.

Stan Shackler practically groans. "I really don't want to talk about it."

"Sorry."

"But I should be done soon. I have to be done soon or else I'll forever hate my career. But I really really don't want to talk about it. No offense."

"None taken," Billy says, viewing Stan Shackler along the lines of a cat who wears a bell that warns potential prey, this shrill alert excusing the thousand leaps and swipes, the constant springing forward, the frankness of attack.

"I'm sure it's brilliant," Gretchen says.

"It's not, it's shit, okay. Now we have to go because it starts soon."

"What's starting soon?" asks Billy.

Stan fidgets. "Can we please just go?"

"*Fitzcarraldo*," Gretchen says.

"It's a film by Werner Herzog," Stan informs Billy.

116

"I know," Billy says, then he asks, "Is it the movie or the making of?" though he's seen neither, though he knows both plots.

"Not *Burden of Dreams*," Stan snips. "*Fitzcarraldo.*"

"The only Herzog I've seen is *Even Dwarfs Started Small*," Gretchen says.

"The fact that you've seen that film is amazing," Stan tells her, captivated.

"He did *Nosferatu*, right?" Billy says.

Stan nods with critical indifference. "His most commercial film. I, for one, prefer Murnau." Stan pauses, sort of simulates a burp as if digestion is a personal quirk. "It's not cinematics, if that's what you're thinking."

"Thinking what?" Billy asks.

"About my dissertation."

"Oh."

"And it's certainly not economics. Now Gretchen, let's go. Kinski awaits."

"We're watching it in my room," she tells Billy.

"My roommates are only interested in Tom and Jerry," Stan explains.

"Join us," Gretchen says.

Billy shakes his head. "That's all right." And off they go, Stan shuffling along, Gretchen falling in behind, Stan glancing back as if Gretchen is a scribbled note he fears has slipped his pocket. Billy watches them disappear into her room, Billy alone in the hallway, the self-styled outsider, surrounded by images of anxiety and relief, by the man who holds his throbbing elbow instead of a golf club, by the woman who takes a deep liberating breath on a mountaintop—*Welcome home*©.

14

B ILLY JOURNEYS into the lounge where the more social normals
gather. They sit on couches and chairs that are durably comfortable
and designed for the mildly deranged. It's arts and crafts meets Bellevue, a
Mission-style institutionalism. As with all the rooms, the nexus is the
television, though this television is equipped with a VCR and a collection
of movies, mostly action-oriented. A few people play cards. Dominos as
well. Betting is done on credit. Billy's arrival is barely greeted. Nobody
talks about potential side effects, not yet, but the slightest shift in physical
current (foreheads touched, joints cracked, skin scratched) is noticed,
always tangential and never commented upon, like a footnote in sign
language.

What they do talk about is money. Or the promise of money.

"I'm going to buy a car. Nothing fancy. Just good solid wheels, maybe a
pickup," says Stewart Slocum, who rocks his left foot up and down,
probably a preexisting condition from the onslaught of adolescence.
Stewart (he prefers "Stew") has the kind of metabolism that excites the
air around him. Calories get burned through his tongue. "A rig that'll
work for me, oh yeah, something sweet." He punctuates his speech with
odd nonsense interjections—*Be-baa!* and *Yoopie-do!*—as if the Marine
Corps has a special clown unit.

"What kind of vehicle can you get for two grand?" asks Yul Gertner.

"A decent one."

"I'd rather take the bus and keep the cash," Yul says. His head is shaved
like his famous namesake, but instead of the King of Siam he resembles a
thumb on constant futile hitchhike.

Rodney Letts struts in, beelines for Billy. "I just took a half-hour shower," he announces like this is big news. When wet, his hair is disturbingly long; when scrubbed, his skin is newborn-rodent pink.

"You missed your nose," Yul tells him.

"That's a permanent thing."

"Oh."

"You know the problem with buying a car," informs Craig Buckner, midthirties, the guy shuffling a deck of cards too many times, shuffle, shuffle, shuffle, cutting the deck then shuffling some more, enjoying the shuffle more than the idea of dealing and playing cards, every *ffffllllllppp* and *cheheeheyip* causing his fellow players a wince of impatience. "The second you put your money down your investment is halved if not quartered. You buy a new car and you own a used car. You buy a used car and you own shit."

Luke Sillansky groans, "Just fucking deal."

"Who's the one who dealt a straight flush?"

"That was pure chance."

"Well, I'm just being thorough."

"I'd rather hold cards," says Luke Sillansky, of the plain face battered into something interesting, like a hubcap hammered into a bowl.

"I bought a car on three weeks' worth of dylazphil bendotrine," Herb Kolch tells them. "Dytrine was what they were calling it. Paid three grand. I got a Jetta."

"Jettas suck," Yul says.

"It was a good car."

"Please."

"I was thinking of a Honda Civic," Stew says.

Yul shakes his head. "Civics suck, too. I'd rather blow my three grand on fun."

Freddie Melendez, looking over the movies, suggests *The Thing.*

Everybody's seen it a hundred times and Freddie moves on, disappointed.

Rodney Letts eyes Herb with competitive respect. "You did Dytrine?"

"Yep."

"In Austin?"

"Yep."

"I heard about that one."

"Well, I was there, dude." Herb's tongue holds a dose of braggart. He's middle-aged, with long salt-and-pepper hair and a pre-trendy tattoo, faded blue like a nasty nautical bruise.

"What's Dytrine?" Billy asks.

"An antispasmodic," Herb says. "I don't think it ever got FDA approval or maybe they're still working on it, but this was seven years ago and none of the trade rags are mentioning any further R&D." He leans forward, warming his hands on the campfire of a story. "In the beginning we were dealing with routine stuff: drowsiness, constipation, dry mouth, irritableness, nothing special, nothing out of the ordinary."

These suggested side effects flicker on the wall like a bear silhouetted on a tent. Stew licks his lips. Yul yawns. Craig finally deals, asking, "What are we playing again?"

"Gin," Luke says.

"How's that go again?"

"It's fucking gin."

"Is it like crazy eights?"

"It's nothing like crazy eights. Don't tell me you don't know how to play gin?"

"Uhm."

"You're the best shuffler I've ever seen, a goddamn shark, and the only game you know how to play is go fish."

"But," Herb continues, undeterred, "three days into the study, someone sneezes. We're sitting around, just like this, talking our shit, and this guy sneezes. No big deal, right? A sneeze. And this guy, he sneezes four times, still no big deal, and before anybody can say gesundheit, God bless you, whatever, this guy's going into some sort of seizure, twitching and groaning for like ten seconds, doing crazy shit with his face, and we're watching him and we're thinking, okay, the ball has dropped, a sneeze is going to kill us, explode our fucking brains or something. We all hold our noses and look around for a nurse, too freaked to even speak, and this guy, the guy who sneezed, he's going all loose like it's his last breath, like it's

120

that death rattle you hear about, and he collapses in his fucking chair. It's like a shotgun blast to the head. The guy doesn't move. He just lies there, all crumpled up, and we're watching him and we're wondering what the hell should we do, because nobody wants to do anything that might trigger one of these suicidal sneezes. Then the guy, the fucker, he smiles. He's alive and he's smiling like he's happy but embarrassed. We ask him, You all right? What the hell was that? And he gets up and he's holding his pants, you know, that boner part of the pants, and he says he's had an accident and he has to get back to his room. We're like, What happened? And he says, I gotta go change my shorts. Now we're thinking he's pissed or shat himself—all possible with an antispasmodic—and that's been our biggest fear, incontinence, because there's no dignity in that, no matter how much you're paid, so we ask him which hole, and he's like, No man, I just blew a load into my pants."

"No."

"Come on."

"Yeah, right."

"I do not lie," Herb says, pulling his long hair back as if no secrets are hidden in his hairline. "He blew a load. And now we're all looking around like where's the pepper and everyone starts pinching out nose hairs and staring into bright lights and doing whatever tricks they've got for sneezing. Soon enough, the room's a circle jerk of sneezing. Forty percent had the side effect. The doctors called it spontaneous sternutatory ejaculation. SSEs. Unfortunately, I landed in the wrong percent. I just blew snot."

"They should market that," Stew says.

Freddie holds up *Alien* for a vote. Nay.

"But we also shat blood for three weeks," Herb tells them.

"Oh."

"And some people went sort of blind in one eye. Temporarily."

"But three grand for getting off. You should pay them," Yul says.

"We actually qualified for minor unanticipated duress, two hundred bucks."

"I'd take that MUD any day."

Herb disagrees. "I mean, it was all fine and dandy for the first few days. People said it was the best orgasm they ever had, what they imagined multiple orgasms would be like, but by the end of the study they were wearing clothespins over their noses. Because after a while it became a hassle. When they felt a sneeze coming, they'd cover their prick with a Kleenex. It was like having a cock cold. They were blowing through underwear. I kind of felt sorry for them. They'd sneeze and sort of slump."

"Still," Stew says.

Philip Crouse, quiet until then, mumbles, "I once made ten grand on a MUD, but it was major instead of minor." He says this from the sofa, his head drawn back like his neck has no spine. Words seem to come in the form of bubbles that float above him then fall back and explode on the hard squint of his eyelids. The effort alone holds Billy's attention; he's a stutterer without the stutter.

"Nobody makes ten grand on a MUD," Rodney objects.

Herb Kolch agrees.

"I still have the check," Philip Crouse says.

"Now I know you're lying, because who wouldn't cash a check for ten thou."

"It's my talisman."

"I don't care what it is, *man*."

Rodney shakes his head. "I'm sorry but nobody makes that kind of MUD."

"I have the proof."

"Then show it."

"Okay." But Philip Crouse doesn't move; instead, he talks, and everybody is held by the elliptical trail of words, by the slow descent of meaning and the splatter-back of memory. Billy imagines the Ancient Mariner in his youth, when he BB-gunned a seagull. "This MUD I would wish on none of you. Ten grand was cheap. It was a basic feed and bleed, same setup, same Phase One thing except this was through a uni— university hospital that got huge government grants to study such and such, which the university then sold to pharma—pharm—to companies for such and such and such and such, and so on, and yeah, recruiting students but paying with scholarship money, cost effective, like some people play football and some people play guinea pig."

"That can't be legal," Billy says.

"Football players got banged up worse. Usually we'd do a study a semester, sleep stuff, psycho mind stuff, occasionally harder stuff like this ACE inhibitor for high blood pressure. I can't remember what they were calling it. Flumox—can't be right. Flumoxide, Flumo—xidine, Flumox—celsior." Crouse puckers like he's trying to turn spittle into soap. "Early on, maybe the second day, yeah, I wake up dizzy with the whole bed, the whole room, spinning and there's no way I can walk or do anything but puke and puke and puke from motion sickness, imbalances in the inner ear, I guess. I'm crying it's so bad, spinning and crying and puking and wishing everything would stop. If I had a gun, I would've done myself in right then and there though I'd a missed a bunch of times and taken out a few doctors. Right away they pull me from the study, immediately off the drug, but this crap must've had the half-life of plutonium because it's done something to my—the head because two days later I'm still spinning and puking, and they don't have a clue, and slowly I'm going nuts and I'm pleading for like tranquilizers and morphine but they're scared about dangerous interactions—what a joke—so they give me nothing and tell me I have to tough it out. Three days, four days, still spinning just as hard, eyes closed, spinning, room dark, spinning. Fifth day this orderly comes in with a paintbrush, a can of black paint, and a stepladder. On the ceiling over my bed he paints a big black dot. He tells me this should help, and I'm like, thank you so much, who needs morphine when you have *this,* and he tells me to stare at the dot, focus on the dot, spot yourself on the dot, whatever, a focal point, he tells me. I'm so pissed because I want drugs not some crafts project. I would've strangled him but I'm spinning so bad, so fuck it, I stare at it, stare at this dot, and it actually does help, it's the only thing that helps. If I look away for even a second, I'm thrown around, and when I close my eyes, I'm back in the spin cycle." Crouse pauses and opens his mouth wide like a giant mama bird might fly down with a worm. "I don't really remember sleeping. I'm sure I did but it was like a deeper extension of that black dot. For five weeks I had a staring contest with the ceiling."

"This is getting heavy," Yul says.

"I prefer the sneezing story," Stew says.

With great effort, Philip Crouse lifts his head from the back of the couch. Now the words seem to dribble down his shirt. "Try staring at one thing for five weeks, staring like your sanity depends on it. On the second week I thought I caught the dot moving, crawling a few inches like a big hairy spider kind of growing, and sometimes I swear the thing was dangling right over me, within my grasp, or its grasp."

"This isn't shit I need to hear right now," Luke says.

"Are hearts wild?" Craig Buckner asks.

"Nothing's wild. It's gin."

"I waited for this thing to come down and finish me," Crouse goes on.

"Oh, come on," Yul heckles.

"What about your parents, your friends?" Stew asks.

"I talked to them on the phone and told them not to visit because I didn't think my black dot liked company. Then I start getting bedsores, and the orderly comes back with a paintbrush and paints black dots all over the room so I can move around, stumble to a chair, and begin staring again. He paints dots in the bathroom, in the shower, and I jump from spot to spot like it's a game and these place are safe."

Freddie waggles *The Thing* again but nobody bites.

"He even paints dots on the window so I can get some light, and I almost convince him to paint a dot on the tree outside. Then I ask the orderly to Magic Maker a dot on my forehead so I can see myself in the mirror, see what I look like. Not pleasant, I found out."

"Maybe because you had a dot in the middle of your forehead," jokes Yul.

"I'm smelling serious bullshit," says Herb.

Philip Crouse slackens his jaw. "Fine, don't believe me, but this is the truth. The third week, the fourth week, and I'm like one of those wildebeests swiped down by a lion, all faraway and fine with it. That was me. I'd been pounced on and I was barely breathing, not thinking, hypnotized, peacefully waiting for the end. Then, on the fifth week, in the middle of the night and for no apparent reason, the dot turned back into plain old paint."

"Oh, come on," Herb shouts.

"The next day I was on my feet."

"You're talking too pretty for real pain," Herb accuses.

"After five weeks, all I could do was make it pretty. I remember being discharged and going down the hall and seeing these rooms with bed-ridden people, must've been four, five of them, staring at their dot. I knew everything around them was spinning. I understood. I was almost jealous of them."

"And you were paid a ten-grand MUD?" asks Rodney.

Philip Crouse nods.

"With ten grand you can get a decent vehicle," Yul says.

"But he never cashed the check," Stew says.

"Now that really is too pretty," Herb critiques.

"I could live a year on ten grand," Rodney says. "Two years maybe."

"I'd hit Thailand and live like a king," Freddie says, fantasizing with *Terminator* in hand, the first *Terminator,* which gets a majority nod and is slipped into the VCR, the TV going from blue to black to the FBI warning against unlawful duplication.

"I'm never cashing that check," Crouse tells them. "I don't know if there's a statute of limitations, if after a few years they clear the account or if it sits there, ten thousand dollars with my name and they're wondering when check one-nine-five-eight-five will land. I think you'd notice ten thousand dollars missing or not missing. Or maybe not. Maybe to them it's a dime. I don't know, but I'm not cashing it."

"That's just stupid," Herb says.

"You're probably right. Ten thousand dollars *is* a lot of money."

"No shit."

"It's just." Philip Crouse leans down, depleted. "It does hit me that that's a lot of money, especially living like I do. But I need it alive," Crouse says.

Just then Lannigan comes running into the lounge, hands on face, screaming, "My eyes, my eyes, Jesus, my eyes!"

Panic slips from every mouth, motionless and speechless, peering from half-parted lips like children sinking low in nighttime sheets, a sliver of noise illuminated beneath the door. Billy rushes forward only in his imagination; otherwise, he stands still, gaping not so much at Lannigan but at implication, at the ullage between soul and bystander. "They, they burn!" Lannigan screams. In an awful instant, fingers curl deep within orbits and bring forth chunks of eye meat. Moans of pain-on-pain torment rip apart sight as white flesh crumbles. A fleck of yellow lands on the carpet. Body pure torment, Lannigan lowers his hands, slowly lowers his hands, and reveals—*oh God, this is going to be awful*—the gore of hard-boiled eggs for breakfast. "Got you," he says.

"Fucking prick," Yul Gertner shouts.

Lannigan licks his palm. "You guys should've seen yourselves."

Luke Sillansky throws his cards at him. "Jerk."

"Pretty good, huh?" Lannigan asks.

The room is silent.

"You guys really thought I was poking out my eyes?"

But attention has roved toward the television where a cyborg from the future drops down into 1984—evident by the hairstyles, the clothes, the cars—and naked from time travel, approaches an unwitting Hell's Angel and separates him from his still beating heart.

"Was it really any good?" Lannigan asks again.

People cheer.

Lannigan turns toward Billy. "Was I any good?" he asks, desperate to know.

15

T HAT EVENING, Billy stands in front of the pay phone with defeat. A certain peace has existed without the phone. There's been no undercurrent of tinnitus in all things ambient *(Is that the phone ringing?)*, no intimate electrical impulses invading his ears, no loud potential in Bakelite. The readiness for a dozen possible voices has been relaxed, and the guilt over losing contact has been put on hold. No messages to leave, no calls to return. No cult of the phone. *Reach out and touch someone* always struck him as a creepy religious campaign, a crusade against heathen incommunication where nobody is beyond saving for just ten cents a minute. *Friends and family. I just called to say I love you.* But here he is, in front of the phone, wondering if he should call, wondering if tomorrow the drug will take hold and turn him into a version of Philip Crouse. This might be his last opportunity. And he needs to talk to her, to Sally. He needs to explain himself, needs to apologize. It's not for reasons of guilt or shame. No, it's far more narcissistic, he realizes. It's the idea of a person existing in this world who might hate him. Billy can't abide that. His misanthropy has always been one-sided.

Too bad he has to call collect.

Sally accepts the charges, though not without muttering, "Typical."

"I'm on a pay phone and I don't have enough change," Billy explains. Nothing from the other end.

"Sally," he says. "I'm sorry. Really. Sorry. Seriously. I'm sorry. Sally?" The alliteration briefly frustrates him. "I apologize." He tries stringing words into a sentence—"I know how shitty me leaving all of a sudden without warning was"—but they sound as eloquent as his handwriting.

More nothing.

"But I had to go."

Nothing still.

"Just disappear for a while."

"Your friend Ragnar has been around," Sally finally says.

"Really? Ragnar was there? You saw him?"

"Yep," she says. "Two nights ago I come home to find a cat nailed to the door. A dead cat. Poor thing had a collar with a tag. His name was Billy and he belonged to Ragnar and he was nailed to my door for all the neighbors to see. Luckily they thought it was some freaky Chinese thing."

"A dead cat?"

"And last night somebody was waiting in my apartment, just sitting there in the dark and for a second I thought it was your sorry ass with your tail between your legs, but no, it was him. He asked me where you were and I told him I had no idea and he said, too bad, I'd be your stand-in if you didn't show up soon. Then he shoved me, Billy. A pretty hard shove, too." Sally cracks near tears. "I swear I'm bruised. You know I've got a lot on my mind without your problems shoving me around."

"What did he look like?"

"He shoved me and you're asking what he looked like? Oh, he was positively dreamy, how's that, Billy? You know what, you're a real prick. Think about someone else for just a second, think about me, think about what you did to me, just leaving, and I'm stuck packing up this place like I have any free time. I don't even know why I'm talking to you."

"You're right. I'm sorry."

"Stop saying 'sorry.' 'Sorry' is not some magical word."

Billy grips the receiver like the floor could collapse any moment. "Sally, you're in grave danger. Maybe I—"

"*Grave danger?* Oh Billy. I'm kidding about Ragnar. The prick stuff I'll stand by, but Ragnar, I'm kidding. Nobody's been here. I thought I was being obvious enough with the whole cat-crucified-on-my-front-door thing, but maybe not, maybe you're that delusional. Nobody's been here. No phone calls. Nothing."

"No phone calls?"

"You sound disappointed."

128

"Maybe they know where I am then."

"And where the fuck is that?"

"I can't tell you," Billy says.

Sally groans. "Time out and listen to me, just listen, because this is my field of expertise. I did some research. Ragnar & Sons is a totally professional operation. Aboveboard. They don't operate out of some dark alley and they're not going to hurt you. They might want to hurt you—God knows I understand that—but they're not going to hurt you. They just want their money. Hurting you is bad for business. Hurting you won't get them paid. These aren't bookies who depend on street cred and can't afford deadbeats running around their hood. The worst they'll do is go to court and try garnering a percentage of your pay."

"But you saw their letters to me. What do you call that?"

"Creative intimidation," Sally tells him. "You probably got an over-eager client rep that's trying to make an impression on his boss. That's all. If he can squeeze money from you then he looks good. He's in a win-win situation."

"I don't buy that. I talked to this guy on the phone."

"My bet is he's a twenty-two-year-old pencil dick who's seen too many movies." Sally, when annoyed, slips into the corners of her Brooklyn upbringing. "Do everyone a favor and get over yourself. Even if this fucker's a kong, no excuse for being a jerk and leaving me in the lurch."

"You're right."

"I realize our relationship was casual, and in a week the hole would've been on the other ass, with me leaving for Cambridge, but—"

"Why can't you say Harvard? Why can't anyone say Harvard?"

"Fine. Harvard. But let's think about my recent situation in purely technical terms. Nothing personal, just business. Okay? You know what I've been doing since your sudden departure? Let's see. Packing up the apartment. Alone. Finding storage space. Arguing over the security deposit with our pleasant landlord. Rendering the corpse we call furniture. God knows how the couch ever crawled in here. Closing accounts and paying bills. All alone and all while I'm working a full day and all with the unfortunate but now necessary help of my parents, who are so smug and controlling I feel positively Tibetan in my plight."

"I tried to get rid of most my stuff," Billy says.

"Which wasn't much," Sally shoots back.

"True."

"The point is, while the rest of the stuff is mine, you certainly enjoyed my stuff, slept on my stuff and cooked on my stuff and maybe took advantage of my stuff, free of charge. You kind of squatted on my life, Billy. And hey, no problem, I liked the company, I really did. But now I feel like you were using me."

"I'm sorry."

"Enough with sorry. All I'm saying is you could've given me your help for a couple of days."

"The whole Ragnar situation was—"

"Billy—"

"—heating up."

"Enough with Ragnar."

Sally's doorbell buzzes (always a horrible sound in Billy's book).

"Hold on a second," Sally says.

"What?"

"It's the door."

Judging by the tonal quality of her footsteps and the muffle of the security intercom and the unlocking of the door, Billy figures Sally has placed the receiver on the coffee table. Sally loves the phone too much for a cordless model; she prefers the umbilical restraint and enjoys worrying the elastic around her fingers as she walks around the apartment like an all-banter cabaret singer. Billy imagines his head resting on the coffee table, near the pile of magazines and the three remote controls, just another bit of endless clutter.

Then he hears a scream.

"Sally?" he says, testing the air.

Something like a plate shatters.

"Sally."

Billy hears her pleading, "Please don't hurt me."

130

He hears a deep voice shouting, "Where's Schine?"

"Who?"

"Don't be smart with me, bitch."

A slap of skin and Sally starts crying, an uncharacteristic noise from her mouth, both odd and ordinary, like a popular song played on an ancient instrument. It makes Billy sick.

"One more time. Where is he?"

"I swear I don't know."

"Sally," Billy almost yells. They must be near the coffee table, and Billy pictures, briefly, the phone sneaking up behind Ragnar and strangling him.

"I know you know."

"I don't."

"You're lying."

"I'm not."

"Sally?" Billy wonders if he should hang up and dial 911? Could he get 911 for Manhattan? Would the local 911 dispatcher put through a long-distance emergency? Should he give up his toehold on the coffee table for the chance of 911? He has no idea. But his indecision films beautifully in the nickel plate of the pay phone, a fun-house mirror effect Billy regrets noticing.

"Then you're going to have to pay."

"But I don't know where he is."

Is Sally pinned on her back, with a knife to her throat or a gun against her temple? Expecting ripped fabric, abused flesh, sobs, instead Billy hears what seems to be giggling. Is he tickling her? The man must be insane.

Billy whispers, "Tell him, Sally."

"I really have no idea."

The voice shushes her.

"I—"

"Shhhh."

"Please."

"It's okay, it's okay. Relax, okay. Just relax." The voice could be stroking Sally's hair and thumbing away her tears. Nothing creepier than psychotic tenderness.

"I swear he's gone," she says.

Again with the giggling. What is this madman doing?

"Then I guess I'll have to leave a message."

"Don't you fucking dare," brave, feisty Sally warns.

"Or else what?"

"Just don't."

"What're you going to do?"

"Get the fuck off me," Sally shrieks.

And that's when Billy really yells. "I'm here! Right here!" He wishes the phone could hop up and down and wave wildly with heroic distraction. "Hey Ragnar! Ragnar!"

Nurse Clifford/George pokes her head into the hallway. "Everything all right?"

"Yes." Billy covers the mouthpiece. "Sorry."

"We might want to keep our voices down."

"My grandparents," Billy explains. "Almost deaf. Very frustrating."

The soft infirmities of family pull her back.

Billy resumes with, "Ragnar!"

"Goddamn it," Sally says, pissed and amazingly unafraid.

"Where is he?"

"Okay, enough, seriously."

"I'm here! I'm here!" Billy tugs the handset's armored cord. "Ragnar!"

"Give him this for me."

"Don't you—"

Billy hears slurping.

"You fucking jerk," Sally squeals.

"Thought you'd like that."

"Ragnar! The phone! I'm on the phone!" Billy yells.

Doorways begin to fill with normals who check on the commotion in the hall, perhaps curious if this is a side effect, seeing Billy jump up and down and pound the wall. They look like children peering between banisters, watching their parents fight.

"God-fucking-damn it!" Billy yells.

132

Nurse Clifford/George reappears, this time unappeasable. "Keep your voice down or no more phone privileges. And ease up on the swears."

"Sorry."

"This isn't a pool hall."

"Sorry."

"Or a locker room."

"I'm sorry."

"Or some football game."

"I get it, okay, Ms. . . . Nurse . . . ma'am."

"Well then, keep it down."

"Okay." Billy returns to the eavesdropping. "Sally? Ragnar?"

More and more normals peer from their rooms: Stew Slocum, Yul Gertner, Craig Buckner, Gretchen with cards fanned in her hand, Luke Sillansky with cards fanned as well, toadying himself behind her shoulder and shaking his head as if rudely interrupted in mid whist.

"Just tell him I'm on the phone," Billy wishes aloud, using more ESP than AT&T. Physical helplessness creeps into his stomach: His insides buckle under the weight and become airless and dusty from collapse. Frustration stings his eyes. Then he hears, "Schine?" over the line.

Billy freezes.

"That you, Schine?"

"Yes," Billy whispers, calmer than expected. "It's me, it's Billy Schine. Listen, I'll turn myself in. I'll offer myself up fully and totally. I can be in New York in four hours, by late tonight, and you can break my legs first thing in the morning. You can do whatever you need to do. But don't hurt her. Please. Don't hurt her. If you do, or already did, I will find you and I will kill you. I will." The words sound unreal, scripted, but the emotion catches his voice. Billy loosens his grip on the telephone as if rather than falling he might float.

"You dare challenge me!" Ragnar bellows, which is followed by a maniacal, uhm, ridiculous cackle, like a professional wrestler.

133

"Well—"

Billy hears another voice, Sally, safe in the background and saying, "Give me the fucking phone, you idiot."

Before departing, Ragnar says, "You might be the biggest tool in the world."

Billy deflates, realizing he's been had.

And then Sally is in his ear. "Hey."

"Your brother?"

"He had me pinned."

Tommy Hu shouts, "You're a dipshit, Schine," Tommy, eighteen, no doubt sporting gel-inspired bed-head and a Bay City Rollers T-shirt and absurdly flared bell-bottoms. Cut him and he bleeds sarcastically. Tommy, the youngest Hu, the only Hu born on U.S. soil, never needed to assimilate, so he disassociated.

"Well, you got me," Billy says.

"I think you need serious help," Sally tells him.

"Why, because I believed you, because I thought you were really being hurt and I was worried? And you think I need serious help?"

"You're Ragnar-obsessed."

"I thought you were being hurt."

"You'll buy anything Ragnar. I should sic them on you for your own good."

"I was really scared for you."

"Aw, poor baby," Sally says. "I wish I could comfort you but I'm in the middle of packing up the apartment. That's why my asshole of a brother is here."

"You mean Ragnar the magnificent," shouts Tommy.

"Shut up." Then Sally, softly: "You know, you ruined a good thing. We were friends and you dumped me like we were lovers, and suddenly, I'm upset, like I'm the woman scorned. I can't say I ever want to see you again, and that is sad. Sad was the last thing I was expecting from us. I was expecting the opposite. You know what I was expecting? That we'd pack up together and maybe order in one more time. I was. But you changed all that. You know what my last memory of you is? You doing what you did

134

the morning you left and me helping you out, which, in retrospect, I suppose is perfect."

"I'm sorry."

"You should see my brother. He's hopeless at packing anything that's not square."

"I'm sorry."

"And I can't stand the feel of cardboard on my skin."

"I'm sorry."

"You know, Billy, there's a point where I'm sorry kind of slips away from apology and lands smack-dab into contempt. I'm hanging up now."

And with that—click. Billy stands there, still listening, as if on the other side of a door. Adrenaline fades and is replaced with a drowsy numbness as well as something far less romantic. Billy hangs up the phone, a miserable invention, he thinks, born with pain, with acid spilling on Bell's thigh while he fiddled his clump of primordial transmission, Bell screaming for his friend who was fiddling a similar clump. *Mr. Watson, come here, I want you!* Watson must have been amazed. The machine captured a man. He probably leaned forward and listened for more music while his mentor burned alone downstairs.

Mr. Watson, come here, I want you!

What perfect first words.

The phone rings.

Billy startles, then, "Hello," answers.

Silence.

"Hello?"

The silence is familiar.

"Sally?"

The line disconnects.

Walking back to his room, Billy pictures Sally sitting on the couch, her finger tapping the liquid crystal display of her caller ID.

"Hey Schine."

Billy looks up and sees Ossap and Dullick.

"You done screaming?" asks Dullick.

"I think so."

135

Ossap flexes his mouth into a frown. His lips seem burdened with a heavy load—"Good"—and his left eye twitches—"because"—and his head jerks as if pulling the words free—"we need the phone"—like a bird with a stubborn worm.

"Yeah," Dullick says, counting change and drooling.

16

ON MONDAY the side effects of Allevatrox have come into ugly bloom.

Though Billy feels nothing, nothing yet, he's seen it in others, like Ossap whose facial expressions would scare small children, eating, talking, walking about like the bogeyman until Dullick—"Ossap!"—tells him he's getting freaky, stretching his neck like some pervert tortoise, and Ossap apologizes, controlling himself for a few minutes until forgetting brings on another spell. Ossap is not alone. Other normals can be spotted chawing their own tongues, rolling their eyes upward, curling their lips like they're yelling in slow motion. Drooling has also hit. Those afflicted carry plastic-cup spittoons, which they consult every minute, a clepsydra in spit, their glands manufactering too much saliva to swallow without getting sick. Conversation with these people is difficult. The akinesiacs and akathisiacs are also being divvied up within the group. The akinesiacs are zombies, slow and stiff, not too far removed from a graveyard and a full moon. And the akathisiacs could be channeling hummingbirds. Fingers fluttering from hands fluttering from wrists fluttering from arms, they are the chorus line of dancers behind an invisible lead in gold lamé. The akinesiacs and akathisiacs, Billy thinks, they're like the Jets and the Sharks.

And that afternoon, there's a rumble.

It's Roger Coop, akinesia, versus Anton Krojak, akathisia.

Roger Coop spends his day waiting for a call that never comes. He's almost always the first to answer the ring—"Yeah!"—stomping from his room—"I got it, I got it!"—and when invariably the call is for somebody

137

else, he screams the name—"Anton Krojac, phone!"—as if an elaborate scam has been perpetrated on his rigid frame.

"Anton Krojac, phone!" he screams again.

"Anton Krojac, you've got a phone call!" he screams louder.

Now Roger Coop is goose-stepping from room to room.

"You know who and where Anton Krojac is?" he asks Lannigan, Billy, and Do.

Nope.

Finally Krojac is found, napping in bed—"Can't you hear, phone!"—and Anton—"Relax, dude"—all electric shimmy, is escorted to the payphone by the plodding Roger who's already laying the groundwork for a short conversation—"Dude, I talk for as long as I like"—and Roger is none too pleased—"Don't dude me, you Croat!"—and Anton wags his arms—"I'm a fucking Serb from Massapequa, you idiot!"—and with the atypical antipsychotic heat coursing through his fingers, Anton grazes, inadvertently—"I swear"—the rigid cheek—"Fucking prick!"—of Roger Coop. Pushing ensues, followed by a series of misguided blows. A crowd is attracted. They watch Roger and Anton clutch like heavyweights in the last round. Roger does rope-a-dope without the rope; Anton throws extravagant punches that startle him more than his opponent. Roger leads with his head (*Oomph!*); Anton counters with his chin (*Arrah!*); Roger falls between Anton's legs (*Yoops!*); Anton trips over Roger's shoulder and pile drives the floor with his funny bone (*Kphuck!*); Roger lies sprawled, exhausted, pinned (*Haaphew!*); Anton rolls over and manages, by mistake, a glancing knee to the groin (*Fwaaah!*); Roger reflexively tenses and stubs his big toe (*Oyooh!*) on Anton's (*Nyumph!*) nose.

At this point, Nurse Clifford/George steps in. She holds, none too subtly, a can of pepper spray. "Okay, okay, break it up, boys." But the boys are already broken up, on their backs, massaging their various injuries and already giggling about the ridiculousness of the brawl. They are men bonded by fight. Nurse Clifford/George leans over and studies them. A little blood, some bruises, nothing serious. She takes close personal aim and sprays their eyes like the pupils are cockroaches. Now Roger and

Anton are lovers in plight. They roll around, writhe, spit, snot, tear, and curse together. The floor could be the beach and tomorrow is good-bye. "No fighting," Nurse Clifford/George informs them. "If this happens again, you will be fined or possibly dismissed without pay." Security shows up—two beefy men who look as if they've recently outgrown a career in bouncing. They wear faux officer-of-the-law shirts a size too small so their guts might appear more menacing. As they lead Roger and Anton away, they seem nostalgic for club days when patrons were drunk and restraint was vaguely sexy.

"Mild agitation," Nurse Clifford/George remarks to the remaining normals. "Not a real surprise." She scans the crowd. "We also have stun guns if something like this ever gets worse, so don't worry about your safety. We have enough voltage to bring down the biggest agitator."

Nobody is relieved.

Do, for one, is having difficulty with urination. He asks Billy and Lannigan after dinner, "You guys having any problems peeing?"

"No," Billy says.

"Because I feel like I need to pee, but I've got nothing to pee, and it's driving me nuts." Do stands by the bathroom door. He rarely ventures outside the room for recreation, and hasn't showered since his inaugural attempt. The smell coming from him is offensively pure, like a newborn's spit-up. His beginning facial hair could be houseflies that have landed on skin and done everything possible to rip themselves free, leaving behind their legs. "It's like I got a few extra drops of pee trapped in the tip of my, uhm, penis." Do blushes. Or blanches. He has combination shame.

"I'm sure it's nothing," Billy tries reassuring.

"It stings."

"Ask the nurse about it."

"I'm not asking the nurse about that."

Do returns to his bed, holding his crotch in gotta-pee fashion.

"Maybe it's an infection," Lannigan offers. "A UTI. Maybe chlamydia. Syphilis. Gonorrhea. Have you been fucking any sheep lately, farm boy? Or maybe it's cock cancer. Maybe a bit of flesh-eating virus got up in

139

there. Or it could be soap, but you'd have to shower for soap, so strike that. I've heard stories—"

"Come on," Billy says.

"—about the urethra which would rattle your balls."

"You're fine," Billy promises as Do crawls under the sheets.

"Whatever you do, don't get a hard-on."

"He's kidding."

Lannigan shoots Billy a hard-truth look. "Billy, man, we've got to be honest with him. We both know what this is and we both know it's not good. How the rhesus monkeys, the test animal for this drug, had the same reaction, a burning sensation, an incomplete feeling toward urination, though of course they couldn't articulate that. No, those little critters just rubbed their rhesus monkey dicks raw, practically tore them off."

"He's lying," Billy tells Do.

"Billy, you're doing him no favors."

"Shut up."

"What, or else you'll sock me?" Lannigan cowers.

"What's the point?" Billy asks, hoping he's speaking in code and Lannigan is hearing, *Why pick on a person like Do?*

But Lannigan hears nothing. "Hey Do," he says.

Do, defensively: "What?"

"You're doing it again."

"What?"

"That thing."

"What thing."

"Oh, maybe you don't even notice it, maybe it's unconscious."

"What am I doing?"

"You just did it again."

"What?"

"Don't worry about it, it's no big deal, barely noticeable."

"So what am I doing?"

"Oh, never mind."

Do looks toward Billy, says, "Billy?" with doubt, like every blink, every breath needs reassurance.

"You're not doing anything. Don't listen to a word he says."

Do turns toward the window. The sun is setting. In the courtyard, that bronze finger berates the last minutes of the visible day, like the night will be long and cold and without meaning.

17

BILLY NEVER sees Gretchen in the lounge. For meals, she lingers toward the end of the line and scouts the greens for the company of her own choosing. Her tablemates have no rhyme or reason, no continuity; there is no searching for friends or acquaintances, no slow-building coalitions. She's like a special celebrity on a cruise ship who spreads her presence around, sometimes pulling up a chair and making the group scoot for space. "Sorry, you mind?" Nobody ever does. Because like Billy, they've all been watching her. They all perk up when she sits down, as though her presence transforms them back into boys. A girl. The only girl. There might be other girls in other colors (the blues, in fact, have three who wear their giant sunglasses and toil together like a Gorgonian Yoko, Jackie, and Greta). But Gretchen is theirs alone. She is her own side effect. During feed and bleeds, she spends a minute eyeing the green medical Barcaloungers, the nine open seats, the eighteen hopefuls who might bookend her, the twenty-five imaginations who wonder what she's thinking. She is full of possible meaning, by dint of her shimmering face, her odd way with angles, her single devastating coup d'oeil for every hundred plain glances. She kicks up questions in her wake.

At least she does for Billy.

He walks down the hallway, slows in front of her room. *Hello. Hey. Remember me? How've you been? Feeling all right?* These lame openings pulse from the doorjamb, the future sound waves from a loser. Gretchen lies in the middle bed. Thick magazines are spread over the sheets like tepees from a fashion-conscious tribe. Cotton balls poke from lacquered toes accompanied by that headache-in-a-bottle odor. Her pose suggests a wet-compress, scarves draped over the lampshades.

"Howdy," Billy says. *Howdy?*

She glances over like whatever she encounters is an intriguing if obvious ploy.

Billy provides his name, for he has no misconceptions of ever being memorable.

"Duh," she says.

"Sorry."

"So how're things, Billy Schine?"

"Fine, I guess. And you?"

"So far all right." She scoots up in bed. "Come on in and take a bed."

Billy obeys. "How're you feeling?" he asks.

"Fine," she says.

"I mean in terms of side effects."

"I know."

"Oh. Sorry."

"I'm bored, that's about it," she says. "But I've been thinking, what happens if you feel good, if you feel more focused and sharper. Wouldn't that be scary? Maybe you're schizophrenic and you don't even realize it."

Billy agrees. "You almost want to feel crappy."

"But I do miss the voices," Gretchen says.

Billy smiles, then laughs.

"Was that a mercy laugh?"

"No, it wasn't."

"Please."

"It was funny."

"Not that funny."

"Maybe we're on the placebo," Billy says, searching for a bond between them even if that bond is inert and innocuous, a sugar pill of connection.

"Maybe. But if that's the case, I think I'll feel gypped. Not that I want what some of these people are getting. Drooling, all that twitching, seems pretty nasty. But placebo is so nothing, you know. I was kind of looking for something. I have enough placebo back at home."

"And that's in New York, home?"

143

"Yeah." Gretchen sort of detaches herself from this line of conversation and turns away from Billy, turns towards the television and the news of the Weather Channel, where a meteorologist stands in front of the jet stream that divides the country in a sine wave, a battle line fought with highs and lows, with cool air dipping and warm air rising, all under the double-breasted command of Stuart James who gives an overly inspired Jonathan Edwards–like sermon on what to expect in the near future. Texas and Arizona will be in the one hundreds. "Hot hot hot," he says. A condemning finger is pointed toward Oracle, Arizona. "The nation's hottest temperature with a blistering one hundred sixteen degrees. Not so nice unless you have horns, a pitchfork, and a little pointy tale."

"I guess this could be a side effect," Gretchen tells Billy. "My newfound obsession with the Weather Channel. I never cared before, but now I find myself loving this channel. It relaxes me." Gretchen pulls up her knees, holds them in a bow of interlocked fingers. Billy tries to snuggle into her thoughts, into the five-day forecast.

"I'm hoping for a hurricane," she says, rocking slightly. "I want to watch it develop over the Atlantic, I want to track its projected path, its possible landfall, its hit-or-miss prognosis on the coastline; I want to see snapped trees and ruined trailer parks, boats deposited in the middle of an intersection, Stop signs bent backwards, people losing everything but determined to rebuild with what is left."

Billy could've been listening to Elizabeth Bishop in a yellow slicker.

"Sorry about that," Gretchen says.

"About what?"

"My rhapsody."

"No need to apologize."

"You have the kind of face that makes me talk," she tells him.

Billy, intrigued: "What kind of face is that?"

"Look in the mirror. Or don't. You might never escape."

Billy, baffled: "What does that mean?"

"You can't force it."

Billy, now really baffled: "Force what?"

But Gretchen refocuses on the Weather Channel where real weather, an

144

hour old, is projected over the continental United States by way of time-lapse satellite imagery – clouds swirl, build, and disssipate, but always gain ground across the country. These fifteen seconds are played over and over again, as though a clue can be discovered.

Billy, insistent: "Force what?"

"An explanation," Gretchen finally says. "Especially if you ask."

"You're confusing me. What is it about my face?"

She grins, thin lips on mysterious logic. "It's a nice face."

"But you said something about never escaping my face."

"That's true. You can't escape your face."

"But you were saying it in a specific way, not in a general metaphysical way."

"Do you ever forget what you look like?" Gretchen asks.

Frustration trumps flirtation. "I don't know what you're talking about," Billy says.

"Do you ever forget how your face shapes up." Gretchen touches her cheeks in the style of a numinous soap commercial. "I mean, you always recognize yourself, of course, but when you're walking down the street and passing people, are you ever unsure how you look? It's like you can see and smell and taste and hear but you know nothing about your eyes and nose and mouth and ears."

Billy, exasperated: "But what about my face in particular?"

"I'm telling you."

"Oh."

"Your face is blank but reflective."

Billy is unsure how to take this.

"Like polished metal," she adds.

"Oh."

"It's like when you hear your voice in a recording and you swear that's not you though you know that of course that's you and what you're really saying is how can you sound like that, how can you not hear yourself if you sound like that, how can you ever talk again if that's how you really sound. Well, that's how you look, to me at least. It's like I can hear myself in your face and I have to talk to drown myself out."

"That sounds awful," Billy says, imagining a mirror and an infinity of reflection.

"It's a nice face," Gretchen repeats sweetly.

Air-conditioning dips down from northerly vents and hits the warm featureless plain of Billy Schine, producing a weather system of flop sweat. Perspiration sends a droplet down the spine, chill inducing and seemingly suicidal in nature, a leap from the nape that lands on the crack of ass. But Stuart James is unconcerned about one man's weather. He's busy gesturing toward Menomonee Falls, Wisconsin, where Charles "The Shroud of Chuck" Savitch is dying. He reports clear skies for the pilgrims who might be gauging their clothing needs. "Maybe a shower in three or four days but otherwise clear if humid. Drink plenty of fluids," he says like the world is in his care.

"Are you adopted?" Gretchen asks suddenly.

Billy, already flustered, now even more flustered: "Me? No. Why?"

"Because you have that look," she says. "That adopted look. My ex-husband had the same look, bruised around the eyes, eager to please but easily hurt, love me because I hate myself."

"Wait, I thought my face is blank but reflective."

"Exactly."

Billy tacks toward clearer wind. "So you're divorced?"

"Three years," Gretchen says as if proclaiming sobriety. "And you remind me of him. I mean that as a compliment. My ex, he found out he was adopted totally by mistake. His parents never told him. They were old-time WASPS, and this was before open adoption and touchy-feely parenting and surrogate birth mothers and Chinese baby girls in every other stroller. This was when adoption was sort of shameful. And he found out because of a high school biology class—he told me the story all the time, told anyone the story; next to him in an airplane and you'd know this story before drinks were served. The class was doing some experiment, you know that experiment where you prick your finger and find out your blood type, well, they did that experiment, and he was an O, and he went home and asked his parents their blood type, and they said A or B or AB or whatever it is that makes having an O child impossible, and that's how he found out. He was fourteen. And he never told them, never called them on it. He waited for them to tell him. And he waited. And he waited. You should've seen their Thanksgivings. It was all subtext. It made me want to scream. Every day they didn't say anything got him more and more angry. After we were married, they blamed me. I probably should've said something. Because what they needed was a fight, you know, with everyone yelling and screaming, but they were way too polite. It got crazy for him. He'd fantasize about getting a rare genetic disease just so he could lord it over them. The funny thing is he never tried to find his birth parents. I don't think it ever really crossed his mind. He was too obsessed with his fake parents pretending otherwise."

"How long were you married?" Billy asks.

"About nine years."

"Why did you split up?"

Gretchen turns in bed and faces Billy, snuggling the space between them like sheets cuddled when alone. "He wanted children. It was all he thought about. It was almost sweet, in a psychotic way, but certainly sweet when I was twenty-seven. It started on the third date. He told me upfront he wanted four children because he thought three was an unfair number, and two was too teamy, and one was impossible for all concerned. It was all he talked about: his four theoretical children. He even had the ideal gender order mapped out: first girl, then boy, boy, then girl again. We had a good time together, even if he was courting my ovaries. He put on a big romantic show, spent serious money on me, which was thrilling, and by the fifth date I agreed that four was a nice number.

"Within a year we were married and right away we tried. And tried. And tried. It was barely sex; it was straight-up baby-making. But nothing happened. Two months, three months, four months and he's suggesting a fertility doctor, and I'm telling him it's harder than you think, so just relax and give it time. Six months and I buy all those awful books with all those awful titles that make me cringe at the cashier. I begin sleeping with a thermometer by the bed and keeping a basal body temperature graph so I know exactly when I'm spiking toward ovulation. But still nothing. A year and we go to a fertility doctor and we learn that my insides have no obvious pathology and his sperm is fantastically motile. I start taking fertility pills. Still nothing. I have a hysterosalpingography and endocsopy performed. Then an endometrial biopsy. A postcoital exam, which is really pleasant. Immunologic testing in case my sera is spermicidal. Over three years my ovaries and uterus and tubes and peritoneum and cervix are checked and rechecked. Half of the New York medical community have their hands up inside my situation. They harvest eggs and do in vitro three times, but still nothing. Maybe my uterine walls have no *blast*-hold, so they stitch in a few eggs and put me on bed rest. Nope. I try experimental therapies. It's a mystery, they say. As far as anyone can tell, my hypothalamic-pituitary-ovarian axis is intact, though my husband starts viewing this partnership as the axis powers of World War Two and he's Eisenhower and every lay is D-Day. He treats my vagina like it's Omaha Beach. I mention adoption but he's bitterly opposed for obvious reasons. I mention a surrogate and he's briefly intrigued until he decides why not just marry one."

Gretchen pauses. She seems more amused than sad, like those married years are a well-rehearsed routine for strangers. Maybe once she was upset, but since then she's divided and multiplied the story until all that remains is archness. Even so, the honesty is thrilling and unexpected. History told is history shared, and perhaps another history is implied, Billy already accepting her bruised heart even if she claims nothing but a little bump. He can't imagine Luke Sillansky or Stan Shackler getting this kind of talk. No, only Billy defends Gretchen by telling her, "Your ex sounds like a jerk."

"Far from it," she says. "He was a nice guy, still is a nice guy, easily the nicest guy I've ever known. He just had fatherhood on his brain. He's remarried now and has his first child and I'm happy for him."

"Do you still want kids?" Billy asks, a gentle inquisitor.

"I wanted kids. Now I'm fine without them. I think you kind of wake up one morning and decide, choose, maybe defensively, I don't know, that you're alone, and you accept that you're alone, not *alone* alone, but without-kids alone, that you're going to get old without children standing behind you, and you embrace it for what it is, which is neither good nor bad."

"Do you miss him, your ex-husband?"

Gretchen considers this for a moment. Her face is lovely under the angle of consideration, her odd disparate features finding anamorphic focus, like she's doing arithmetic in her head and carrying numbers with her eyes. The sun pours in from the window. The hand sculpture glints toward late midday. Billy breathes in deeply and tries breathing in Gretchen, her particulates, her slice of air, not lasciviously but innocently, his nose nuzzling the eight feet between nostril and neck.

"It's like missing warm weather in the winter," she answers. "You understand that it's the natural way of things, that it's winter and it's cold and kind of pleasant, the change of seasons, but you complain because you need to complain about something, and you miss something only because something is not there." Gretchen shakes her head. "I miss his warmth but not his humidity."

Gretchen returns her attention toward the TV. Stuart James is gone, replaced by a history of severe weather in the twentieth century. Billy leans back in the borrowed bed and wishes he could say the right thing, the healing thing, but knowing better, says nothing, hoping blank but reflective is enough.

"What about you?" Gretchen asks.

"What about me?"

"Do you want kids?"

"No," Billy says quietly. "I'll just screw it up. I'll try my best, but I'll screw the whole thing up and I'll never forgive myself."

"You really believe that?"

"Yeah. I just know I'll do something, well, unforgivable in the end. I will."

"Oh baby," Gretchen says with a hint of heart-stopping affection.

"What?"

"That's so sad."

"I'm not trying to sound sad," Billy tells her. "I mean, I'm not trying some sort of sad guy shtick." Billy stops himself. Gretchen is leaning her head on her hand, her face pulled around an upturned palm. The lovely causalness of the pose strikes Billy. She listens with such grace.

Billy turns toward the TV. There's old black-and-white footage of an improperly engineered suspension bridge buckling in a windstorm. The cars abandoned in the middle of the span rock up and down, and a man walks toward the camera as the ground sways improbably under his feet. The bridge is like rubber until the bridge is like rubber no more and falls apart into the river.

"I'd probably be a fine father," Billy says, not meaning a word.

Cars tumble into the water, like playthings tested from a great height.

18

TUESDAY AFTERNOON. Billy sits in the small office of Dr. Honeysack, waiting for the doctor who stepped out for a second five minutes ago. Billy leans back in the chair. He's anesthetized with delay, a halothane of boredom. His brain is a sack of undigested thoughts that trace against the dura mater until somewhere a room forms, the walls covered in posters of Babar and Madeline and Curious George, the floor strewn with brick-colored blocks and trucks and dolls and horseys, the coffee table carrying issues of *Highlights* and *Ranger Rick* as well as *Parenting, Redbook, McCall's*—the waiting room of Dr. Timothy Ecker-hardt, pediatrician. At twenty-one years of age, Billy is by far the oldest child and the youngest adult in this room, the boys and girls viewing him as an exotic hybrid, the parents, mothers mostly, regarding him as a future threat against cuteness. Billy wishes he could help the boys build the block skyscraper bigger and better. His own fingerprints are on all these toys, more toys than he had growing up, this waiting room in many ways his dream room. Put a bed in the corner and Billy would've been a happy child. Every so often Nurse Jones peeks in and calls a name until finally, "Billy, your turn, hon." She leads him toward the examination room. "So you're still with us," she says, almost with resentment, like he's the bitter embodiment of time.

"Yep."

She takes his height and weight as though measuring her aches and pains.

Dr. Eckerhardt soon enters, white lab coat, stethoscope. He touches all the necessary parts, like a potter spinning an already fired pot, and after the exam tells Billy, "You know I think we might be beyond this, old boy."

To eyes under four feet, Dr. Eckerhardt is a thick beard and a huge belly. A baby in his arms might look like lunch. But his voice and eyes are honey.

"Huh?" Billy squirms.

"You're almost twenty-two."

"In seven months."

"I think we've hit the pediatric glass ceiling."

"But you're my doctor." The sound of pleading surprises Billy.

"And you've outgrown me."

"Outgrown you? Look at me." Billy raises his arms. "Nowadays adolescence extends well into the twenties, maybe even the thirties. It's like a fact. I say graduate school is to blame. And increased life expectancy. And birth control. Sure, physically we're developing earlier but emotionally we're going in reverse."

Dr. Eckerhardt smiles, his beard like a kitten curled on his face. "You can always visit and we can just talk. Hell, we can go have a drink together, but in terms of me being your physician, well, that won't work. Nothing against you, it's just your body."

Billy fears tears. He fights the rising tide with sandbags of *don't be such an idiot, such a fool, so stupid.*

"Are you all right?" Dr. Eckerhardt asks.

"I'm fine," Billy says.

"How's Harvard?"

"Good, I guess."

"And your folks?"

"I don't know, all right, I suppose. I try to stay out of their way. Or they stay out of my way. There seems to be an arrangement."

"Never take your parents personally," Dr. Eckerhardt advises.

Billy wants to break down in front of this large man, this concerned adult who has known him for so long, who has cared for him his entire life, always greeting him with hands that tousled hair and squared shoulders, that palpated as if communicating with the soul. Dr. Eckerhardt might understand his frustration. But Billy continues buttressing the rising tide. "So what do I do now?" he asks.

"I can refer you to a primary care physician."

"So that's it, we're done?"

"You make it sound like I'm breaking up with you. You're a young man. You'll find other doctors, better doctors. But I will miss our yearly checkups. And do keep in touch." Dr. Eckerhardt reaches over and pats his knee, no longer searching for an involuntary reflex. "I'm really proud of you, Billy," he says. "Harvard is quite an accomplishment."

"So I should leave?"

"Not yet." Dr. Eckerhardt reaches into the William A. Schine file and produces a stack of Polaroids, the final measurement for every checkup. One by one he passes them over to Billy. It's like a flipbook of winces. A few pictures are given snippets of doctorly narration. "Here we are as a teenager cringing when puberty was mentioned. Here's the small fry who always said, 'I'm sorry, I'm sorry,' like you deserved every sore throat. Someone could be in tears in another room and you'd apologize. Here's the baseball player. The cowboy. The tiny stoic. You rarely cried yourself. Here we are barely standing. No longer standing. Sitting. Slumped. Sprawled. Pretty cute. And finally the newborn with what can only be described as your patented stroke victim gaze of sorry for the bother, sorry for all the incontinence and the feebleness. Always broke my heart, that look right there."

The three-day-old Billy is encircled by arms that tilt the swaddling toward the camera, Billy with puffy slits for eyes and a flat nose, the hours of life emerging from within him, slowly draining his face from the inside world.

"Is that my mother holding me?" Billy asks.

"Yep. And here she is when she first visited my office, eight and a half months pregnant." Dr. Eckerhardt hands over the last Polaroid. Doris McMinn Schine, soon to be Mom, stands with her stomach thrust forward, the proud pose of pregnant women everywhere. She seems so young, Billy thinks, though she's already in her forties. Her complexion is sparked by the camera's flash. Her green eyes have an almost competitive zeal, as if she could hold her own against any form of glare, even an on-rushing headlight.

"How was she then?" Billy asks. "I mean, about having a baby."

"Oh, she was excited," Dr. Eckerhardt says. "And nervous, like all mothers-to-be."

Nervous won, Billy thinks.

"You can keep these," Dr. Eckerhardt tells Billy.

"Yeah?"

"Absolutely, my parting gift." He stands up, grabs his camera. "Now, one more shot, our graduation picture."

Billy waves away the idea.

"Get over there."

Billy relents for the pleasure of the doctor. He takes his normal position against the giraffe height chart as Dr. Eckerhardt snaps open the camera and frames the boy now grown into a man. "One, two," a flash on three and from the narrow mouth of the Polaroid a gray tongue slips free.

Dr. Eckerhardt snatches it, flutters it dry, and gives it to Billy.

No matter your technological life span, if you've lived through horse-drawn carriages becoming automobiles or the Harvard Mark I calculator becoming the Internet, no matter if you think you're living through a space station becoming an airport on the moon, this small achievement still seems miraculous and can transfix great-grandfathers and great-grandsons alike, as the emulsion streaks, and the fog lifts, and the image emerges just minutes after the fact—Billy forcing a stupid grin—and for a moment you're put in the mind of a primitive tribe rich in awe and mystery, even if afterward, on the street, you toss the pictures into the first garbage can you pass, let them spill into the trash of nostalgia, feeling a mile too late that maybe that was a mistake.

"Sorry," Dr. Honeysack says upon his return. "I ran into someone."

"No problem," Billy tells him.

"Okay, I just wanted to ask you a few questions about how you're feeling." Honeysack leafs through files on his desk and taps a computer keyboard. While Billy and he are roughly the same age, Honeysack seems older, more mature, a doctor for Christ's sake. Billy wishes his own face would start bearing some miles. "So," Honeysack asks, "how are you feeling?"

154

"Fine."

"Physically fine?"

"Sure."

"Mentally?"

"Fine," Billy says. "Nothing to report as far as I can tell."

"As far as you can tell?"

"Yeah."

The sport of conversation has come late to Dr. Honeysack, and while he might be an enthusiastic participant, he lacks the grace of a natural talker, much like a person who takes up tennis at a late age. "You know," Dr. Honeysack says with net-crashing insincerity, "you can tell me anything. The thing is, we want a detailed profile of this drug. Even the smallest discomfort is worth reporting. Nothing is insignificant here. Nothing is meaningless. So think hard." Honeysack drums the tips of his fingers together like he's praying with a beat.

"I basically feel the same," Billy says. "Honestly."

"No small changes?"

"Like I said, I feel the same."

"Nothing at all?"

"Do I look awful or something?"

"No, you look fine. By the way, there's no right or wrong answer here."

"Well, I feel fine. I basically feel the same."

"And how's that?"

"How's feeling the same?"

"You feel nothing different."

"Okay, annoyed," Billy says of the conversation. "Just recently."

"There we go. That's something. Annoyed." Honeysack writes this down.

"Very annoyed," Billy says.

Honeysack underlines the word. "Let's talk about annoyed."

"Please, let's not."

"No, annoyance is a real response. Annoyed. Agitated. Short-fused. Frustrated. Superior. How would we define your annoyance?"

"Wait," Billy says. "I never said anything about superior."

155

"So inferior?"

"Just annoyed."

"But being annoyed has a sense of superiority, of being above the annoyance."

"Can we just stick with 'annoyed,'" Billy says, even more annoyed.

"Sure. Sure." Dr. Honeysack scribbles a longish note. "It's just that—"

"Maybe I was being glib about my annoyance."

"Glib? So you've been feeling glib lately. Insincere? Offhanded?"

"You're like a thesaurus."

"What's that?"

"Nothing. Okay, I have been feeling glib. Of late."

Honeysack smiles. "Suddenly we have annoyed and glib."

"True."

"Anything else."

"Worried," Billy says.

"About what?"

"My roommate mostly. John Rami. I'm worried about him." Worried because Do still hasn't showered or shaved or brushed his teeth, and the smell from his bed is starting to shout like a man trapped behind glass that is slowly filling with toxic green smoke.

"How so?" Honeysack asks.

"He seems fragile."

"Does this make you worried about yourself?"

"No, just him."

"You don't feel like you might be next?"

"Should I?"

"I'm not telling, I'm asking."

"No," Billy says. "I'm just worried about him, about his state of mind."

"Anxious?"

"No, worried."

"So maybe a heightened sense of empathy?"

"Maybe." Billy pauses. "And still annoyed."

"Uh-huh."

"Very annoyed."

156

"Got it." Dr. Honeysack makes a note then rolls his pen in his palms, almost disturbingly, as if warming the ink for a more intimate procedure. An angry pimple sprouts among old acne scars on his neck. It's like a high school reunion. And his eyes—Billy guesses Momma Honeysack told her son, repeatedly, that he had the most beautiful eyes, that they were his best feature and he should accentuate them in conversation, because Honeysack squints and stares and uses his eyebrows as adver-tisements. His eyes might be blue, but they're too light a shade, an Is-he-blind? hue. The whites are like blank Xeroxes of light. The dark circles underneath could be gills without water. The whole Honeysack production of *Eyes!* plays sadly, as if Momma is the only person in the audience.

Billy tries disappearing in a question. "Are you married?" he asks.

Honeysack, taken aback: "No. Not yet. But soon, hopefully."

"Dating?"

"I have, but my work has kept me . . . unavailable."

"Must be a grind. You look exhausted."

"Yeah—do I? Yeah. It's been a crazy couple of weeks, kind of disappointing, the last couple of days."

"Have there been setbacks in your work?" Billy asks.

"Not with product, but procedure."

"But you're still going to save a lot of lives."

"Stop a lot of deaths is how I like to think about it."

"Oh."

"Same thing, I know."

"But different," Billy adds.

"Exactly. I've always been more death oriented."

"Oh."

"My father was an undertaker."

"Really."

"Yep."

"He must've hated your choice of career."

"Why do you say that?"

"An undertaker kind of depends on people dying."

157

"Oh, yeah, right. No, he was supportive. I think he thought it was the more respectable end of the business."

"Sure."

"And with my research, when I picture a potential patient, he's always dead, and I'm reversing the trend. I'm stopping that process. I'm buying him time until the time is right for him to be saved."

"Because you hate your father," Billy says flippantly.

"Huh?"

"I'm kidding."

"I loved my father."

"I was just being annoyingly glib."

"Oh, yeah, right. Anyway." Honeysack checks his watch. "A bit of a tangent."

"But interesting."

"I suppose."

"To go from mortician—"

"Undertaker."

"Sorry. From undertaker to doctor. What do you think your children will do?"

"I don't have any children."

"Let's pretend."

Honeysack frowns, turns his attention toward his clipboard.

"A priest," Billy offers. "I think that would be the natural progression."

"I'm not Catholic."

"A pastor then."

"I'm not very religious."

"And your grandson would be a serial killer, karmicly speaking."

Honeysack glances back to business. "Physically, how've you been feeling?"

"Physically, fine. Basically," Billy answers.

"Basically?"

"Yeah."

"Define 'basically.'"

158

"I'm bored, but I think that must be natural around here."

"How are you sleeping?"

"Poorly."

Honeysack scribbles this down.

"But I normally sleep poorly," Billy says.

"Are you sleeping more poorly?"

Billy considers the question. "Maybe."

"How about waking up? How are you waking up?"

"Slowly."

"Is it hard to get out of bed?"

"That's always been a struggle."

"Getting up?"

"I'm not much of a morning person."

"Any fatigue, drowsiness, during the day?"

"I think I'm always fatigued."

"So you've been tired during the day?"

"Sure."

"Napping?"

"Well, yeah, but there's not much else to do around here."

"So 'lethargic' perhaps?"

"I suppose."

"Anything else? Any headaches?"

"No."

"How about your stomach?"

"Fine."

"No nausea?"

"No."

"So fine?"

"Yeah."

Dr. Honeysack checks his paperwork, searches for any forgotten questions. He does this under the soundtrack of "Okay," which stretches all the way through the straightening up and closing of the manila file.

"Sometimes I do hear voices in the shower," Billy says, curious.

"Voices?"

159

"Like somebody's calling my name, looking for me. Always in the shower. Or in air-conditioning."

"Voices in the shower and air-conditioning?"

"Yeah."

"Calling your name?"

"Yeah. Or singing a song."

"A song?"

"Often a show tune. Rodgers and Hammerstein. Irving Berlin."

"Is the voice recognizable?"

"No, it's just a voice."

Dr. Honeysack reopens the file.

"Sort of an echo of a voice," Billy explains.

"And this has been happening recently?"

"Yeah."

Dr. Honeysack jots this down with enthusiasm.

"Is that of interest?"

"It's all of interest."

"Everything is of interest?"

"Absolutely."

"Have other people complained about voices?" Billy asks.

"Other people don't matter."

"So everything about me in particular is of interest."

"While you're here at least."

Billy nods his head and says, "I have of late, I know not why, lost all my mirth," hoping Honeysack will recognize the kidding *Hamlet* reference. But he doesn't.

"Lost your mirth?" he says.

"Yes," Billy answers, trapped.

"Interesting choice of word."

"Which one?"

"So before this trial began, you were more mirthful."

"I suppose," Billy says, wondering if he should come clean with *Hamlet*.

"You're feeling depressed," Honeysack clarifies.

"I hate that word. Maybe I used to be happier. I guess that's what I'm

160

saying, if I'm saying anything. Lately I've become sick of myself. It's like I'm trapped inside my body, not in some transsexual way, but in a claustrophobic way, like my body is this small narrow space I've crawled into and now I'm stuck." Billy wonders how much of what he's saying is true, but Honeysack seems intrigued. "I do all these things, all these physical things, unconscious things, amazing and complicated things, and I'm like, How do I do that? Like walking. Or breathing. Even farting seems like a miracle of biology. I'm like a hermit crab who's found this beautiful intricate shell and hates himself because he knows he's a slimy little shit."

"A hermit crab?"

"Maybe that's silly."

"So feelings of self-loathing—"

"Not that word, please not that word."

"Sorry."

"Write down whatever you want, but not self-loathing."

"Okay," Honeysack says. "One more question, and you very well might've already answered it, but here it is anyway."

"Shoot."

"Would you say you're feeling optimistic or pessimistic?"

"About what?"

"Things in general."

"Since I came here?"

"Just optimistic or pessimistic at this particular moment in time."

Billy naturally leans toward pessimism. Always. How could any half-intelligent person be otherwise? Hope in all forms should be distrusted. Hope is dumb breakaway glass shattered on the softest head. Survival maybe, blood and thunder, but not hope. While Billy can appreciate the technology of hope, the well-crafted mechanism of religion, the internal wiring of promise, the silicon of love, he has no idea how the gizmo works. In all likelihood hope would lay in his hands, unresponsive, the On button hidden from sight. He'd end up hammering nails with hope or employing hope as a paperweight, until somebody would finally tell him, "Hey, you're using hope all wrong." Hopelessness is what Billy prefers. It has a simpler design and fewer moving parts.

"Pessimistic," Billy says.

"On a scale of one to ten."

"A scale?"

"Yes."

"Let's say five," Billy says. "My pessimism is half-full."

19

THAT NIGHT, during dinner, Billy sits with Sameer Sirdesh, Sameer who has brought along an album of photographs which he shares with Billy, the two of them side by side, Sameer occasionally bumping Billy with a wayward elbow, like a sign of boyhood chums if not for the bully of a drug. The album has a single photograph per page, slipped under plastic. All show a beaming Sameer posed near the shoulder of a celebrity—Sameer and Brad Pitt, Sameer and Harvey Keitel, Sameer and Tom Hanks—the movie stars smiling with patience, with the price of fame, with Sameer, who in some cases has managed to slip an arm around unresponsive shoulders. "This is me with Meg Ryan," he tells Billy. "Lovely woman. Great woman. This is me with Jim Carrey. Wonderful man. Very nice. This is me with, uhm, I forgot."

"Jeff Goldblum," Billy says.

"A gentleman," Sameer says. "And this is, oh."

"Meryl Streep."

"More beautiful in person, I can tell you," Sameer says.

He leafs through page after page, Sameer always looking the same, always with a wide warm smile like the day is his, like the sun is his alone, like the American dream is under his arm and it is polite and gracious and much thinner than you'd think. "I have many more back home," he tells Billy. "This is just one book."

"Impressive," Billy says.

"Every night I'm looking for them."

"Must be exhausting."

"Oh no," Sameer says.

"Hey, Judi Dench."

163

"Who?"

"That woman there."

"Oh yes. Very wonderful, lovely woman," Sameer says, never noticing the tremble in his hands, the dozen missed attempts of fork landing in mouth. He continues showing Billy his full-moon orbit of stars, Billy drifting away from Gwyneth, Julia, toward his fellow normals, toward Ossap, who, while busing his tray, jerks and crashes plates to the ground, toward Stan Shackler, mystery Ph.D. who reads Baudelaire and Baudrillard in unison, toward all of these superficially afflicted souls who report to work not with a thermos and lunch pail but with whatever ails them. Billy wonders if he's finally feeling something. Small hallucinations seem to have made an appearance. Peripheral vision contains the creepy-crawlies of the woods, where phantom moths flitter near ears and field mouse shadows quicken corners. Freckles and moles resemble blood-sucking ticks—after an hour of contemplation, they pulse ever so slightly. Eyelids, when half-closed, divulge amoebalike forms living inside the lashes. Yes, Billy thinks, maybe something.

"Garth Brooks, very nice, stood for two pictures," Sameer says.

From the table behind Billy overhears a triumvirate of nameless complaint.

A: "Anybody freaked about their nose."

B: "What about your nose?"

A: "Well, like I feel like my nose is in the way. Wherever I look, there's my nose. It's like I'm like a prisoner to my fucking nose, like my nose has eaten my face. Driving me nuts, not least of all making me all cross-eyed."

Sameer alights on Kevin Spacey. "This man, very charming," he tells Billy.

B: "I've been tasting my tongue."

A: "Tasting your tongue?"

B: "Have you been getting that?"

A: "No, just the nose thing."

B: "I swear to God I'm tasting my tongue, and it's making me sick. Even now, talking is like talking with my mouth full, like I have this slab of raw meat in my mouth. And the texture, it's nasty. It might be the worst thing I've ever put in my mouth."

C: "What's it taste like?"

B: "Postage stamps."

A: "Ugh."

B: "But I can't stop tasting it."

"Mary Poppins," Sameer says of Julie Andrews. "Delightful and kind to me."

C: "You know what I'm getting?"

A: "Is it your nose?"

B: "Your tongue?"

C: "No, but if I tell you, don't think I'm weird?"

A: "Please, it's the drug."

B: "Yeah, the drug's the fucking weirdo."

C: "I've been getting a taste in my mouth, but it's not my tongue, it's my breath. It has this freaky taste, almost like an aftertaste."

B: "What?"

C: "I'm not queer, okay, but I've been getting a taste of semen in my mouth. I don't why. I don't even know what semen tastes like. I don't. I mean, I know what it smells like—"

B: "Maybe you should just stop talking."

C: "No, seriously, I have an idea of its taste, you know, kind of salty, right, and that's the taste I have in my mouth. It has a definite comey quality. I can't explain it, it's just there all the time."

A: "I can't smell it."

C: "I'm brushing my teeth all the time."

B: "Maybe your roommates are doing awful things to you while you sleep."

C: "Here, smell my breath."

B: "No fucking chance."

Sameer Sirdesh arrives upon the last photo, him with a smirking Harrison Ford. "He was very difficult," he tells Billy. "Five different times I tried, always no or nothing, just kept walking, but he's a busy man. Then this night, a beautiful night, he said yes. See, his arm is around me. He even asked my name. 'Sameer,' he said, 'you are one persistent bastard.' And I said, 'Yes, Mr. Ford, I must be persistent for a person of your stature.'" Sameer beams on the beaming Sameer in the photograph, beam on beam, beaming and twitching upon the slightly crooked composition, Billy realizing Sameer must've held the camera himself, pointing and shooting from the crane of an outstretched arm, Sameer now lowering his head for a closer view of Indiana Jones, Han Solo, Sameer clicking his eyes as if recapturing the image in the palsied fist of his face—Sameer on a magical night in Manhattan, when Harrison Ford finally relented and gave him the minimum of his embrace, which must've been everything.

Huddled in bed, Do no longer reads comics but his Bible instead. Billy is always amazed by people who casually read the Bible, on subways or airplanes, like the Bible is the latest thriller. He's curious if they read the book through and through and then over again, if they have favorite parts, applicable sections, assignments for the day. What do the words do for them? Or is their presence alone enough, like a sense of security, a gas mask of devotion? Billy finds their belief admirable, even comforting— piety as trickle-down theory—but he can't help an aside of condescension, a patronizing *Oh, one of those*, that he despises in himself. After all, faith is a beautiful thing. And he's glad his roommate has something to fall back on since, by all appearances, his spirits need bolstering. Do is tucked within a sarcophagus of sheets.

Billy watches him flip through his Bible and check pages like an accountant. Do glances up, examines the clock, then glances back down. Every minute another glance up, his finger tracing down the page, eleven minutes in all before Billy asks what's up.

"Nothing," Do says.

"You seem to be timing yourself."

"I just noticed something."

"What's that?"

"The Gospel of Luke has twenty-four chapters."

"So?"

"Well, the clock kind of gives you chapter and verse. I've never noticed that before. And just when I noticed it, it was three-oh-seven in the afternoon, or fifteen-oh-seven, which in Luke is: 'Just so, I tell you, there will be more joy in heaven over one sinner who repents than over ninety-nine righteous persons who need no repentance.' Interesting, huh?"

"I guess."

"And right now is: 'And the son said to him, "Father, I have sinned against heaven and before you; I am no longer worthy to be called your son." ' "

"So," Billy says.

"Time is telling us something."

"Does every chapter have sixty verses?" Billy asks.

"No."

"So how about all that other time where there is no corresponding verse?"

"Silence can say something, too," Do says.

Stage left, Lannigan storms into the room. He's pleased with himself. He's just met with Honeysack and he's convinced the man that his teeth were feeling wobbly. "You should have seen me," he tells them, wired with performance. "It was genius. I played it very subtle, like I wasn't really sure but I thought they were loose, like I could pull them from their roots. 'Gums bleeding?' he asked, and I said yep, though I wish I had flossed beforehand because then they would've been bleeding for real. Maybe next time. But he was interested. Oh, man. The teeth thing was new to him." Lannigan taps his incisors like a wolf checking for tone. "I told him I was scared to bite into a grape, that I was convinced I was going to wake up choking on my own teeth. I totally sold the side effect. I was Brando on Novocain. Almost convinced myself, which can happen when you're immersed in a role, when you're emotionally dedicated. He was writing down everything. I told him how I was nervous because being an

167

actor my smile is everything and he seemed concerned. I almost started crying."

"I told the doctor the truth," Do says.

"What?" Lannigan says. "That you've developed an irrational fear of showers."

"Give it a break," Billy says.

"I'll shower soon," Do promises.

Lannigan opens the bathroom door. "How about now?"

The bedsheet coffin remains sealed. "Now is not the time, but soon."

"Isn't the Bible filled with hygiene tips? Thou shalt bathe regularly."

"Shut up," Billy says.

"Sor-ry." Lannigan shadowboxes. It's obvious he's never boxed before; he's a dance-floor pugilist. "Oh man, I was on fuego with Honeysack. Next time I might do a massive breakdown for the good doctor. I can cry on cue like nobody's business. It's one of my greatest strengths as an actor, turning on the old waterworks. My specialty ever since I was a kid on the monkey bars. I'd fake fall, cry cry cry, and everyone would hover over me and think about taking me to the hospital. At that point I'd hop up on my feet and laugh and go on playing. Ouchie, they called me. I don't need glycerin drops or a sliced onion or any sense memory. No Stanislavski, Meisner, Strasberg for me. I can just cry, anytime, anywhere. I mean gut-wrenching stuff. Oscar caliber. And I can cry any style. I can give you the welling up, the single tear, the uncontrollable sob, the joyous dissolve, the angry howl, whatever you might want. I tell you, if the movie business had body doubles for crying, I'd be a rich man, because I can cry perfect tits and tight little asses." Lannigan points to his forehead, where a farmer will shoot a pig. "It's a breeze. All I need to do is flex this muscle right here, and tense my jaw so my ears pop, and this feeling of sadness comes over me. It's almost like a yawn, a stifled yawn that builds and builds behind my eyes, not because I'm thinking about my dead sister or my dead cat or all my dead friends, but because I'm stretching my face into a weepy position."

As Lannigan talks, he begins tearing up. His throat smothers speech. Words seek breath through the nose. "I get into this spot and my eyes follow suit." His vocal cords tighten. "And I'm crying for no reason, and whatever I say sounds like it's coming from the bottom of my heart." He's keening now, high-pitched and awful, chest wracked with hyperventilation, like his lungs can only stand small sips of air. He presses his palms into his temple, rocks back and forth. Tears choke him. Even his snot seems poignant. All the energy in the room gravitates toward Lannigan. He's magnetized with grief.

Billy would rather see him having sex or being ripped apart by bullets.

"Whatever I say," Lannigan continues, composure recovering, "sounds so real, so weighted because my tears are a hundred percent true. This is where my acting becomes untouchable. If only they made movies or plays where the lead is constantly crying." He wipes his eyes, pinches his nose clean, takes a deep shaky breath. "Sometimes I cry in public and wait for somebody to come and comfort me, which they always do."

"How charming," Billy says.

"My family is not big into crying," Do says, more to the ceiling than to Lannigan or Billy. "I saw my father cry once. It was when my grandfather died. Not like my father was so crazy about my grandfather, not like any of us really liked him. My grandfather would slap us hello thinking it funny. He'd slap my cheek, not hard but hard enough, and he'd laugh and say, 'Try convincing me you deserved otherwise.' I think he thought my father was soft on me or something, on all of his sons, which is a joke if you knew my father. He could get into the most Incredible Hulk–like rages. But I guess my grandfather only saw that Bruce Banner side. He never hit us, my father. He'd come close but he always stopped, at that last second, stopped"—Do imitates a hand frozen in midair—"and we'd wait for the follow-through. I swear you could see him considering one little smack, like what's the big deal, and just when you were ready for it, thinking this is it, today is the day he's going to hit me, he'd pull back and smash up something in the house. It was like, I don't know, like he was battling his . . . instinct." Do's mouth makes *instinct* sound deceitful, as if lips should be wary of teeth.

"You're losing me," Lannigan says, playing a movie executive hearing a pitch.

169

"What?"

"Your little story about papa crying."

Billy wishes Do would give up on the story, wishes Do would shut up for his own sake. There is danger in such sincerity, especially with Lannigan in the audience. Keep this to yourself, Billy thinks, do not reveal yourself to the likes of us.

But Do is unaffected by the interruption. He seems determined to tell the story, like the ceiling might tumble from above if the words fail. "When my father cried, we were coming back from my grandfather's funeral. I was the only son joining him because my brothers were working and whatnot, and being older they already had their fights with dad and they were no longer talking to him. It was just me and him. I was twelve, maybe, and we were driving home from the cemetery on the outskirts of where my father grew up about forty miles from where I grew up. I guess he was feeling nostalgic or something because he was talking more than he ever talked, normally being a pretty quiet guy. He was also dying, not that he knew it then, not that any of us knew it, but he had cancer in the pancreas, and he must've been feeling pretty lousy because in less than six months he was dead, and I remember him driving like every bump scraped his knees. Most of the people at the funeral probably figured he was hungover, which he probably was, because he was a fierce drinker, but I think it was the cancer that was making him look so bad."

"The fucking pancreas," Lannigan mutters. "What does it do anyway but get cancer? You go through your whole life never hearing about your pancreas until the doctor mentions it one day and tells you, oh, by the way, it's going to kill you."

"Produces insulin," Billy explains.

"Still a stupid organ," Lannigan says.

The words continue from Do's mouth. "During the trip back from the funeral my father told me how much he hated his father, he told me how my grandfather was a primo jerk. And however you feel about me multiply that by a million and you've got him, he said. So I asked him if he was feeling even a little sad and he told me, no, his grave had been dug long ago, and it just needed the dirt to be kicked in. Then he got quiet, spooky quiet, like he was going to scream and scare you, which he did sometimes, thinking this was hilarious. Instead he started telling me about the only time he ever saw his father cry, years ago, when he was a boy. My grandfather took him deer hunting, and I guess they hiked in and camped so they could get an early start on the day, and I guess this put my grandfather in mind of his own father, my great-grandfather, one hard turd, my father remembered my grandfather telling him, viscious, mean, drunk on sacramental wine meaning self-righteous, my father told me. He told me how my great-grandfather was kind of infamous north of here, near Vermont, where he was the enforcer for the largest apple grower in the state. He'd convince the competition to sell their orchards by killing their dogs and brutalizing their migrant workers and setting suspicious fires. Not a nice guy. Eventually he ended up hanging from a tree. The police said suicide even though his hands were tied behind his back. Or legend goes. My father never believed this. The Ramis have that impulse, he told me on that trip home, and he mentioned a half dozen Rami uncles and cousins and how they killed themselves with a rope. Fail-safe method, he said. If it doesn't break your neck, it'll close your throat. Two deaths in one, he said, because we were mean enough to say screw you to the first, and then my father got quiet, like the story was finished, and that made sense. We're not a family who talks about family, especially dead family. I thought that he was done, that he had talked himself out, but ten minutes later he picked up again."

"Too bad," Lannigan says.

"About how they were camping, he and his father, the night before they hunted. My grandfather began telling him about his own father, about the time he was roughly his age, my father's age, maybe ten years old, when his father showed him how to fix something, I can't remember what it was, or my father couldn't remember what it was, some toy or something. My grandfather took this toy to his father and his father showed him how to fix the toy. Something along those lines. And after he fixed the toy, his father, my grandfather, he said thanks and began playing with the toy right there, a car I think, if cars existed back then. Maybe a cart, a toy cart, something with wheels. And seeing my grandfather play made my great-grandfather cry for no good reason. Just cry. That's what my grandfather told my father. He wondered what was so sad? A son playing with his toy? How could that make you cry? And as he was remembering this, my grandfather started crying, trying to figure out what could've been so goddamn sad about a boy playing with a toy. And that's when my father started crying. Right there in the car with me after the funeral. He teared up remembering his father crying. That's the only time I ever saw him cry." Do stops. He looks as if he's woken up from being hypnotized and perhaps has acted foolish.

"Too many fathers," Lannigan critiques. "And I would've liked some tears at the end. That would've been a nice touch, you crying."

Billy looks up toward the ceiling and its punch holes of acoustic tile that beg for a scream. He won't add anything to this conversation. No. He won't tell Do and Lannigan about his own father, a man who seems on the constant verge of tears. He won't tell them about the last time he himself cried in front of his father, when Dad and Mom were gardening in that small backyard they treated like a farm, no lawn, just seasons of soil into vegetables into soil again. Abe and Doris were preparing against a late spring frost, a large tarpaulin being spread over the dirt, the two of them on either side of the plot, unrolling the blue plastic like an artificial pool. Billy was fourteen. He watched them from the narrow strip of grass that bordered the garden, a sketchpad and pencil in hand. His assignment for art class was to draw a tree—that's all, a tree—and there was a tree in the backyard, in the corner, a maple, an oak, an elm, Billy had no idea. But he won't tell Do and Lannigan how the day was beautiful, cool and sunny, a day where runners would run a couple of miles beyond their normal distance. The idea of frost seemed ridiculous, but the local weatherman was convinced, so here were Abe and Doris, and Billy, too. The trunk of the tree was easy to draw, though he spent too much time on the bark's fingerprint, particularly the whorl of a knothole, until finally the trunk looked right, and the pencil could sketch upward. Abe and Doris began pegging down the corners of the tarp while Billy tackled boughs, limbs, branches, twigs, leaves, a tangle of perspective, branches crossing branches, like fingers intertwined. He won't tell Do and Lannigan how difficult it was to get right, to get really right, so that the space came alive. He took out his eraser, erased a whole section, leaving behind bits of rubber dust, while Abe and Doris finished securing the tarp and moved on to the tomatoes. Billy tried again, but once again the drawing frustrated him. His tree was flat. There was no bend, no attenuation, no sense of dimension. He erased again, determined to eliminate any trace of a line. The paper became worn, and he thought about a fresh sheet but his trunk was so good, so perfect, he was determined to save it. Abe and Doris covered the tomatoes in burlap, carefully bagging each vine that grew along a green stake. Billy lightly penciled in a limb, but already the curve was wrong and looked nothing like the real thing. He erased again. Abe and Doris, side by side, moved down the row of tomatoes, never talking, their hands simpatico, their shoulders bumping without apology. His perfectly drawn trunk survived the eraser, a stump haunted by a ghost. Billy floated his pencil over the paper and glanced up at the tree then down at the lineaments of failure while Abe and Doris took on the last plant, tying the burlap around the base. He won't tell them about disappointment and defeat and failure and how Billy felt so lonely that he started crying, how he shook his head, feeling foolish for crying over a ridiculous tree, for crying at all. He had no preconceptions about being an artist and could've cared less about the assignment, yet here he was, crying. His palms covered his face. His head lowered down into the safe house of elbows on knees. His parents progressed toward the smaller shade garden, near the back fence and that untamable tree. He won't tell them how he was bawling now like a silly child, how Abe picked away fresh weeds and Doris joined him, how their gloves dug together into the dirt, how neither one seemed to notice their son for they had things to do, how Billy waited for a hand to fall on his shoulder, how they eased up the unwanted shoots until the roots gave way, how a little pile had grown by the time Billy gave up and retreated inside.

There's no way he will tell his roommates any of this. Instead, Billy watches Do glance up at the clock and back down to his Bible and the

173

corresponding verse in Luke. Billy imagines fathers falling in a forever descent, Rami men extending backward from Do, Rami unbegetting Rami, back to the old country (wherever that might be), back to the old old country, to Palestine, to Eden, back to the beginning where Adam tells Cain and Abel about the only time he ever saw his father cry.

20

THE STORY of fathers mixed with the institutional quality of this place, the wear and tear of boredom, the daily pills, the sickly clean smell, the bland food, the long bright hallways, the open doors repeating the same dazed scenes inside, the nurses far removed from saving lives, the overall weirdness of time in the clocks, almost like breathing—at best unconscious, at worst conscious—tugs Billy toward a phone that rang three years ago.

"Billy Schine, please, this is Abe Schine, his father."

Of course Billy recognized the voice. There's that nervous cadence, that lag between brain and tongue as if every word is poorly chosen and needs further clarification. His father is the king of redundancy. Abe has always been the preferred title, father and all its cozy derivations dropped years ago, not from some liberal notion of parenthood but simply because those terms never really applied. Once, when Billy was five, he tossed a "sleep tight, Daddy" at Abe, and Abe flinched and said, "Just call me Abe from now on. No more 'Daddy,' just 'Abe.' In Hebrew, you're halfway there, so stick with 'Abe.' Okay? Good night."

So Billy said, "Hey Abe," to the phone.

"Billy?"

"Yes, Abe." Patience was already frayed.

"I need your hand, help. A favor. You think you could come home?"

"I'm kind of busy."

"Just for the day. Thursday. Three days from today. Not even a full day, just late morning and afternoon. You can be home by the eleven o'clock news."

"I don't know," Billy said in a deep breath of no fucking way. "It's kind of crazy around here. I'm totally swamped, tax time and all." He said this as if his temp work was wrapped up with April 15, but at the time his job involved copyediting a teen clothing catalog which, with its spunky portmanteaus and youthful brand of syntax, was impossible to correct. How do you tackle words like *coolicious* and *awsum* and *fway*? Where do you begin when you find a sentence like this: *So pretty boy, right, u know who I'm sayin, yeah, absotootely, he's goin wow when he spies u to the 9s in this floral pantsuit number with matching visor and kicks ($49.95), go girl camo we call it, cause once he shwees you, bang! he's already dead.* All Billy could do was red pencil in {*sic*} with a question mark. {*sic*}? {*sic*}? {*sic*}? It was like his mantra, {*sic*} by every purposeful mistake, {*sic*} becoming the rule of his own {*sic*} life. It could've been tattooed on his forehead.

"We need you." Abe said.

"Well—"

"It's your mother. She's ill, not well, quite bad actually. She's sick," he said. Immediately cancer came to mind. Or a stroke. Or a heart attack. Surgery, chemotherapy, radiation swirled in the aftermath, as well as hospital stays and months of recovery and perhaps, in the end, hospice care followed by dying words, a funeral, flowers on a grave. Billy was ready. He was prepared. He had been expecting this phone call from either his mother or father with news of the other's declining health. He had rehearsed his reaction, had scripted his speech before their last breath, had staged his changed relationship with the lone survivor. All the years of coldness might thaw in the eleventh hour. Maybe a bit sentimental, but feelings needed prompting and who gave better cues than the Grim Reaper. Under time's scythe they might end their chilly truce and finally make peace. Not that they were ever at war. War involved battles and there were never any battles in that household. But there were tensions. It often seemed like the domestic version of mutual assured destruction: whoever launched the first shout could very well destroy the world.

Billy asked, "What's wrong?" He was unsatisfied with his tone (too curt) so he added, "Is she okay?" which sounded better, warmer, more genuine, which, upon recognizing the improvement, made him feel shallow, leading him to mutter, "I hope."

"She has Alzheimer's," Abe said.

"Alzheimer's?"

"Alzheimer's," Abe repeated with a vague hint of his first tongue. Billy was stunned. Within the inventory of parental decline, he had never considered Alzheimer's. It loomed so much larger than his mother, like one of Sameer's celebrities was posing by her side. *That's my mom with Alzheimer's.* The actual awful effects—the slow attack on memory and function, the backslide into geriatric pediatrics—sounded like a metaphor gone gangrene.

"I can't believe it," Billy said.

"I know," Abe agreed. "Terrible."

"I'm in shock."

"Yes, terrible."

"I can only imagine."

"Well—"

"My God, I am"—weighted pause—"so sorry. For you. And her, of course. But you, my God, so hard. Not fair."

"Well—"

"Just tragic, you know."

"I know."

They could've been inventing a new language, beautifully inarticulate.

"So you'll come home?" Abe tried again.

Billy—"Absolutely"—answered without hesitation. "I'll come home right away," he said. "I'll even stay for a while. I will. I want to. To be there. I do. Really. We'll face this thing, together, as a family, which is important, I think. The three of us. We'll be a team. I want to spend as much time with her, with you, as possible before she gets"—Billy was shocked by the natural quality of his words—"worse. No, I'll come home. Definitely. Maybe I'll move back, and help, and everything, until whenever." The sentiment, the decency of his reaction, moved him within the vicinity of tears.

"Uh-huh" crawled through the line.

"I'll try getting a flight tomorrow."

"No rush," Abe said. "We just need you Thursday, April twenty-second, twelve noon."

177

"But I can come tomorrow. No problem. Work is barely work."

"But Thursday is when we need you."

"What's the big deal about Thursday?"

"She goes into a nursing home, assisted living, and we—"

"A nursing home?"

"Assisted living."

"Already?"

"Yes."

"That seems soon."

"I tried for as long as I could," Abe said defensively. "I really did try hard. When she became more"—he skipped trying to find the right word—"I took leave from work and stayed with her, but she's now beyond my care. She needs around-the-clock professional assistance and I have no choice. I can barely—"

"Wait, how long has this been going on?" Billy asked, stomach roiled.

"She's soiling herself, not eating."

"Abe, how long has this been going on?"

"The soiling and not eating? About three months."

"No, Abe, when was she diagnosed?"

"Diagnosed?"

"Yes."

"About four years ago," he said matter-of-factly. "But I suspected long before. She was becoming different and of course forgetful. Scattered. In a way it was a relief because I thought she might be leaving me for somebody else. I thought she was having a lover, a torrid affair that was making her crazy. I thought that. I thought she was leaving me for a while."

"Four years ago?" Billy repeated.

"Yes, four years. I even followed her I was so convinced she was loving someone else. I was so crazy I followed her and caught her in the park by herself eating dirt. Eating dirt. Who eats dirt but the insane? She was eating dirt like a sick animal. So I ran over and she saw me and I was a nobody to her. I took her home. The next day she remembered nothing. Makes me think about all the days I didn't follow her."

178

"Eating dirt?"

"Or worse."

"And that was four years ago?" Billy asked.

"The dirt, then the doctor, the diagnosis, yes, four years ago. Roughly."

"So you've known for four years?"

"Officially, yes."

"And you didn't call me?"

"We didn't want to bother you."

Billy sagged, emptied his lungs until they were deflated, allowing sadness brief lodging in his chest, outrage as well, the space measuring four years, Billy holding his breath and waiting for the burning to begin, the burning that might anneal hope for the simple promise of the next breath when his heart would push away his parents and temper lament for the sake of air.

"Billy?"

"I'm glad you're telling me now," he said without bitterness or irony.

"We thought you should know."

"So Thursday."

"Yes, and if you could rent a car."

True New Yorkers, his parents never learned to drive. They relied on buses.

"I don't know, Abe," Billy said. "I'll try, but I don't know."

"We need you now," Abe told him coldly, as if activating some familial sleeper cell.

"I'll let you know if I can make it, but if I can't, I'll try to visit soon. I will. But Thursday I'm not sure about." The pain in his voice might as well have stemmed from his appendix, vestigial and serving no useful function. But why should he help them? Let them be abandoned, denied. Let them finish their life the way they lived it, on their own, in exile, without anyone else crowding the picture except for that out-of-focus boy who occasionally lingered in the back. Four years without a word until they needed him for an errand. Four years of ignorance in New York, in exile from exile, as his mother dwindled, as his father no doubt clung to the last of the warmth, his alone. What did Philip Larkin say in that poem, something about parents and how they fuck you up? But Philip Larkin is nowhere to be found within the parents of *The Oxford Dictionary of Quotations*. There is Charles Dickens. "You don't object to an aged parent, I hope," he wrote in *Great Expectations*. No, Billy thinks, there's no objection, except that aging should be a shared thing, a slow progression, communal in nature between parent and child, often the circumstance that bears most fruit, seeing Mom and Dad inch toward death, toward the end time when they will pass into memory. And what if parents object to a young child for no apparent reason. What if every step brings a headache, if every hour of need robs them of time together, family like a zero-sum game, mother and father pitted against wife and husband, and what if, exhausted, the latter throws in the cards and lets the child play in the corner by himself, lets the child fend with only the nuts and bolts of care, like some genetic boarder who earns his keep with quiet compliance. No, Billy doesn't begrudge them growing old. But he is jealous of death's last unimpeachable word.

Billy thinks Oscar Wilde has a point: "Children begin by loving their parents; after a time they judge them; rarely, if ever, do they forgive them." As does Francis Bacon: "The joys of parents are secret, and so are their griefs and fears." But Billy gives Horace the final say: "What do the ravages of time not injure? Our parents are worse than our grandparents and they have produced us, more worthless still, who will soon give rise to yet a more vicious generation." Billy translated the words himself.

21

O N WEDNESDAY, the fifth day, Billy has to escape his room. Since
after lunch, Lannigan has been standing in front of the bathroom
mirror, shaving. The decent beginning of a beard, certainly more than Billy
could muster in double the time, is shaved in increments. After each
particular pass of the blade, Lannigan peeks into the room and asks, "How's
this look?" He goes from Viking to heavy metal rock star to Amish to hipster
to swinger to Hitler to nothing. Water is splashed on his face as if he's
advertising the cooling effects of aloe vera, then he snoots his upper lip for
stray nose hairs. Yep, a few. Out come the tiny scissors and—snip snip—all
gone. Then he trims the thin side-curls from around his ears and cleans up his
eyebrows. He stares at himself for a good three minutes before he grabs a bit of
forelock and—"What the hell"—cuts. Cuts again. After every few cuts he
again asks, "How's this look?" without needing an opinion, only a con-
firmation of his own patented wackiness. Do barely acknowledges Lannigan.
He reads his Bible and checks the clock for Luke time. He's a hermit without a
cave, only a bed, hoarding the stink underneath like shame is his nourish-
ment. Words no longer appear on his mouth. For the last few days he's been
silent. But there's something in his eyes. If they were a movie they might be
saying "Please kill me now!" but since they are far from a movie, they submit
to another minute of misery, another appearance by Lannigan with the latest
fistful—"How about this?"—of hair.

Please, leave, Billy tells himself.

But where?

Just go.

And, finally, he crawls out from under indecision.

*   *   *

A glance into Gretchen's room. She's not there, but Billy basks in the evidence. The bed is disheveled. The TV hums with weather. Socks are curled on the floor like a litter of newborn kittens. Billy departs before his pause can be certified as anything but a casual look-see. Farther down the hall he passes Ossap and Dullick's room. Dullick and Ossap sit on the same bed, Ossap twitching like he's saying *no-no-no-no*, Dullick obsessively rubbing his left hip like he's got a boo-boo that's lasting forever. "We should go sooner," Dullick mutters. "We need to go sooner, the sooner the better, the faster we're gone from here. I know blah-blah-blah but I'm sorry, we should go sooner."

"Your arm," Ossap says.

"What?" Dullick's right arm is slowly lifting in the air, like a question's unsure answer. "See?" he moans. "I didn't feel that. I didn't even know that was happening. We've got to go sooner."

Ossap elbows Dullick and gestures his chin toward the doorway.

"See," Dullick answers. "You're a mess, too."

"No, the hall."

But before Dullick can turn around, Billy is gone.

In the lounge *RoboCop* plays to an audience of seven. Their attention easily wavers—both socially and pharmaceutically—and they talk over the movie to the point where the half-man, half-machine crime fighter is like a hotel bar pianist who only gets acknowledged during particularly jazzy bursts of violence.

No easy seats available, only scoot-overs and sit-ups and do-you-minds, Billy goes over and browses the board games. All the classics are here. Stratego. Monopoly. Life. Risk. Trivial Pursuit. Stacked together, the boxes are a montage of rainy days and rec rooms, the worn spines holding the abuse of nothing else to do. Clue. Masterpiece. Othello. He wonders if children still play these low-tech games, or are adults the only enthusiasts, inviting friends over for marathon sessions of Scrabble and Boggle while upstairs their kids blow apart a nasty breed of graphically intense zombie. Chess and backgammon are, of course, in attendance. They're like the Old and New Testament of board games—chess for the Jews, backgammon for the Christians. The boards themselves are pressed from cheapo cardboard and seem almost blasphemous. These games deserve jewel cases, Billy thinks. Even worse, on the flip side of chess is checkers, which is akin to a conversion in Scientology.

Billy takes backgammon from the shelf. He feels like playing himself.

On the TV, Officer Murphy goes through his transformation into steel, while on the couch, a crew-cutted Karl McKay, self-professed all-American type though his lusterless eyes would make the Secret Service wary, says, "I once did some government work. NASA. Medical-experiment stuff. Not like old Robo here, nothing that extreme."

"Oh, really," Yul Gertner cuts in. His shaved head is being eclipsed by a crescent of bald-guy hair. "You mean they didn't turn you into a cyborg prototype of a douche bag."

Nobody reacts to Gertner anymore.

"I went to Mars. Theoretically."

"And I went to your momma's anus." Gertner, it is agreed, can only heckle.

Billy sets up the backgammon board as Karl McKay eagerly explains his work for NASA. "It was at the Ames Research Facility in Moffett Field, California, a superb, top-notch facility. Really the best. Best scientists, best equipment, best food."

"The best of the best?" Gertner bites.

"All the real astronauts get tested there."

"Where do the fake ones go, your parents' basement?"

"They were looking for normals, normals in good shape, athletic and health conscious and focused, not your random person off the street guinea pig but somebody who in body mimicked the physicalism of an astronaut."

Gertner tilts his head. "Physicalism?"

Billy is thinking the same thing.

"It was a rigorous process just to get into the study," McKay continues—

"Because of the physicalism, I bet."

—unperturbed. "Me and five other folks were signed up for a hypothetical mission to Mars. They even had jumpsuits for us. Really cool.

Our mission was called Harmony Three, even had patches, just like the real deal. Our job was to simulate the physiological effects of zero gravity over an extended period of time."

Gertner rolls his eyes while Billy rolls the die to see who goes first.

"They kept us in bed on a six-degree decline so blood would go to our heads like we were floating in space. They kept us this way for thirty-five days and tested things like muscle mass and bone density and experimented with all sorts of ways they might counter the effects of no gravity." Karl McKay nods, which spontaneously fires the antipsychotic muscles in his jaw and causes his chin to jut-jut-jut. "Like they packaged us in these inflatable cuffs that pulled the blood away from our heads. We were like the Michelin men. From start to finish we were covered in gauges and tubes and clamps and electrodes."

"Anal probes?" Gertner asks.

"They injected us with radioactive dye; they x-rayed us; they made us breathe through a bag; they had us pedal a stationary bike while still on our backs. Not once were we allowed to compromise the six-degree decline. Six degrees sounds like nothing, I know, but trust me, six degrees is something you feel."

Billy chooses white for himself and red for him, the him of superhuman backgammon ability, the him of understanding the doubling cube, the him of a vaguely European style of throwing the dice, the him of knowing the odds and fearlessly leaving a piece open and disdaining the easy 3–1, 4–2, 5–3, 6–4 combinations, though the fantasy him will occasionally accept these rolls like a complimentary glass of perfectly adequate gewürztraminer offered by the lady of the house who watches her husband's high-stakes game from behind the latest issue of *Paris Match*, the one with the cover of the minor royal jumping half-naked from the bow of the race-car driver's yacht into the turquoise of the Italian Riviera, while the inset picture has her husband, the grand duke, frowning as if this file picture from a 1997 Bahraini royal wedding perfectly captures the future news of his wife's pendulous breasts lifting unenthusiastically toward the sky and surrendering under the noses of two million readers. Billy grins. Maybe it's the drug he's playing.

"But the thing is," Karl McKay—knee kick—says. "You're really well cared for. You almost feel like a, like a baby, a premature baby in that incubator thing. All these lights surround you, UV lights, sun lamps, though they have the room temperature nice and cool so you're never hot but perfectly cooked. You shit and piss in bed, which you fight for the first few days because it's like steering into a tree on purpose, but once you get used to it and just let it happen and let the nurse clean you up, you begin forgetting about it and you sort of let your body do whatever it wants whenever it wants. They change your sheets twice a day. And the best is when they bathe you. They slip you onto a gurney and wheel you into this stainless steel box. Only your head is outside, like a magician doing that saw-the-assistant-in-half trick. Inside are hundreds of jets, and they start shooting a warm soapy spray, pounding you all over, but gentle. It must be a thousand jets because they hit every pore. Meanwhile your hair is being washed and your face and neck are being sponged, and you're like nothing but pure pleasure. It's not sexual or anything. It's just nice. It's like your mother scratching your whole entire body right before you go to bed."

"Maybe *your* mother," Gertner tosses in.

Billy, in jail, fails to roll himself free, and the him of summers in Maine filled with marathon backgammon tournaments between brothers and sisters and father when father was between three and six drinks scoops up the dice and drops them with the minimum legal amount of wrist. Up comes doubles, ones, which is ideal for closing the board and leaves Billy behind bars—"Nooo," to himself—as the him of failed careers and endless charm brings his boys in from the cold and begins removing them from the board, occasionally glancing toward the imprisoned white piece and almost wishing for the bad roll and the smallest chance of comeback drama, this slight empathetic imbalance the cause of a hundred heart-breaking defeats in a myriad of sports.

"And at night," Karl McKay goes on. "When they turn off the lights, the ceiling has those glow-in-the-dark stars but better than store-bought glow-in-the-dark stars; these are like glow-in-the-dark stars specially made for NASA. The stars are arranged the way they'd be seen from the southern hemisphere of Mars, and in the distance, a little brighter than any other star, is Earth."

"What'd they pay?" Rodney Letts asks.

"Four thousand."

"Not bad." Unlike most of the group, Rodney has never looked better. Regularly bathed and closely shaved and more-than-decently fed, his ID hangs like the interstice between who he was and who he will eventually be again. The temporary turn of appearance has given him a regal flare, as if the most basic comforts are the provenance of kings. Except for his skin. Or maybe because of his skin. His skin is dry, beyond dry, sprouting small wildfires of rash. A nurse has given him his own personal tube of lubricant which Rodney applies with foppish regularity, squirting a dollop into his palm and rubbing his hands together and—*aaaaah*—hydrating like Munch's famous painting retitled *Fast Relief*.

"I lost three inches on my length," Karl McKay says.

"So that leaves you with half an inch." Gertner high-fives himself.

"Of height, and I regained it."

"You're lucky because the government can fuck you up," Rodney says.

Hyper Stew Slocum nods. His drug-related akinesia turns the nod into an autistic rock, his hips doing the work of the neck. "Yeah, like I heard about this government study," he says. "They inject you with something and then tattoo the sole of your foot. When you die the undertaker will bury rocks in the casket and send your body to a government lab for dissection. For this they'll pay you ten thousand dollars. Hard cash. All they care about is how you are when you're dead."

"Bullshit," Herb Kolch says.

"It's what I heard."

"Have you guys heard about the heart stop study?" Rodney asks.

"The one in the hollowed-out mountain in Colorado?" Stew asks.

Herb Kolch practically spit-takes his own excessive saliva. "Oh, come on."

"Go ahead, laugh, but it exists."

"The one I heard about happens in Texas," Rodney says.

"I heard Bermuda," Karl McKay offers.

186

Rodney gives them his version. "The one I heard about pays you twenty grand to stop your heart for three, four minutes, so they try this new super-duper heart attack relief medication on you. There's something like a one-in-five chance you'll die, like forever die."

Billy turns away from the backgammon and the him of you're good, very good, but I'm better. He thinks of Honeysack and his research.

"What I heard," Karl says, "is that the chances of dying, of real death, are one in three. They stop your heart and submerge you in liquid nitrogen, and it's in Bermuda because the laws are much looser there."

"Please," Herb Kolch says.

"What do you call cryogenics?" Karl says.

"Ridiculous."

"But it's real."

"I know it is," Herb says. "But it's not happening in Bermuda, and it's not submerging someone in liquid nitrogen so maybe in the future they can be cured or cloned or whatever. I know what you're talking about. I've heard it myself. It's a twenty-five-, thirty-thousand-dollar study, and that's roughly the chance of not surviving the thing. But this isn't about thawing a person in a hundred years. This is short-term stuff, a half hour, an hour, ninety minutes maybe. They lower your body temperature until you're basically dead, like frozen on the inside with ice water in your veins, and then they can do whatever they want to you."

Billy imagines himself dead, or not quite dead. Near dead. Floating upward, toward the stick-on stars over Karl McKay's spaceship bed, into the black perithanatic beyond, hoping for some white light in the distance even if the white light comes from some chemicals in the dying brain, those receptor sites sucking in the sentimental end, a voice reaching for him like a hand, warm and knowing, saying come live with me and be my love, drawing him in among the rest and only letting go when the world below kicks in the door and flips on the lights and mutters another good morning.

RoboCop, full of fury, blasts away at the bad guys in an abandoned factory. The gore is enough to cease conversation in the lounge and refocus attention on the screen. One of the baddies has just been drenched in toxic waste. His flesh is melting; his throat is swelling a tad too graphically. Billy recognizes the actor from another movie, *Fame*, the sweet curly-haired redhead who sang the body electric, but now he's staggering down the street and pleading for help from his baddie buddies who scream when they see him. Billy can practically feel the impact of the truck as it smashes into the *Fame* kid and bursts him like a goo-filled balloon.

Back in his room, Billy interrupts Lannigan crouching near Do's bed. Lannigan is naked and entirely hairless, a primal sort of man. Head, chest, legs, arms, armpits, eyebrows, groin, have been shaved. His prick hangs down without the proscenium of pubes; it seems imbued with the discomfort of possible audience participation. In fact, all of Lannigan, regardless of the nudity, seems too intimate, as if a small army of hair maintains the borders of personal space.

"I got carried away," he tells Billy.

"I guess so," Billy says.

"I couldn't stop." His eyes seem to poke through a mask. "My hair got shorter and shorter until I said fuck it and shaved it. It felt good, all light and cool, like I had lost ten pounds." Lannigan rubs his shower-cap scalp. "It doesn't look bad, does it?"

"No, not bad," Billy lies.

"Sort of exotic, I think."

"I'd say 'otherworldly.'"

"I've always wanted to shave my head. My armpits, that was a bit more random. My head felt so smooth I wanted to see how smooth I could get, the smoothest possible me. I worked my way down. It is amazing," he says, running his fingers over his chest. "It's like I'm underwater." Lannigan hops up and stands as straight as possible, stretching up on his toes and reaching with both hands, looking like an alien reaching for his distant star. "Hey, I'm impulsive," he says, back on his heels. "I shaved my entire fucking body for no reason. I would've shaved my ass crack if Do had agreed to help."

Do is turned toward the window.

"What can I say, I'm nuts." Lannigan caveman-walks into the bathroom and inspects himself in the mirror. "Okay, the eyebrows might've been a mistake," he says soberly. "I shaved one and I was screwed." The eyes squint within an endless stretch of forehead. "Do I really look this awful?" he asks Billy.

"You look like you just shaved your entire body."

"It would've been fine if I just kept the eyebrows," he says. "That was stupid. I mean, I have Voltimand coming up, and I was hoping to understudy Rosencrantz or Guildenstern. Maybe even Hamlet. Why not? I was born to play Hamlet. I'd be a great Hamlet." Lannigan glances back at the mirror, sullied flesh unresolved. "How long does it take for an eyebrow to regrow?" he asks.

"I have no idea," Billy says.

"A while maybe."

"Maybe."

"What an idiot I am." Lannigan sighs. He could be leaking away an idea of himself, the spontaneous character, the free spirit, leaving behind the person in the mirror who is easily embarrassed. "Maybe I can chalk this up to a side effect," he says.

"Whatever. But put on some clothes."

Lannigan remains naked. He hunchbacks to the door and with silent-movie aplomb inspects the hall. "Maybe it's time for some streaking and freaking."

With that, he is gone, no longer Voltimand, Billy thinks, and never Hamlet, but Tom O'Bedlam, shorn of reason, amphibian in desire, jumping from the land of hot pursuit into the green mantle of the standing pool.

22

WHEREVER BILLY goes, the TV follows, and wherever a TV flickers, another bit of Chuck Savitch is revealed. ABC, NBC, CBS, FOX, PBS, UPN, WB, CNN, MSNBC, CNBC, FNC, PAX, E! have devoted reporters and precious airtime to the story. News programs fly through the night with all the wonderment of Santa's reindeer—come *Dateline*, come *Nightline*, come *Primetime Live* and another *Dateline*, come *48 Hours*, come *20/20*, come *Extra* and *Inside Edition*—delivering the story, gift-wrapped and bowed, into every home. *A&E* has rushed into schedule a week of biographies concerning saints, martyrs, and miracles. Tonight, St. Catherine. The *700 Club* is on the scene, Pat Robertson and the white-haired black man whose name never sticks recommending their VHS tape on the Rapture ($19.95). All the angles are being covered. Pre-millennial anxiety is mentioned by a gaggle of pundits as a possible culprit, along with OJ and Monica and the twenty-four-hour news cycle and the lowering standards of American journalism which they rail against with rouged cheeks and pancaked complexions, like Shiites flagellating themselves on whips lashed with silk.

It's all the normal crap, Billy thinks.

Flip around and you see the same portrait in different colors.

Click.

Pilgrims gather around the home of Lily Savitch, mother of Chuck. Filmed from above, the crowd sit on the lawn and sing and pray under the hot Wisconsin sun, the shadow of the helicopter in buzzardlike relief. They're keeping vigil. They're witnessing. They're waiting for a glimpse or maybe an audience. "The Lord shows up so rarely in this day and age," says Frank Vernon from Chester, New York. "You seek Him where you can. Even if it's not Him, it's Him, if you know what I mean." Though they're from all over the country, they might have shopped in the same stores. They could be related, the atmosphere family-reunion friendly. Children buddy up. Picnics are shared. Every day new friends are delivered into the crowd's loving grasp.

Click.

"Every hotel, motel, bed-and-breakfast within a twenty-mile radius is booked solid with you folks and pilgrims," Tyrone Ophuls, mayor of Menomonee Falls, tells a reporter. He wears a wide tie on a wide stomach hanging below a wide smile. "All our restaurants are packed. Business is booming well above our normal October-in-August fest traffic. I hear Milwaukee's doing well too. On average ten tour buses are arriving every day and charter flights are coming in from all over the world. Yesterday, Hungary; today, Colombia. The Chamber of Commerce is estimating fifty million dollars will be pumped into our local economy, maybe more, depending on the, well, longevity of the event." The mayor seems widely pleased with his tact. "You know most small towns only get this kind of attention when, God forbid, something awful happens, a multiple homicide, a school shooting, something like that, so we feel fortunate for the positive circumstance behind this coverage. Menomonee Falls is a lovely community."

Click.

"Hey, have you heard the latest about Chuck Savitch?" a late-night host asks his bandleader. "No? Well it seems the guy picked his nose and"—grin—"spread the word of God under the kitchen table." Rim shot and the audience groans.

"You're going to get some letters," the bandleader says.

Click.

The modest front of the Savitch home is covered with 1) candles, votive candles along with large colored candles that melt on a hardpan of their brethren, encasing the stoop in red, blue, green; 2) a quarter-life-size crèche pulled early from Christmas storage; 3) bundles and bundles of flowers, mostly lilies of the valley and palm fronds and holly; 4) notes taped to the wrought-iron banister and aluminum siding, also children's

191

drawings in thick crayon, and devotional pictures, and banners as if Christ is the best football player ever; 5) six wooden crosses leaning like an uncompleted trellis; 6) photographs of loved ones too sick to travel positioned along the perennial border of pansies and geraniums blooming with despair. The bay window curtains are always closed, though the fabric is near sheer and works like a scrim. "He's in there," says Bruce Nole, from Missoula, Montana, as people around him sing hymns and lift cell phones for friends and family back home. "You can feel it, sometimes see it, him right behind those curtains, watching us on TV."

Click.

The talk show guest, a university professor of popular culture, nods and smiles like he'll always get the joke long before the punch line, nods and smiles as he waits for the end of the question, which is dragging, which is typical for this serious interviewer who squares his question—"Which is to say . . ." "In relation to . . ." "What I mean, I guess . . ." "So the whole issue, really, in hindsight is . . ."—and smiles and nods along with his guest, though his smile is more uncertain, like he's in under his head, leaning forward, leaning backward, telling a long flamboyant story around this one question hoping he might hit upon a single good idea, which seems to revolve around mass hysteria vis-à-vis religious fervor combined with millenarianism and, of course, the self-perpetuating media event, the feeding frenzy, the need for eyeballs that stick, and the obvious strength of the ratings for this story, a story for our times, the host punching his final words about, "What. This. All. Means. In. This. Day. And. Age?"

"Well," the guest—

Click.

Neighbors of Chuck have been infused with the entrepreneurial spirit. They rent their driveways to satellite vans. They sell sandwiches and lemonade and cookies. They charge two dollars for bathroom privileges. "What with all the hassle, all the traffic around here, we might as well make something," says Peter Lauffesen, local resident, standing in his yard surrounded by fifty folding chairs that face the Savitch house. Every chair is taken, five bucks a day. It's a better deal than his neighbor Geoff Carlson who charges seven.

Click.

"I usually have terrible asthma," says Frank Toffelson, a local resident and friend of Chuck. "And come summers allergies can kill me, especially this summer, high pollen, high rag, a tough summer for me. But three weeks ago, and this is before we knew anything about what this thing looked like, we just knew Charlie was sick, so I went on over and dropped off an apple pie my wife baked—we're all friendly—and when I walked into that house, the air seemed different, like purer, cooler too, and I wondered, I remember wondering, did they put in central air-conditioning? I gave them the pie and since then I've had no allergies." Then he stares into the camera. "Go ahead and make fun us, all of you out there. I know what you're thinking because I thought it myself. Rubes, right. Religious nuts. But what you are seeing is love. That's what you're spitting at."

Click.

The oncologist and the older sister of Chuck stand in front of the attached two-car garage. A small podium has been constructed for an informal press conference, a sort of state of Chuck address. Dr. Nathan Vartan, of Mercy Hospital, bobs over the microphones like a ferret wondering if these black eggs have gone bad. Nancy Savitch Karansky lingers behind his right shoulder, more family representative than spokesperson. She stares at the only place where there's no camera: her feet.

The doctor reads from a prepared statement, at times embellishing his words poorly. "Our treatment of Charles Savitch has progressed to the point of pain management. That means palliative care." He spells *palliative*. "We're not trying to cure him, as some rumors have, uhm, rumored, we're trying to make him as comfortable as possible." Dr. Vartan blinks rapid-fire, like his eyelids are Morse code beating *Get me out of here.* "The truth is, his condition is grave. Charles Savitch is dying. He's made it clear that he wants to die in his childhood home surrounded by friends and family. It's a sad situation for everybody involved. Mr. Savitch is saying his good-byes. How long will this last? Hard to say. As a doctor I take no stock in prediction. His condition is deteriorating daily. The tumor is suffocating his ability to function, but the tumor itself is located in the

193

cerebrum, in the lobes, while the brain stem, in particular, the medulla oblongata, is still persisting under the assault. It's like a fire on the fifth floor but the mechanicals in the basement are still working. As you can imagine, it's a terrible way to die, especially for the loved ones, but I feel I must remind the people of the media, *again*, that beyond the personal tragedy there is nothing unique about Mr. Savitch's condition. He is one of the thousands of people with a malignant glioma and one of the millions of people with cancer. His signs and symptoms are neither rare nor special, certainly not miraculous. His clinical features have been wholly characteristic of the disease. His MRI, unfortunately famous, shows nothing more than a typical glioblastoma multiforme in both hemispheres of the brain. I will remind you, *again*, that the rate of incidence for this disease is four-point-five persons per one hundred thousand people. Our initial strategy in terms of treatment was hampered by both the location and size of the tumor. Mr. Savitch chose—I think rightly—a nonaggressive approach knowing the slim chance of a therapeutic success. Let me make this perfectly clear, *again*, that in no way was his treatment precluded because of a coincidental resemblance to anybody living or dead. We gave Mr. Savitch his options, none very appealing, and he decided on refraining from an aggressive course of action. He wanted to spend his remaining time with friends and family, free from what can be debilitating care."

Dr. Vartan pauses, a dramatic pause, which he plays for rage. He tightens his face and clenches his mouth. Every word that follows is strained through colander teeth. "But let me tell you, ladies and gentleman of the media, you've made a dying man's life even worse. You've robbed him of his remaining freedom. He's trapped in his own home, unable to savor the outdoors, his greatest joy. All he can do is watch TV, and thanks to you people here, he's constantly reminded of his situation. Being from the great state of Wisconsin, it reminds me of another period from our past when something else ran wild. It seems we've entered a comparable age but instead of McCarthyism, we have the media shouting and pointing fingers and claiming to report nothing but the facts when the whole system is corrupted. So I ask, in a similar vein, have you no shame."

Dr. Vartan folds his slip of paper, steps back. He reaches for Nancy

Savitch Karansky; she flinches as if his hands are too severe. "If I could add something," she says, reluctantly approaching the microphones. "The doctor is not talking about you pilgrims. My brother is touched by you people and says thanks for the kindnesses and prayers. Thank you."

A voice off camera shouts, "Will you release the most recent MRI?"

She glances around, lips wallowing, and then says, "No."

The doctor bends forward. "These are not press releases. These are diagnostic tools and as such are the sole property of the patient. As everyone well knows, the MRI now in circulation was stolen from the hospital and sold to a tabloid. It was not released to the public nor will subsequent material pertaining to the patient be released."

"Unless authorized by the family," the sister interrupts.

The doctor corrects himself. "Of course. Unless the family so desires."

"But does the latest MRI reconfirm the image of Christ?" somebody shouts.

"You mean the Shroud of Turin." The doctor grins, obviously pleased the subject has been broached. "That's what we're talking about, right, the Shroud of Turin. This cancer resembles, if it resembles anything, the Shroud of Turin. And as we all should know, the Shroud of Turin has been scientifically proven a fake."

"So are you saying the MRI is a fake?"

"You're putting words in my mouth. What I'm saying is all this excitement is over a similarity with a known fake."

"So this MRI is the real thing?"

"Yes, absolutely. The cancer is real. But the portrait of Jesus Christ could just as well be a portrait of a butterfly or a cloud formation or Charles Manson for that matter."

Nancy Savitch Karansky frowns.

"It's ambiguous stimuli," the doctor continues. "It's the equivalent of a Rorschach, but in this case the projection of Christ has been made and that's all anyone can see. You know what I see, as a doctor. A late-stage tumor."

"Excuse me but can I say something?" asks Nancy Savitch Karansky.

"Certainly."

"Charles Manson is not the person in my brother's brain. He's a good Christian. I don't want TV reporters saying Charles Manson could be up in there. Let's stick with Jesus at least."

A shout of, "Any truth to the rumors of blood weeping from the eyes."

"Not really," the sister says.

"Absolutely not," Dr. Vartan clarifies. "And those aren't eyes, they're tissue contrasts, light and dark spots, shadows."

The sister turns to the oncologist. "Actually, I have a question."

"Sure."

"Has anyone ever come across a pattern exactly like this?"

"No. But all neoplasms are different. They're like fingerprints." He offers his frustrated hands, stares into his palms, shakes his head like he's been thrown into the Dark Ages and he's explaining an eclipse. "Look," he says, "as humans we're biased to recognize an image within disorder, and Christ is certainly a very visible, very hopeful image. Nevertheless, at some point image has to give way to ideas and the idea here is that Mr. Savitch is a very sick man, a dying man, who deserves some peace. We can't invest images with hard truth."

"So are you saying Christ is just an image?" is yelled.

"I'm not here for a theological debate. But I will say that I think Christ as an idea is fundamentally more important than Christ as a historical fact."

"And what's your religion?"

"My parents were Episcopalian."

There's a groan from the Baptists.

Nancy Savitch Karansky edges in front of Dr. Vartan. "With regards to the earlier question about blood, I'd like to clarify that the house has had some strange leaking, particularly in the pantry, sticky yellowish stuff on the walls, like sap."

"How about the rumors of healing?"

"My mother has been feeling better. She's had horrible arthritis in her hands and I swear she could probably play jacks right now. And my best friend said her migraines eased up when she was having coffee in the house. Yeah, people've been feeling better. Even the twelve-year-old dog seems spunkier."

196

"Psychosomatic," the doctor says.

"Psycho nothing, they really have. Maybe not on the level of miracles, but it's still early and it's still something and it's still special." Like time-lapse photography—those filmstrips in biology class of a flower exploding or a dead mouse melting—Nancy Savitch Karansky transforms in less than a minute. Her bearing becomes more confident. Her pupils go from soft to steely. The clouds could be speeding over her head as she rises into her new role. "From now on," she tells the collected media, "I don't want anybody listening to this man here. For now on you only listen to me."

Click.

The front door of the Savitch home opens and two attendants appear holding the MRI in a baroque gold-painted frame. It's paraded through the crowd. It's a sin-clearing Zamboni looping the lawn in ever-tighter circles and leaving behind glistening flesh and chills. Hands stretch for the slightest brush. Sickly children are raised aloft by desperate parents who bat them toward the icon, the small hands reaching back toward their parents. The feeble and the infirm, the terminal, strain for their moment to kiss the lips, one of the attendants discreetly wiping away the plexi before the next person puckers. People faint. During the nightly prayer service, the bay window curtains slowly slide open and reveal Charles Savitch lying in his rented hospital bed (courtesy of Hogarth Medical Supplies in Milwaukee). He's like living stained glass. The crowd inhales forward. Nancy Savitch Karansky, dressed in blue, sits by his side and clutches his hand with less sibling grace and more self-promotion. She seems to squeeze the fame from his fingers.

Click.

The Catholic Church, like a bad joke, has sent forth a priest, a psychologist, and a canon lawyer. "What we might have here," says Raymond Dellacorte, spokesperson for the archdiocese, "is a victim soul whose suffering benefits the community around him. He absorbs their pain, takes upon himself their hardship. The scapegoat of Leviticus. There is a long history of victim souls that the church has recognized. Audrey Santo is the most recent example and perhaps most famous. She's been featured in *People* and *Dateline*. A movie is in the works. What we're doing here is convening a commission to investigate the possibility of victim soul status. Because of the progressive nature of the disease, the process has been put on fast track."

Click.

Victim soul or not, who will land the exclusive interview is the buzz among television types who talk about television on television. Word is the Savitch family is ready to open up, and with the right offer they're promising unlimited access including a chat with Chuck himself. The competition is fierce from network to network, the brightest lights pitching their services. Serious money has been offered by syndicators. "In the high hundreds of thousands," an industry source reveals. A pay-per-view outfit is floating the idea of a tent revival with Muhammad Ali and various ailing superstars in attendance. "We could get these people for nothing," a source is quoted. "The buy-in would be epic." Bids are rushed due to the terminal quality of the event—everyone wants a breathing Chuck; everyone agrees Chuck is essential. "Without Chuck," a former head of programming tells a cable personality, "this deal isn't nearly as attractive. He's the keystone. Or capstone. Whatever. The entire package would have to include rights, that way the entertainment division could pay big bucks while the news division could maintain its integrity. You'd have something like a six-month broadcast delay between the interview and the docudrama. The local affiliates could double dip with lead-ins and follow-ups on their evening newscasts. It'd be a real revenue maker with possible overseas appeal. But you need to air Chuck, the interview, while he's still alive. You need the thing fresh. Chuck dead is depressing. Just another cancer story. Chuck alive, now there's tension. Chuck alive is full of questions. Maybe even Chuck *Live*. Oh man." The former head of programming (famously fired from a half-dozen jobs for poor public behavior) claps his hands. He's become a raconteur who specializes in his own decrepitude. "I could pitch that like Sandy Koufax," he says.

Click.

The Savitch family has decided to go with a living legend of broadcasting, the face-lift formerly known as the Elizabeth Cady Stanton of network news. Immediately the promos begin—the teases, the flirtations of something special happening next Wednesday at 9 P.M., 10 P.M. central, when all your questions will be answered. Billy—*click*—watches this, watches all of this—*click*—it's inescapable—*click*—the publicity flooding the airwaves—*click*—and Billy knows—*click*—that despite himself—*click*—he'll tune in—*click*—and embrace this farce—*click*—for no good reason—*click*—except that there's nothing else to do—*click*—but watch.

23

THERE WAS nothing holy in Doris's brain, no Son of God interred, only a slow wiping away of the neural face. But there was a pilgrimage, if humble, on a beautiful spring day, when the weather was just getting warm and Doris was scheduled for admission into the limbo of assisted living. During the flight home, Billy tried recalling his last visit for any clues of Alzheimer's. It was two years ago. He had returned to Cincinnati for the non-holidays—Christmas and Hanukkah canceled out in his family. No matter his relationship with his parents, being alone in his apartment was worse, and he had hoped, like he always did, that maybe things would be different, that time apart, and distance, and age, and even the season would bring about some charity. He envisioned a week not of love, but of understanding. After the first five minutes he realized what a crock. His parents tensed up and Billy became tight-lipped but hard-edged. Instantly the three of them regressed into simply surviving the remaining days together, like a vacation gone bad. But on the plane, Billy searched that last visit home for a loose thread auguring further unraveling. His mother had been quiet, yes, but she was always quiet around him. Nothing unusual there. Growing up, Billy would hear Abe and Doris talking excitedly, and when he'd enter the room, they'd clam up and greet him formally and wait for whatever he wanted. Maybe her eyes carried a bit more fear; they gravitated toward Abe for reassurance, as though a gun-toting madman hid in the closet and had told them, "Act cool and nobody gets hurt." But this reaction still was well within her bounds. Had she been moody? Hard to say because Billy was so moody. He assumed she was suffering from him. How about forgetful or confused? Sure, but once again, this seemed normal. She was always distracted around him, tripping through motherhood with little inspiration. Billy was a series of chores she really should write down.

His parents lived in the middle of the postwar housing boom in Cincinnati, when developers plowed fields into towns and packaged the American dream in quarter-acre lots. Over the years these basic ranch houses had gone through small adaptations, crawling from the primordial muck of the working class and into the more complex biology of the middle class. Second floors were added; carports were turned into family rooms; backyards were jammed with aboveground swimming pools. In some cases, next-door properties had been bought and razed and mansions sprung up in their place—not really mansions but ideas of mansions, with white columns and stone lions and giant brass knockers. There were special names for these estates. Shenandoah. Candymore. Perisailles. Billy could've laughed at the topiary, the slopped turrets, the Palladian windows, but he would've been laughing at the easiest sort of target as well as the sweetest sort of pride.

He pulled the rental car into 220 Cypress. As with every homecoming, the house seemed lesser. Today it verged on the size of a Monopoly house on Baltic, its rent too cheap for all his complaining. His parents owned the last remaining ranch house totally untouched over the last half century. Rumor was the local historical society had been pushing for landmark status, claiming this was *the* prime example of preplanned, mass-produced housing in the area. The neighbors, Billy guessed, must've been pissed.

His father answered the door. "Good, you're here," he said.

Billy raised his arms. "In the flesh."

"We're all packed." The bags were waiting by the door.

"Okay."

"We should go soon."

"Could I get settled?"

"They said early afternoon."

"It's eleven-thirty-five A.M." Billy said.

"Exactly why we should go."

"Let me just use the bathroom and maybe get a drink of water."

201

"Fine. Then we should go because they're expecting us."

Billy surrendered with "Sure."

He followed Abe into the living room where Doris sat on the couch. Abe quickly joined her, as if the space was up for grabs and Billy might leap in. He touched her knee and whispered, "He's here. We'll be going soon."

Doris had no reaction.

"She's ready to go when you are," Abe said.

To Billy, his father never really aged. The man always looked the same, whether forty, fifty, or, as he was now, sixty-four. Neither youthful nor elderly, he was just Abe with dark eyes bruised by shadow. He might've been obsessed with time—already he had checked his watch twice—but time had no need for him. The lines in his face, the cleavage of worry, were unaffected by wear. His hairline was forever receding but never balding. His paunch, his waddle, were present in the earliest known photos, the pre-Billy photos that covered the house. It was as if Abe had been painted on wood instead of canvas, like a Bruegel, one of his less exciting seasons. *The Glass Cutters*. But in the background, away from the primary action, you could catch glimpses of quiet tragedy and undetected suffering, an Icarus falling behind Abe's shoulder. His poor wife looked horrible. She had lost weight, but it was weight you'd never mention. She was sunken and sallow. A wick could've been buried in her head. But she seemed more relaxed than she normally did around Billy. There was no register of his presence, no frowns, no nervous asides, no opportunistic shame floating around the room. It was just Doris rocking with her hands clutched together and singing two notes back and forth, *LA-la, LA-la, LA-la*. There was an honesty about the years and their toll on her. Mothers show their age, Billy thought, while fathers stay moored in the present until that last moment, that day when you visit and notice too late that they've turned into dying men.

Abe checked his watch again.

Doris was the calendar and Abe was the clock.

Billy crouched into his mother's line of sight. "Hey Mom."

"She doesn't talk much," Abe explained.

"Nice to see you."

"She just groans. But they're happy groans. Usually."

"I'm sorry I've been away so long," Billy told her.

"It hasn't been that long," Abe replied.

"I'm talking to her."

"It's not worth the trouble."

Billy turned toward Doris. "I should've come home sooner."

"This is soon enough," Abe said.

Billy noticed Doris's clenched hands. Bright colors were visible through her fingers. Every so often they twisted the colors and a creak of plastic could be heard. "Is that a Rubik's cube?" Billy asked.

"Yeah."

"My Rubik's cube?"

"I suppose. I really don't know. One day she had it and she's had it ever since. The doctor told me that that can happen with Alzheimer's patients, that they get fixated on something. I think it relaxes her, like knitting."

"Of all things," Billy said.

"I tried taking it away from her."

"Why?"

"Because it seemed a cruel joke. A mind-bender? A puzzle? But she got upset." Billy watched her turn the colors with all the devotion of the rosary. She could've been meditating on fifty-four mysteries, eighteen rows of three, saying a prayer with every new combination. The Rubik's cube. It had been a brief glory for Billy; in his youth he could solve the thing in less than four minutes—198 seconds his record.

"Have you forgotten where the bathroom is?" his father asked.

"No."

"Because we should go soon."

After pissing, Billy peeked inside his old room. Besides the bed and bureau, it had been stripped bare. Shelves were empty. The strange childhood mishmash, the archaeology of toys and hobbies from his different periods—the Stone Age of stuffed animals, the Copper Age of action figures, the Bronze Age of board games, the Iron Age of nunchucks and rock star posters—was gone. Only meager evidence remained. The walls carried the forensics of Fun-Tack. The rug was still stained with cranberry juice that Billy improvised into a bloodbath for green army men. Otherwise, nothing endured. What was he expecting? A shrine? Not likely. This was right, he thought. Give his entire youth to Goodwill. But maybe his parents could've used this space for a guest room, an office, a media center, storage even. At least slap on a fresh coat of paint and new carpeting. No crimes had been committed here. There was no need for it to look like a murder scene.

"I heard you flush," his father called from the living room.

"Yeah?"

"So let's go."

His parents sat in the backseat, Abe with his arms draped around Doris, his head resting on her shoulder, his mouth cooing sweet nothings while she stared straight ahead with oh-say-can-you-see posture. They were like flag and flagpole. She flew his heart and he proudly embodied her love.

Billy almost gave the rearview mirror a small salute.

The Whispering Pines Assisted Living Center was near the airport, on the other side of the Ohio River, where the sprawl of Cincinnati slipped into Kentucky and nobody was sure of their home state. Buckeye or Bluegrass? North or South? Urban or rural? In the middle of this mild confusion stood Whispering Pines. It was located among low-story apartment buildings and chain hotels and various support services for the airport. It was the sort of flipbook community glanced from fast-moving cars, never noticed unless you needed gas. But Whispering Pines might catch your attention. Eight stories tall, constructed in white postwar brick, the roof was topped with a massive central air-conditioning unit. It resembled the head tefillin for a moon-faced Jew who had forgotten all that came after *Baruch*.

"Here we are," Abe said.

Along the side of building was the signage for the previous occupant. The letters remained behind in ghost form—*Marriott*—while down the street its new incarnation rose in a glory of tinted glass.

Billy pulled up in the circular driveway where a revolving door seemed like a game of chance for the elderly. Abe helped Doris, and Billy unloaded the bags then parked in the lot behind the building. Walking back, he noticed a plane circling high above and another plane ready for landing. Either thanks to the wind or the tonal properties of turbojets or just his mood, the engines sounded like they were failing.

The lobby had probably changed little since its Marriott days. The visitors lingering around inside could've been the waylaid travelers of yore who had time to kill because of a missed connection or a delay or a bad storm. None of them were happy to be here and all of them were happy not to be here long. Billy glanced about for his parents. No sign of them. He went to the reception desk. A man asked, "How may I help you?" with the Kentucky side of life.

"I'm looking for the Schines."

"They just checked in and went up to their room."

"Where's that?"

"Six-ten, sixth floor. Are you family?"

"Son."

"Let me tell you your mother is in excellent hands. It's a hard, hard thing, what she has, what you're going through, a hard, hard thing, but we will do our best to somehow make it easier, for you and your family, because it is tough, Lord, is it tough, and I feel for you, we all do." The man was almost teary.

"Sure," Billy said.

The elevator seemed to hum the first bar of *Oklahoma*, a sort of mechanical, breath-defying fermata, all the way to the sixth floor, where the doors opened and the wind came rushing through the plains. Room 610 was a double with its own bathroom. A curtain divided the beds. On one side was Doris; on the other side was an old black woman who looked like a bundle of twigs anticipating a match. Three women, probably daughters, hovered over her; they were force-feeding their loved one some sort of mush, laughing a bit too loudly as they mopped up her messy chin.

"Look Mom, they sent you a cute young man."

"Dessert."

"Hi ladies," Billy said.

One of the daughters came over. "Whatever you do," she told Billy, "do not, and I mean *do not*, allow them to put in a feeding tube."

After Abe got Doris settled, he asked Billy, "Should we be worried?"

"About what?"

"The ring. Do you think stealing might be a problem?"

Billy was not surprised by his father's mild unoriginal racism. "I doubt it."

"Because I've heard stories." Abe reached over, uncurled Doris's left hand from the Rubik's cube and slipped the ring from her finger. "See how easy it is," he said. "It pulls clean because she's lost so much weight. And she'll never protest, never scream. God forbid the Rubik's cube but the ring is for the taking."

"What comes around goes around."

Abe leveled his eyes on Billy. "This was our dowry, our due."

Billy regretted the introduction of family lore. "I know, I know," he said.

"This bought our freedom, always remember, this half-carat delivered us."

"I know. I'm sorry."

Billy knew the story (Christ, he knew the story). He was more biographer than son. Abraham Schine, twenty-five, and Doris McMinn, twenty-nine, met in 1958 under the marquee of the Winter Garden Theatre. It was the year Mike Todd died in a plane crash while his wife, Elizabeth Taylor, was spared by a timely cold; the year Cheryl Crane, daughter of Lana Turner, stabbed and killed Johnny Stompanato; and the second smash year of *West Side Story* on Broadway. Abe and Doris, single-ticket holders, stood as strangers outside the theater during the Wednesday matinee intermission. Both had left their jobs early, sudden illness the excuse, Doris with a stomachache, Abe with a headache, though the true cause was the infectious combo of Leonard Bernstein and Jerome Robbins. They lingered under the sun-bleached lights and risked discovery by bosses or coworkers, but they needed air after hearing "Something's Coming" and "Tonight." The usher paraded about with a handheld xylophone chiming the three notes for the second act. The crowd started filtering inside. Abe and Doris stood alone for a moment, on opposite ends of the marquee. They waited for the other to move first, to break this unspoken sideways spell. Finally, the usher stood there and hammered one note and Doris gave up. On her way inside, she dropped her Playbill (on purpose) and Abe raced over and (of course) picked it up.

"Quite a show," he said.

"Oh, yes," she replied.

That was that, they were in love.

Abe gestured toward Billy. "See this." He was holding up the ring.

"Yes. I know," Billy said.

"This is our Exodus."

Instead of Passover, his father celebrated the story of the stolen diamonds. During meals, before bed, Abe would recite the particulars. The family store—Schine Brothers Gems—was on Forty-seventh Street with all the other diamond merchants. For eighteen months, Abe and Doris secretly dated, knowing their parents would be against the match. Irish Catholic, Orthodox Jew, they were the original Jets and Sharks. They would meet in Times Square and take in the various entertainments, arcades and shows, lunch at Howard Johnson's, until one day they were discovered and, as predicted, they were forbidden from seeing each other again. After crying, they obeyed, disappointed in their lack of romantic resolve, but not surprised. This was the real world. They were too old for rebellion. Soon enough, the Winter Garden marquee changed to *The Unsinkable Molly Brown* and Liz Taylor was remarried (Eddie Fisher, no less), and Cheryl Crane was cleared of all murder charges. Just when Abe and Doris were settling into their chosen roles—he a fiancé to the right woman, she an unmarried aunt—the film version of *West Side Story* hit the Rivoli. Memories flooded back. The movie was even better.

"Natalie Wood," his father would say. "Who knew she had that voice?"

"She was dubbed," Billy would tell him. "Marni Nixon."

"Well she did a good job sounding like Natalie Wood."

A month later, Abe snuck inside the vault of the family store and grabbed his disinheritance. The amount was respectable without being brazen: forty grand worth of diamonds. This was the price on their heads. This was the cost of exile.

"But the smallest we never sold," Abe told Billy.

"I know. A thousand times I know."

Abe continued, his eyes alternating between Doris and the diamond ring, like the facets subtitled her impenetrable face. "The smallest we saved for ourselves, didn't we. Just under half a carat, a mêlée, not a centerpiece, but the look, the clarity, flawless, and the color grades D, and those two things I was taught above everything else." Abe squinted. His eye was threaded for a loupe, like nut and bolt, though now he cut decorative glass for a living. "This came from the alluvial beds of Southwest Africa. In water, it blazes. No blemishes, only a few pinpoint flaws, character marks really. Otherwise ideal. If I had the proper tools, I could show you specks of another mineral deep within the carbon. Invisible bits of weakness." Abe breathed on then buffed the diamond against his shirt. He slipped the ring back onto Doris's finger. "Thirty years old and I was a thief and a pariah and for a moment a perfect ten on the Mohs' scale. I love you, Doris, with all my heart, I will always love you." But Doris was too included to notice.

After escaping from New York, Abe and Doris settled on Cincinnati with no roots, no connections, creating their own country with a population of two. This is part of the story that never went said, that Billy filled in on sleepless nights. For years they must have waited for the authorities to find them, to charge them with robbery, but the knock on the door never came. Day jobs supported their true ambition: themselves. Neither trusted the other's friends so they surrendered them without a fight. Every morning they woke up with their sole reason for bravery; every night they fell asleep with their lonely choice. Happily ever after was imperative. A lapse in affection, even for a second, might prove devastating. They were Tony and Maria shopping for discount socks, Romeo and Juliet washing chipped dishes. When they tried having a child, and success seemed doubtful, they dropped the subject without issue because failure might introduce strain and strain might threaten everything. Years passed. Then a miracle happened: the feared symptoms of early menopause—hot flashes and nausea—were the signs of pregnancy. Doris was forty-five, Abe was forty-two. They excitedly prepared for parenthood. And when the boy was born, William, they held him and cried and for a moment forgot themselves, forgot their struggle and sacrifice, forgot their essential love. All they had abandoned, their families, their histories, faded in the background. The ether of passion and romance condensed into a far more complex compound—a screaming infant. Mother and father glanced up in unison. They recognized their mistake too late. What had they done? Self-devotion was everything. They had given up too much to replace it with a son. Right then they pulled away as if the child's heart pumped nitroglycerin and the merest rattle could destroy their fragile world. A safe distance would have to be maintained, an emotional two-mile radius.

In room 610 at the Whispering Pines Assisted Living Center Abe rubbed Doris's hand. Billy stood in the corner inspecting the metaphysical space around his shoes. He knew there was no room for him here. Soon enough he would say good-bye and he understood it would be for the last time. The view from the window was of the parking lot and the small, minimally maintained garden for family visits outside. Of course he should come back and visit, like a decent son, but he decided right then that he would let them be. He'd stay away and allow regret its foothold and contempt the place of perhaps not being loved. Billy went to the edge of the bed. Abe finger-brushed Doris's hair while Doris worked the Rubik's cube. As she turned the rows and mixed up the colors, her diamond ring caught the afternoon sun and broke the light against the wall. Billy reached down and touched her foot under sheets. Her toes curled. Just a reflex.

24

T HERE IS, Billy thinks, a comfort here, in the routine, in the hourly drift, in the purposeless purpose of the AHRC. The slight twist of a side effect (a ghost shadow here, an imagined murmur there) reminds him of the drama going on inside his body, a sort of suspense as he waits for the next creep. Otherwise, he's sleepy and pleasantly removed from the process of survival. The sticky details of life are gone. All he has to do is swallow and bleed.

Meals, like lunch on Thursday, simply appear on his tray, well balanced and nutritious, the daily values hitting 100 percent and measured for a healthy diet of two thousand calories. Done. No longer is there any panic when morning, noon, or night rolls around and a decision has to be made. What to eat? Just feeding himself can crush Billy with bother. Particularly lunch. Lunch is the bane of his mealtime existence. So many questions seem involved with lunch. An early lunch or a late lunch? A big lunch and then a small dinner or a small lunch and then a big dinner? Maybe no lunch and then a really big dinner? Lunch puts him in alimental limbo where he wanders the streets hoping for an answer. Make a fucking sandwich, Sally might say, Sally always decisive, Sally's desire providing breakfast and dinner. But for lunch, Billy is on his own. Here in the AHRC lunch is delivered hassle-free and today it's macaroni and cheese, which Billy accepts from the cafeteria staff—"Thank you so much"—as if love did the melting.

Comfort continues back in his room, as Billy digests with cable television and air-conditioning. These luxuries come without charge. No bills will follow. No tabs will remind him how fast the month ends. No due dates. No checking-account fears. No need for stamps never in supply. And on the opposite end of comfort, there's no litter, no recycling, no separating the garbage into paper, metal, plastic, and glass, no questions about what is deemed salvageable. No trash piling up in the corner. No worries about cockroaches and mice. Consumption has no refuse and the supplies are endless. No grocery shopping. No thousand products for the same thing. No going to the store for just a roll of toilet paper and trying to make this purchase with dignity. No milking the last skim of soap. No cleaning. No false promises of tackling the grime tomorrow. Billy can sit in the bathroom, like he is right now, and do his business with pure ease of mind. On Monday a janitor will roll through with a wet mop. Towels will be laundered without lugging a duffel to a Laundromat five blocks away, without begging for quarters, without the washer-dryer politics and the lame attempts at folding. Twice a week bedsheets are changed while Billy is somewhere else, the only evidence of this mysterious event being a fresh green shirt on a crisp pillowcase.

Even Lannigan is of some comfort. His foolish full-body shave is almost endearing, as is the way he talks to himself right now. "That's a good question," he says though neither Billy nor Do has asked him anything. "I was fascinated by the character." He speaks barely above a whisper but loud enough to be heard. "This character," he continues, "is a character I've never seen before on-screen, and I really wanted to sink my teeth into the part. More for my soul than for anything else, because, honestly, my last few movies have been soul crushing. Successful, sure, but not deeply satisfying projects. And for this role my soul had to be totally invested. I needed my kidneys, my liver, my heart; all my internal organs had to be on board for my performance to register. It was almost like I needed to be one of those swamis who can control their pulse. I needed that level of control. Transcendence." Lannigan smiles like a newborn who leaves you wondering if it's anything more than gas. "I'll tell you, and this is the God's honest truth, I've never been so scared about a part, about doing justice to a part. Because this is great writing. It is. This is, this is, well, art. I honestly believe that. This is Shakespeare if the guy were living in Hollywood and his first screen credit was *Hamlet*. You know I'm doing

Hamlet, my *Hamlet*. Very exciting, but that's another question. Anyway, this script set a very high bar and I could either rise to the occasion or crash and burn in front of the whole world." Pause. "Well, thank you." A longer pause. "I really wasn't fishing for a compliment but that's very nice of you."

"What are you talking about?" Billy asks, more charmed than annoyed.

"Huh?"

"What are you going on about?"

"You were listening?"

"You were talking."

"Softly," Lannigan says.

"Loud enough."

"I was interviewing myself. Sometimes I do that. I just know I could give a really great interview if given half the chance. I could be funny or earnest. I could talk about the jobs I had before I made it big. Waiter, of course, but also a masseuse with absolutely no training. For real. I just faked it, rub-rub-rubbed like I knew what I was doing, even improvised this Nepalese deep-tissue technique. And I was good. I had clients who swore by me. And I was also a private eye for a year, another job that requires no certification. A dog walker, then a dog trainer, though that was me being cocky. A model, but not the glamorous kind. An assistant stylist. A personal shopper. I was briefly but fondly part of a posse when a friend of an acquaintance became famous for like a millisecond and needed bodies to bulk up his club presence. Okay, that's a lie, but you see, I can lie as well. I can spew the most fabulous bullshit. Right now I could lecture on anything for an hour. Give me a topic. Anything. Israel. Uhm, Diet Coke versus Diet Pepsi. I'm on a roll. Screw expertise, it's all about presentation." His browless eyes are manic, like lamps without shades lighting a nighttime of obsessive work. "I have such good answers to questions nobody asks."

Yes, Billy is fine with Lannigan.

Do is all right, too. Sure, he's a mess, but Billy feels protective of him and defends him against Lannigan's jibes. He's sort of his man Friday if Friday were a Monday morning in New York. Every hour or so Billy asks for the time in Luke, and Do obliges, and they try reading in the words something meaningful. They've also discovered Lannigan's weak spot: the Health Channel, in particular, *Inside the Operating Room*, a show that goes into graphic detail on different varieties of surgical procedure. Today is cosmetic surgery day. This causes Lannigan to cover his face and scream, "C'mon, we're not watching this." But Billy and Do hold firm, like they're backing away Dracula with a crucifix. Soon enough Lannigan abandons the room for less squeamish environs.

"Much better," Billy says.

"Much much better," Do answers.

They stay tuned against his return and watch three hours of plasty. They absorb an hour of liposuction, where the patient, Nathaniel, a lawyer from San Bernardino, wants to do away with his love handles. "I work out," he says in a prologue that shows him running on the beach, lifting weights. "But no matter what, I have this spare tire. I've been told it's recalcitrant fat and beyond my control." The entire liposuction process is shown, from consultation to surgery to post-op results, with the bulk of the time spent in the operating room where a doctor brutalizes Nathan's unconscious flesh with something misnomered a "wand." It's the same with Kimm's eye tuck and Charlotte's cheek sculpting and Todd's hairline resection and Pat's nose job/chin implant/ ear pin. It's like an afternoon talk show under the knife. Next week is breast week. It must be sweeps, Billy thinks.

"Billy," Do asks during dermabrasion.

"Yeah?"

"Does your mouth ever water when you smell shit?"

"Uhm."

"Or is that an insane question to ask? It is, isn't it?"

"Well, no."

Yes, Billy likes Do.

And there's always Joy, Joy after breakfast, Joy, like now, after dinner, Billy talking with her through the span of his blood. "I'm starting to like it here," he says. "I'm content. Interesting people. Decent food. TV. Mind-altering drugs. It's like college all over again."

"Wait until Saturday," she says.

"PK day?"

"Yep."

"It'll give us more time to chat," he says.

Joy disconnects the test tube from the cannula.

"Can I feel it?" Billy asks.

"What?"

"The test tube."

"I suppose." Joy hands it over, and Billy palms it like some sleight of hand will commence and the object will—*voilà!*—end up in her ear. But Billy knows no tricks.

"It's warm," he says.

"What'd you think, it'd be cold?"

"Can I keep it?"

"Absolutely not."

"You could take another," Billy says. "And I could keep this one."

"It's hazardous human waste material," Joy tells him.

"That quick, huh?"

"The second it leaves your body."

Billy hands back the test tube with exaggerated care. "What do you do with the excess blood, after all the research has been done?"

"I really don't know."

"Is it buried deep in the desert, in yellow skull-ridden drums, or is it just poured down the drain?"

"We're finished. You can go, Mr. Schine."

"Alas," he says. As he leaves, he passes a *Time* magazine tossed aside on a countertop. On the cover is the MRI of Charles Savitch, SECOND COMING OR COMING ATTRACTION? written across the bottom. "Jeez," he says to Joy, "*Time*, she is a-slumming."

"No dawdling."

"Can I just read this article?"

"Take the whole magazine but leave."

"A gift, thank you."

"More like a bribe for you to go."

"I'll take it any way it comes." Billy departs, pleased.

Yes, he thinks, these daily moments with Joy are pleasant.

And, of course, there is Gretchen. Billy passes her room, peeks inside, "Hello."

Gretchen lounges not quite lovely in bed, the weather swirling in front of her, like Isis if Isis were in the witness protection program after ratting out the syndicate of gods. She spots *Time* in his hand and asks, "Is your mail being forwarded?"

"I borrowed it from Joy."

"What's on the cover?"

Billy breezes in under sail of Charlie Savitch.

"What is it, the disease of the year issue?" Gretchen's hands are all gimme. As she rips through the pages—in some cases, literally—Billy imagines touching the tip of her nose, feeling the pinch of arrowlike cartilage, her face the bow. "Are you getting excited for the big interview?" she asks.

"Not really. But I suppose I will."

"I can't wait," she says.

Kiss her, Billy thinks, disarm her jaw with a little kiss, a tester kiss, a floater, almost filial, no tongue, no lip even, just kiss her cheek or forehead and immediately apologize, if need be, though who knows, she might raise her chin and lock her hands around his neck and hum an electric trill of climb-deep-inside-my-throat, and in the pause before full-on face sucking, romantic banter might percolate (Billy: "I don't know if what I'm feeling is a side effect or the real thing." Gretchen: "Love is the biggest adverse event there is") as he strokes her hair and smiles on the strange circumstances of fate, while the weatherman points to the radar and the turbulent swath of green that's soaking the Midwest and is heading toward the northeast.

"Can you believe this?" Gretchen says of the picture showing the pilgrims in front of the Savitch home.

Billy nods, the idea of the kiss having passed.

"What are they expecting?" she says. "Cancer as salvation, as a gift from God?"

"Who knows?" Billy watches her skim the article, *Time* spread in front of her face like this is an X ray of her own head, and it shows his own face shadowing her brain, an all-encompassing thought, his eyes and mouth inhabiting her desire, lips puckering into a prompt that would lead him toward her bed—*Billy, come here, I want you*—and have him gently lower the magazine from her grasp and reveal, in humdrum glory, the original. But Chuck is Chuck, and Billy is Billy, and he asks Gretchen, "If you could have any disease, what would it be?"

"What disease would I want?"

"Yeah."

"I don't want a disease," she says.

"It could be from any era," he explains. "Tuberculosis, the plague."

"I'm sorry, but I don't want any disease," Gretchen says.

"You never think about it?"

"No."

"Even as make-believe, like a poet with consumption in the nineteenth century."

"No, sorry."

"Like for me, it's Lesch-Nyhan syndrome. That's what I'd pick."

"Excuse me?"

"Lesch-Nyhan syndrome," Billy repeats. "It's a hereditary condition that affects purine metabolism. It does all sorts of horrible things to you, the most horrible being a tendency toward self-cannibalization. You compulsively bite your fingers and hands, your arms, whatever your teeth can get their grip on. You basically try to eat yourself. Lips, tongue, toes."

Gretchen flinches. "How gruesome."

"Even worse, it only affects children."

"You eat yourself to death?"

"No, you die from a host of other things."

"I've never heard of the disease."

"It's rare, thank God," Billy tells her. He only knew of the disease

216

because of a book his parents had, a circa 1950s child care book aptly titled *Is Your Child Sick?* It listed symptoms, the possible diagnosis, and the best treatments, and wedged in the middle, like a slice of fatty ham, were fifteen pages of pictures in black and white. The last picture was of a boy restrained in bed and surrounded by doctors. A black bar covered his eyes. To a nine-year-old Billy, it was frightening, that Lone Ranger mask without the *William Tell* overture, without Tonto and "Kemo Sabe," without "Hi-yo, Silver, away," none of that which pleased him on lazy Saturday morning when the local public TV station dipped into the past, *Flash Gordon* not far behind, *Superman*, shows that thrilled fathers now thrilling sons. But this black mask didn't disguise anything. Suffering was not a secret identity. And Billy, haunted, found his father and said, "I think I might have this."

His father, instantly bothered: "What?"

Billy showed him the boy.

"Lesch what?" Abe said. "Don't be silly."

"I think I might have it," Billy maintained.

"You don't."

"But I might."

The weight of a ridiculous belief sagged Abe's shoulder. "It's very rare," he said.

"But I think I have it."

"You're being silly. You're a healthy boy," he said with what seemed like disdain.

"But I could get it."

"You're not going to get it."

"There's still time."

"You would've been born with it," Abe said. "It would've been instantly known."

"I'll fight it," Billy promised. "I'll do my best not to chew up my fingers. At night you might have to tie me to my bed."

"Enough, Billy."

"I already chew my nails. Who knows what's next?"

"Billy—"

"But what would you do if I got it?"

Abe's eyes were as anonymous as that boy's black bar. "What would I do? What could I do? It's a silly question. You're not sick. You're fine. Now enough of this and give me that book."

And that was that.

But instead of going into that with Gretchen, Billy simply says, "I don't even know if Lesch-Nyhan is relevant anymore, what with sonograms and amniocentesis."

"But why would you want a disease like that?" she asks.

"I don't know," Billy says, realizing he's wandered far afield from flirtation.

"You shouldn't wish that sort of thing on yourself," Gretchen tells him. "Even if you're being provocative or something, which I can appreciate, nothing good comes from being sick. I keep on thinking about the people who might take this drug we're testing, you know, down the road might benefit from our participation. Not to be schmaltzy, but I feel like I'm one of a thousand helping hands lifting them up to their feet and brushing the confusion from their shoulders. It's like when they take their meds they'll be taking a little piece of me. Okay, maybe that's schmaltzy, but we're healthy, thank God. Don't begrudge it. At some point you'll get sick, and you'll die—don't worry, you'll have that opportunity. But right now you're healthy. You should be glad for it. I, for one, am glad you've got all of your fingers and all of your toes."

Gretchen tilts her head toward Billy, hits the mark where her face does wonders with light. Eyes ripple as though a mirage from the heat between the beds, the air near his chest wobbling until his sternum feels like it's collapsed into a wormhole and this woman could climb in and pick and choose any Billy from any moment in time because she owns them all and understands every last one.

And though he doesn't kiss her and soon enough leaves for his own bed, he thinks, yes, this place isn't a bad place to be.

25

T HERE ARE scars, though not many, in *The Oxford Dictionary of Quotations*. There is John Bunyan and Mr. Valiant-for-Truth who says of his scars, that they will be carried with him, to be a witness for the battles he's fought. There is Lord Macaulay talking of Boswell's *Life of Johnson* and that dazzling face seamed with the scars of disease. And there is Shakespeare and Henry's Saint Crispin's Day speech where the happy few, the band of brothers, will strip their sleeve and show the scars gained on the feats of that day. Billy lies in bed, nearing a nap, his head filled with scars, literary and worse. Perhaps *Bartlett's* has more scars, but the *ODQ* only has three. Frank Gershin, Billy thinks, has them all beat.

That morning in the lounge, Friday morning, Billy watched a docu-reality program about maternity wards in various hospitals nationwide. "Maybe they'll show some vag" was the crowd's impetus for staying tuned, but the impetus soon gave way to the natural drama of labor and delivery as well as the power of good editing. All the normals were on edge as woman after woman gave birth under a variety of circumstances. There was consensus concerning its miracle, its positively science fiction quality. Then Stew Slocum jumped to his feet as if catapulted by cushion and said, "I'll show you labor and pain." He pulled his shirt over his attention-starved head. Across his chest was a tattoo of claws ripping through flesh and rib cage. The gore was rendered with all the precision of *Gray's Anatomy*. A section of collarbone was visible and an angry red eye of an unknown beast peeked below a bloodied nipple. "I was under the needle for two full days," he told everybody with pride. His sternum was sunken, the pallor of collapsed soufflé, and while Billy could appreciate the art, the torso brought to mind rickets instead of viciousness.

"You look like a sack filled with hungry rats," Yul Gertner told him.

"Fuck you," Stew said. "It's awesome and you know it."

"Do you have an asshole tattooed on your ass?"

"No, I have your momma's face down there."

"Thanks, she's dead."

The animal within Stew sagged. "Seriously?"

"Seriously."

"Oh."

Then Frank Gershin spoke up, Frank who always wears a long-sleeve turtleneck under his green jersey and normally sits like a quiet observer from a more civilized land. His eyes have seen things, they insist. "Tattoos, pierces, brands," he proclaimed, "are for everyone and their mothers nowadays. Nothing there but a bandwagon of ink and studs and spikes. I hate them all. All the modern primitives, the body manipulators desperate for outrage. It's a tired empty trend. You might as well be cattle with a brand from the circle jerk ranch." Stew Slocum crossed his arms as if the beast had burst through his rib cage and there, snuggled in his hands, was a kitten.

"You wanna see something real?" Frank Gershin asked. "Something that isn't badass but true?" He stood up and removed his green jersey, folding it neatly, then did the same with his turtleneck. Nobody cared about an emergency caesarean anymore. Frank Gershin's torso was punctuated in scars, not scars like apostrophes and hyphens, but scars like angry globular periods from an epic pen. Deep and circular, they covered his body, the healed-over tissue devoid of personality, as if pores had released blisters of magma brewing below the surface. Frank raised his arms, turned around. His backside held similar grammar.

"What the hell is that?" Yul Gertner said.

"Gunshots."

"Were you in a war or something?" Billy asked.

"Nah, all of these were done on purpose," Frank told them. "Except this one." He pointed to his left pec where a meaty scar was puckered in a brutal kiss. The wound was even nastier on the other side, like a rose, a pink American Beauty with its bloom spent. "This one is the first one I got. My younger brother gave it to me. A hunting accident. He got overeager and confused me for a deer. I think it hurt him more than it hurt me, the way he cried."

"That's quite an accident," Billy said.

"Yeah," Frank replied, rubbing the wound like a worry bead. "But the rest were done on purpose."

"That's sick," Stew said.

"That's right that's sick," Frank said.

"How do you get shot on purpose?" Billy asked, leaning forward, wanting to touch this human Braille and perhaps read the pain.

"I know this guy in New York who specializes in trauma. Found him on the Internet a couple of years ago when I was fooling around with sites about gunshot wounds and came across this link, which led to another link, and then a chat room, and finally a warehouse in the outskirts of Queens. It's this guy's studio. He's South African, was a medic in some mercenary unit. He's a whiz with trajectories and ballistics. Hand loads all his own ammo."

"Trauma?" Stew asked.

"Yeah."

"Like really being shot?"

"Yeah, but my traumatist runs a very professional operation. He dopes you, shoots you, stabilizes you, treats you, and if you need further care, dumps you in a hospital. He has an EMT unit on his payroll. All his wounds are very clean, and he can give you whatever you want."

"Is this like the latest rage?" Billy asked.

"I hope not," Frank said. "But there are its enthusiasts. The first night I met him he was about to do a Joan of Arc on this Goth heretic nut. I show up and do all the secret password stuff and the warehouse door slams open and there he is, a fist of a man, head like knuckles. All he's wearing is a red Speedo and a pair of flip-flops. His accent is like the Nazis conquered England, and he takes me around his studio, which is part firing range, part hospital, and totally soundproof. As he's doing this, Ms. Joan

221

Wannabe is getting her legs and thighs painted by an assistant who uses some special flammable gel that burns at a low but disfiguring heat. She's naked except for a bulky flame-retardant bra and panties. Very freaky. The South African sits me down and shows me his trauma portfolio. It's filled with photographs of low-caliber wounds that cost in the low thousand-dollar range, depending on placement. Arms and legs are cheaper than torsos, he tells me. He explains the difference in caliber and jacket, the signature impacts of specific ordinances, a three-fifty-seven magnum versus a thirty-eight special. He gives me a lecture on Baretta, Colt, Luger, Ruger, Webley-Scott, Martini-Henry, Mossberg, and Snider, which is his favorite, because it's obscure and leaves the sweetest sort of exit wound. This guy knows his stuff. He tells me about the popularity of historical trauma, an Al Capone, an Andy Warhol, a Bonnie and Clyde—for couples only—a Dillinger, a Jesus Christ. And, of course, the Joan of Arc.

"We tour his small burn unit, small surgical theater, small recovery area. All this adds to the cost, but real hospitals would ruin the work and plastic surgeons he considers the worst kind of art restorers. He mentions the chance of death but explains how a single death would put him out of business so he's anything but reckless. All the while he's talking, Ms. Joan Wannabe is pointing to the areas of her upper body that she wants burned. She sees me staring and she smiles and tells me this traumatist is an artist. He goes through his more exotic menu. Bow and arrows for the cowboy, Glocks for the hip-hopster, a Tupac is mentioned, a Biggie Smalls, and for the connoisseur, he has access to a world-class gun collector who has museum-quality munitions that he's willing to loan. You can get shot with a flintlock, a harquebus, a Kentucky, a tommy, a Henry, an Enfield, a Springfield, a Krupp, a Remington. He even has the pistol that killed President McKinley in 1901 and one of the machine guns that got Sadat. The only condition is the collector gets to watch, kind of gets him off, the traumatist tells me. This is crazy, I'm thinking, and I'm ready to bolt. The traumatist goes over and injects morphine into Joan, and she's lifted a few feet off the ground by wires and pulleys, her arms forced upwards. A ladder is brought over. He tells me in no way will he do fabrications of faux cancer surgeries or amputations or eye removals for the sake of a conversation piece. Like that's what I'm thinking. He has standards, he says. All of his work is the result of real injury. He inspects the prep work of his assistant and adds a few more brush strokes. Now I'm ready to leave before anything happens, but Joan, she's hanging there and I'm stuck on her eyes. Two assistants come over with fire extinguishers. The traumatist checks his watch. Joan is shivering. And I'm like, leave. But her eyes. Every second pounds from her eyes, like a hammer working metal into a bowl that will soon be filled with something precious. Sorry. But it was something, the flame, the smell, those eyes staring like they're giving you a gift. I've been hooked ever since. I'm wearing about sixty thousand dollars worth of trauma, but you get to the point where you want every inch covered."

"I don't think so," Yul Gertner said.

Frank Gershin slipped back on his turtleneck under the screams of a soon-to-be teenage mother, the doctor telling her not to push, not yet. "You get shot and you know something has happened to you, something that will stay with you a thousand feet per second. I felt it when my brother shot me and I feel it now. This is real stuff, boys. No matter how well prepared, the fact is, you've been hit and you're bleeding and you're hurting and there's always someone on the other end."

Billy lies in bed, near asleep, *The Oxford Dictionary of Quotations* splayed on his chest like hands performing CPR, pumping compressions of Shakespeare and Milton and whatever else might revive him. His skin has never felt so bare. And as he fades into a nap, an image appears, not of Frank Gershin and his scars, but of Frank Gershin's brother, little Bob or Jack or Tim, walking the woods with his older brother, excited by the prospect of a deer. And maybe, in the buckless boredom, little Jessie or Fred put his brother in the scope, just fooling around, lined up his older brother in the crosshairs. Fingers slip, Billy thinks. Muscles jerk. Voices scream a second too late but they can echo forever.

26

BILLY IS roused from sleep by Roger Coop, eternal keeper of the phone, a Tantalus condemned to reach for a call that never comes. "You've got a fucking phone call," he tells Billy.

"Me?"

"Unless there's another Schine around here."

"Do you know who it is?"

"Do I look like your secretary?"

"Could you ask who's calling?"

"No fucking way."

"Okay, is the voice male or female?"

"This isn't twenty questions. Answer the phone or I'll hang up."

"No, yeah, okay."

Billy rolls out of bed and into the hallway where the receiver hangs down like an unwritten form of pay phone misdemeanor. Ragnar skids his stomach, Ragnar skip-tracing his ass to Albany. Or maybe Sally asking what she should do about all of his books, Sally slightly recovered. Billy stares at the phone's black pendulum, still holding Roger Coop's bitter displacement. He picks it up, hears heavy breathing and background chatter and a few violent coughs. Ragnar, he thinks, definitely Ragnar.

"Anybody there?" comes over the line.

It isn't Ragnar. It's something worse.

"Abe?" Billy says.

"Billy?" Abe says.

"Yes, Abe."

"Billy, is that you?"

"Yes, Abe, it's me."

"It's your father calling."

"I know."

"Where are you, Billy?"

"How did you get this number?"

"I called you not long ago and your lady friend gave me this number."

Billy curses caller ID. He thinks of Sally's cool revenge as she constructs a dozen book boxes.

"I got a shipment of stuff from you," Abe says.

"I moved," Billy says.

"I thought for a moment you were coming home. I thought I would come home one day from visiting Doris and find you, waiting for me, but it was always just the boxes. I started wondering if something was wrong, if these were personal effects. That and the flowers you sent. I started thinking, so I called."

"Were the flowers nice?" Billy asks of Ragnar's floral threat.

"Sure, lilies. Very nice."

Billy wishes he knew what lilies looked like. "What'd the note say?"

"Thinking of you or something like that. Always in my mind. Can't really remember."

Behind Abe, voices chatter, disrupted by the occasional announcement over a loudspeaker.

"Where are you calling from?" Billy asks.

"An airport bar," Abe says.

"You going somewhere?"

"Me? No. Not me. But there's a Marriott not far from Whispering Pines and it has a free shuttle to and from the airport."

"Oh."

"I come here after a visit when I'm in no mood to go home. All those bus transfers. Too much. So I come here and walk around and sit and read and watch the news. Sometimes I sleep. Sometimes I spend the night like my flight's been canceled and I'm stuck here, that way I can get back to Doris first thing in the morning without two hours of commute. It's not a bad place to be, plenty of bathrooms, water fountains with good cold water, bookstores, food courts. It's one of the few places where a man can still get a shoeshine. The people, they assume you're like them and you're traveling and you're just waiting for your plane. It's not a bad place for an old man."

It sounds too depressing for words, and while Billy almost serves his father a thick slice of mockery ("I hear Charles de Gaulle is beautiful this time of year") he relents, knowing (*a*) the effect would be lost on him, (*b*) the idea of his father pleasantly wandering around the Cincinnati airport trounces any humor, and (*c*) he could hear himself in his father's words. It's one thing to see yourself in your father's face, the same eyes, the same chin, but it's another thing to hear yourself in your father's words, in gestures and phrases, in those small recognizable ways that dislodge you from the inside. Instead, Billy says, "You're not old."

"I'm old enough."

"You should come to New York. We can spend the day at JFK." Billy is half-serious. "Come for the weekend and we'll hit Newark and LaGuardia as well."

"I knew JFK when it was Idlewild," Abe tells him. "There wasn't a better name for an airport. Shame about the man but too bad we had to lose Idlewild as well."

"You all right, Abe?"

"That's why I'm calling you."

"How's Doris?"

"She'll outlive me."

"What'd you mean?"

"I mean she's stronger than I am. Always has been. I fear the time when I'm no longer here for her and that kills me, her being alone, untended to."

Billy catches laughter, odd, almost mechanical laughter somewhere near his father. A tattered parrot could be perched on Abe's shoulder, the original owner having died years ago and all that remains are recycled expressions of affection. "What the hell was that?" Billy asks.

"What?"

"You didn't hear that?"

"What?"

"That laughter."

"That's the gentleman on the bar stool next to mine. But he's not real. He's a robot who sits here and tells jokes with his other robot friend. Not robots, animatronics is what the bartender says. They're the regulars here. They sit together and tease each other and pretend to drink beer. People seem to find them funny. After every hour they repeat their routine. I know all their jokes by now, as does the bartender. He says it's part of the theme of this place and one day soon he's going to crack a bottle over their heads and give them the bum's rush even if they're worth a fortune in electronics."

"I think it's based on a TV show."

"I think that's right."

"And what're you calling from, a cell phone or something?"

"I got one so Doris can always be in touch, not that she calls, that part of her is gone, but she still answers the phone, that part is still intact, the answering part. I call her when I'm on the bus on my way home. I talk to her and I know she's listening because I can hear her breathing."

For some reason the fact that his father has a cell phone depresses Billy.

"You know what I was thinking, Billy?"

"What's that, Abe?"

"I was thinking you should go to Forty-seventh Street and visit the family store. You should storm in and tell them who you are, the offspring of Abraham Schine and Doris McMinn. That would be something. Kick open the doors—no walk in quietly, yes quietly, with dignity, and stare down all those Schines and Sappersteins and curse their hard hearts. Find my brothers and tell them how happy I am, how glad I am I barely escaped their clutches, how I lived for love and they lived for something much harsher and look at them now. I'm sure they look awful. Oh yes, you really should. Today. Or tomorrow. But soon. I can imagine their faces. They might take great pride in their handshakes but they have no honor. Tell them that exactly. That their idea of family is as bad as what we barely survived. I'm sure we're a Wanted poster in their minds. Tell them you went to Harvard and maybe dress like you're a big success and could buy the store because I bet their sons are working the counters and hustling estates, waiting for the grande dames to keel. Offer them an outlandish sum. Oh yes, you must."

Billy hears the laughter again, though explained, no less creepy. He considers telling his father that he already visited the store (Schine Brothers Gems in shimmering rhinestone) a few years back. He went in on the sly and posed as a boyfriend looking to become a fiancé and told the black gabardine behind the counter he was willing to spend twenty grand on an engagement ring. Perhaps the salesman was a relative, bearded and bespectacled but with a surprising sense of humor that contradicted his appearance, as if his warmth came from someplace ancient. He brought forth his merchandise and said, "Some lovely tombstones for the bachelor." He explained the varieties of cut and setting, using his pinky as pointer, then he called over a raven-haired beauty, Sasha her name, who possessed a glorious left hand and an intriguing Russian accent. She slipped on the rings and presented her paw as if ready for a waltz. "I like the baguettes on this one," she purred. Billy agreed, as did the relative Schine who eyed Sasha up and down and teased, "Sometimes I think you weren't our wisest hire for men seeking wives." She greeted this with a blazing bit of smile. Around the counter came another salesman, another possible Schine, but younger, with payos instead of a full-grown beard. He edged by the first salesman, affectionately bumping his shoulders and saying, "Is Sasha ruining another engagement?" Billy played along, Sasha as well, with easy nonbinding flirtation. The older salesman joined in and muttered, "If you want her you'll need a minimum of four carats." Billy was tempted to give himself up, in the company of these men and this pretend bride, reveal himself as the son of Abe, quietly whisper the truth—*I am Billy Schine*—and leave these black coats less villainous. Instead he told the salesman, "I'm going to have to think about it." The salesman, disappointed, gave him his card—Lev Halevy, sales associate. "I know we can find you something, so call me when its time." That was that. Outside, Billy stood in front of the store and hated himself for saying nothing of consequence, his heart pounding with ridiculous adrenaline, his feet stutter-stepping with notions of going back inside before finally giving up.

"Billy?"

"Yes, Abe."

"Where are you?"

"I have to go," Billy says, spotting Roger Coop down the hall.

"I'm glad you called," Abe says.

"You called me."

"The flowers, they were nice. You should know, I'm terribly alone. Even when I'm with her, I'm terribly alone. Please come home, Billy. We need your help."

"I really have to go," Billy says.

"Come home, Billy."

"Abe—"

"I have the right pills."

Billy winces, like a hacksaw is the only way to unshackle his hand from the phone.

"But we'll need help with the plastic bags. That's what the Hemlock Society suggests, pills and plastic bags, to be certain, absolutely certain, of the act."

"Abe—"

"Please come home."

"I—"

"Together in bed, that's the way we want to go. On our anniversary. Do you remember the date?"

"September fourth," Billy answers.

"Year?"

"Nineteen sixty-one," Billy answers.

"That's a good boy. It'll be thirty-eight years married. Too bad we couldn't get to 2001, then it would've been forty. I would've made her a gift of rubies though I probably could've only afforded a garnet. But September fourth will be our day. We'll empty the pills into ice cream and mix in some alcohol, rum, I think. But I'll need help getting her back home and into bed. And once we're asleep, we'll need help with the plastic bags."

Billy laughs, unfortunately laughs, awful but he laughs as hollowly as the robotic barflies near his father. "Sorry Abe," he says, "but I'm not going to kill you. Maybe if I were younger, but not now, not in my late twenties."

"But I have it all planned. You do nothing but slip the bags over our heads and fasten them with rubber bands, all of which I'll provide."

229

"Abe, please."

"You'll be doing us a favor."

"I don't know how to say this, Abe, but our relationship isn't really strong enough to handle me killing you and Mom. I'm sorry." And this is the truth. Billy wishes he loved them enough to kill them, to kiss their foreheads before easing them into death like a good euthanizing son. "I could also end up in jail. No, no, no. It's a supremely poor idea."

"We want to die together, not like this."

"We are not having this conversation."

"I can try it on my own," Abe says. "It just might be messier."

Messier strikes Billy as highly disturbing. "Abe, listen to yourself."

"I'm serious."

"Please don't be serious," Billy says. "And let's think about me for a second. I'll be orphaned." Orphaned? A twenty-eight-year-old orphan? "Okay, maybe not orphaned," Billy says. "But parentless in one fell swoop. I'm not prepared for that kind of, well, swoop. No, I need more time. Because September fourth is not far away. For my sake, let's lay off the double suicide for now."

But Abe is unmoved. "We want to be cremated," he says. "We want our ashes mixed together and divided into four equal parts and spread in four different locations: one in front of the Winter Garden Theatre; one while riding the Cyclone in Coney Island; one while cruising the Circle Line; and one on the observation deck of the Empire State Building."

"Jesus Christ, Abe, you're describing a montage."

"I'll put all our wishes in the note."

"I won't do it," Billy warns. "If you do this, I'll bury you in separate plots divided by a highway."

"You won't do that, Billy, because you're a good boy."

"You can't do this to me, lay this on me."

"Come home and help your mother and father."

"This is crazy," Billy says, drained. "Just hold off. Promise me that you'll hold off until I get back in touch with you or come home or whatever."

"No matter what, September fourth is when this is happening."

"Be flexible, for Christ's sake."

"Come home, Billy."

"I don't know if I can come home for this."

"I love my wife, Billy."

"Believe me, I know."

"Come home, Billy."

Back in bed, Billy in shock, the kind of shock that transforms the future into a series of impossible knots, ad nauseam ad infinitum, Billy closing his eyes, Billy rubbing his eyes until blackness grinds with galaxies of rubbed-on light, like a thumb on liquid crystal, like the final scene in the movie *2001*, before the intergalactic four-star hotel room, before the baffling fetus conjoins with the atmosphere of earth, when David Bowman travels through jet streams of color, the speed of light scored by the otherworld, Billy rubbing through this retinal space, not wanting to stop for there's pleasure in this abuse, a self-created itch, rubbing long after a mother would say, okay, enough of that.

27

BILLY WAKES up a day closer to his parents' projected death. All night long scenarios streamed in his head, of going home or not going home, of calling the cops and reporting an upcoming crime, of bundling faces in plastic and bags stamped *Grand Union*. What should he do? Maybe if he had been home more often and experienced their decline he'd have no problem with the chore. A William would be by their bed, a Liam would be sobbing, a Bill would spoon-feed the toxic mush while a Will would read from *Goodnight Moon*. But this was Billy and all of his suicide scenes were baroque, filled with clumsy measures and Rasputin survival, lips still breathing, Billy panicking and reaching for a pillow, the hands underneath battling him. No good. An imaginary to-do list—finish study, fly home, kill parents—haunted sleep. Eulogies were attempted— "My parents loved each other very much, very very much"—like an essay requiring a minimum of words, but the chapel in his mind was crowded with the homeless seeking shelter, not solace. And then a darker thought: how much could he sell their house for?

Today is also Saturday, PK day for the greens. Today Allevatrox's dose life will be gleaned through blood, lots of blood, a small sample drawn every thirty minutes from 9 A.M. until 7 P.M. For ten hours the greens will remain seated except for twenty quick trips to the bleed room and, when necessary, the bathroom, which will be closely monitored for loitering.

Billy showers, fingers in ears, pressing against what the water might say.

"Precision is essential," the head nurse tells them once they've sat down and swallowed their morning pills. "This should move like clockwork, in and out, in and out, in and out, one after another." She might be snapping her fingers but she looks dubious of their ability to breathe let alone to coordinate themselves in such a fashion. "It'll be a long day for all of us"—*me in particular*, her eyes flare—"so let's be patient, let's be orderly, and let's be professional. Today you earn your money. Tomorrow you can sleep"—*you bums*, her lips smirk.

Billy sits between Ossap and Dullick. Not that he planned it this way. After breakfast he insinuated himself with Gretchen by saying, "Hey," with causal coincidence, as if he had bumped into her instead of targeted her. She walked stiffly, her elbow nearest him like a tiller expecting a guiding hand, but Billy was unsure of the direction and just followed the current. He asked her, "Shall we sit together?" immediately despising the stuffy auxiliary verb. But she didn't seem bothered. She said, "Sure," and they found two seats together in the back row. Suddenly a marathon of bloodletting turned into a date. Billy glowed while watching the other greens file in, no doubt envious over his match. Do dragged in his compost stink. Lannigan, hairless, performed a death row march from whatever movie was running in his head. Rodney Letts carried a pillow, a blanket, and a magazine and settled into what could've been a deck chair on an ocean liner. "I should've brought my book," Billy said, but before Gretchen could respond, all-American, faux astronaut Karl McKay popped up from the seventh row and waved for her attention, which he got after an embarrassing half-minute flail. Gretchen said, "Crap, I promised I'd sit next to him." "Just blow him off," Billy told her. "I can't, he brought Battleship with him." "The game?" "He wanted to play me." "I thought you were a solitaire person." "Not exclusively." "Well"—Billy was near pleading—"how about we play Twenty Questions. Or a game of I Spy. Here I'll start: I spy a big loser who wants to sink your battleship." Though she grinned—a klieg flash on an otherwise gray face—she stood up and said, "Sorry, I promised." Billy grumbled, "I should've brought Stratego." "Yup," she said. "Stratego and you would've had me." Karl McKay, on his gentleman feet, offered Gretchen the red game case with a small absurd bow. Billy seethed. That's when Ossap and Dullick walked in, always last, always huddled and whispering. They searched for seats roughly together—there, in the back row, on either side of Billy.

"Hello," Billy said.

Their answer—"Right"—had the soft nougat center of *fucking prick*.

The dose room faces the courtyard and the bronze hand expressing the morning sun. Billy spots Joy. She's running from the parking lot. Her left arm holds her chest while her right arm crooks a canvas bag, swinging wildly, four times more unwieldy than her bosom. Strain is translated into a smile, as if she realizes the sight she must make, rounding the sculpture and skipping over the shadow of the finger with girlish dexterity.

Billy, glad to see her, almost waves.

"Hey jerk-off."

Billy turns toward Dullick.

"No, the other jerk-off, jerk-off," Dullick tells him.

Ossap leans forward, his face in mid twitch. The second hand of his internal clock seems to stick every so often, as if struggling with its sweep and getting caught on the more dominant minute and hour. "Yeah?" he says.

"I forgot my spit cup," Dullick sort of says, his mouth steeped in slaver, a pool under his tongue so the words belly flop into *I orgah eye ih up*. Reluctantly, Dullick swallows, then he shivers. "It's like I'm drinking backwash," he says. "My mouth is like the end of New Year's Eve."

"You're an old toothless cat," Ossap teases.

"Maybe your cat. My cat never got that way."

"Oh, he'd just pee on the brisker."

"It was a warm spot and he was arthritic."

"Lie there in his pee snuggled against that brisker."

"Poor Mickey Deans!"

"How about my Carr crackers and Wheat Thins!"

"You and or ucking—" Dullick glances toward Billy with newfound hostility. "Ut da uck"—swallow—"you looking at?"

"Nothing."

"Yeah, asshole," Ossap joins in. "What're you looking at?"

"Nothing, I swear."

Dullick: "Fucklips listening to our conversation?"

Ossap: "Fucking jerk fuck."

"I can't help it," Billy says. "I'm sitting between you two. I'll switch if you want."

"No," Dullick tells him. "Stay put and keep watching because trust me you're seeing something, something you own't underdand undil ees ooh ate."

Billy leans back, away from the crossfire. A thought strikes him: what if Ossap and Dullick are representatives from Ragnar & Sons? What if his phone had been bugged and Ragnar knew all along Billy was coming here? What if Ossap and Dullick have been subcontracted for his death? They're certainly suspicious enough. And those four duffel bags. Maybe they carried brass knuckles, rope, silencers as long as cattails. After all, this would be an ideal place for an unforeseen adverse event, perhaps involving a razor blade and wrists. And so what if the idea of sending hired guns into a two-week drug study just to off a piker like himself seems a bit, well, overboard? Billy, in his present state of mind, entertains the high concept.

"I bet you think you can read us like a book," Ossap scowls.

"Trust me," Dullick says. "You don't know uhding."

Pharmacokinetics is like an odd relay race. The first green in the first green row gets up and heads into the bleed room and only after he returns does the second green get up and go. Et cetera. Et cetera. Up and down. Up and down. It's roughly a two-minute lap from beginning to end. There's a strange mechanical quality to the movement, like an extravagant time-keeping device Torquemada might have invented.

Up Ossap.

Up Billy.

Into the bleed room he goes. He sits down and presents his arm. Joy reaches for his cannula and empties a few drops of blood into a test tube then barks, "Schine, nine-twenty-six," to an assistant who transcribes the info onto a label and places the test tube into the *William A. Schine* container. The first slot of twenty is filled. That's it. Billy is done.

But in the process, Billy manages a snippet of conversation with Joy.

"You were late," he says.

"No talking," she says.

"I saw you rushing through the courtyard."

"I'm working."

"Did you get in trouble?"

"Of course," she says. "Now leave."

Schine, 9:52

"Why were you late?" Billy asks.

"No talking," Joy says.

"Sleep in?"

"I wish."

"Traffic?"

"Around here? Please. You can leave."

"I'll see you soon."

Schine, 10:29

"Why were you late?" Billy asks again.

"My son, if you won't shut up," Joy says.

"He all right?"

"He's fine, he just thinks he's sick."

"With what?"

"Everything. He might as well be allergic to sleep. Now leave."

Schine, 11:01

"Was he faking, your son?" Billy asks.

"You're the only one who insists on talking," Joy says.

"Just being friendly."

"You're not making any friends here."

"I can't just be quiet."

"Well, try. Now go."

Schine, 11:36

". . ."

"Don't say a word," Joy says.

"I didn't," Billy says.

"But you were going to."

"You're the one who started."

"This is a long day for me."

"Do you get a break?"

"A small one for lunch. Leave."

Schine, 12:04

". . ."

Schine, 12:39

". . ."

"So you're not talking anymore," Joy says.

"You said 'shut up,'" Billy says.

"Well I was right, shut up."

"Are you smiling?"

"Because you're done."

Schine, 13:08

It's not Joy but her assistant who lords over his assistant, the lowly assistant's assistant, the assistant yelling orders in hopes of covering up his clumsy tug on the cannula and his excessive bloodletting, the assistant's assistant racking the test tube with an exaggerated, overladen dip of his hand, as the assistant, the maestro, rips off his latex gloves and yells, "Next."

Schine, 13:43

"Did you have a nice lunch?" Billy asks.

"If a bologna sandwich is nice," Joy says.

"Not bad."

"But not nice."

"They served us chicken salad sandwiches. It was like a picnic except for all this bleeding."

"You're done."

"I'm saving the potato chips for a snack later."

Schine, 14:18

"What's your son's name?" Billy asks.

"Rufus," Joy says.

"Means red-haired."

"I know."

"Why was he sick?"

"Because he misses home. Go."

Schine, 14:45

"Where's home?" Billy asks.

"New York. The Bronx," Joy says.

"When did you leave?"

"July."

"Why did you leave?"

"Are you interviewing me?"

"Just small talk."

"I got a better job, okay. Now adios."

Schine, 15:17

"The public schools are better here than the Bronx," Joy says.

238

"I can imagine," Billy says.

"Why can you imagine that?"

"Maybe because it's the Bronx."

"The Bronx has never been better."

"So why did you leave?"

"Because it still stinks. Now go."

Schine, 15:43

"You married?" Billy asks.

"Was. Yourself?" Joy asks.

"Could you imagine me married?"

"Good point."

"Who would marry a person like me?"

"Somebody deaf."

Schine, 16:07

"Why are you here?" Joy asks.

"Get away from things, I guess. Make some money. Hole up, shrivel up and disappear. I don't know, but it's not all that bad bleeding into a test tube and being cared for by a nurse named Joy."

"I wouldn't say cared for."

"Then attended to."

"And I'm not a nurse. I'm a phlebotomist."

Schine, 16:42

"How old is Rufus?" Billy asks.

"He's almost nine. School's just started and he's not a fan. He's been playing sick for the last three days, telling me it's something deep in his belly that won't show up on any thermometer. Insists on sleeping with me and he's a kicker."

"He sounds like a character."

239

"If by that you mean nightmare, yes, he's a character."

"But you love him."

"Of course I do. My God, that's never a question. He's everything to me."

Schine, 17:10

". . ."

"No talking, Mr. Schine?" Joy asks.

"I'm getting tired. And please call me Billy."

Schine, 17:48

"I think it's nice that you let Rufus sleep with you. I don't think it's wrong, I just think it's nice. Something you'll remember, you know, how he crawled into bed with you, something you'll tell him when he's older, all those fake stomachaches disguising bad dreams. 'Mommy, mommy' as you pat the bed. Jump on in."

"You all right?"

"Maybe I'm losing too much blood."

Schine, 18:11

"In eight days my father's going to kill my mother and then himself," Billy says.

"What's that?"

"My mother has Alzheimer's. It's in its final stages, I guess, and my father wants to end her suffering as well as his own, hence the double suicide, or murder-suicide, or mercy killing, depending on your politics."

"Are you being serious?"

"I think so."

"So what're you going to do?"

"I don't know."

"Are you really being serious?"

"Depends on my father."

Schine, 18:50

"Are you really being serious about your parents, because I can't tell," Joy
says.

"That's often been the problem with me. Too many jokes."

"Well you should go home and be with them—"

"And help them? Because they want my help, or my father does."

"Leave here, go home, talk to them."

"My father wants me to slip plastic bags over their heads."

"That's gruesome."

"I'm pro–assisted suicide, but I don't know if I'm capable of that. I
picture a yellow grocery bag. You know, paper or plastic? Plastic please."

"That's not funny."

"But those are the problematic details."

"Is your father in poor health?"

"Physically, he's fine, but no way can he survive without her. You've
almost filled the entire test tube."

"Oh crap."

Schine, 19:18

"You can call someone, you know, and tell them about your parents. Do
you have any brothers or sisters, any relatives who could help you deal with
the situation?" Joy asks.

"No, just me. I'm sorry to lay this on you."

"That's all right."

"No cause, no cause."

"What's that?"

"Nothing."

"The least you should do is go home."

"I don't think I can."

"You're not close with your folks?"

"Never have been."

"Either way, the death of a parent is the hardest thing."

"Death of a child, that's harder."

"Go home, Billy, that's my advice."

"Don't tell anyone, okay? Not that there's anyone to tell."

"This is the last draw, but stay longer if you want."

"No, I'll go."

"Leave this place and go home."

"Yeah, maybe."

Billy gets up and leaves as Joy removes her latex gloves and throws them into the garbage bursting with sluffed hands, fingers gone limp.

28

MIDMORNING Sunday, Billy, bored and curious and a bit disheveled in his thoughts, decides on attending the AHRC's nondenominational service. It's run by Carlson Dickey, a security guard. He greets his flock of blues, reds, greens, oranges, and yellows with a welcoming handshake and a suggestion to take any seat but preferably up front. "We don't stand on color around here," he tells Billy. "Grab a Bible from the table and make yourself comfortable." He wears his blue-gray uniform and nonlethal utility belt, his curly dirty-blond hair tonsured by the officer's cap tucked under his arm. He looks like a cherub grown old and fat, falling from a frescoed ceiling and landing in a pile of mustache and eyes accustomed to the slow arc of a softball.

The first few rows carry nine normals—no matter how virtuous, a small sum, Carlson Dickey seems to suggest as he cranes his neck out the door for the hope of more bodies. Do is here. He traces his index finger along the onionskin pages of his Bible as if searching a phone book for a name he can't quite remember and has no idea of the spelling but he'll certainly recognize it when he sees it. Do is the only other green. For the sake of balance and spectrum, Billy sits between a yellow and a blue.

"Hey," he says.

The blue, deep in sunglasses, whispers, "Did you hear anything about doughnuts?"

"No."

"Told you," the yellow says.

"What about doughnuts?" Billy asks.

"I heard they give you doughnuts afterwards."

"No chance," the yellow says.

"Maybe he's hiding them and after the final amen he'll pull out a big box of Dunkin' Donuts. I'm thinking three per parishioner if he got the party box."

"You're delusional."

Billy, inspired, opens his palms and pronounces, "Blessed are they which do hunger and thirst after righteousness, for they shall be filled with lightly fried dough."

This does not go over well.

"That's not funny," the yellow says.

"Not at all," the blue agrees.

"Don't dis Jesus."

Billy apologizes, thankful he censored his near-riff on the potential glories of a jelly-injected communion wafer, a two-in-one sacrament, delicious too. *Mmm-mm Jesus.* But really, this is just bad-boy blasphemy, the sort of desperate-to-be-noticed iconoclasm he despises in himself. It's not that he's religious. There was no God in his home, his mother and father adopting the separation between church and love. The only religious training he received was a circumcision and that was for aesthetic reasons. "Officially," an adolescent Billy once asked his father, "I'm not a Jew, right, because my mother's a gentile." Abe frowned. "Don't say that word." "What word?" "'Gentile.'" "Goy, then." "Not that word either." "Okay, fine," Billy said, "but in terms of your people's law, right, I'm in the same boat as Mom while you're waving from the promised land." "Oh, I'm in the boat, too," Abe told him, "the front of the boat, and your mother's in back." "Where am I then?" Billy asked. "Lucky for you, you're not in this boat, if we're talking boat as religion. No, you're on the shore, free to choose whatever boat you want. But we, we dug our own grave, or boat. Okay, enough of this talk." *God bless them*, Billy thinks.

Ossap and Dullick come through the door, and Billy sinks as they eyeball him suspiciously and pick up Bibles like some primitive form of bludgeon and nod toward Carlson Dickey, who seems satisfied with this slightly greater number, with Dullick and Ossap who sit down and bend over, either praying or plotting.

The pulpit is a latter-day lectern draped in a purple sheet, the fabric satin and a tad too erotic for the proceedings. Carlson Dickey steps up to the lectern, rustles papers, relocates his Bible, clears his throat with phlegmy gusto like he's coughed up vertebrae. "Welcome to our Sunday service," he says, reading poorly from prepared text. "This is something new for the center, something I've been campaigning for, what with you good people being stuck on Sunday with nowhere to worship, so I asked and asked and asked and finally they said yes and here we are on our third Sunday. I'm so proud and happy that you can be here with me on this day of the Lord. I'm still learning, and I'm certainly no preacher, as you can see, just a lowly security guard." Billy can imagine Carlson Dickey taking a nail for Christ. "But together we will share in our common faith, whatever denomination that might be, and honor God in our humble fashion in our humble setting."

After a few prayers and a hymn ("Amazing Grace" photocopied and handed out, Carlson Dickey gets to the reading, which is from Daniel 1:3–16:

Then the king commanded his palace master Ashpenaz to bring some of the Israelites of the royal family and of the nobility, young men without physical defect and handsome, versed in every branch of wisdom, endowed with knowledge and insight, and competent to serve the king's palace; they were to be taught literature and the language of the Chaldeans. The king assigned them a daily portion of the royal rations of food and wine. They were to be educated for three years, so that at the end of that time they could be stationed in the king's court. Among them were Daniel, Hananiah, Mishael, and Azariah, from the tribe of Judah.

But Daniel resolved that he would not defile himself with the royal rations of food and wine; so he asked the palace master to allow him not to defile himself. Now God allowed Daniel to receive favor and compassion from the palace master. The palace master said to Daniel, "I am afraid of my lord the king; he has appointed your food and your drink. If he should see you in poorer condition than the other young men of your own age, you would endanger my head with the king."

Then Daniel asked the guard whom the palace master had appointed over Daniel, Hananiah, Mishael, and Azariah; "Please test your servants for ten days. Let us be given vegetables to eat and water to drink. You can then compare our appearance with the appearance of the young men who eat the royal rations, and deal with your servants according to what you observe." So he agreed to this proposal and tested them for ten days. At the end of ten days it was observed that they appeared better and fatter than all the young men who had been eating the royal rations. So the guard continued to withdraw their royal rations and the wine they were to drink, and gave them vegetables.

Carlson closes his Bible and leans into the pulpit for dramatic effect, forgetting the unlocked wheels of the lectern and sliding forward and then almost tumbling backward. Ossap and Dullick snot with laughter. Resettled, Carlson begins: "I'm going to jump right into my sermon because my sermon today is on Daniel. In case you forgot, he's the prophet who was cast in the den of lions and lived not because he pulled a thorn from one of the lion's paws, I think a common misconception, but because he had total faith in the Lord and the Lord gobbed up the lion's mouth so that Daniel lived. Daniel is the first great"—he glances at his notes for the word—"apocalyptist. He was the interpreter of Nebuchadn-uhn-uhm-nay-dennezzar's dreams and the reader of the handwriting on the wall and the man behind the visions about the four beasts and the ram and the goat and the seventy weeks and the contemptible person and the end of time and the final consummation. All that stuff is from Daniel. I was thinking about Daniel when I was thinking about what I might say today. Daniel came to mind because you have something in common with Daniel. You do. Like in our reading where the best representatives of the Israelites— *those without physical defect*—were taken to the king's palace, that's kind of like you here. Daniel's request of having one group eat the fatty royal diet and another group eat the nice healthy, surprisingly hearty vegetarian diet is something like a parallel design study. You have the old way versus the new way, the standard treatment versus the experimental treatment. And I was thinking, you're kind of like prophets as well. You're providing

246

signs of the future, your blood, your body, lighting the path ahead. You're the first comers. Yes, you're prophets. Small prophets perhaps, but prophets are better than deficits. Because of you a grain of the future drops down the hourglass. You're everyday prophets, no lottery jackpot, but instead, pennies and nickels, loose change saved up until something is earned. Dependable prophets. Even in failure the world has gained because of you and a better world will come. Truly. I believe that. It might be hard to believe now. Impossible to believe. 'Me?' you might say. 'No. I'm here for money. Five years from now I don't care what I've done,' you might think. 'My memory of this place will last as long as the cash.' But guess what, your blood lives on. It does. A single drop has raised the level a little higher, not much higher, but a little bit higher, a billionth of a billionth of a billionth higher. You won't be remembered for it, but you have changed the world. That's a fact. Your blood is in the system. God is knowledge and knowledge is speaking through you even if your tongue is gobbed up with sin, even if you feel you are the contemptible person. You are part of the whole and the whole is God. A part and a whole. Think back on Daniel's parallel study. Faithless versus faithful. Not nonreligious versus religious, but faithless versus faithful. Ask yourself, who is healthier? Regardless of your idea of who or what God is, or how God should be worshiped, ask yourself, who is healthier? The disconnected or the connected? Even if there is no God, even if you die and are greeted with nothing, who is healthier five minutes before they die, in the unspeakable horror of that moment, who looks to comfort the weak and the frightened but those who understand that we are all made in an image of one thing and that one thing is faith? Who understands that we are all reflections of love and not mere reflections of ourselves? Who possesses comfort in the last second of life and who screams? If you were the palace guard, who would you choose as the healthier?" Carlson Dickey steps away from the pulpit like the question might be settled with fists. "Let us pray," he says.

After the Lord's Prayer—nope, no doughnuts—the congregation of normals departs. Billy notices that Ossap and Dullick loiter with Carlson Dickey, Dullick genuflecting his eyebrows and Ossap playfully jabbing the Hargrove Anderson Medical security patch on Carlson Dickey's arm.

Is Ragnar everywhere? Billy wonders.

Back upstairs, Billy gives a glance into Dr. Honeysack's office. Honeysack sits hunched over his desk like paperwork has flatlined for the last time. Billy says, "Hey, doc," enjoying the patently ridiculous notion of this man ever being known as doc—he's as folksy as brushed steel. The overhead twin fluorescent tubes do his complexion no favors; his skin could be absorbing light for a long lonely night of glowing in the dark. His return of "Hello" carries the telltale pause of *I have no idea who you are.*

"Billy Schine," Billy says, presenting his ID badge for further proof.

"Right-right-right."

"Working on a Sunday, doc?"

"Is it Sunday?"

"Sure is. I just attended your nondenominational Sunday service."

"Certainly not mine," Honeysack says.

"It was interesting."

"A security guard, right?"

"Yep."

"That guy's been a royal pain about having some sort of service. Next thing he'll push for is a chapel. He's hanging on his last straw."

"A thin rope."

"That's right," Honeysack says. "He's been here only three months, thumping his Bible nonstop. Driving a lot of people crazy, me included. You see him and before he even speaks, you want to shout shut up. He's not long for this job. Acts like St. Francis with the research animals and half the time he's not even allowed where he ends up. One thing for a researcher or a doctor to go on about the concept of God, but we don't need a security guard preaching to us." Honeysack seems startled by his own bitterness. "Sorry," he says. "I'm thirty-six hours without sleep. Anyway, I didn't peg you as the religious type."

"It was just something to do."

"I'd rather have root canal."

248

"I think it's interesting. You ever read Dante?" asks Billy.

"In college, probably."

Billy, arms crossed, leans against the doorjamb—doorways, it seems, are his favorite place for a pose. "I remember this one bit from the *Inferno*, actually I'm probably remembering the Doré engraving more than the book. There's one engraving of a soldier, a really bad guy his entire life who's been killed in battle, and a devil is ready to drag him down into the pits of hell because this is a guy they've been eyeing for a long time. Then an angel appears and says 'whoa' to the devil because the soldier, with his last breath, has fashioned a cross with his arms. It seems that this is enough to save him, this one gesture." Billy illustrates with his own arms and imagines the soldier slipping away into death and feeling, in those last few seconds of life, a warm blinding faith stronger than fear, his muscle straining against armor, struggling to express this newfound light before his soul empties into the ground. Billy eyes Honeysack dramatically, like Honeysack is a series of lines incised in metal in need of ink. "You know, people have been talking about your work, your real work."

"How's that?"

"They're talking about your research, with embellishments. They're convinced it's happening in a hollowed-out mountain somewhere or an ice cave or some banana republic where cash is king."

Honeysack shakes his head wearily. "They're always talking about it. The thing's become normal lore and I'm afraid it's going to stay normal lore. Where have they put the payout, I'm curious, a half a million?"

"No no, just in the twenty-thousand-dollar range."

"Any good names?"

"Huh?"

"Like 'freeze and seize,' or 'frosty the dead man,' or 'blood on the rocks,' all of which I've heard. Or my personal favorite, 'no fucking way is this ever going to happen in my lifetime.'" Honeysack smiles without humor. His thin upper lip is unable to register any emotion but strain. It's a rubber band wrapped around a cluster of unpaid bills.

"No," Billy says. "They had no great names."

"'Honeysack's folly,' that's what they should call it." A blush of heat colors the doctor's gauntness, particularly around the problem areas of his skin where acne damage lingers as shame and anger. "Think the FDA would let us try our procedure on a real person, say somebody on death row, a murderer? Like your Doré guy. You give him a choice, either get killed by lethal injection or participate in some radical medical research. If you survive, which is a good chance, then your sentence is reduced to life in prison. Think the FDA would be interested? No. Of course not. They'd scream ethics. They'd mention all sorts of awful tests done in the fifties on convicts. And, yes, they were awful, but still. The FDA would even claim cruel and unusual punishment regardless of the fact that this person is about to be strapped down and killed like a dog, his life going down the drain without any purpose. They'd scream ethics, and in return, we might scream morality. We might even scream redemption." The word elicits a roll from Honeysack's earthbound eyes. "Yes, redemption," he says for his own sake. "Fuck God, but why not redemption? Penance? A massive act of contrition? Why not? There is some truth in that stuff. Even if the state is hell-bent on killing the guy, on going ahead with his death sentence, given the choice, do the study and maybe do some good and then get executed, well, I bet the guy would side with us. I do. Or at least a workable percentage would."

"Sounds reasonable to me," Billy says.

"Instead we waste their lives. And I should say I'm against the death penalty."

"Me too."

"I've given money to causes that fight the death penalty," Honeysack says.

"I haven't, but still."

"What kind of stupid phrase is 'death penalty' anyway?"

"Like life is a game."

"Death is too ultimate to be slipped in with 'penalty,'" Honeysack says.

"I agree."

"I'm not trying to make martyrs of these men," Honeysack says.

"Of course not."

"So forget redemption, how about death reparation, giving something back?"

"You should run for office," Billy says.

"It's frustrating. You can get so close, you can practically prove your thesis with all the animals you want, but if you're doing something truly radical, you can never make that, that—"

"Evolutionary leap," Billy fills in (a tad smugly, in his opinion).

"Fuck evolution," Honeysack says, as if evolution is the bane of his existence, as if evolution stole his girlfriend and wrecked his car and leaves laughing messages on his voice mail. "This is about practical medical science. Evolution is just a bad childhood game of telephone done nonstop, an endless whispering loop between simpleton cells. I have no need for evolution."

"It was just a metaphor," Billy explains.

"Yeah, a metaphor." Honeysack says this with equal disregard. "Can I ask you a question?"

"Sure."

"Do you believe that something can be unnatural? Because I don't. The only time unnatural is ever mentioned is in relation to something man has done, but if man is a part of nature, how can his expression, whatever that might be, be unnatural? Whatever we do, by definition, is natural. Cities, cars, airplanes, global warming, hell, abortion, bestiality, you name it, it's all natural, isn't it, if it comes from us? It might be self-destructive, unhealthy, illegal, repugnant, but it's still natural. How can anything be unnatural? Nature has no opposite."

"Man has become its opposite," Billy says, going along for the Socratic ride.

"I mean, you can say unethical, immoral, unseemly, but don't say unnatural."

"Strike unnatural from all dictionaries," Billy pronounces with a flourish.

Honeysack laughs—it's a geeky hiccup of delight. "Sorry, it's been a long day."

"And it's still early," Billy says. "So I'll be going."

251

But Honeysack keeps talking. "You know who'll end up doing something like our stasis study." He pauses, dejected. "The Chinese. They'll do it. They'll use prisoners, no problem, and they'll succeed, and they'll develop some marvelous new drug, and the FDA will scream at us and ask why couldn't we have been first. Mark my words, it'll happen. We'll be forever stuck doing the most innovative Nobel Prize–worthy treatments on pigs and chimps."

"I'll do it," Billy says, the words slipping free without tweak, always wanting to be offered up to Honeysack, battler of death, theriac against the poison of too many thoughts, of Abe and Doris, of Ragnar and his punishing debt—elaborate me, Billy thinks, into something that sticks.

"What's that?" Honeysack asks, not listening.

"Your study, I'll do it."

Eyebrows briefly lift, then fall, like caterpillars going nowhere. "No, it's too dangerous," Honeysack says. "Ideally you'd be an accident victim, not in perfect health."

"Wouldn't my health raise the chances of success?"

"But failure might kill you, and success certainly wouldn't save your life."

Billy leaves the doorjamb, steps into the office. "Not that I'm about to kill myself but—" he stops himself. Temporary death shimmers like the grandest of all temp jobs, a dip in the pool of timelessness where all of history sinks. "I have confidence in you, but if the study fails, it won't be the greatest tragedy in the world. If it succeeds, great. Maybe I'll get a little money, or a lot of money, which will be very helpful in my particular situation. But if it fails, that's all right. Not that I have a death wish. I don't. Doing this would be the opposite of a death wish. I mean, I really could really use the money. And maybe a certain kind of focus would follow, you know, after the fact, when we're all having a celebratory drink. Cheers, I survived. It might be the sort of depth of experience I as a person need right now to settle things in my head a bit. Otherwise I'm so—" *shallow, ridiculous, worthless,* Billy thinks, but the right word seems impossible. "I just need something like this," he tells Honeysack.

Honeysack shakes his unenchanted head. "It won't happen."

"Why not?"

"Honestly, your psychological profile would raise some flags. A person rationally choosing this would be deemed irrational. That's why we need people who don't have a choice, people already wrapped around a telephone pole."

"But maybe it will save my life," Billy says. "Maybe I'm already wrapped around a telephone pole."

"Won't happen," Honeysack assures him. "And at the end of the day one person proves nothing. We need a range, and a range, the FDA tells us, is too dangerous in this case. They like the results, sure, but they hate the idea of tossing the results into the realm of public trauma. Too risky. Too many losses, too many lawsuits. Too difficult to find subjects willing to consent while they're bleeding out in wrecked cars. No, I think as research, we're done. Five years and we're done in two days of deliberation."

"Maybe you just want to see if it works," Billy says.

"What's the point?"

"Curiosity. Satisfaction."

"Too risky."

"I won't tell a soul," Billy says, fearing the chance slipping away. "I'll sign any release form. I'll pledge eternal nonliability. I can guarantee nobody will miss me. If it doesn't work, cremate me and spread my ashes somewhere nice. If it works, I'll be a bit wiser and richer, and you'll know that your research meant something."

"Yeah, by almost killing you."

"Semantics," Billy says.

"It would be something," Honeysack muses aloud. "In concept."

"Absolutely something," Billy says. "At least something to think about. So think about it." Billy turns around and leaves. In the hallway, under the glare of advertised affliction, he wonders if anything he just said was true.

29

"B ILLY ?"

It's Do. His voice is a surprise. Lately, he's been quiet, saying nothing except yes or no, letting conversation pass through him as if words have the weight of neutrinos. His meals are eaten without comment; food is barely touched, just bread and water and whatever starch is being served. But his odor still screams. Showerless since that first morning, he hasn't brushed his teeth or shaved or spritzed any deodorant under those odor-catching hair traps. The bathroom has been avoided except for the essential business and that's handled with as much speed as possible, then it's quickly back to bed, the sheets pulled up to his chin. He smells of wet leaves leavened with sweat instead of rain. It's the primal funk of man, of gym bags tossed deep into closets and forgotten for months.

Billy glances away from the Sunday afternoon breast augmentation on TV where an already well-endowed woman is adding another letter. It seems there's no blurring of breasts when breasts are informative, even for these moneymakers, and Billy wonders if fourteen-year-old boys pop boners to these antiseptic orange tits on the operating table. "You want me to change?" Billy asks.

"Not if it keeps Lannigan away."

"I agree." Billy smiles hoping he might prove himself an ally.

"You're smart, aren't you?" Do asks.

"What do you mean?"

"You're reading that big important-looking book."

"This book is cheating," he tells Do.

"No, you're smart, I can tell."

The surgeon squeezes the newly implanted breasts for the sake of uniformity then steps back and regards the drape like he's hanging a velvet painting.

"Where are we in Luke," Billy asks, changing the subject.

Do consults his Bible. "Sixteen twenty-three: 'And in Hades, being in torment, he lifted up his eyes, and saw Abraham far off and Lazarus in his bosom.' "

Billy pauses at hearing his father's name. "Really?"

"Yep."

"Lazarus as in *the* Lazarus?"

"Different Lazarus. That Lazarus is much earlier, around seven in the morning."

"Oh."

Do turns over on his side. "Billy?" he says.

"Yeah."

"You ever think of yourself as bad?"

"Bad?"

"Yeah."

"I certainly don't think of myself as good."

"But I mean bad, like really bad."

"I've done some bad things," Billy says. "I've been a jerk to a lot of people."

"Really bad?"

"Bad enough."

Do shakes his head a bit too vigorously. "No, I mean really bad, evil bad, like bad through and through." His voice trembles. His eyes seem to channel a deeper spirit within. "Like I have these thoughts about women, when I'm passing them on the street or anywhere, I think about how their breasts must look under their shirt, saggy or firm, round, pointy, I think about what kind of nipples they have, dark or light, big or small, like it's a secret they're keeping from me. Then I think about their privates, their vaginas, and I imagine all those vaginas behind pants and under skirts, shaved or bushy, blond or brunette, and I look at their eyebrows like I'm looking at squints of their vaginas, and I just want to reach out and grab them. I have to stop myself and tell myself no because I can feel my hand reaching. In buses. In any crowded place. Even with the nurses here. I want to know those secrets. I have to know. I can imagine the whole thing, the actual moment where I grab them. It's like a flash of what might happen, just seconds away, and I'm always relieved and kind of shocked when they walk by me without anything happening. The problem is, there's always another woman in the distance. And they have no idea what kind of person they have next to them."

"They're just thoughts," Billy tells him. "We all get strange thoughts."

"These kinds of thoughts?"

Billy treads lightly. "Sometimes, sure. They pop into your head, but it doesn't mean you're an awful person, especially if you don't act on them. It just means you're nineteen years old."

"I've never had sex," Do says.

"Even more reason why you have these thoughts."

"I could have," Do says, "plenty of times, but I didn't. I stopped. I said no because I was scared of what I might do because I know, I know what I might do. I've imagined it. I've done it in my head a hundred times. Now I'm a nineteen-year-old virgin and that seems worse, you know, a big joke. It's something you can never lose, being a virgin at nineteen. That fact stays with you for the rest of your life."

"It's not a big deal," Billy says.

Do balls his hands into fists; the whole room seems to squeeze around him. "These thoughts are constantly screaming in my head and they're always the worst possible thoughts. They always storm in before I can stop them. Like I think about raping nuns. Is that sick or what? It's not as if I spend my whole day thinking about raping nuns, it's not my number-one thought, but when I see a nun, a nun in her habit, young or old, rape kind of slams into my head, me raping this nun." Do grinds his face into splinters.

"Calm down," Billy says.

But Do is on an unfortunate roll. "Or with African-Americans, when I meet them or walk by them or whatever, like with Joy, with her I'm nice and friendly, but in my head, in my head, I'm thinking 'nigger' all the time. I can't help it. It's an echo between my ears. 'Nigger nigger nigger.'

256

Sometimes it's almost on my lips. I hate it, I hate that word, but I cannot not hear it. 'Nigger' so loud in my head I'm sure she can hear it. They all can. Nigger—"

Billy says, "Okay, okay," hushing him. "But that word is just a word, a very charged word, maybe the last powerful word, but thinking that particular word doesn't mean you're an awful racist, it just means you're intrigued by the word. It's just about the worst word you can say. That's all. It's that temptation to scream in a theater. I mean, do you hate black people?"

"I don't think so."

"Are you a member of your local KKK?"

"Of course not."

"So there," Billy says, pleased with his reasoning.

"But it's nonstop. This nigger stuff is nonstop. I get all the awful words in my head. All the wrong words. 'Cocksucker.' 'Cunt.' 'Faggot.' They're in there, just waiting. And they ruin everything nice. I have an older brother who has these great kids, a boy and a girl, and I really love these kids, I live for these kids, even though I'm not crazy about my brother. But say I'm wrestling with them, goofing around, and my brother and his wife are in the kitchen or something, and say they come in and see me rolling around with their kids, I swear they look at me funny, like I'm some kind of child molester, like I'm touching them in the wrong places, like I'm too physical with them. I can see it in their eyes, and maybe they see something I don't see, you know, because I am always aware of where I'm touching them and I try not to touch them anywhere I shouldn't. It's constantly on my mind. Be careful, be careful, stay above the waist. I get scared I might get an erection, which can happen for no good reason, and I'm like, you're so sick. These are kids. But I can't help it. I'm thinking about it so much that I can't turn off the thought that I might hurt them, that I might do something horrible."

"Uhm . . ."

Do is near tears. "My thoughts, they ruin everything," he says, frustrated. "It's got to be that I'm an evil person. All these crazy thoughts, what else can it mean. Out of the blue murder comes into my head. I'll be

257

in a mall and I'll be walking around and doing nothing and all of a sudden I'm carrying an imaginary machine gun and I'm mowing everyone down. I can hear the screams; I can see the blood. I go to Mass and pray to be good, or if not good, at least forgiven, but I know I'm just saying the words. I volunteer and give myself to charities, but I know I'm just pretending. I want to get married, I want to have children, but I know I'll manage to mess things up royally. I start thinking about incest and all the awful things I might do to my children, to my wife, the hell I'll put them through. Some day I know all the bad will outweigh any good I might have done and this evil inside will fly free and you'll read about me in the newspaper." Do looks as though he can already read the headline.

Billy lies there, unsure of what to say, hearing some of his own fears expressed with such inner turmoil, as if Do is one of the research animals who will not survive the high dose of doubt, part of the fifty percent who convulse while the other half merely shudder. "You're, uhm, you're not insane or anything," Billy says, unsatisfied by the words.

Giving comfort has never been one of his strengths. In the face of other people's emotions he often shuts down and simply stares, hoping his silence will be read as quiet empathy instead of helplessness (or worse, coldness, which is his own opinion). It's not that he's apathetic; it's just that he's uncertain of the terrain. The topography of *shh-sh-sh* rises above him with dizzy awe. "They're just thoughts," he tells Do, "sick thoughts, but just thoughts. If we were liable for every single thought, we'd all be in jail."

"You try living with these thoughts," Do protests. "It's exhausting. When you sleep, you dream these horrors and they're all nightmares. You never have a moment of peace." Do rubs his eyes with the heels of his hands, then drags his fingers over his cheeks, his nose, his mouth, his chin, leaving behind a reddish wake.

"You seem to me a nice guy," Billy tries.

"That's what everyone thinks and it drives me crazy."

"Maybe they're not wrong. And remember, you're on a pretty heavy-duty psychotropic drug right now. It's got to be doing something to your brain."

"No," Do almost screams. "This has nothing to do with anything here. This is not something new. Even when I was a kid I had these thoughts, that I might be bad, really bad, son-of-the-devil bad. I did. I read Revelations and thought this book was about me. It was the only part of the Bible I enjoyed. All the monsters, the seals, the signs. I even had a friend check my scalp once for the three sixes, you know, the mark of the Antichrist. I was so sure. I'd try strangling people with my eyes, impaling them, throwing them from windows, drowning them. I would give teachers heart attacks. I would explode the heads of bullies. Airplanes and I'd blink engine failure. I probably killed my parents a hundred times. When nothing happened, I was always disappointed. No, these thoughts have been with me long before this place. Do you know what it comes down to? It comes down to who I am every minute of the day. Every minute of the day is a test whether my thoughts will just stay thoughts and not see the light of day."

"I think maybe you should talk to someone here," Billy says gently.

"Oh, they already know," Do tells him with matter-of-factness. "They've known since the beginning of the study. They can see it in my blood, in the genes, the bad gene; they've isolated it and they're ready to put me under lock and key and study me even more. They know I know. He knows, Honeysack, the nurses too, the security people, Carlson Dickey, they all know, me included, so there's no need to say anything. You should see how they treat my blood. It's like acid. They wear gloves because it's such toxic stuff. Oh, they know. And I've known you've known forever, which is fine. Lannigan doesn't know yet. All the researchers are frightened and interested because this is all so new, my kind of blood. They're calling in experts. Reputations will be made because of what's inside me. I'll be shocked if I ever leave this place. But right now we're pretending that we know nothing, that we don't know what we really know." Do seems pleased, his left foot churning under the sheets, and though the conversation has taken a dramatic turn, paranoia is easier for Billy than the previous anguish, the fear and sadness. Yes, delusions are preferable. Do seems to feel the same way because right then he calms down and settles back into bed, a lump once more. "They know," he says, relieved.

"Look," Billy says. "I'm five feet away from you and I'm not nervous. I think of you as a gentle person, I do, maybe too gentle and that's why these thoughts hurt you so much. It's the normal subconscious shit that most of us barely notice, or if we do, we're semi-proud to be so twisted, but for you it kills."

"How do you think of yourself?" Do asks.

"What's that?"

"Are you good or bad?"

"I don't think in those terms," Billy says, avoiding words like *Manichean* or *Zoroastrian* though they persist in his head like precocious students who moan *pick me, pick me*. "I'm more of a believer in gray."

"But deep down you must have a sense."

"A little bit of both," Billy answers.

"But say there was a gun at your head."

Luckily, at this point, Lannigan storms in giddy with something, which is finally made clear when Billy notices the dark stain around his groin. "I just peed my pants," he tells them. "Right in the middle of the lounge. I was talking with some guys, shooting the breeze, and suddenly I peed my pants. I put on a show of being upset, like what the hell is my body doing. You should've seen their faces."

30

THAT NIGHT, Billy lies awake in bed, thinking about bad and good, his thoughts slouching toward his parents. The word *messier* has caught his imagination, of Mom and Dad ending things with a shotgun and a lurid splatter on the wall. He should get up and go, hop on the next plane, that's what a good son would do. But a good son would've done so much differently, starting three years ago, five years ago, the goddamn beginning. It's all too late, he thinks, if not for that word *messier*. How long would it take for the bodies to be discovered, for the smell to seep into passing noses and neighboring yards, for the growing pile of mail to elicit curiosity from an already curious home? Weeks? Months? The bodies getting messier. Bills unpaid and the power turned off. Grass growing into suburban hay. Windows broken by Saturday night teens daring themselves into existence. Abe and Doris melting into myth and mattress. Until, finally, their discovery followed by a search for the son, the bad son who let this house turn into a tomb. Billy gets up. Lannigan and Do are sound asleep. Do makes small moans of containment, like inside his head a hand is teasing a puppy's cage. Billy tiptoes toward the door, his feet balanced on a tightrope of silence. In the hallway, the fluorescence stings his flesh as if skin has sublimated from vapor into solid without the cool liquefaction of morning. He glances left and right. No nurses, no security personnel. He listens. Nothing but the natural analog of the well-worn world.

Standing there, now crouching, he thinks, *okay, now what?*

That's when he starts sneaking into rooms. He inches open doors and edges through narrow shafts of light and creeps in and stays still until his eyes have absorbed the darkness. He waits for the nocturnal rhythms to

261

settle in around him, for the snores to breathe him into their dreams. The heads on pillows emerge in various shades of scotopic gray. He's ready for shouts of "Who's there?" and a speedy exit, but once he's certain he's gone undetected, he ventures forward, like a defrocked tooth fairy who can't give up the game. Going from bed to bed, he watches the faces sleep. They look so peaceful, almost lovely. They seem to hold a reflection of childhood. Billy is filled with benevolence. He wants to touch hair, tuck in sheets, kiss foreheads, smooth over any nightmares. A person sleeping is the sweetest saddest thing. Maybe because you're alone. Maybe because the sleeping person is gone from you. Maybe because you're both ghosts. Who knows?

He touches Gretchen's door (he could be testing the temperature for a fire inside) before slowly pushing it open. The TV is on. Maybe she's fallen asleep with the weather. Wider, wider, wide enough for his head to crook in and Billy sees her bathed in boob-tube blue, the watery light reflecting against her face with the sensuality of skinny-dipping which—she smiles. Christ, she's awake. "Hello," she says like a mind reader who senses her own presence in your every thought.

"Hi."

"Prowling around, eh?"

"Can't sleep," he says.

"Me neither. You might as well come in."

"Okay," Billy says, taking the bed nearest the door. A bass line of *act cool, act cool, act cool* pounds in his head, which seems the antithesis of acting cool, which, after further deliberation, leaves him dorky. "You're not watching the weather," he says.

"No. I'm newly hooked on a sports memorabilia home-shopping show. For the last half hour I've been watching two guys vigorously praise the wise investment strategy of baseball trading cards."

"Oh."

"But I love anything on late-night TV."

"Me too," Billy says.

"Public access—"

"The best."

262

"And the weird movies you find."

"And watch," Billy says. "You actually watch those late-night movies whereas other times you wouldn't bother."

"Very true." Inspired by the company, Gretchen begins traveling up the dial, pausing long enough on each station—A&E—so the show can sink in—*Law & Order*—and tease Billy with her taste before she moves on—Bravo—coyly—*Inside the Actors Studio*, Christopher Walken—but with consideration, like she's part of the Nielsen family—VH-1—their temptress daughter—*Behind the Music*, Rick Springfield—who understands the power of consent—E!—as she cruises the early A.M. offerings—*True Hollywood Story*, Adam Rich—clicking higher—MTV—languidly steering the remote—*The Real World*, Hawaii—serially unsatisfied—Court TV—while Billy watches her—*Trials of the Century*, Fatty Arbuckle—the cathode-ray tubes as flattering as candles—The Food Network—her tongue curling from the commissure of her lips—*Emeril Live*—her pupils wet with light—The History Channel—no doubt catching Billy in the corners—*World War II: The Bombing of Dresden*—and basking in her own rating share—AMC—while around her the room breathes with shadows—*Jules et Jim*—with Jeanne Moreau racing across a railway bridge dressed as a man—Comedy Central—Gretchen sliding her left leg from the sheets with the intrigue of a bare ankle glimpsed from under a hoop skirt—*Talk Soup*, scenes from *Jerry Springer*—as she climbs into the high two figures, the business loop of public access and pay-per-view and home shopping—QVC—and curls her toes and cracks the knuckle of the little piggy who had roast beef—Luxelon Floral Embroidered Twin Sweater Set, $49.95—and moves up into the scrambled neighborhood of the tenderloin.

Gretchen stops.

The vertical hold might be unhinged, the tones blurred, the frame fractured down the middle, twisting, trembling back and forth, but Billy instantly recognizes the world of subscriberless porn. Behind this waving curtain live the basic mechanics of sex. Billy's pretty sure they've entered the blowjob section of the fuck. The TV is a sonograph of *hmm-ooh-aah*.

"What do we have here?" Gretchen asks.

263

"The Disney Channel, I think," Billy says.

"You think?"

"*Pinocchio* is my guess."

"He must be fibbing his brains out."

"But she doesn't mind."

Bodies are split down the screen, half here, half there.

"Almost dirtier this way," Billy says.

"Certainly more acrobatic," Gretchen adds.

In front of them the amoebalike stud demands, "Oh yeah, suck my balls, baby," as if the line has been written expressly for this moment, as if somewhere between lip and shaft there's a cue, and Billy briefly thinks of Sally and their last sexual encounter. Porno words as a final good-bye. She's probably in Cambridge by now, the apartment in New York no longer holding any traces of their life together, just scratches on the floor, nail holes in the walls, his books probably returned to used-book stores from whence they were born, like salmon spawning another generation too cheap, too poor, to buy new, a dog-eared begot. Billy listens to every thrust, every grunt, as if hearing himself. The only natural sound emitted is horribly intimate and beyond control.

"How romantic," Gretchen says.

Billy squints. "I have no idea where the bits end and pieces begin."

"It's like spin art," Gretchen says. "With pink as your only color."

While they talk, the fractured couple contemplates their next move.

"I want to fuck you."

"You want to fuck me?"

"Oh yeah, I want to fuck you bad."

"Then fuck me bad, fuck my cunt."

"Oh, I'll fuck you."

"Fuck me now."

"I think they want to fuck," Gretchen says.

"I'm getting that impression," Billy says.

Billy stares at Gretchen, almost challenging her to ask *What?* My God, she's not beautiful. Her skin shimmers against *yes yes yes*, the light worthy of La Tour. Not beautiful and looking innocent the way people who've

264

seen everything can look innocent, as if all fault has been beaten from them. Her face finds purity in a smirk. Billy wishes he could touch her. If only they were in the same bed then he could play accidental footsie, could reach across the divide with his pinky and investigate her enthusiasm. Maybe other men would've gotten up and climbed into bed with her, but Billy is more subtle, shy until the first kiss. Okay, timid. Wimpy even. In the beginning. He depends on incidental contact, the bump that lingers, the handshake that sticks, the soft agreement that reclines. He tries seducing Gretchen by telepathy. He pushes the space between them, opens up his pores hoping he might feel small bruises of air.

"Billy?"

He—"Yes"—answers perhaps too quickly.

"Where do you suppose her legs are?"

"I have no idea."

"Or her head for that matter?"

"I don't know," Billy says.

He can fall in love so easily. Maybe not true love. Not undying commitment. God no. It's more the words, the verb form embraced by pronouns—*I love you*—the profound simplicity of the sentence. *I love you.* Amazing, the power of that syntax. In high school, in college, in studio apartments after too much drink he could suddenly drop *I love you* between belt buckles and bra straps. Not as a line. He just wanted to hear himself say the words.

"Fuck me up the ass."

"You want me to fuck you up the ass?"

"Yeah, right in my asshole."

"Your tight asshole."

"Uh-huh."

Thus follows a series of particularly violent seizures. At one moment the reception lands upright and roughly intact and remains frozen in place for one, two, three seconds and counting, the man and woman clear as a bell, the man pumped up, seemingly more interested in his delts and pecs, the woman constantly flipping her dirty-blond hair—they both grimace with phony pleasure as they fulfill the anal requirement of their contract, until finally, thankfully, this modern-day Paolo and Francesca fall back into the whirlwind.

"I better go," Billy says.

"You're leaving?"

"I should at least try sleeping."

"Are you tired?"

"No."

"Then why go. I can change." Gretchen waves the clicker. "Here, the weather."

"No, I should go. It's late."

"You can stay if you want."

But a feeling has come over Billy, a self-defeat in the face of love. He thinks about kissing her good night, maybe under pretensions of tucking her in and being sweet, but instead he waves and nods and slips away. In the hallway, in that harsh forensic light, he kicks himself for leaving. He should've stayed. Please, she had him watching scrambled porn. Is there a clearer message? Billy clenches his fists and grimaces as if electrocuted by this missed opportunity. He's always the gentleman by accident, and in retrospect, the rake. He thinks about turning around—just turn around and storm back in and tell her you forgot something, meander toward her bed and lean down and kiss her, barely implicate your tongue and curl your hand behind her head and leave your other hand flat on her chest, copping balance. Sounds good. Almost sexy. Maybe cheesy. Too silky smooth. Or he could stumble back in, all flustered and confused, and confess, "I'd like to kiss you very very badly," with an endearing stammer. Better. More honest. Practically the truth. But now just another rehearsed line.

Billy is spinning in circles when down the hall a door opens up. He spots Dullick sneaking out and creeping along the wall's edge. Four steps into his mission Dullick realizes he has company. "Schine," he startles.

"Hey."

"What the fuck you doing out here?"

"I couldn't sleep."

"Now what, you're guarding the hall?" Dullick farts. It's a toot of

266

interrogation, a gassy *Hmm?* He blushes. The big man is in poor shape, pale and sweaty and far from terra firma. Another fart escapes him, longer and more portentous. "Sorry," he says. "The food is killing me."

Billy nods his sympathy. Dullick is dressed in black and he carries a walkie-talkie. Maybe the absurd fantasy of Ragnar is a possible reality. Maybe this is the night of Operation Billy Schine. "What are you up to?" Billy asks.

"I could ask the same thing," Dullick says. Then he tilts his head and freezes, like he's heard a twig snap in the intestinal forest. Clearly, danger lurks in those dark places. Dullick spins around and scurries back to his room.

Billy goes to the door and eavesdrops. "Abort, abort" is hissed into the walkie-talkie, followed by desperate clawing toward the bathroom.

31

MONDAY IS the last dose day for Allevatrox; from here on in, all they do is bleed and give evidence of the drug scattering from their system. By Friday, they should be clean enough for discharge. The green normals swallow the after-dinner pills with celebration even though they still drool and twitch. The end is near. Money will follow. The nurse with the penlight and the tongue depressor checks Billy's mouth for the last time, and as a flirtation, Billy hides the pills in the back corner of his cheek. She spots them like cavities. "Cute," she says. "Now swallow." In the bleed room, Joy is gone. Ron, her replacement, tells Billy it's her day off. Ron has rough hands, as if blood is pulled from the ground. Billy begrudges him his sample.

That night, Billy watches the moths thwump the window like drops of light-hungry rain. He can see Do in the reflection. His hands are tucked in the Bible and his lips move silently through the minutes of Luke. A few moths take on a head of steam and slam the glass while others flutter and search for a way inside, going up and down, resting, and starting again. But Billy is more interested in Do. Earlier, he had thrown up. After dinner he had slipped into the bathroom, and the sound through the closed door was unmistakable: the ratchet of finger on epiglottis, the first few false gags, then the splashdown of fried chicken, peas, mashed potatoes, and butterscotch pudding for dessert. Billy and Lannigan exchanged looks. Lannigan seemed pleased, as if overhearing gossip; his hand covered his mouth with *what-do-we-have-here*. Billy moved toward the bathroom door, quietly because Lannigan had a point. Vomiting is a private affair. Billy overheard mumbling, almost a chanting in tongues made even more

Gregorian by the acoustics of the toilet bowl. It was a relief when another stomach-emptying aria interrupted the recitative.

Lannigan hopped out of bed and went to his section of the bureau where his toiletries (a city compared to the towns of Billy and Do) stood. He grabbed the Right Guard skyscraper, shook the can until primed, and paraded toward Do's side of the room. He began crop-dusting the sheets, holding his nose the whole time.

"What're you doing?" Billy whispered.

"Taking advantage of the situation," Lannigan said.

"Don't be a jerk." Billy knocked on the door. "Do, you all right in there?"

More mumbling, this time sounding like a didgeridoo.

"Should I get a nurse?"

Do shouted back, "No! No-no-no-no."

Lannigan stopped with his aerosol assault. "What we really need is an exorcist," he said. "This is beyond BO. This is closer to demonic possession. This stink stars Linda Blair." He returned to his skyline and picked up a phallic-shaped bottle of cologne. "Holy water," he said, "by Calvin Klein."

"Come on, Lannigan, enough."

"I agree. I have had enough."

Billy opened the bathroom door, pulling and peeking inside, a sort of neighborly *yoo-hoo*. Do was on his knees, leaning over the toilet and force-feeding his hand down his throat. Most of what could come up had already come up. Only spit remained. The bowl was a mess of what was once considered food but now resembled subhuman slop. Smelling like internal mildew, mustiness made chunky, it instantly reminded Billy of the fine line between puke and digestion. Do kept pushing his fingers deeper, reaching as far as yesterday's lunch. "Okay," Billy said. "I think you're done." But Do was undeterred. He tortured up empty gags, which he treated with contempt, as if somewhere the Gestapo were screaming *Speak!* Billy reached down and thought about patting his shoulder or gently rubbing his head, but those moves seemed too intimate, too paternal, so he flushed the toilet and told Do, "Let's take a break for a second."

Do's ID dangled in the bowl. This ten-day-old Do circled the drain and smiled for the camera, while the Do above him, incalculably older, took in the small drama of his official likeness spinning faster in the whirl, nearing that black hole and its end pirouette. But the chain held. The ID floated back to the surface. "There's more in me," Do said. "I know it. I can feel it. I didn't get it all. Not everything. There's more."

"You got most of it," Billy promised.

"Not nearly."

Billy handed him a wad of toilet paper. "Just do me a favor and sit back."

"I can still feel it in my gut." Do pinched his belly.

"Feel what?"

"They're slipping something extra in my food. I've seen them do it. They're preparing me. Getting me ready. You'll see. Soon enough everybody will see and they'll take me away forever. I need to get this out"—he began treating his belly button like pull tab—"because otherwise they'll be able to track me wherever I go."

Billy sat down on the bathroom floor, hoping he might impersonate comfort with proximity. "Do, it's the drug. You're having a bad reaction, that's all."

"It's not the drug. It's me."

"I think I should get a nurse," Billy said.

Do grabbed his arm. "Don't you dare."

"But this is getting serious."

Do glared, his heavy brow like knuckles on a ledge. "If you tell anyone, I'll never forgive you. That might not seem like much coming from slime like me, but know for the rest of your life there's somebody in the world who will never forgive you."

"Okay, okay."

Lannigan's voice, desperate for attention, broke through the bathroom, Lannigan standing over Do's bed, sprinkling the sheets with drops of cologne, chanting, "The power of Christ compels you" over and over again like a priest battling low-thread-count cotton.

"Lannigan, shut up," Billy shouted.

"The power of Christ compels you!"

"Shut the fuck up, I'm serious." Billy tried screwing his face so he might communicate the gravity of the situation, the absolute bad idea of the joke, but the high priest only continued.

"Don't listen to him," Billy told Do. "He's an idiot."

But Do was newly calm. The liquid tremble had washed away. What was left behind was colder and far more troubling, a certain smooth resignation, Billy thought, implacable, like a stone no longer submerged in a river but holding all the years of wear. Even Lannigan must have been struck because he stopped his little homage and tilted his head like he could hear what dogs hear. A slight tectonic shift. A high-frequency yell. Do said nothing. He just wiped his chin, got up from the floor, walked past Lannigan and crawled into his newly perfumed bed.

The cologne odor still lingers, bonded unpleasantly with funk. Billy watches Do's reflection in the window, wondering if Do is watching him, if their eyes are meeting or if Do is focused on the moths and the black beyond. Billy goes over and closes the thick curtains, explaining, "Bedtime," so Do might not suspect his dead harvest moon face is the culprit.

"You feeling all right?" Billy asks.

Without moving, Do gives the impression of nodding.

32

THE NEXT morning, Do is gone.

Nurse Clifford/George surveys the turned-down sheets, the decoy Do. His green jersey has been stuffed with laundry and his sweatpants have been shaped with toilet paper and towels. Headwise, he's an undershirt. Nurse Clifford/George picks up his ID necklace and reacquaints herself with the face of the vanished. The smell must be factored into her look of disgust, but mostly she's beady with suspicion, her chin weighted down with the early shape of the day. "If this is a prank," she tells Billy and Lannigan, standing side by side, sudden compatriots in the case of the missing roommate.

"No prank here," Billy says.

She gives Lannigan a long hard stare.

Lannigan touches his chest, *Moi?*

"You didn't hear him get up and leave."

"Nope," Billy says.

"You heard nothing?"

"Groans," Lannigan recalls. "Oh, sorry, that was me. I had a good night."

"Did he say anything about leaving?" she asks.

"No, but he was upset," Billy offers.

"Disturbed," Lannigan embellishes.

"How so?"

Billy takes the question, knowing Lannigan's opinion is not appreciated. "I think the drug was having a pretty bad effect. He was getting kind of delusional. He thought stuff was being put into his food, that he was being watched, that he was going to be institutionalized or something. He was really pretty manic."

"Is that your professional opinion?" the nurse shoots back.

Billy shrugs.

"Sorry," she says, glancing down on the impersonation of clothes. Billy can picture her cutting onions and remembering all the times she should've cried. She has a How-did-I-get-this-way look, a when-did-concern-become-a-chore pout. Funny, how a whole life can slip through a glimpse. "Certainly reeks," she says.

"Bloodhounds would find him in a second," Lannigan tells her.

Nurse Clifford/George bends down and checks under the bed, the execution of which gives Billy an undeniable view of her backside, that slippery bit of skin between pant and blouse with its underwear elastic and last trace of vertebrae, the pale smooth small, the torso's nape, sexy in all cases though Billy must admit feeling lewd for noticing.

"Do people sometimes hide under the bed?" Lannigan asks, thrilled.

"If this is a joke."

"Like scared little boys," Lannigan continues.

That's when Billy sees it, near the front door, curled up like a worm dried by the sun—a particularly nasty worm. He picks it up, needle-side up, and says, "Uhm," knowing this is explanation enough.

Lannigan stops kidding.

The nurse puts on rubber gloves before accepting the cannula.

"He really pulled out his cannula?" Rodney Letts asks during breakfast.

"Oh, yeah," Lannigan says, relishing his first-hand status. "Pulled it right out." Lannigan has taken primary ownership of the story. The news spreads through the cafeteria, from color to color, all mouths on Do and all eyes and ears on Lannigan and Billy like they're the bereaved. "Weird because I thought I heard a muffled scream last night, but thought nothing of it, thought it was a bad dream, but now," Lannigan shudders. "Obviously."

Billy only communes with his scrambled eggs.

Let Lannigan bask.

A cursory search of the premises has been conducted, the night staff rounded up and questioned—nothing—the surveillance tapes scanned—

nothing—closets and storage rooms checked—nothing—all the normal hiding places checked and rechecked. Do is still unfound.

"Think he's still here?" Rodney asks.

"Definitely," Lannigan says.

"Maybe he busted out."

Lannigan shakes his head. "He didn't take his shoes or his wallet."

This new information murmurs the air.

Joy says to Billy, "I hear your roommate's missing."

Billy nods. As always he's fascinated with her work, watching as she finesses his blood from the cannula, her hands so warm and soft, even under latex. "How much would it hurt to yank this thing out?" he asks.

"If done right, not at all."

"If done wrong?"

"A little bit, if the vein pulls, if there's pressure." Joy racks his test tube. "You know, I don't think I can even picture this John Rami character."

"He's the guy who smells."

"Oh him. I remember him. He covered his face when I took his blood. Unlike you, he couldn't bear watching."

Nigger, Billy thinks, terribly, *nigger nigger nigger*.

A more thorough search goes on after breakfast. The HAM security team sweeps the building, led by Carlson Dickey, who seems to have taken this personally, huddling his team in the hallway and saying, "We've got to find this individual ASAP because every minute is a minute too late." The loudspeaker announces his disappearance and says thanks in advance for everybody's patience. "If anybody has information on Mr. Rami's where-abouts, please contact the floor nurse." But no luck. There must be hundreds of hiding places, Billy thinks. He imagines Do jammed in a closet, Do huddled in a pile of laundry, Do hearing all the activity inspired by his disappearance, no doubt confirming his fears and leaving him certain in his belief.

"You have no clue?" Honeysack asks Billy. The doctor stands by the door and tries to look cool and casual, but he overthinks the masquerade with a series of minor adjustments, easygoingness as complicated as a golf swing.

"No," Billy says from bed.

Lannigan is in the lounge, the oracle of Do.

"We've pretty much exhausted our search," Honeysack says.

"All I know is he was in bed last night."

"You think he's all right, mentally, I mean."

"He made himself throw up after dinner because he was convinced you guys were putting something in his food. He was convinced he was going to be institutionalized. And with all this searching around for him, I bet he's even more convinced. The more you look for him the more he's going to stay hidden."

"But we can't stop looking."

"If you don't look for him, you'll find him," Billy says.

"I'm too tired for that kind of logic."

"I was thinking more along the line of quantum mechanics."

"That's the last thing I need right now."

"I told you he wasn't well."

"Look around. They're plenty of unwell people here."

"Just be nice when you find him," Billy says.

Honeysack frowns. "Of course we'll be nice. You think we'll be mean or something? He's our patient, or our pseudo-patient; anyway, he's our responsibility. We just hope he doesn't do anything stupid."

After lunch, Ossap and Dullick storm into the room, Ossap breezing past Lannigan's empty bed (Lannigan having embraced the search for Do the way a son embraces a mother's missing earring) while Dullick closes the door and barricades it with his bulk. "Your roomie has made everybody a little too nosy." Ossap speaks through a barricade of facial tics. "People are in our room, kicking around our stuff, looking for this jerk, this jack-off, this fucking"—he wavers—"yeah. It's fucking with me, it's fucking with us, and we're already sick and tired." He thrusts a thumb toward Dullick, who yawns and stands more horizontal than vertical. "So if you know where this cock-chomper is, you better tell, because we don't need to be

275

fucked with right now, not now, no, not now, with this little game of hide-and-go-seek disturbing our peace."

"Who are you guys?" Billy asks.

"Who are you, Mr. Roam-the-halls-in-the-middle-of-the-night?" Ossap counters.

"Nobody."

"Well, same here."

"So you're not here for anything in particular," Billy asks.

Ossap looks toward Dullick. "No," he says with a hedge. "Are you?"

"No."

"Okay then."

"Okay."

"You're just here, right?" Ossap asks.

"Yeah," Billy answers.

"That's the same with us," Ossap says.

"You're not working for anybody?" Billy asks.

"No. And you?"

"No."

Dullick says, "I think I'm going to throw up," and rushes from the room. Ossap walks toward the door, elbows splayed like a flightless bird. Before leaving, he turns around and asks Billy, "So a pride of African elephants on the Serengeti would mean nothing to you."

Billy, puzzled: "I wouldn't say that."

"Then what would you say?"

"I don't know, they'd make a majestic sight?"

"Wrong," Ossap tells him. "Go fuck yourself."

It's raining. No wind, no thunder, just rain falling like static. Billy watches the downpour from bed. It must be coming down an inch an hour. Any harder and the drops would lose their integrity. It's the kind of rain where, if you're outside for a second, you're instantly drenched. There's no running here. A dash to the car is as good as a swim. In that way, the rain is almost carefree, giddy, like Gene Kelly. Billy wonders if rain was ever so happy before 1952? But with Do missing, and his parents inching closer to their romantically proscribed date, pathetic fallacy is what gets Billy on his feet for a closer, more indulgent view of the summer squall.

Give rain a bit of thought and you're soused.

No other weather, not even snow, is as dangerous.

The middle of the sundial courtyard is flooded, thanks to its slight concave quality, another design flaw. The hand sculpture has been transformed into the centerpiece for a fountain. Water pours from the palm into a shallow pool around its base, the index finger pointing as if daring for lightning. The storm's bruised light does wonders with the bronze. It's like an odd optical harmonic, metal hums the eyes. Billy squints and unblurs the individual drops of rain, his head unconsciously nodding their descent. As he stands there, curious when the torrent will stop, this firework finale of rain, surely unsustainable, he catches a sense of *you're not alone* on his left. He pivots and sees Do in the thick accordion folds of the curtains. Do stares straight into the fabric. His arms are tight on his sides, his face is blank, his body is naked. The Bible is held tight to his chest, like some flotation device.

Billy, softly: "Do?"

Do doesn't move.

"Do, it's me."

Do remains committed to his invisibility.

"I'm not going to tell anyone so you don't have—"

"Leave," Do mutters.

"Where are we in Luke?"

"I'm out of time."

"Is this where you've been hiding?"

"Yeah."

Billy is briefly thrilled, the winner of the find Do contest.

"Now leave," Do says.

"You must be exhausted. And hungry. Why don't you lie down for a bit and I'll get you some food and something to drink. I won't tell anybody."

Do squeezes his eyes like a boy wishing away a bad thing. "Leave," he says.

277

"Even if they do find you, they're not going to do anything except maybe kick you out, which is what you want anyway, so put on your clothes and I'll get you a snack. They had Pop-Tarts for breakfast."

"I'm not an idiot," Do says.

"I know."

"Aren't you scared?" Do says.

"Of what?"

"Being next to me."

Billy shakes his head.

"I'm seeing you dead right now," Do tells him. "Ripped to shreds. I can see your head and it's three feet away from the rest of your body and you're a geyser of blood and it's awful. I can't help it. It's what I see."

"But I'm here," Billy says. "I'm not ripped to shreds."

"I don't want to hurt you."

"I know, I know." Billy tries investing his words with as much truth as he can muster. "And you won't hurt me, I know that too. You won't hurt anybody. I know that about you. I'm smart, remember. Now you can stay here for as long as you want. I'll sneak you food and water and tell you the coast is clear when you need to go to the bathroom. Because I know about hiding. I used to hide all the time when I was a kid. And this is a genius spot, so obvious, so right under their noses. I was pretty good at hiding too. I once told my parents I was going to a friend's house for sleepover but instead I stayed home and hid. I knew every great hiding place in that house." Like the top shelf of the linen closet, the cabinet under the bathroom sink, the corner wedge behind the television set, those spots where Billy would hole up and listen as his parents went about their day without him. He never heard anything but the mundane. "What do you want to do for dinner?" "I don't know." "I love you." "I love you too." "Now dinner?" "I have no idea." "Pasta?" "It's always pasta but pasta is fine." "Pasta then." "I love you." "Me too." Billy would wait for an opening, creep toward the front door, and slam himself home.

"Would you shut up," Do whisper-shouts.

"Yeah, sorry," Billy says, heading back toward bed. "I won't tell a soul."

*　　*　　*

278

During dinner Do remains the topic of conversation. Billy practically bursts with his secret, though now he has drifted into the realm of accomplice. He sits with Gretchen and Stan Shackler, mystery Ph.D. candidate, and Stan has changed the subject away from Do and toward something more to his liking: his reinterpretation of Nietzsche's idea of eternal recurrence. "But my spin on it," he says, primarily to Gretchen, "is the idea of the eternal rerun. See, Nietzsche's eternal recurrence posited that we are destined to live our lives over and over again the same exact way every time, that this life is the first run so we better be bold and make good strong choices because those choices will stay with us forever, that the true über-man would rejoice in this fact."

"And what's your eternal rerun theory?" Billy asks.

Stan Shackler raises his hands as if what he really wants to do is direct. "That with the onslaught of recording devices and reproduction equipment, with photography and video, the digital revolution, with all this entertainment around us, TV, movies, music, we as a race are no longer original. We've lost the first-run quality of our lives. Instead, we're living in the eternal rerun, the cliché, the hackneyed. At least Nietzsche thought this life was the first life. But I don't think that's the case anymore, not in this day and age, when we sit back and consume our life. The only way we can stomach this fact is by being superior to the material."

"What does this have to do with Do?" Billy asks.

"He's playing the escapee, the guy who snaps. Do's big bold choice is something we've seen a thousand times before. Because there are no more original gestures left except maybe blowing up the world. If originality is our god, then god is dead. Rugged individualism, that's long gone. All that we have left that is uniquely our own is DNA, hence the recent obsession with the human genome. It's the last gasp of the original, a little mark here instead of there and eureka, this is I. But I would argue that the death of originality is a comforting thought because when we are presented with true originality, with true genius, which still exists in the corners, we shrivel up inside and die. We can love it, we can pursue it, that rare great contemporary work of genius, but its presence is debilitating. Old master painters, they're fine because they have the added element of time, they're

279

already in syndication, but new masters, they're devastating. Current greatness makes us feel unspeakably small. On the other hand, the cheesy, the predictable, the bad TV show, the bad book, the bad movie, they're uplifting for we know we are better than that. Originality is what crushes the soul, not its opposite."

"Do you take this philosophy to heart or is it just something you flog?" asks Billy.

"Definitely take it to heart."

"So you surround yourself with mediocrity?"

"Hard not to in this society."

"You avoid the latest greatest movie?"

"No, I don't avoid it. I go. But while watching it I'm hoping the film stumbles, just a little bit, and if the film doesn't stumble, if it is truly great, or at least to my thinking great, I leave the theater feeling lesser because I'm nothing in comparison to the fiction on that screen, whereas a sitcom can fill me with metaphysical joy. Same with a great book, a great piece of music. Give me pulp and pop."

Billy notices Gretchen's body language leaning in the direction of this Ph.D. "Is this what your dissertation is about?" Billy asks.

"I refuse to discuss it."

"How far along are you?"

"No comment."

"But you're almost done?"

Stan Shackler flinches. "Please."

"Well, how many pages have you written?"

Stan Shackler gets up from the table.

Gretchen smiles.

"At least tell us how many words," Billy calls out.

The long day of Do nearly done, Lannigan says from bed, "He might be gone, but his smell lingers on."

Billy looks toward the curtains for a flutter of discontent.

"Where do you think he is?" Lannigan asks.

"I have no idea."

280

"Do you think he's gone totally nuts?"

Billy keeps his eyes on the curtains. "No."

"How can you say no. You saw him, the guy was losing it."

"It's the drug."

"Yeah, maybe," he says. "If I'd known he was so on edge I wouldn't have been so over the top." Rue suits Lannigan poorly, like a pair of tight loafers his mother insisted he wear. "I was just fooling around. I should never have offered to suck his cock for fifteen dollars."

"You did *what?*"

"I'm not even gay. I thought it was a joke. I was just expressing my inner swishiness. I've always had a gay sensibility and I'm fine with it. I just don't dig the whole penis-in-asshole part. I thought Do would've known I was joking. I was being locker-room queer, you know, like I'll suck your cock if you want for fifteen dollars. I thought the word *cock* was universally recognized as a joke. But maybe he didn't get it. Do *is* kind of an idiot. Sweet, but dense. A big old loser. If I said to you, I want to suck your cock, you'd know I was joking. I just think that Do is—"

"Lannigan?" Billy says.

"Yeah."

"Shut up."

"What?"

"Just shut up."

"What did I do?"

"Do me a favor and don't say another word."

"Fine."

281

33

ALL NIGHT long Billy is focused on the thick curtains and the small sways of fabric, Do as intermittent breeze. He could be a child's monster haunting the room's crannies. Every second implies *Boo!* But Do stays on the lam, no doubt starving and bladderful and scared. Billy is tempted to join him and turn this into a game of sardines. Lannigan would be next, then Gretchen, all the way down the hall until the curtain is bowed with bodies giggling at the approach of the last remaining player.

In the morning, Billy opens the curtains and stares down the inside seam to where Do stands, unmoved since yesterday. Billy pretends to admire the sun on the courtyard. "It's going to be a beautiful day," he tells Lannigan, hoping he might convey a sense of warmth and understanding, an ally-ally-in-come-free sentiment.

"I'm sick of this place," Lannigan says from bed.

"Well, we only have two more nights."

Lannigan scratches new-growth hair, particularly itchy around the groin. "I hope Do's all right," he says.

"I'm sure he'll be fine."

"I was just kidding around. Nobody should ever take me seriously." Lannigan's fingernails kick up a fury of sheets. "Typical the worst side effect I suffer from is my own stupid fault."

In the bleed room, Joy puts in a fresh cannula for the last few draws. "Still no sign of your roommate?" she asks Billy.

"No," he says.

"Are you all right?"

"Yeah."

"You're so quiet."

"How's Rufus?"

"He's fine."

"Good."

Joy tapes down the cannula, then draws a test tube of blood.

"I'll miss this," Billy says.

"You might be the only person who's ever said that to me."

"I will though," Billy says. "I'll miss this whole place. I wish they could extend the study, just keep it going, you know, or allow me to matriculate into the next phase. Sign me up forever. Let me be the first-in-man man. I'd do it for room and board, that's all. They could do anything to me, use my body for some scientific good. Crunch me, you know, like numbers. Break me down into base data."

Joy crooks her head as if peeking around Billy's words, to the source of the blather. "Are you going home to your parents after this?" she asks.

"Probably, unless something comes up."

"Like what?"

Gretchen, he thinks, a new life with Gretchen once the first kiss has been gained. Run away with her in the style of his parents, abandon family ties for the sake of love. Or there's Honeysack, Honeysack and his test, Billy strapped down and killed and possibly brought back, the first successful bypass of certain death, like da Gama going around the Cape of Good Hope, Billy living on as tricky currents navigated. Or dying in those waters. Yes, dying. The first death, the building block, the old college try. But first casualties are often remembered, even if in footnotes, William A. Schine a notation in the History of Great Endeavor, a trail for scholars with nothing better to do. No matter, this is more appealing than a Ragnar dispatch. Gretchen, Honeysack. "I don't know," he says to Joy. "Something."

Joy stares at Billy longer than his eyes can accept. She says, "I feel for you, I do. But your parents need you even if you don't need them and trust me, not going, not doing anything, will leave you worse off. So suck it up and go. You don't have to help them with their"—her forehead buckles into a staff of sad music without notes—"chore, but be there even if being there is selfish, so you can say to yourself 'at least I was there.' I know it's hard. But trust me, the other way will be harder."

Billy is briefly thrown by the sentiment, but he recovers and tells her, "I didn't realize I was on a couch," hoping he might defuse her sympathy with sarcasm.

"Fine, make fun of me," she says.

"I'm not making fun of you."

"Yes, you are."

"Am I really?" Billy asks, honestly unsure.

"It doesn't matter. Just go home, to your parents."

After breakfast, a new group of normals arrives, replacing the reds discharged earlier that week, a giddy mess. "They're coming, they're coming," Lannigan cheers from the window, seeing Corker lead a vanload of recruits through the courtyard. Billy hopes Do is hiding well in the curtains, but to Lannigan the curtains are a mere paranthetical to the action before him. "Finally," he says. He rushes over to his bed, to his duffel bag stashed beneath, and pulls out a squeeze bottle of ketchup smuggled from the cafeteria.

"You in?" he asks Billy.

"In what?"

"Our madhouse scene." Lannigan heaps his left palm with ketchup. "I'll be the victim, you'll be the perp. You can batter me into a delicious pulp."

"I don't think so."

"Come on, I need somebody."

"Let's not," Billy says, thinking of Do.

"No, let's."

"Why freak them out?"

"Freak them out? It's all in fun." Lannigan spurts a half-dollar-sized dollop on the bald bony knob of his forehead. He opens wide and loads his mouth with what seems to Billy a disturbing amount of condiment, then he primes the plastic bottle and slips it under his right armpit. Ready, Lannigan approaches the window. After a moment of actorly calm, he begins pounding the glass with tomato streaks of gore. This is followed up with a knocking of the forehead against glass, self-mutilation painted in broad B-movie strokes. The ketchup bottle under his right armpit splutters like a bagpipe player with a severed aortic artery. Just when Lannigan is ready for the pièce de résistance—the exploding mouth trick—he notices Do, his gobbed-up mouth mumbling, "Oh!" a second before Do springs forward and grabs Lannigan by both hands.

Ketchup falls to the ground.

Lannigan's eyes bulge as if a glassblower bugles the optic nerve.

Billy steps forward but still keeps a distance. "Okay, Do, settle down."

Do is unmoved. He squeezes Lannigan's hands into a tight bundle of fingers.

Lannigan yells, "You're hurting me," spitting phantom wounds on Do and himself.

"Do, stop," Billy ridiculously commands, like Do is his monster.

Lannigan begins kicking, but Do's shins are harder than toes.

"Enough," Billy says.

Lannigan begins screaming, "I found Do! I found Do! He's in here!"

Do bends down until his eyes are level with Lannigan's bunched-up fingers.

"He's in here!"

Billy wonders if the people in the courtyard think this is part of the show.

"Quick, hurry! I found him!"

Do moves closer, as if prepared to be blessed by Lannigan, pulling those clenched fingers toward his eyes, wide open, like black targets, the pupils never flinching from the approaching fingertips, while Lannigan squirms like a child refusing a parental hug, Do's eyes an inch away, now closer, Billy shocked by what he's seeing, but frozen, as if shock insists on fulfillment as fingertips enter eyes, forks for the eggs, the tips going in deeper and Lannigan crying, "Please stop," his hands transformed into hilts for jabbing swords, Do down on his knees, a disturbing liquid, like viscid tears, on his cheek, Lannigan retching, overpowered, his fingertips wiping clean the windows of the soul, "Stop him," he screams, then he goes limp, Do clutching his hands in place, the two of them dancers dancing Greek myth, a blinding pas de deux, Billy thinks, the thought striking him as absurd and releasing him from shock, Billy rushing over, a hand on Do, a hand on Lannigan, an incompetent referee until security storms in.

They must see the ketchup everywhere, all over Lannigan and Do, on the floor and window, and think a blade has been used on Lannigan, his head sliced open, his mouth looking like the tongue's been bitten clean through. They skid to a stop as if coming to an edge of a cliff. They take in Do, naked and imposing; they take in Lannigan weak and screaming. They rush Do.

"It's not what you think," Billy shouts.

Security tackles Do, flinging him, punching him, headlocking him, riot police on a bull.

Lannigan melts into a corner. He holds his hands like they've been dipped in acid.

Billy, the bystander, shouts, "Don't hurt him."

Security beats Do until blood and ketchup mix.

Lannigan wipes his fingers on his pants and then vomits.

Nurse Clifford/George runs in and plunges a hypodermic into Do's arm.

"He's already unconscious," Billy shouts at her.

But the nurse, adrenaline exhausted, backs into a bed and leans there, the aftermath too queasy for words. Security steps away from Do. Their arms are still ready for a lurch, like Do could be a madman in a movie and a final jolt is coming, time slowly giving way to the fluid on their hands and the fears of some kind of contamination, their heaving chests slumping into the fatigue of their own thoughts. Lannigan goes weeping into the bathroom, shuts the door, the nurse and security surprised by his spryness, considering his obvious wounds. Billy looks down at Do, *poor Do* a mantra in his head. His nose bleeds, his upper lip swells. His eyes are thankfully closed. Down lower, his penis rests against a mound of pubic hair like a gift from a forlorn lover. *Poor Do.* Billy goes to his bed, rips away the top sheet. Do covered seems to break the room's hush.

"What happened?" Nurse Clifford/George asks, shaken.

Security huddles amongst themselves, motherfuck blooming from the middle.

"What happened?" Nurse Clifford/George asks again.

Billy crouches down near Do. Touch his head, Billy thinks, comfort him, he thinks, stop thinking, he thinks, now kneeling, now thinking about acts of sweetness and how they might be portrayed, a hand caressing hair, a whisper of you'll be all right, a pillow crafted from lap. Poor Do.

In the bathroom a shower hisses.

Two orderlies arrive, a gurney on the way. There's no need to force Billy aside; he backs away accordingly. And soon, Dr. Honeysack is on the scene, "Jesus Christ," on his lips.

On the radiator by the window the Bible rests.

10:16 A.M. "He who hears you hears me, and he who rejects you rejects me, and he who rejects me rejects him who sent me," the time in Luke, no help, Billy thinks, closing the book and watching Do being lifted onto a gurney.

34

D O GONE, Lannigan leaves soon after. "I thought this would be a casual two-week gig," he tells Billy as he packs up. "Get out of the city during the height of the summer and do my thing and get paid decently. I didn't sign up for blinding." Lannigan shudders, balls his hands into blunted fists. No more Voltimand, now he's Lady Macbeth with eyes red-rimmed. "Shaving my entire body was my own stupid idea, but poking a guy's eyes out, that I never intended. What was he thinking?" Billy shrugs no idea. "I mean that must've killed. I could feel his eyeballs kind of roll against my—fucking awful. And my god-damn fingernails. Why was I growing them long?" Lannigan zips up his bag like quick stitching on a scar. "I don't need this in my life right now, the sight of that, that memory, that sensation. He must've been nuts. Did you see him when he was laid out on the ground?" Billy nods. "He almost looked content. I never thought my body would become an instrument for something like that. I can still feel it on my fingers, you know. Christ, he was strong. I couldn't pull away. I tried." Lannigan's bag thuds from bed to floor. "I'm gone." He gives Billy a wave instead of a handshake. His face seems shuttered and newly mournful, as if the marquee of Brad Lannigan, the show, is no longer running, Billy's, "So long," one more spray of graffiti on the stage door. "I hope he's all right," Lannigan says before leaving. "I mean I hope he can still see. Do you think so? I'm doubting it after what I, yeah, awful. Not my fault. Drug must've been doing something crazy in his head. I just hope he's all right. I wonder where they've put him."

This is the question Billy poses to Dr. Honeysack after Honeysack calls him into his office for a little talk.

"Who?" asks Honeysack, frazzled.

"John Rami."

"Oh, him. Terrible what happened. Certainly unexpected. We sent him to the hospital and they're keeping him under observation. The eye is a fairly resilient organ. He'll probably recover his sight, or some of it, at least. But we paid him in full and we'll pick up his hospital bill and maybe cover any other counseling that might be required. But whatever happened to him happened on his own accord, that psychotic break or whatever, that was his own thing. Now on to—"

"How can you say that?" Billy interrupts. "Of course your drug was responsible. In fact, I thought you guys would've called off the whole study after an incident like that."

"Not my drug, not my study. I want to be clear about that."

"But your company's."

Dr. Honeysack levels his eyes on the real world lingering just to the right of Billy's shoulder. "He was on placebo, okay. Once a volunteer washes, we access their file and check their dose just in case, so we can anticipate other possible reactions within the test group. John Rami was on placebo. He was taking sugar pills."

"Placebo?"

"So we're in the clear," Honeysack says.

"You know what 'placebo' means in Latin?"

"No. And I don't care."

" 'I shall please,' " Billy says. "It's vespers for the dead."

"Oh," Honeysack says without interest.

"Why the fuck would you people use that word for a sugar pill?"

"Don't be mad at me. You think I came up with the word?"

"Placebo isn't nothing," Billy says.

"Hey, but suggestion can only go so far," Honeysack claims. "Our hands are clean in this matter, legally. John Rami had a preexisting condition, a mental crack that after nineteen years finally broke. Maybe we were a catalyst, but you can't prosecute a catalyst."

"Yes you can," Billy tells him. "A shove is a catalyst."

"The behavior was his own."

" 'Placere,' to please. He was under the influence of—"

"Nothing," Honeysack says. "He was under the influence of influence. I also accessed your file so I could sleuth your status, and you're on placebo as well." Billy is disappointed but not surprised; all of his side effects seem so trivial, like an overactive imagination. "Brad Lannigan," Honeysack continues. "Also on placebo. Never would you find three roommates on placebo. It simply wouldn't happen. So I'll tell you what I think, and I'll tell you because I want you to trust me. What's going on here is something called a calibration study. A calbrat. Roughly every five years we have one and they help determine the effect of environment on the normal population. It's like weighing the container before putting in the contents. Calbrats give us a sense of the adverse effects of just living here for a few weeks. We get a baseline of stress and its manifestations, usually constipation, lethargy, coldlike symptoms, sore throat, sniffles, the stuff that always shows up regardless of the drug. But sometimes in these calbrats we study suggestion. Personally, I'm not a fan, not a fan of any kind of calbrats. They're a waste of time and resources. At the end of the day a regular study can divine real side effects from imagined side effects by simply crunching the placebos. Anyway, nevertheless, Hargrove Anderson takes great pride in their calbrats. It's a marketing gimmick. They load maybe ten, fifteen percent of the study group with actors and these actors perform the expected adverse events to gauge the effect of proximity on placebo. Quantifiable, I'm not sure. Sexy promotional tool, perhaps. But they claim to get a reliable percentage of unreliability in an average study, placebo or nonplacebo."

"Actors?" Billy says.

"Not always the greatest actors either. I've witnessed some horrible side effects."

"Was Lannigan one of these actors?"

"I have no idea. For the sake of double-blindness, I'm out of the loop. I should say, this is just a guess, but it's an educated guess."

"So nobody's on anything?" Billy asks.

"In my opinion."

"So whatever we've been feeling these two weeks has been phony."

"Not phony," Honeysack says. "Just free-floating."

Billy shakes his head, half-pleased, half-depressed. "So we're the ass-holes who get high on oregano, drunk on grape juice. We can't even suffer legitimately."

"But the conclusions are as important as any real study. Or at least some people think so." Honeysack leans forward, as if the air is clearer below this innocuous conversational smoke. "But that's not why I want to talk to you. I want to talk about something else."

"What's that?"

"We have a window."

"A window?"

"A window of opportunity. A very small window but a window nonetheless."

"What kind of window?"

"For us to do something."

"Us?"

"If you're game."

"Is this for your deep-freeze study thing?"

Honeysack frowns. "That's not what we're calling it."

"Do you have a name yet?"

"Not yet. But we have an opening—"

"A window."

"—to test our work."

"To preemptively kill someone before they die."

"In a matter of speaking."

"Manner," Billy says.

"Manner?"

"Yeah. In a *manner* of speaking, as a *matter* of fact."

Honeysack grimaces.

"So what are you proposing?" Billy asks.

"What an idiot, of course *manner*."

"Do you want me to get into a bad car accident or something?"

"The trauma itself isn't necessary."

"Oh."

"We'd like to prove our thesis before they drop our research and take the write-off. 'It's a good idea impossible to execute' is what they've told us. Trauma care will always insist on the best possible treatments before our experimental procedure can be attempted, and as a *matter* of last resort, our work will fail more often than not. It needs to get in early and take hold in order to slip the patient into this hypothermic chrysalis."

"To buy some time."

"Exactly, then the ER can determine with a bit more leisure the best course of action. Problem is, we've come up with a breakthrough that can't be tested properly. We can't use it because we need the proof and we can't get the proof because we can't use it. The danger in field-testing this thing without informed consent is that if it doesn't work, then hospitals will get sued. We can show eighty percent success in animal studies but animals don't have lawyers. But we have a window," Honeysack tells Billy again. "And we have discretionary R&D money left over, and we have access to the proper equipment, and we have a moment where nobody's looking, and hopefully, we have you."

Billy smiles. "So you want to use me."

Honeysack glances down like his lap is vibrating. "Yeah."

A skid of unease in his stomach, thoughts locking up on slippery desire, if all this talk should be acted upon for what? the dubious hope of self-transubstantiation, his own flesh becoming his own flesh? or if he should turn away and apologize to Honeysack for words once again said without meaning, Billy, unsure, asks, "What would you do to me?"

"I promise you won't feel anything. We'll knock you out. It'll be like having your wisdom teeth removed. Then we'll flush your aortic artery with something we've developed called Sal-Gid, a solution we chill to forty degrees Fahrenheit. Then we'll wait. Your body will start to shut down all unnecessary function and just service the essential trunk. Vitals will slow down to almost nothing, an in-between state, a stasis. We'll keep you this way for thirty minutes, and then we'll start bringing you back, gradually, by degrees, until you're like all the happy dogs we've seen who are none the worse for wear."

"So you kill me."

"No, not at all. Or if so, just barely. It's like we're pushing the Pause button. The things we've done to dogs and chimps, inflicting massive trauma on them, breaking them up pretty bad and then flushing them with Sal-Gid and putting their demise into a sort of superslow motion while we move twenty-four frames a second, it's like that but without the trauma."

"Do you know Frank Gershin?" Billy asks of the man and his canvas of scars.

Honeysack nods. "Unbelievable, huh? See, Sal-Gid would be a perfect application for military use, for hospitals in the field, for people just like Frank Gershin coming in all shot up, of course in his case by friendly fire, but that's beside the point."

"Frank Gershin?"

"Yeah, he got those wounds in Desert Storm."

"He was in Desert Storm?"

"Yeah."

"I thought it was something else," Billy says, curious where the truth lies, Kuwait or Queens, if the truth even matters. "So when would you do it?" Billy asks.

"Our window is Friday afternoon, the day of your discharge."

"That soon?"

"It's that or nothing."

September 3, Billy thinks, the day before his parents' scheduled death. He could beat them to the punch and be spared the news, spared the survival, spared the rod of their spoiled life. Funny how stars can line up, how circumstance can scream. If he lives, he lives, and maybe in recovery, whatever recovery that might be, he'll know what they felt, heart stopped, heart restarted, and he'll feel in that banal but awe-worthy repetition, beat upon beat, a sense of who they were. "What would I get paid?" Billy asks.

"We might be flexible on this but we've come up with thirty thousand dollars."

A thousand dollars a minute for thirty minutes of death, Billy calculates.

293

"We think it's a good offer. There's a chance something could go wrong."

More than sixteen dollars a second.

"There's a chance you might die, not a big chance in our opinion, but a chance."

In the other direction, sixty grand an hour.

"And death would be a big problem for us, for you, of course, but for us as well."

$1,440,000 a day.

"Particularly in terms of explaining your death."

$10,080,000 a week.

"We might be able to chalk it up to a coronary occlusion or thrombosis or something. That's a thought. You just dropped dead, sudden death syndrome, something congenital. We could do the autopsy ourselves and nobody's the wiser."

$40,320,000 a month.

"But we want to cover all the bases."

$483,840,000 a year.

"So what we were thinking, me and my colleague, is that on top of all the release forms we're going to want you to sign, if maybe you could"—Honeysack grins as if the words about to be spoken must be summoned from his bowels—"well, if you could write us a suicide note. Just in case. That way, worst-case scenario, we could chalk this whole thing up to a depressed man. That's what we were thinking. A classic overdose, which we could pull off no problem. Nobody's suspicious of a dead body in a hospital. We would simply bypass the normal operating procedure. Keep it internal. My colleague would do the death certificate, and we'd notify next of kin and give over the suicide note and there, done, finished. Because at the end of the day, a doctor is as good as a cop."

$174,182,400 in federal taxes.

"But you're not suicidal, right?"

$58,060,800 in state and city taxes.

"Because that's very important, that you're of sound mind and body.

Otherwise it'd be unconscionable for us to let you do a test of this severity." The small office is ripe with Honeysack, a bitter, soaked-in smell, the brown rings on white Oxford armpits like a half-drunk cup of coffee forgotten on a radiator. "You're not suicidal, right?" he asks.

"No," Billy answers. "I'm sane."

Honeysack smiles unnaturally. "That's what I thought. You're as sane as they come. You're just playing the percentages and you understand the odds are in your favor, hugely in your favor. You're perfect for our test. Smart, educated, sensitive to the need for extreme secrecy. Because we have a window where we can actually do this, a small window that's about to close for good."

"Friday afternoon?" Billy asks.

"Yep, from three to six. Three hours but we'll only need one."

"What happens afterward, if everything goes well?"

"Worst-case scenario, and I mean that in the best case, you'll go to my colleague's house for observation. He has a nice guest room. Best best case you'll be groggy and sore and probably still spend the night in his guest room, just in case."

"Okay then," Billy says.

"You'll do it?"

"Yes."

"This is great." Honeysack rah-rahs his fists.

Billy wonders if he should bow. Honeysack has never been so animated, not necessarily a positive development. His face is more suited for a courtroom sketch. And what has Billy done by saying yes to this suddenly giddy doctor? The chances of death churn like the reels in a slot machine, the payout tray ready for 120,000 quarters. Yes, the money would be nice, and the odds are more than decent. Absolutely, the money is the thing, Billy thinks. Pay away a large chunk of Ragnar and gain peace of mind. But in the spinning cherries, oranges, lemons, bars, and bells, there is another symbol, a metaphor, a cheesy image of almost dying, of being reborn. Should he endorse such hackneyed crap? Should he allow himself such self-indulgence? There must be a special level in hell for those who die for the sake of their own gesture, perhaps the eighth level, among the fraudulent. No, the money's the thing, Billy assures himself, good old-fashioned greed. But in that deep breath, as the coin slips in and the lever is pulled and the three wheels blur blue-red-yellow-orange-blue, there's the other thing, the thing that speeds between loss and gain.

Billy gets up from his seat. "So Friday."

"Friday it is."

As Billy leaves, Honeysack stops him. "Billy?"

"Yes, doctor?"

"Don't forget that suicide note."

35

THROUGHOUT THE day, Billy thinks about his theoretical suicide note. He borrows, rather begrudgingly, a pen and a few sheets of yellow tablet paper from Nurse Clifford/George, who seems to fear a prank with the pen, who hands over the pen like its future debasement is dangerously close to her fingertips.

"You can keep it," she says.

In the newfound privacy of his room, Billy arranges himself in bed with *The Oxford Dictionary of Quotations* acting as desktop. How should the note go? What should its tone be? Good-bye cruel world or the world is too much with me or I have not loved the world or O world! O life! O time! The pen conducts the air over the paper. God knows what his father is composing back home, probably a three-hundred-plus-page note with chapters and illustrations. That whole house is a suicide note, Billy thinks, their whole life a sentiment of adieu adieu on a fog-heavy marsh as vengeful family approaches with torches blazing and dogs barking. Theirs is the sorrow of impossible love that's moved to Cincinnati. Billy figures they're doing what they should've done a long time ago, when they had the power to truly devastate family and put a notch on the annals of grief. Now it's too late.

Billy wants his suicide note to be explanatory and apologetic, to carry a sweet sense of nobody is to blame, this is the best thing for everybody concerned. But who is his nobody; who is his everybody? Who will mourn his death? Who will even remember his life? Who will do anything more than mutter "too bad"? Sally? Ragnar? Friends in New York, friends from college, friends from high school, all of whom knew Billy as the friend of friends, always on the periphery of the group, the eighth, ninth phone call, hearing news third-hand, never an usher or groomsman, but, if a big enough wedding, why not invite Billy Schine? He's the perpetual alternate. What should he say to these friends? *Guess what, I'm dead.* Who will read this suicide note anyway? It's not likely to be published in Class Notes. At best, his death will register an In Memoriam, a small jab of mortality within those words of self-regard.

Billy is interrupted by Gretchen. "You excited for tonight?" she asks standing in his doorway wearing bunny rabbit slippers and her silk peach bathrobe. She resembles morning gone eccentric, a younger Miss Havisham who's been jilted from bed.

Billy, flustered: "Excited?"

"For the big Chuck interview."

"Oh yeah, that's tonight."

After all the heavy promotion—*Finally, Chuck Savitch will speak, and believe us, you won't want to miss it*—the idea of not watching the interview seems impossible. It's like rubbernecking in traffic and you screaming from a distance but as you get closer you slow down and participate in the mess because you deserve your due after all the waiting, the sea of red brake lights teasing you with the same halting solemnity as the voice-over artist—*Chuck Savitch, in his own words. Hear what he has to say.*

"You're going to watch, aren't you?" Gretchen asks.

"Probably."

"Probably?"

"I'll probably watch."

"Oh," she says. "Because I'm definitely watching it." Gretchen sizes up the postmortem of the room. "You have a single now."

"Yep."

"I heard the amount of blood wasn't to be believed."

"It was mostly ketchup."

"I heard blood was shooting from John Rami's eyeballs."

"Not really."

"Awful."

"That's true."

"But now you have a single."

"Lucky me."

Gretchen bends down slightly, like she's watching her head against the low frame of a bad mood. "You all right?" she asks.

"Medium," Billy says.

"Medium what?"

"A little depressed."

"Well, it's almost all over."

"Maybe that's what I'm depressed about."

Gretchen does a dégagé with her cotton-tailed left foot. "About leaving here?"

"Maybe."

"Maybe you're coming down from the drug?"

"I seriously doubt it. Can I ask you something, honestly?"

"Honestly." Gretchen plants her left foot on the ground; she could be an allegorical statue, a sort of Eros trampling on bunnies. "Sure," she says. "You can ask me anything, honestly."

"Seriously."

"Seriously. Honestly. You might want to watch those adverbs."

"I'm serious."

"I'm getting that. And I should be honest. So go ahead and ask."

"Are you really participating in this study or are you pretending?"

"Pretending what?"

"To be here."

"That's the strangest question I've ever heard," she says. "I'm here. I'm like you. I'm like everybody else."

"So you're not an actor?"

"Please," Gretchen says with distaste.

"Not that you would tell me if you were."

"Acting is a great profession which is unfortunately made up of actors. But I'd tell you if I was an actor."

"So you're not acting here?"

"Like really acting? No, of course not. Why do you ask?"

"I've heard things."

"About me," she says with matter-of-fact terseness.

299

"No, not about you."

"No?"

"About this place."

"Not about me?" She seems almost disappointed.

"About actors performing side effects," Billy says.

"Why?"

"To test their effect on people."

"Why do they care about the effect actors have on people?"

"To see how susceptible people are to suggestion."

"By actors? I'm confused."

"Never mind."

Gretchen shrugs and smirks without smugness, nailing the prick of her loveliness. "I just came to see if you wanted to watch the Chuck interview. I always find it better if you have company for these kinds of things; otherwise, it seems pathetic. But obviously you have bigger things on your mind."

"Just the two of us?"

"If you want to bring some of your actor friends, be my guest."

"What time?"

"Any time before nine."

"Okay."

Billy skims his blank suicide note. "Do you know what Hart Crane said before he killed himself? He was on a cruise ship, drinking heavily, and he climbed up on the rail and turned around behind him and said, 'Good-bye, everybody,' then leapt. That's all he said. 'Good-bye, everybody.' Supposedly witnesses reported that he was last seen swimming strongly."

"I'm embarrassed to admit I have no idea who Hart Crane is."

"No reason you should. He was a poet in the twenties. Wrote this epic about the Brooklyn Bridge. Here." Billy opens the book of quotations and settles on Crane and a tidbit from *The Bridge*:

> *"And why do I often meet your visage here,*
> *Your eyes like agate lanterns—on and on*
> *Below the toothpaste and the dandruff ads?*

And did their riding eyes right through your side,
And did their eyes like unwashed platters ride?
And Death, aloft—gigantically down
Probing through you toward me, O evermore!"

Billy tries putting Gretchen's eyes in those lines, eyes that might span time, that might hoist the dread in his chest and swing him like a boy on wires imagining himself a bird, not Poe, but Warwick in the tunnel, on the rails, Billy reading aloud, knowing this is just a glance from the poem long ago read in college, long forgotten, Hart Crane mostly remembered as a romantic suicide, the delusion of a poet convinced of his failure, Whitman's doppelgänger, the professor said, Billy looking toward Gretchen as he finishes the lines deemed worthy of quotation, searching her eyes, thinking, despite the mixed metaphor, let your eyes hear me in these words, please, in the negation of a negation.

"Pretty, I suppose," Gretchen says, unmoved.

"It's just a piece of a much longer work," Billy tells her.

"Well, not much without its context."

Billy silently agrees.

During dinner, meatloaf and mashed potatoes, Billy is in the midst of listening to himself give a long eulogy, an honest eulogy about himself ("*He was not a particularly cheerful person yet he had a certain joie de misérables, a more individualized weltschmerz, a kind of schlock luftmensch, which, with its enthusiasm, was infectious if a tad taradiddlesome*") when tablemate Luke Sillansky says, "Now she's just mocking me."

She must mean Gretchen. Billy's ears perk into the conversation.

"To go to Barry Pica," Sillansky says with disbelief.

Billy spots Gretchen a few tables away, and yes, she's sitting with Barry Pica, laughing with Barry Pica, resting her hand on the shoulder of Barry Pica. Barry Pica, the not-ever-worth-mentioning? He's the dregs of the dregs, friendless even here, his desperation for popularity making him ill suited for even lackey status, only a few minutes of cruel fun. Historically speaking, he's the tap on the shoulder you dread, the reason you avoid high school reunions, the person you might feel sorry for if he had a nanosecond of self-awareness. Barry Pica, already nicknamed "That Fucking Idiot," seems to have his entire past unwittingly taped to his backside. The worse thing is that he's always happy and preternaturally optimistic.

"It must be mercy," Stew Slocum says, his knee going nuts under the table.

"You don't give mercy to a prick like that," Sillansky rants. "Give him an inch and he'll follow you forever. That guy makes mercy a dangerous thing. A halfway friendly hello is like saving his life."

"Aren't we touchy," Slocum says.

Sillansky stabs a wedge of meatloaf and holds the fork near his mouth like a gruesome microphone. "All I can say is I'm glad I got my licks in early."

Billy (what was that, what was that just said about licks, what's this small bit of information so casually dispensed that spins Billy, that blanches him if not publicly certainly privately, that recoils his insides and whiplashes the air he breathes, with Sillansky chomping away on spongy meat as if nothing has happened, as if the earth remains steady beneath his feet, while Billy rocks as if every atom is reforming, recasting him into a ridiculous state of flesh, his ID tick-tocking the twelve days before this second, now a few seconds ago, when Billy was naïve, by far the worst offense) thinks maybe he misheard.

But then Herb Kolch agrees.

"But you were after me," Sillansky brags. "I was first. You got my sloppies."

"You're like extra hot sauce. But Pica, man, he's anchovies."

"I like anchovies," Rodney Letts says. "Maybe I should go next."

Craig Buckner jumps in. "She's obviously scraping the bottom of the barrel."

Rodney grins. "I like bottom scraping."

"She only blew me," Buckner says. "But I'm glad."

"Yeah, right," protests Kolch.

"Yeah, right, that's right. I don't fuck sluts."

"She let me pretty much do whatever I wanted," Stew Slocum boasts.

302

"I hear Gertner had quite an experience," Buckner says.

Sillansky curls his lip. "And I thought Gertner was the lowest."

"That woman," Kolch mutters.

"But Barry Pica is easily the lowest," Sillansky says.

"How about if she does me?" Rodney asks.

"You?" Sillansky's off-kilter eyes crumple. "She'd need a fucking jackhammer to get any lower than you."

They all laugh.

Billy sits dumbfounded during this exchange. Of course he's upset. Or not upset but disappointed. Okay, crushed. While he and Gretchen have never graduated from flirtation, he thinks maybe she likes him, and vice versa, and yes, he thinks, or thought, that maybe tonight, during the big interview, something will be said between them and fingers will intertwine like suspension cable, and Billy will forsake Honeysack for Gretchen's sake, the two of them meeting up after the study, yes, standing by that bronze sculpture, bags packed, two thousand dollars richer, and saying, "Where to now?" perhaps tackling this question side by side. Yes, he fantasized. Nothing sexual, nothing about her sharp nakedness and stern mouth and variety of moles and freckles on her arms and neck that hint at bigger mysteries. His fantasies had run more rose-colored, embarrassing in light of recent revelations. A silly montage. A love-will-save-the-day sort of thing. How could he be so dense? He dreamed of kissing her while everybody else, evidently, was screwing her. And these guys here, not quite the cream of the crop. How many have had her? Do they assume he's a statistic as well? Hearing them talk, their camaraderie, their locker-room misogyny, Billy senses he's missed something else. These people have evolved into chums while he stands half-formed, part acquaintance, part stranger.

Stew Slocum slaps the table with excess hilarity.

As always, Billy is the last to know.

Gretchen squeals with delight. "Can you believe this?" she asks.

"No," Billy answers from the neighboring bed.

The interview is not going well. It started well enough, with a brief video introduction for those people living in caves: the chronology of

Chuck, birth, typical childhood photographs, school, the town he grew up in, the normal fluff seen thousands of times. It then tackled the last frenzied month, the MRI, the tabloid story, the sensation of Chuck, the doctors, the pilgrims and their firsthand accounts of something special happening here, something unmistakably holy. This was followed by the famous reporter inside the now internationally known ranch house on 410 Cedar Lane, touring the home with the sister and mother of Chuck who recounted warm stories about their Chuck growing up, showing the small backyard with the rusted jungle gym—a real terror, he was—going into his childhood room still decorated with heavy metal posters and barely clad women which instantly date Chuck 1987. From the bedroom the camera panned toward the window where outside, gathered on the front lawn, a crowd sang hymns and held signs of Christian support. The famous reporter asked if they could have ever imagined such a scene, the two women shaking their heads, never in a million years. Next came Chuck himself. He was hospiced in the living room with a state-of-the-art hospital bed, a large-screen television, a DVD player, a VCR, all these goods donated by local Menomonee Falls businesses, even the full-time nurse who smiled as she took Chuck's pulse and wiped the spittle from his slack lips. There were glimpses of the day in the life of Chuck, his meals and massages, his constant care, his medication, his friends visiting, *rock on,* his uncle who wore a Savitch Towing and Plowing T-shirt and baseball cap, *you stay strong, boy.* There were tidbits of all the mail he's received, ten pouches worth, none of them get-well cards but instead notes of inspiration, some enclosed with drawings from children, Chuck crayoned in a smiley-faced heaven, Chuck holding hands with a stick-figure Jesus. Other letters sounded like résumés of pain, with photos attached of loved ones too sick to travel but please say a prayer if you could. "They break your heart," the sister said, holding them with the regret of a casting agent who has already filled the lead. Then finally, after all this and a round of commercials, there was the interview.

And it's not going well.

Chuck is bedridden between mother and sister. His mouth is lolled open, and it seems his neck is unable to support the psychic weight of the brain tumor. He's just proclaimed himself, in soft but unmistakable words, the left gonad of God.

The famous reporter squints through her third eye-tuck. She appears a bit uncomfortable in this setting, considering the celebrity homes she normally visits, the retreats and estates and mansions, not this kind of place where dreams come to die. Her facelift has a hard time registering meekness. "What do you mean by that?" she asks with professional seriousness.

"That's the cancer talking," the mother of Chuck answers.

"Of course, Mother," the sister of Chuck says.

"It's doing something to his brain."

"Obviously, Mother."

"And the morphine. The poor boy is on morphine. For the pain."

"Mother, please."

"And he's always been a joker, oh Lord, yes. I think he was probably having a joke on you. Right honey, one of your jokes. But I tell you, it's the first thing he's said in a couple of days. We think the cancer's gotten into the talky part of his brain. But it's nice to hear him speak even if it is off-color." She beams down on her son and gently rubs his head. "You wicked wretch. You've been saving up your strength for that!"

"Mother, please." The sister of Chuck battles the daughter of embarrassment.

"What?"

She gestures toward the famous reporter.

"Oh," the mother says. "Sorry."

The famous reporter smiles. "That's quite all right."

The mother shakes her head. "I still can't believe you're in my living room."

"Mother!"

"You might act all sophisticated, like this is no big deal, but that's your generation." She turns toward the famous reporter. "They think our little town is a mile away from Hollywood. But me, I'm old-fashioned and I'm sorry but I'm starstruck. Oh, the people you've interviewed. I bet you've got the best gossip. Maybe later, hmm."

Gretchen claps her hands. "This is unbelievable."

"Sure is," Billy says with less enthusiasm.

"Why so glum?"

"I'm not in the greatest mood."

Billy looks toward the TV where Chuck is in close-up. A question has just been asked—"How do you feel about all this attention?"—and Chuck lies there, staring toward the distance, his eyes empty, his strength sapped from his last reply. Breathing is rough on him, white-capped with moans that spill drool and glisten his chin. There are no more jokes left, no wiseass comments, only a certain dumb seriousness that transforms his features until Billy realizes what he's seeing is unspeakable. It's the slow nothing. It's probably where his own mother is right now, holding a shiver of what was once there, a tiny bit of life huddled in the cold corner, clawing for warmth. The question is repeated. The mother of Chuck reaches over and strokes her son's hand. Sadness is under her normal good cheer, this brawny woman, large and loving and probably pretty tough, a woman not unfamiliar with bars and bad men, a storyteller, a laugher, perhaps of Bavarian stock mixed with the mongrels of America. She's proudly unsophisticated. She's easy with herself and easy with her son, easy with the knowledge that his smile is what she lives for. But the sister is tense. She's all speak, you bastard. Dressed up, made up, a hundred times rehearsed in her own mind, she grips her knees and seems to telepath the right response to her brother, the perfect response, and as usual, he isn't listening. Now the silence is becoming awkward. The sister wedges her face as if nothing but ice stands before her and she must break through it to escape. Damn her brother and mother, they can stay behind and freeze together.

"Blessed and moved is how we feel," the sister says for him. "We feel like we've been given a gift, a gift from God that we're sharing with the whole world. And it is moving people. People are moved. People are touched. They feel the presence of God right here. We all do. It's a radiance." She raises her hands beatifically.

"Well," the mother begins.

But the daughter keeps talking. "They say he might be a victim soul,

306

that he takes on suffering for other people, that's what they're studying, the church officials. They says it's a pretty strong case, what with the evidence outside, all the people who've claimed, well, not healing, no, there's been no substantiated proof of that, not yet, but a vast improvement in mood. It's hope, I think. A lightness of spirit. That's what Chuck here has done."

"Excuse me," the mother says. "Can I get one thing straight? He's 'Charlie.' He's never been 'Chuck.' He hates 'Chuck,' ever since being called Up-Chuck in third grade. I'd like to make that clear once and for all."

" 'Chuck,' 'Charlie,' it doesn't matter, Mother. What matters is what he represents. He's a vessel for God's true light. It's Him saying I'm here with you."

"Great, so God gives my boy cancer."

"He's a victim soul, Mother."

"I'll still be burying my son, my only son, in the near future."

"Mary did the same."

"I'm no Mary."

Charlie lies there, a net for this rally.

The famous reporter jumps in. "Charlie, do you feel like a vessel of God?"

The question passes through him.

"I'm sorry," the mother says, "but like I warned, he isn't talking much anymore, with all the pain medication and the tumor growing. You're tired baby, aren't you. So tired. Close your eyes if you want. I don't blame you for not saying anything even if you could."

"Mother!"

"Nancy, enough."

The sister suddenly gets up. "I think we should stop the interview. Can we stop? My brother's not having a good day and obviously my mother isn't either and this just isn't working out the way it should, so let's stop."

"Fine, leave," the mother says. "I've let you handle things long enough."

"This interview is over," the sister says to the camera. "You can edit around this and just keep the inside look. Maybe we should open up the curtains and you can get a shot of the pilgrims' reaction. Or better, they can come in and have a moment with Chuck, a laying of the hands, and you can witness their being overwhelmed by the spirit which is really nice."

The mother of Chuck grabs the daughter's arm. "Look at your brother," she says. "Look at him. That's your brother and he's dying. He's dying in the most awful way. I know you had your problems with him, but he's dying, and he's not dying for your sins, or my sins, or anybody's sins, he's just dying, plain and simple. Next year this bed will be gone, the people outside will be gone, the reporters will be gone, all this hoopla will be gone, and all that will be left is a grave. A victim soul. I don't mean to belittle anybody's religion, but that's silly. Maybe suffering has a bit of grace to it, but don't tell that to the person suffering or to the mother of the person suffering because you'll end up with spit in your eye."

"Mother" is yelled with the tenor of Judas.

"I don't mean to spring this on you," the mother says to the famous reporter who is far from upset. "But this has gotten out of hand. Maybe for a second I enjoyed the attention. I know Charlie did. I thought it was worth it if he was happy because I knew what lay ahead. But we're at what lays ahead, you know, and I think it's high time we flip on all the lights and tell people to go home or drink somewhere else, this bar is closed."

"Mother, this isn't about you."

"Oh, yes it is," she says.

The family of Chuck has been replaced by the famous reporter who sits in the studio and chats with her co-anchor. She shares with him her impressions of what they have just seen and how the more complicated personal story often lurks behind the public story. They both nod thoughtfully.

That's when Billy gathers his nerve to just say it, not now, not yet, wait a second, like a stuntman judging the wind, the overall rightness of the moment that once taken can't be taken back, heart racing, eyes closed, deep breath, jumping, "Did you sleep with Sillansky?" His tone is far from cool. He hears the thud in the question, the voice-cracking honesty.

Gretchen turns toward him. Her face shimmers with a Jeep Cherokee storming across the American West. "Has he been talking?" she asks.

"He and a few others."

"I thought my ears were burning," she says.

"So it's true."

Gretchen narrows her eyes, tilts her head toward one o'clock as if this is the hour of someone else's reckoning. "I plead the Fifth, prosecutor."

"Barry Pica? Don't tell me that's also true."

"Okay, I won't."

"I mean, Sillansky, fine, but the rest of them?"

"Are they all talking?"

"Of course they are."

"Good," she says curtly.

Billy goes from prone to upright. "Can I ask why?"

"Maybe it's a side effect."

"Can we be serious?"

"About what?" Gretchen asks.

"About why you slept with all these guys."

"Do you want to know why them or why not you?"

"Leave me out of this."

"I did actually."

"Look," Billy tells her. "I'm your friend, right, I mean, we're friends, and I just want to know why you'd do something like this because it doesn't seem healthy."

"Healthy?" she says, confounded.

"Maybe that's not the right word."

"Try another word. I'm dying to know what it is."

"It seems . . . sad," Billy puts forward.

Gretchen flinches as if slapped with open-palmed pity. But she quickly recovers. "Well, maybe I like sex. Maybe this is a dream come true, being the only woman with all these men. How would you feel if you were the only man surrounded by women? Not bad. Kind of thrilling. Maybe this happened by accident. Maybe I was expecting to feel something, you know, from the drug, and when nothing happened, maybe I came up with

309

my own idea. I got bored. I saw all these men. And I started thinking about them. In two days they'll go home, back to their non-normal normal lives, and invariably they'll tell stories. They'll tell their friends about their insane time here, testing experimental drugs, the side effects. You know, the money might be good and easy, but you don't do something like this without knowing you're getting a good story. It's the main reason I came. I wanted one of those stories that make people go 'huh?' The story is the biggest perk. You know what I mean? The story sort of premeditates the exploit. It's like jumping from an airplane knowing the only reason you're really jumping from an airplane is so you can tell people you've jumped from an airplane. That's half of the fun. It's the same here. Then I got here and it's just boring. I'm getting nothing out of it. And I started thinking about the men, how they were flirting with me like I was some great beauty, and I thought maybe I'll give them a story, or add something extra to their story. I could almost hear them with their friends back home. The craziest thing is I fucked this chick, I did, seriously, dude, the wildest fuck of my life. Duh, duh, duh, duh, duh. The sex itself was a joke. Trust me, the sex was nothing. And seven guys is the grand total. But for me, the excitement comes after the fact, when I imagine them remembering me a week, two weeks from now. And they will. Absolutely. Even without telling the story, they'll remember me. I'll pop into their heads. I'll be that flash during the daily grind. Oh yeah, that girl, that crazy girl in Albany. I'll sneak into their dreams. I'll become their sex-movie moment they'll replay at will. You ask how could I with Barry Pica, well, precisely because he's never going to forget. I'm his sexual highlight."

"More like punch line," Billy says.

"You don't really believe that. You probably couldn't name the people you went to high school with but until your dying day you'll be able to remember the people you slept with there. I don't know. It's like every time you sleep with somebody new, you lose a bit more of that awkward virginity. Unless you're a rock star or a super stud, you remember, but even Wilt Chamberlain never lost count. He knew the number. He could probably sit down and list maybe not the names, but the bodies. Don't tell me you don't remember every lay let alone every kiss."

310

"That's probably true, but remembering is the by-product of passion and affection and drunkenness and idiocy and intimacy, all those things that get you into bed. To sleep with someone just to be remembered seems, I don't know."

"Don't you want to be remembered?"

"Not by people I'd rather forget."

"I want to be remembered," Gretchen says quietly.

"For being an easy lay?"

"But in their minds I'll become much more than an easy lay. Think about your own one-night stands. Don't they carry a certain fond recollection, a kind of Oh-my-God-did-that-really-happen magic? Even the bad ones, after a time, become youthful indiscretion. I think they can have more staying power than a six-month relationship; more mystery, that's for sure. Maybe you cringe but you cringe with delight. And you men in particular, you're insanely nostalgic about your sexual past. Even if you're happily married, happily dating, you boys are always reaching back and remembering the ones who came before. Ha! A pun. Don't tell me that's not true. I had an ex-husband who presented me with a list before we got married, a list I didn't want but a list he wanted in exchange for my own list. It's not a criticism, not at all. It's almost sweet, how you boys will chase memories and spread your genes in retrospect. It's what preserves monogamy, I think. In my book, adultery is a fundamental breakdown in imagination."

"You've given this thought," Billy says.

"I have," Gretchen says.

"Maybe too much thought," Billy says.

"That might be true. But it's not like I've slept with a ton of men. I was very faithful to my husband. And before I was married, there were only eight other men. But I'm getting older, you know. Or old enough. And maybe I'll get married again, though I doubt it right now, but maybe. In the meantime why not leave behind miniature relics of myself while I can. And this place is ideal. Everybody has been screened for AIDS and STDs. Everybody is basically clean. And the best part is I'll never see any of them again."

"I get it in concept but not reality. I mean, Barry Pica? It's like you're a whore who gets paid in occasional happy thoughts."

"Fuck you."

Billy, having already jumped, fallen, landed alive if wounded, hobbles toward the edge of another precipice. "But I care about you," he tells her, immediately despising his voice. "I like you," he says, determined to go forward. "I've liked you since the van ride. There's something about you that clicks. I see you and I feel something snap in place."

"Sounds as romantic as a dislocated shoulder," Gretchen says.

"I'm trying to be serious."

She smiles without affection. "You're sweet."

"I'm not normally called sweet."

"Maybe I'm screwed up enough to consider you sweet. And I like you too. But my project here, I don't want it following me home. I'm not interested in strays. It seems to me this can only work if it stays my own secret. Otherwise, it becomes part of my past. I don't want that. And you're sweet, funny, and smart, but you're young, and you're looking for something big, something huge and special, something life-changing, whereas I'm looking for something much, much smaller, something I don't think you'd even notice." Gretchen stretches and yawns like tiredness is a waterfall she's stepped into. "Now I'm exhausted and need to get some sleep." She turns off the TV, the bedside light.

"So that's it?" Billy asks in darkness.

"What?"

"You have no feelings for me?"

"It's not that. It's more a matter of scale."

Billy gets up. "It's so cold, your little history project."

"The past is a cold fire but at least it burns." Hearing herself, Gretchen can barely contain—not glee, Billy thinks, her lips are too lopsided, her eyes too bright with understanding, as she curls up in bed and begins gathering sheets to her stomach, hugging them the way some people sleep, Gretchen alone, Billy standing by the door, hand on handle—no, not glee, he thinks, and not melodramatic snickering though the words certainly slant in that direction and she knows it, and he knows it, as he glances back in the style of a forever-leaving lover, but there's no ridicule in her face, only—Billy opens the door and is greeted with light which slants into a third of the room, never touching Gretchen though the messy edge bleeds into her like a distant tucking-in—what, he wonders, what is there, as he waves more good-bye than good night (fingers frozen in half-mast), and steps into the hallway, gently closing the door behind him and walks back to his room, passing Rodney Letts who insinuates cunt-licking with his tongue and looks hell-bound for Gretchen's room and his own piece of history—what was he feeling, sad, lonely, sympathetic, thinking of the past coldly burning in Gretchen and her barely contained resignation.

"Rodney," he says.

"Yeah?"

"In all honesty, if you go in there, I'll break your leg."

36

T HURSDAY AND the AHRC is giddy with lasts, every hour kissed good-bye and every minute tied up with a bow, the air outside, the life surrounded by that air, beckoning like a memory soon to be revived. Billy stands by the pay phone. Twenty dollars bought him fifteen dollars in change from the usurious Nurse Clifford/George, plus he has his own meager pocketful. All totaled, he has nearly seventeen dollars. As he slips in the quarters, he can smell the heady odor of the U.S. Mint, the thousand touches of commerce, the daily transactions between customer and till and the laughable inconsequence of such tender.

He dials (513) 555–1313, the number like one of those movie numbers that instantly bump into the elbows of the audience—*That's fake*—but in this case puts Billy in contact with Cincinnati information which then passes on the number for the Whispering Pines Assisted Living Center. Billy dumps in the rest of his change for credit. A receptionist answers and he asks for Doris Schine's room. "Is this Abe?" she asks pleasantly. "No," Billy says. "It's his son." The receptionist embraces the moment with quick connection. Billy waits, waits, waits for his father to pick up. He's determined to say nothing of value—no rolling his tongue around suicide, no final sentiments, no explanations, no teary good-byes. Nothing is on the menu except hello. He just wants to hear their voices, have a sense of Mom and Dad, be in the same room with them even if telephonically. He wants to feel the weight of what might soon happen.

Finally, the phone—dropped-knocked-dragged-banged—is answered. "Hello?" Billy says.

Silence.

"Hello? Hello-hello-hello?"

Breathing, Billy hears labored breathing, or not labored but dismissed with groans, as if every lungful is a small disappointment.

"Mom?"

Still nothing.

"That's you, isn't it?"

There's licking, or lip smacking.

"It's me, Billy. Is Abe there?" Stupid to ask a question, Billy realizes. It's miracle enough that the rare synapse fired and she answered the phone. Embrace that, he thinks. But the licking is disheartening, like a treat gone sloppy, so Billy talks against that sound, talks despite the empty sound of his own words. "Abe must be at the airport, or on his way from the airport. Do you know that? He hangs around the airport when he's not with you. Strange, huh? Yeah. So. Anyway. You know I'm sorry about all this. Really. If I'd known earlier I would've done something, or said something, but I didn't know earlier, I didn't know until it was too late. My fault, probably. I'm sorry I'm not by your bedside or something, but Abe's there, or usually there, and I think I'd be in the way. I'd spoil it for the two of you. I'm just calling to say . . . I hope what you're going through doesn't hurt much. I hope you're not feeling anything, you know. I hope it's like sitting on the beach and looking at the ocean, something like that, though I'm sure it's not, but I hope it's quiet, peaceful. You know Abe wants me to come home to help with the, well, the end, I guess, move it along for the two of you, but I was calling to say I don't think I can do that. Not that you can leave a message. Besides, I might beat you to the punch. But I wanted you to know that I've been thinking about you."

Yes, he has been thinking about her, thinking about her face in particular and how it must've changed over the last few years, Billy aging her in his head, like those children who go missing for years and are beckoned with computer renderings of how they might look right now, after adolescence, the softness gone hard, the parentless life. Doris was never beautiful but she was shamefully vital, the sort of woman who would never complain unless all the air was gone and even then she would muster a deep breath and make due. Stout, red-haired, and easily freckled by the burning sun, she would've survived the Oregon Trail without a word. But

315

Doris in bed, holding the phone, lives without context. For Billy, her face is only a concept of time, like a pumpkin opened up for Halloween and enduring the front porch until New Year's Eve. He can no longer remember what was carved. All he can recall is the blade.

Billy huddles the pay phone, his breath fogging nickel. "You know what my strongest memory of you is?" he says. "I'll tell you and then I'll hang up because all I wanted to do was say hi. But my strongest memory, the memory I can close my eyes around and fall right back into, is when I was eleven years old and the next-door neighbor, their daughter, Becky, Becky Malone, remember her, remember when she had chicken pox and you insisted that I go next door and play with her so I might get chicken pox too and be done with it. I was like no way because she was older and maybe I had a tiny crush on her, having her so close, you know, as a neighbor, even though I never said a word to her, but I was kind of in love with her. I always thought one day we'd talk and she'd have that oh-my-God-you-were-under-my-nose-the-whole-time sort of reaction. Anyway, I remember you dragging me next door, you ringing her doorbell, me squirming under your grip, and Mrs. Malone answering—she was not a fan of our family, then again, who was. You know people called our house the crypt because they thought of us as being sealed up inside. Every time the doorbell rang and nobody was on the other side, that was a dare. Well, Mrs. Malone, she sees you, sees me, has a sick daughter and dinner to fix and she's annoyed with what-do-you-possibly-want. That's when you ask if I can play with Becky. She's like, no, she's sick, and you tell her that's the point, that you want me to get chicken pox and be done with it. I'm old enough to be painfully embarrassed and I also know that Mrs. Malone has a good mouth on her and this is going to be her gossip, those crazy Schines, nothing you'll ever hear, but I will at school, through the trickle-down of scorn. You tell her—"

"Younger is better with this sort of thing." Billy's mother leveled her practical green gaze on Mrs. Malone.

Mrs. Malone defended her own brand of sensibility. "But Becky's in bed."

"It'll be just a minute."

"I don't think so."

"We'll be in and out."

"She's feeling miserable."

During the exchange, Billy became intimate with the rhododendron by the front door. Its natural beauty seemed like an outcrop from the world inside that house. The plant's leaves were as waxy as Mrs. Malone's skin and when in flower matched the woman's preferred eye shadow.

"Any older and it gets serious," Doris continued, undeterred. "And God forbid he goes into adulthood without being exposed. So if you wouldn't mind, it would be a favor for his future health."

Mrs. Malone stretched her lips around her teeth and clicked, "I don't suppose I can say no." She moved inside as if a salesman had worn her down and she'd suffer the pitch but buy nothing. The house was clean and bright, decorated up to the minute instead of the Schines Cuban missile crisis hue. Though the two houses had the same design, Billy took in the rooms wondering how they possibly translated next door. A sunken living room? A sun room? This home spoke French. Every inch of wall space was covered with photographs of Becky and her older football-hero brother, pictures matted like an advent calendar revealing all the days of skiing and sailing and the big game in 1982.

"Becky won't be pleased," Mrs. Malone said. "Girls this age can be so vain."

"We could blindfold the boy," offered Doris.

Mrs. Malone thought she was joking, though Billy knew better. His mother was simply being reasonable, this reason often reflecting a naïve no-nonsense manner. Her son was a series of problems to be solved until the problems were no longer hers. She never complained, never bitched or moaned, but she went about him like he was a minimum-wage job that offered barely enough.

Becky's door was painted pink, like an Easter egg. Inside the room the theme of pastels continued, with frilly curtains and a princess bed holding a scratching beauty no suitor would kiss. Becky Malone looked medieval in her plight. Pustules, red and angry, some raw, some white-tipped, some

317

bleeding together to create a superpustule, covered her skin. How she might recover seemed impossible to Billy. On her hands were large skiing mittens, a soft defense against nails opening up craters. Billy noticed they were taped on, like boxing gloves. Becky had no chance of slipping them free unless she used her teeth. "Mom, why are there people in my room?" she asked, attitude masking hysteria. Her throat was smoky with chicken pox.

"This is your neighbor," Mrs. Malone said.

"So?"

"Well, he wants to get chicken pox so he can get them over with."

"So?"

"So he's going to spend a little time with you."

Becky's eyes burned brighter than her skin. "You've got to be kidding."

"Chicken pox can be serious with adults," Mrs. Malone explained.

"You don't think this is serious?"

"I don't mean it that way."

"Look at me!"

"I know, honey."

"And you're letting in visitors."

"It's just—"

"Are you charging admission?"

In the midst of this squabble, Doris whispered, "Breathe deeply," and scooted Billy toward the infectious bed. He obeyed against his better judgment and future schoolyard repercussions, obeyed, as always, because he had little else to offer his mother but gentle compliance. He drifted toward Becky, blond Becky, thirteen years old, who often wore her hair like those long pretty streamers that hung from the handlebars of her bike that she pedaled around the cul-de-sac, circle upon circle, whirling the air pink. But today she was furuncle red. Billy apologized with his eyes. But he was also in Becky Malone's room, which was kind of exciting, near Becky Malone's bed, which was kind of exciting, in the presence of Becky Malone's nightgown, hundreds of flowers and the cutest frill, which was really kind of exciting, her exposed scoop of chest covered in nipplelike bites. Billy breathed in deeply. Oatmeal, he smelled, and balm.

318

"What're you looking at?" Becky spat.

"I'm sorry," Billy said.

"Get closer," Doris whispered.

Scabs were drying into scars and Becky Malone screamed.

"Oh honey," Mrs. Malone said, going toward her daughter.

"I can't stand this another second."

"Honey—"

"How could you have done this to me."

"I was just being neighborly."

Billy turned toward his mother. Often, when eye-to-eye with her, he'd wait for some recognition of affection—this was his mother for heaven's sake—and when nothing flashed between them, he would look away. However, today, as mother and daughter embraced in front of them, with shame and anger and abiding comfort, Billy thought he recognized something in his mother's face, a sense of inarticulate regret. Doris offered him her hand, not out of warmth but out of escape, that we should leave this world and return to our world, and Billy went toward fingers that, once found, gave up the clutch for the sake of hustling him along.

"Hopefully the chicken pox took," she told him on their way home.

"Of course," Billy says on the phone, "I didn't get chicken pox. And Becky's face never quite recovered, and that girl had the most beautiful skin. Not a pimple throughout high school and she was covered in pockmarks." Billy listens for a sign of change under his mother's breath, a rhythm of subaerial understanding, but nothing is different. His story was far from fluent. It was nothing like his memory which could open the door of that house, that room, where Becky cried, a butterfly finding herself inside another chrysalis, unexpected and cruel, where Doris held out her hand for him. His words fumble from intention, spiral away from sentiment and land hilt-wise against its target. Just another strange story about dear old mom. "Anyway," Billy says. "I'm just calling to say hi and maybe I'll—"

There's a sound, an extended beep from one of the twelve touch-tones, and Billy thinks maybe she's accidentally resting her chin on the keypad, stretching number 7, 8, or 9 into oblivion, obviously not hearing it, or if hearing it, not minding it, this shrillness, not moving away but remaining still. Maybe she's fallen asleep. Maybe she's screaming over him with a well-placed finger. *Enough!* Or maybe it's something else, a last desperate attempt at saying something. Who knows, but the tone doesn't stop. It keeps going. One obliterating note. And Billy stays on the line and hums along in slight sympathetic vibration until the automated operator informs him he'll need more money, and soon after, he's disconnected for lack of change.

37

THAT LAST night, a noise. Around two in the morning, a noise in the hallway, and Billy rustles awake. This is not a place that creaks, like an old house. This is new construction, and after a few days, all the night noises have been cataloged. The central air—*ka-duum*—pumping in its fresh batch; the toilet communicating with another toilet that's been flushed—*chaaa*—like a communal cleansing breath; the courtyard spotlight clicking near the window—*ki-ki-ki*—in a halogen pulse. These are the normal noises, the AHRC's REM. But Billy bolts upright when he hears something, something, he swears, being dragged in the hallway.

No matter how murderously baroque, Ragnar comes to mind, Ossap and Dullick revealed. There must be a chemical reaction in the brain that brews a killer in a midnight noise. Receptor sites suck up old fears until you're a boy again with your various escape plans. You could jump out the window. You could lock yourself in the bathroom. You could pretend to be asleep. You could hide in the closet. You could cover yourself under the sheets and lie real flat, barely breathing, as if nobody's in this bed, nope, nobody here. Billy calculates the probable order of death, the homicidal feng shui of a psychopath. He'll likely move down the hall, from room to room, and slit throats with the routine of a hotel maid. This would be the fourth room. There should be screams, bloodcurdling, canary-in-coal-mine screams. Unless, of course, he's the only victim. The dragging continues down the hall, fading with a creepy old lady *hush*.

And that's the only noise.

Until now.

Ninety-three minutes later and Billy hears whistling outside the window, gentle entreaties coming from the courtyard, loving calls, kissing lips, enthusiastic claps, barking—yes, he hears dogs barking. All of this seems like midsummer night's dream stuff that sneaks through the heavy curtains. On the other side could be the frantic backstage of sleep. It's the sound of anxious wooing. Certainly better than the earlier *hush*, but equally mysterious, and while Billy is curious, he's also comfortable and goes through the sort of profit and liability reasoning more often associated with a full bladder and a warm bed. If he gets up any chance of sleep will be squashed. Then again, he's already awake and piqued. The floor must be cold. But not *that* cold. Just close your eyes and tomorrow will prove these noises ridiculous. But if you get up, you'll be satisfied. And feel stupid for the effort. Either way, do something. As it always seems, this debate goes on longer than necessary, to the point of false countdowns (in five seconds) and mini-motivational lectures (*go go go*) until finally (*fuck it*) Billy rolls out of bed.

Time: 3:23 A.M.

Parting the curtains (the anticipation in finding the seam and inching back the fabric and peering outside is almost sensual, and Billy lingers, giving the moment more oomph, knowing this is performance, suspenseful foreplay in the style of edging your fingers along another's waistline even when there's no question the pants will be removed), he catches the source of the noise: nearly a dozen people bustle about the courtyard in chaotic synchronization. It's not far from woodland sprites, Billy thinks, from Puck and Co. if they were clad in black and their heads were sheathed in ladies' pantyhose, if they were incognito goblins scurrying around with ponytails of empty feet. Billy spots two vans parked no doubt illegally near the HAM sculpture. It's like the great bronze finger has finally hailed its ride. A few of the goblins are hunched over, tapping their knees *here-here-here*, while others run about waving their arms, pointing, giving thumbs up, gesturing *come come come quick*. All this action is being documented by a goblin with a video camera lashed to his right hand. Sensitive to every jiggle, he seems to be doing a form of cinemagraphic tai chi. The overall strangeness of the scene allays any need for explanation. Billy just watches, dumbfounded but pleased, feeling certain this has nothing to do with him.

No, these goblins are after different game. They're herding animals,

322

mostly dogs, from the center's east wing. Beagles scamper free as well as mixed breeds with strong traits of Labrador and German shepherd and some sporting pointer. There's a golden retriever with its belly shaved; a cocker spaniel with a cone around its neck. The more energetic dogs speed around the courtyard in frantic circles, their hind legs hitched in tight serpentine. The fast chase the faster, their mouths nipping *It!* They tackle, roll, yap, bound toward grass where pissing and shitting must be more pleasurable for they muster an endless supply. They're beasts stoned on smell. But a majority of the dogs are far from enthusiastic. They are the ones in the midst of experimentation, nurtured with disease and recovery. They barely move. Instead, they lie down, or worse, step-step-step, collapse, and struggle to get up again. They limp. They shiver. They lick worn bits of overly kenneled fur. Some wear backpacks in the mode of sporty dogs who jog and hike with their sporty owners. But these dogs are the sportless; they carry the machinery of their own demise.

"I feel like"—Billy turns around—"we're on a sinking ship"—and sees Gretchen standing by the door. Lit from behind, she resembles a ghost who is sick of the haunting part. Despite everything, Billy is glad for her company.

"It's unbelievable," he says.

"Who are they?" she asks.

"No clue."

Gretchen drifts toward the window. "Animal rights, I'd guess."

"Yeah."

"Do you think security has any idea?"

"I would seriously doubt it," Billy says.

"Yeah, stupid question."

More animals are brought into the courtyard: rhesus monkeys clutched none too gracefully, Chimps hugging their rescuers sweetly. Cages are lugged from indoors and dramatically opened for the camera. Out flee rats, mice, gerbils, bunnies, the jetsam from a sinking ship. More dogs are brought forth, lame dogs who must be carried. The goblin videographer rushes over and films a pit bull convulsing in somebody's arms.

"This is awful," Gretchen mutters.

"Look at that dog," Billy says of a largish breed with a cone around its neck and a scar on its shaved chest.

"That's a Bouvier des Flandres," Gretchen tells him. "That's a real breed."

"And how about that one?"

"That's a vizsla, another expensive dog."

"And that?"

"A basenji."

Billy thinks of Eden, and he's Adam pointing to an animal in the distance and saying, "Dog," and Eve shakes her head and says, "No, Chesapeake Bay retriever."

The goblin videographer is summoned to the HAM sculpture. Across the wrist a banner has been unfurled (unreadable from this angle). Under the impressive thumb knuckle, two goblins, short and tall, stand in the camera's headlight. They must be making a statement because they flamboyantly gesture toward the AHRC behind them and the pitiable animals all around. The taller goblin holds a hairless rhesus monkey, which he thrusts forward, much to the displeasure of the monkey who leaps out of his grasp and lands on the head of the shorter goblin. Its claws instantly dig. The rhesus-affixed goblin tries pulling the monkey free, but the monkey has a good grip on pantyhose and hair, ripping both apart. The taller goblin tries helping his friend by grabbing the monkey's scruff, but stocking and scalp are like taffy and the monkey isn't letting go. The afflicted goblin now screams (audible through the glass) as the taller goblin yanks and pries. The fellow goblins briefly stop herding animals and watch this struggle, some obviously amused, and the videographer keeps on filming like this will be perfect for the blooper reel. Finally, the monkey abandons its position and leaps for the higher ground of the sculpture, springing from thumb to index finger. It hugs the bronze trunk like a memory gone weird. The shorter goblin dabs his head while the taller goblin tends to the worst of the scratches.

That's when Billy recognizes them. "Ossap and Dullick," he says.

"You think?"

"I'd bet my life."

324

Behind them, the third floor begins to bustle.

The hallway fills with shouts and naked feet slapping.

News filters in of the night nurse found tied up.

Word is the lounge has the best view, but Billy and Gretchen stay together. They watch Ossap and Dullick as they do another take for the camera, their statement this time more subdued and lacking in props. Ossap speaks while applying pressure to his forehead; Dullick rips his black shirt for a makeshift bandage; Dullick reaches for Ossap; Ossap swipes Dullick away; Dullick, shirt ruined, crosses his arms; Ossap, frustrated, divests himself of the tattered pantyhose and screams at the videographer who removes his own pantyhose and hands it over for the sake of anonymity. Thus Carlson Dickey, the security guard preacher, is revealed. He starts filming take three.

"There's security," Billy says.

"What do you think they're saying?" Gretchen asks.

"I have no idea."

In the hallway, the newly freed night nurse screams, "Everybody back into your goddamn room, right now, no screwing around! We have a situation here!"

Yes, Billy thinks, a situation. The friskier dogs have noticed the rabbits. They are now giving chase. The rabbits don't stand a chance. They're too drugged, too chemically cooped up for evasive maneuvers. They're ripped apart, torn open, played with until lungs stop squeaking, then abandoned for the next flash of fur. It's a massacre. The courtyard, the massive dial of that clock, might as well be the floor of a timeless abattoir. The goblins try their best. They kick the dogs halfheartedly (animal abuse not their natural instinct) and scoop up the injured bunnies and run for the vans. They're all running for the vans, bringing as many animals as they can muster, like this is Saigon, 1975. *Move move move!* Those left behind are urged toward the safety of the woods, but the dogs, the mice, the rats, the lone rhesus monkey atop of the bronze hand have no understanding of freedom, not in this world. They watch the vans speed away with little more than passing curiosity, more interested in the cool night air, the moon, the sirens in the distance flashing the horizon red, the brief recess of life unbounded by prescription.

"Run away," Gretchen says, like a filmgoer talking to the screen.

Billy reaches for her hand, and she accepts it, neither one saying a word. He holds her without flirtation, fingers cupping fingers, nothing more, nothing less, their palms creating something a few degrees warmer than normal body temperature. They stand like this not forever, no, obviously not, but long enough so that time loses its grip and surrenders to heartbeats with no sense of the clock, only the immeasurable rudimental damp of a first touch. The remaining dogs chase down the last of the rabbits. Mice bump into nothing as if searching for the walls of a maze. The monkey balances itself on the raised index finger and reaches up into the air, wanting something higher than bronze. Billy and Gretchen watch this, holding hands, until the night nurse, a schoolmarm of the imagination, orders Gretchen away.

38

T HE NEXT morning, the final morning, the specifics of last night trickle in.

It seems Ossap and Dullick accosted their roommate, Stew Slocum, in the middle of the night. Bum-rushed him, Stew tells people during breakfast, though in truth he was sound asleep and duct-taped to his bed. Similar assaults happened on other floors. Every color was involved, some in teams, some solo, all coordinated precisely. Carlson Dickey was rumored to have disabled the entire night security staff, a notion Billy thinks absurd until Dr. Honeysack's confirmed it after breakfast. "That's true," he says. "Supposedly he had a gun, a toy gun it turned out. That's our top-notch security for you, immobilized by a water pistol."

"So who are these people?" Billy asks.

"Animal rights nutcases," Honeysack explains, unconcerned, other business glinting behind his sleep-deprived eyes, his pupils like self-concocted speed pills. "Some extremist branch of PETA. SHAME is what the banner said: Stop Heinous Animal Medical Experimentation. It's a new one on our enemies list. But anyway."

"I bet they came up with the acronym first," Billy says. He pictures the group brainstorming around a table, tossing out words and deferring their meaning until later. "I bet they had a problem with the *H*."

"Yeah, right, anyway." Honeysack leans in for privacy. "So about today."

"They couldn't stomach SAME."

"One o'clock is when your group is cleared to leave, but we can't pick you up until two, so you'll have to wait outside till then. I've already okayed it with the staff, told them your ride will be late. Not that they

327

care; they have other things on their mind. So two o'clock be in front of the AHRC." Honeysack looks at Billy like Billy is his dealer, like Billy is the only one with the goods that might sustain the doctor for another day. "Okay, you got it?"

"Got it. You know, 'heinous' is a lousy choice."

"Have you done your note?" Honeysack asks, teeth gnawing a knuckle.

"Yeah," Billy answers. " 'Inhumane,' small *i*, big *H*, that would've been better."

CNN has discovered the story. Desperate for news, they already have *Exclusive Tape* of the incident, delivered to them by way of a militant group of animal rights activists, SHAME their name, the same SHAME who broke into Hargrove Anderson Medical's Animal Human Research Center in Albany, New York, late last night. This is a mouthful for the reporter on the scene who's perspiring through his suit. The man is hairy with sweat, like a werewolf transformed by the sun, his face unleashing a growth of nonstop drips. He might be live but he looks as if he wishes he were dead, *Peter Barnes* bannered below his wilting jacket. Billy, packing up his suitcase, is amazed by the evidence of heat outside his window. For two weeks the weather was only circumstantial.

The CNN video begins inside the east wing of the center. Flashlights poke around darkness and reveal stacks of cages with dogs inside, barking and wagging tails like possible ASPCA adoptees. Some pooches have only the strength to register a whimper. Others say nothing though their eyes reflect red. On the tape, whispering can be heard, as well as latches being released and paws clicking the floor, a Morse code of *huh? huh? huh?* Through random beams of light the animals bustle around the lab, and a SHAME goblin whispers, "show them the steak," like meat is an idol these restless natives worship. More cages open, more dogs stretch their legs. The camera gets jostled by an overly excited hound that practically licks the lens. "[Beep] nipped me" is muttered. A quick shot of the steak-bearing goblin: dogs surround him, his torso climbed like a tree with a squirrel atop. Growls commence. Mice, rats, gerbils, rabbits are loaded into duffel bags, Billy recognizing them as the type Ossap and Dullick

328

carried that first day. Then—jump cut—they're outside, in the courtyard with the vans and the herding goblins and the wrist of the hand sculpture slit by the SHAME banner. Ossap and Dullick make their statement: "We say SHAME on Hargrove Anderson Medical for their cruel treatment of animals. Death for the sake of science is still death. Torture has no rationalization. As the Hippocratic oath states, 'Do no harm,' but it seems Hargrove Anderson and dozens of other multinational pharmaceutical corporations follow a hypocritical oath of 'Do no harm to profits.'" A bit of blood marks Ossap's forehead, like he's been henna-blessed by a Hindu priest. "In a hundred years we will be ashamed of our diet today." The final sequence is the quick piling into the vans, the peeling tires, the whooping of triumph from the goblins inside as the AHRC fades in the rear window and the dogs inside the van begin barking in what might be the beginning of a fight.

Peter Barnes is back live. Shaved of sweat, he already sports a five o'clock mist as he reports on the latest development. Security was found bound and gagged but uninjured. The loose animals are being rounded up, a spokesperson for Hargrove Anderson Medical assuring the public there is no safety issue, no CDA concerns, no danger of sick animals on the loose. Already several of the SHAME participants have been caught. PETA in a press release has denied any responsibility though they support their fellow liberators. And finally, more details are sure to follow as this story continues to unfold, Peter Barnes, CNN, Albany, New York. The morning slips through the TV, through the loop of CNN where roughly every so often Peter Barnes returns with fresh tidbits: names and photographs of the SHAME people; added information on the chronology of the raid. But Billy keeps watching for the ten seconds of video that show Ossap and Dullick standing in front of the bronze hand while behind them the AHRC looms, in particular, the west wing, its windows pressed with faces, bodies barely visible, like shadows of shadows.

The TV holds last night while the courtyard contains its aftereffects. Police stand around and take pictures and point in various directions. A groundskeeper shovels up rabbit remains and hoses blood into pink skims, the nozzle a gun. A researcher leans a ladder against the hand sculpture and entices the rhesus monkey with a banana, almost comedic in its yum-yum unpeeling, its offering bringing not-so-funny capture. A posse heads into the woods for strays, and every now and then a dog is dragged back. Occasionally a gunshot is heard and soon a man steps from the tree line with a yellow medical waste bag in hand. Billy wonders how many dogs are still out there.

Gretchen stops by his room. She's dressed in the clothes she wore two weeks ago, as if clothes could bookend a masquerade.

"They're shooting some of the dogs," Billy tells her.

"I know."

"Must be the ones who don't come."

Gretchen crosses her arms. She has the look of reality soon regained. "I just want to get home and eat Chinese food in bed. You know what I mean?"

"Yeah."

Gretchen sits down on Do's old bed. All the edge is gone from her face; she is unlovely from all angles. "I feel like I've been watching one of those nature shows," she says, "with the wildlife footage of elephants and tigers, and I'm thinking how beautiful the world is, and I almost feel hopeful, like regardless of who I am at least I live in a world like this, that is, until the end, when the narrator says his *but*—there's always a *but*—and they begin showing what's happening now, the deforestation, the poaching, the acid rain, like all the previous footage was dug up from a time capsule buried only yesterday, and right now, these animals, their lives, this world, is gone. I try to change the channel before that *but* hits, not in denial, but it's not something I need confirmed." Gretchen shrugs. She nails her beauty mark like a gymnast whose poor routine is redeemed by a perfect dismount. "You know what I mean?"

Billy nods.

"I just want to get back to the city and curl up in bed."

"I love you," Billy says matter-of-factly. The words, once said, seem empty and leave him defensive of feeling.

Gretchen grimaces. "Please don't say that."

"But I do."

She glances down, as if the floor has a diagram of impossible dance steps. "That's ridiculous, Billy. You don't know me. Two weeks in this place is hardly real, let alone real enough to fall in love with somebody. Once you're back outside, you'll see. But let's not have this conversation, please."

"I know what I know," Billy says. "It might not be much, but I love you. I'm not expecting anything like trumpets or fireworks, I just wanted you to know."

"We can sit together in the van," Gretchen tells him.

"I'm not going back to New York."

"Where are you going?"

"Elsewhere," Billy says.

"Oh." Gretchen's tongue traces against the inside of her check, as if feeling for an unseen flaw. "You know why I didn't sleep with you?" she says. "Because I liked you too much to include you in my project. Or maybe I thought you'd remember me better unrequited."

"I don't care about the guys you slept with here."

"I'm so relieved."

"And I lied," Billy says. "I do want trumpets and fireworks."

"Well, that can also be the prelude to war."

"Just say the word and I can be in the van with you."

"I can't say that word."

"It doesn't have to be a big word," Billy nearly pleads.

"Turn down the melodrama, please."

"That's an unfair thing to say to somebody who's trying to say something."

"Billy, I don't love you. I mean I think you're nice and sweet, but that's all. Nothing more. Nothing earth-shattering."

"I thought you didn't want anything earth-shattering."

"You're too young for me."

"I'm not that young."

"When you get to my age you'll understand how young you are."

"Please, you're not that old," Billy says. "You know what I wish? For the first time in my life I wish I had a cell phone, then I could give you my number and if you were ever watching TV, watching one of those nature programs and that big *but* was approaching, you could call me and I could talk you through the bad bits." Billy thinks of his pocket suddenly ringing *The Rite of Spring*. "I'd give the number to nobody else. It'd be a line solely dedicated to you."

"A cell phone. How romantic."

"I was just trying to be original."

"But alas, you don't have a cell phone," Gretchen says.

"True."

"I could give you my number but it'd probably be fake."

"I'll take that." Billy grabs the pen and folded-over suicide note from his suitcase.

"Just one number has to be wrong," Gretchen tells him.

"Make them all lie, I don't care, but write it down."

Gretchen relents and scribbles her name and questionable phone number across the top-right-hand corner. "There," she says. "Seven perfectly random numbers."

"I'll call every day."

"I already feel sorry for the chump on the other end."

In the courtyard, the dog hunters return for lunch. Two of them lug a deer carcass, a good-sized buck with six points.

"Look at that," Billy says.

"Maybe a case of mistaken identity," Gretchen says, smiling through the truth.

39

L UNCH IS leftovers, the greens in civilian dress and already breaking with the recent past, like graduates who have learned nothing and must make their way alone in the world armed with this knowledge. Nobody talks much. The SHAME news event is discussed in terms of *I was there, I saw the whole thing, I knew those guys,* their own brush with fame springing from someone else's notoriety, a sort of new American celebrity, Billy thinks, hearing people ready themselves for Peter Barnes's microphone, *Hi Mom!* blinking behind their eyes. Billy keeps to himself, eating nothing, doctor's orders. Gretchen sits at another table, no worse for his love, holding court one more time, as if plates are commemorative-issued, her face stamped beneath spaghetti.

"Fucked-up place," Frank Gershin says from across the table, speaking to nobody in particular, speaking, it seems, to the scars beneath his shirt.

"Where are you going to get shot next?" Billy asks.

Frank glances up, startled. "What?"

"Your next bit of trauma."

"Not sure. I'm thinking head."

"Get shot in the head?"

"Yeah. An Oswald."

"That'd be a gut shoot. I think you mean a JFK."

"Yeah whatever. I'm thinking right here." Frank lands his finger in the middle of his forehead.

"Wouldn't that kill you?"

"Nothing's killed me yet," he says, getting up.

*   *   *

333

The greens, cleared for discharge by way of cashier's check, collect in the courtyard where vans are parked and ready. Corker is there for those heading back to New York, and there are other Corkers who will take people to train stations and bus stops and various points of departure. A few normals with their own cars linger before exiting for the parking lot. It's like the end of summer camp, Billy thinks, or assumes, having never been to camp. Hands are shaken. The rare hug is dispensed. Good-bye to Karl McKay and Stew Slocum and Yul Gertner and Herb Kolch and Frank Gershin and Barry Pica and a host of others, never to be seen again though some make promises and exchange phone numbers, Billy amazed by the mysterious chemistry of friendship. Rodney Letts, blue plastic bag slung over shoulder, spots Billy lurking along the periphery of good-bye. He grins and walks over. Already he's losing his better looks, like he's leaving Shangri-la through a soot-covered duct.

"Ready for the city again?" he asks.

"I'm not going back," Billy says.

"No?"

"No."

"Smart of you. Who needs the city except people like me who need people who hate the city so maybe they'll toss me a few coins. I'm like the opposite of a wishing well. But I want to thank you. Your piss saved my butter. Now I've got two thousand dollars, which is like a year for me."

They shake hands.

"Do you know this whole study was bullshit?" Billy says.

"It's always bullshit," Rodney tells him, misunderstanding the question. "But the money's real, and the clean sheets are real, and the showers are real, the three squares a day." Rodney taps Billy on the shoulder. "I'll see you later," he says as if this too is bullshit but at least his hand is real.

The vans begin filling up. Corker stands arms crossed by the open door, nodding Peter Swain and Sameer Sirdesh inside but keeping his eyes straight ahead, like he's in a staring contest with the AHRC where maybe he thinks a woman is watching him, up from her reception desk and near the window and wondering if she should ask him to pick her up a dozen authentic New York bagels—please please, ask me anything, his dark eyes

334

plead, not even noticing Gretchen who steps inside without looking back toward Billy who is mentally rehearsing his wave, a small sad wave, a wave of what could've been, just a slow raising of his hand, an opening of his fingers, an expression of five, no more, no less, the sentiment running to his mouth (rueful) and his eyes (mournful), but she has to look back or find him from the van's window for this action to commence, Billy waiting as Corker uncrosses his arms and gives the AHRC one more minute to open those doors and unleash a sprinting skirt who's finally come around, one more second as Corker slides shut the passenger door and crosses around the front, glancing back, glancing back, getting to the driver-side door, opening the door, pausing, seeing Billy.

Billy waves at Corker.

Corker waves back.

Billy, with time to kill, decides on a walk down to the Hudson. A well-worn path through woods advertises the river, the water squinting against the sun's highest point. Billy drags along his suitcase. At first, the heat was a novelty, his pores stretching like they've been on the couch for two weeks, but now it's an annoyance of sweat. Air is processed through pine trees and dirt and moss and the underlying mindlessness of water as the path opens up on a stretch of chain-link fence. On the other side is an embankment for train tracks followed by shoreline. The river is narrower this far north but none the less impressive. Billy sees a large brown boy, shirt tucked into his back pocket, standing along its edge. He's picking up rocks and tossing them into the water. He seems to be searching for the biggest splash.

"Think of the devil."

Billy turns to find Joy on a tree stump, like a giant toadstool.

"You were thinking of me?" he asks.

"Nobody ever bothers to say good-bye to me."

"There was no bleeding today."

"Yesterday was the all-clear screen."

"You should've told me."

"I thought the removal of the cannula was enough."

"I should've figured."

Joy regards him and his suitcase curiously. "You going by boat, or are you swimming home?"

"I'm being picked up in an hour. Is that the famous Rufus out there?"

"Yep," Joy says, unable to hold back a smile. "He enjoys attacking the water. But if he slips and gets his toes wet, he'll be screaming."

"Is it safe with those research-animal hunters around?"

"They stopped. I guess a few of them were getting overenthusiastic."

"I saw them dragging out a deer."

"A bad idea from the start," Joy says. "So you going home?" she asks.

"Yes," Billy lies. "Just waiting for my ride."

"Are your parents still going through with it, their thing?"

"Tomorrow, supposedly. Yeah. Tomorrow is their thirty-eighth wedding anniversary. I'm sure my father loves the idea of dying on that day, you know, too hard to pass up on that symmetry. But today might be the bigger day. Today is the day they ran away from their families and eloped. Tomorrow might be their wedding anniversary, but today is the bigger anniversary."

"You flying home?" Joy asks.

"No, I'm taking the train," Billy tells her, thinking she knows he's lying. "But I'll get there in time. I will. I'll get there and stop them." Billy kicking open the door, rushing into their bedroom, slapping the deadly ice-cream mush from their hands, ripping open the plastic from their mouths, fuck it, while he's there laying his hands upon Doris's head and healing her, reaching for Abe so the group hug may commence—all of this lives in the lie as if lying is the lingo of superheroes.

"That's good," Joy says. She reaches into her pocket and pulls out a pack of cigarettes, crumpled by its intimacy with her thigh. "You want one?"

"I don't smoke," Billy says, disa—"Screw it." He accepts the pack and excavates a misshapen cigarette, which he strokes straight, then lights, the most pleasing aspect of the smoke. The taste in his lungs is cool and minty, like a choke of ice. It could be a brand of Nordic tobacco. "What is this?"

"Menthol," she says.

"It's almost disturbing."

"Well I like the taste."

Billy takes another drag. His head is already spinning around a cold peppermint center. "Disturbing in an interesting way," he clarifies, flicking away the dead ash, which is very satisfying, as he flicks again, could flick forever, already impatient with the slow rate of ash.

"When's your train?" Joy asks.

"I'm not sure." There are, he finds, at least a half-dozen ways to grip a cigarette, none of which seem ideally suited to his fingers. "So what do you think happens when we die?" he asks with a sort of existential crook of his hand.

"Either you go to heaven or you go to hell," Joy says.

Billy can't mask his disappointment. "You really believe that?"

"I do."

"So you pray and go to church and read the Bible?"

"Yep."

"Jesus Christ as your savior?"

"Uh-huh."

"I'm not being critical."

"You are and that's all right."

"I don't believe in anything," Billy says, attempting, rather lamely, an effete smoke ring. "But I also don't believe in nothing. I mean, sometimes I think it's just eternal blackness, and sometimes I think if there is an afterlife it's an afterlife of your own devising, your last thought, whatever that might be, going on forever. I guess I believe in the great big in-between, nothing as part and parcel of something else. But in general, I'm pretty confused about everything." Billy's voice shakes with honesty and nicotine.

"You've had a long two weeks," Joy tells him, her eyes a soft pat on his shoulder.

"I suppose."

"Your thinking is still wobbly."

"Maybe that's true." Billy suffers through a thin last drag then he launches the cigarette with a slick disdainful placekick of his fingers, sending the butt over imaginary goalposts. "But I've been thinking maybe I don't need to go home for my parents' deathbed scene."

"That's cold," Joy says.

"Positively mentholated," Billy replies.

"They're your parents," she says.

"And I'm their son, and blah blah blah. At the end of the day, when all is said and done and Mom, Dad, and Child are old enough to know better, who has the bigger responsibility, you know, who should make the effort to understand and reach out for the other, them or you? Who should go first?"

"Does it matter?" Joy asks.

"Absolutely."

"Why?"

"I don't know, because it does."

"It's not a competition, there's no winner or loser."

Billy distracts himself with a half-buried rock near his left foot, which he toes free, which he then picks up, a good-sized rock with nice heft, jagged from who knows what, a bit of talus from a long-lost mountain, the mountain itself worn down and now rising from the plain of his palm, the ways of geology a mystery to Billy so that what is before him is simply rock, a rock, which, sizing up a tree in the distance, he throws with a decent arm though sports was never an interest, the rock heading toward its target, Billy feeling a certain pleasure in creating speed, in hurling something as fast you can, the rock missing by a few feet, the tree not mocking but perhaps daring him to try again, Billy far too old to take up the challenge.

"So you'll do nothing instead?" Joy asks.

"I don't know if it's worth it to do anything else," Billy says.

"Go home, Billy."

In this light, the Hudson seems like a giant mercury spill. Rufus, bored with splashes, leaves the shore and storms over the railroad embankment like a boy playing his imagination and he's being chased. He slams into the chain-link fence, thwarted. Fingers poke through the diamond-shaped mesh. The boy is big, football big, but soft enough so his belly strikes Billy as an easy target, a stupa of slaps and jabs which the gentle-faced Rufus must accept without protest, the tenth incarnation of fat. Through the fence, he regards Billy with the suspicion of a boy who knows he's not yet a man.

"Rufus," Joy says, "this is Billy Schine."

"Hi Rufus."

"Hey." Rufus starts climbing up the fence with assurance.

"Now be careful," Joy says.

But Rufus is a good climber for his size. He gains the top and lords over the view, teasing his mother with what would be a nine-foot fall.

"Get down," Joy orders.

After a beat of protest, Rufus obeys. Halfway down, he jumps and lands with an action-figure pose, much to the delight of his mother who claps her knees *Come on over here!* Rufus is in no rush. Every step requires an unspoken beg from his mother.

"Look at you," she says, drawing him in like a club chair. "A chain-link fence you know from back home. It's the rest of the stuff that's alien."

"I thought I saw a bear," Rufus says.

"I hope not."

"Or that Bigfoot guy."

Joy puts his hands in hers and says, "Worms could live in these fingernails."

"Have you been smoking?" Rufus asks.

"No."

"Hey, could we get a canoe?"

"I don't think so."

Joy squeezes Rufus as if invisible claws might tear him away from her, and Rufus pretend-squirms but in the end gives way to her nestling chin. Billy looks away, thinking this deserves privacy, this expression. He glances toward his hands, with something like shame.

"You've been smoking," Rufus says.

"Maybe a little bit," Joy admits.

How do you recover from who you are? Billy wonders. How do you come to grips with the facts of yourself? How do you ever accept the diagnosis?

"I'm hungry," Rufus says.

"Maybe we should get some doughnuts and milkshakes."

Rufus hops up. "That would be beautiful."

"You want to join us?" Joy asks Billy.

"I can't," Billy says.

"You have plans?"

"Only immediate."

Joy gets up and prepares for reentry into civilization. "If you find yourself needing a place to stay, I don't know, for the next few days, we have a pullout. It wouldn't be a problem."

"I think I'll be fine."

"Well, just in case." She comes over toward Billy, reaches for the ballpoint pen clipped to her lapel. No paper readily available, she takes his arm. For the first time her touch is latex-free. She extends his elbow, revealing the red prick where the cannula once lay. "Like old times," she says. The ink is stubborn to start. Ballpoint digs into skin. "I can't find a vein," she jokes. Finally, ten digits are traced and retraced, and Joy clicks her cheeks with satisfaction. "Call us if you need something," she says, standing over him like an eclipse.

"Thanks for everything," he says.

"I didn't do anything but my job."

"That's true, I guess."

"Go home," she says, her eyes on him like hands brushing away rubble.

"Yeah."

Joy corrals Rufus for their return to the AHRC.

Billy hears Rufus ask, "What's he doing there?"

"He's waiting for the train," Joy tells him.

"Train doesn't stop here, does it?"

"I don't think so."

"So why's he waiting?"

"I think he's been misinformed."

*   *   *

340

Billy takes in the water, the blue sky, the few clouds, the sun, the every-so-often airplane slicing a thin white contrail that slowly distends into an intestine of vapor, the trees, the random breeze, the branches like creaky playground swings, the birds, the heat, the dirt, the smell, the heat on pine and mulch, the no-see-ums, the bugs, the ants, the mossy green, the brown, the red suitcase, the pose, the bullshit tableau, the chain-link fence, the train tracks, the rocks, the shore, the small waves lapping back on the lone figure taking this all in.

Billy gets up.

He goes over to where he flicked his cigarette and pockets the filter.

Midway along on the path, like a vision from a dream, odd and ordinary, a dog is spread on all fours. Billy freezes. It's a mutt, mostly black Labrador with a white chevron of Ur-canine on its chest. Billy wonders if the dog has seen him, but it seems unfazed, mouth open, tongue dangling wet. Strapped on its back is a saddlebag, the nylon torn and dirty. Billy is curious if the dog is still receiving its automated dose, if the external infusion pump still works in the wild, churning away its noncure. Billy lowers his suitcase. The dog perks. Its ears seem broken, as if as a puppy they met cruel thumbs. "Hey boy, hey boy," Billy calls out. The dog tilts its head, commercial cute. Billy crouches down, pats his knees, clucks sweet nothings. "Come on, come here, boy, come on, yes, you big beautiful dog, you good dog, yes, come here, come on." The dog is not tempted while Billy is a surveyor of possibilities. He fantasizes about stealing this dog away from here. His mind's eye travels the country with this diseased, drugged-up dog, the two of them inseparable. Screw Honeysack, screw Gretchen, screw his parents, he'll be devoted to this dog. "Come here, boy." The dog gets up and shakes. Billy turns up his cooing and approaches, hand available for sniffing. "You sweet thing, good dog, good dog." The dog watches Billy with deep brown eyes, impassive, like Coca-Cola gone flat. Twenty feet away, now fifteen feet, and Billy is already thinking of names. Doug, he thinks, Doug the dog, from Douglas, meaning *black water*. "Hi, beautiful." A straightforward, single-syllable American name. "Yes, you good good dog, yeah." Billy ten feet away and the dog flexes its nostrils. Breathe me in, Billy thinks. Take in this reek and render it your own. Billy floats forward on soft entreaties of "Hey." Close enough now to notice a bit of white around the muzzle, an older dog, perhaps once a pet, Billy is ready for a lick when the dog turns toward the woods and begins walking. It walks without haste. On a rotted tree it shows itself male. Then it keeps walking into the deeper part of the woods, trailing behind a loose rubber tube from the infusion pump, like a leash from a lost owner. Billy doesn't budge until the dog disappears. There goes a new species of animal, he thinks.

40

BILLY SITS in the courtyard, in the shade of the HAM sculpture, his back leaning against bronze like the hand is a tree to laze beneath. The finger is still three hours slow. Maybe there's a day when the time's just right, when the earth is on a particular rotation, when the sun is in conjunction with a gesture and somewhere the sculptor smiles. But not today. Today, thoughts of death are lifted toward the sky. Today, death might die. Who said that? Somebody else, Billy thinks, in so many words, those words no doubt better chosen. Billy closes his eyes. He imagines his head pressing the pulse of the statue, the great big nothing of this monument. He tries feeling for a sign of life, even if a faint echo from where the rhesus monkey scampered. Oh well. No great revelations, only mild pretension. At least the bronze is warm.

Billy is almost asleep when the largest SUV he's ever seen comes tearing down the AHRC driveway. This SUV seems to have swallowed another SUV. It screeches along the curve and stops not with a skid but an extended high-pitched whimper. The passenger window rolls down. Dr. Honeysack waves toward Billy like this car is an embarrassing costume.

"Hey."

"Hello."

Billy opens the backseat door, tosses in his suitcase.

The man behind the wheel is in his early sixties. He wears green scrubs and a lab coat like they're pajamas for an insomniac. He spins around, faces Billy. Smallish and lean, he has a nose suited for tunneling. "Big, huh?" he says. "It's brand new. The Rio Grande, the biggest thing on the road that's not commercially registered."

"Billy Schine," Honeysack interrupts, "this is Dr. Nathanael Marx."

343

"Hi."

Dr. Marx bangs a U-turn and the fat tires hop toward high speed. "This monster's got driver's side airbags, side, top, front, same with the passenger side, same with the backseat. If we wreck, this thing becomes inflated, and if we do wreck, whoever wrecks us will be much worse. Trust me, I've seen it. Oh man, have I seen it. Try seeing what happens when an Accord goes against a Suburban and you'll understand that it's war out there and you've got to keep up with the arms race. I agree, it's absurd. But would I rather treat broken glass to the face or a decapitation? Hmm, let me think."

Dr. Marx barely slows for the security station. Though no music is playing, he drumsolos the steering wheel and brakes with the beat of a bossa nova bass line. He seems to dance with the road. Honeysack, on the other hand, waits for the band to strike up the air bags. "I like to drive," Dr. Marx explains. "I love to drive. As a kid I dreamed of sports cars, especially in med school. The doctors drove all the hot cars in my town. Doctors had the wheels. That was the day when doctors were considered rich. Ooh, a doctor, he must be rich. Funny now. But when you regularly witness what eighty miles per hour does to a Porsche, well, you start shopping for a tank." Dr. Marx catches Billy in the rearview mirror. "Hey man, I'm a fan of reckless abandon," he says. "I just don't want to be stupid about it."

Honeysack turns to Billy. "This man's a legend in the trauma field."

Dr. Marx flinches. "Was, maybe."

"He helped develop the ABCDEs for EMTs."

"Big efing deal."

"And pushed the use of backboards for possible neck and spinal cord injuries."

"Now you're dating me."

"Backboards were not standard before this man."

"Not like they call it the Marx board," Dr. Marx says.

"And the Ambu bag," Honeysack mentions.

"It's not like Ringer's IV solution, or the Swan-Ganz catheter, two pricks I knew. I once met Hank Heimlich at a convention, before he was

Heimlich of Heimlich maneuver fame. Nice guy. Nothing special but nice. Now look at him. His name is in every restaurant. I can't eat a good piece of steak without feeling a bit envious."

Up ahead, a car is pulled over on the side of the road. Dr. Marx decelerates and leans forward. He seems ready for the call immemorial, *Is there a doctor in the house?* His eyes are on constant high alert, never fearful but prepared, and while his intentions are noble—*Must save lives!*—his sharp rodent face has an uncomfortable blood lust. Sadly, the pulled-over car has only a flat tire.

"Trauma," Dr. Marx says, "is a young man's game. And look at our young man in the backseat," he says of Billy. "Our brave young man willing to step forward with us. Cryopreservation is where the world of medicine is going. And the three of us right here, riding in this Rio Grande—feel it, feel it. Do you feel it, guys?" Dr. Marx rolls down his window so the wind can join the conversation. "We are cruising on the forefront regardless of how history might remember us."

Honeysack opens his window a few inches and allows the wind slight coaxing.

"So," Dr. Marx asks Billy, "do you have your suicide note?"

"Uhm, yeah."

"Would you mind if I took a look?"

"I guess not." Billy hands it over. "It's still pretty rough," he says.

"I'm sure it's fine." Dr. Marx unfolds the piece of paper. "*I'm sorry,*" he reads while driving, a multitasker of the road. "*I'm so so very sorry.* That's it, huh? A bit terse, don't you think? *I'm sorry, I'm so so very sorry.* The *very* works well. But I'd like more, just a bit more, to give a sense of your mental state. Why you're sorry? Who you're sorry towards? That kind of thing. More depth, more emotion. I'd like to see more of you, instead of just *sorry.* Your call, but think about it. There's still time. But definitely sign your name, just your first name. That's essential. Anyway, no big deal, you're not going to die, not today. And I've been thinking a coronary occlusion might be the best way to go, the most reasonable explanation." Dr. Marx hands back the note.

"So you don't even need this?" Billy asks.

"No, we do, just in case. And in my opinion the note needs a bit more. But hey, I'm not a writer."

"Neither am I," Billy says.

"I had you pegged for the writerly type. You went to Yale, right?"

"Harvard," Honeysack corrects.

"Harvard and Cornell in my car," Dr. Marx coos. "Not bad for a Rutgers man."

"I'm going to need some more paper," Billy says.

"Just pick it up from sorry."

"You seem to be an expert on this," Billy says.

"I was a doctor in Vietnam," he answers as if natural explanation.

"Were there a lot of suicides over there?"

"Hardly any. Nobody thought of killing themselves in the face of all that. Killing yourself would be a screw-you to the guys who died. But a lot of them wrote notes and hid them in their boots so if they were killed they had their last words on them. We doctors always found them, wrapped in plastic. Shrives, we called them, and they all read like apologies, like the bullets came from their own gun. Heartbreaking stuff, always full of love even when their insides were ripped to shreds. It's what got me into trauma, those notes, me trying to make them moot." Dr. Marx grips the steering wheel extra tight and seems to drive from the corner of his eye as if the road is only worthy of peripheral vision. "What an epic waste, but I guess we all know that, right." He turns toward Dr. Honeysack. "Vietnam was where I replanted my first finger, a wedding band disseverment."

"Really?"

"Yeah. A mechanic got his ring caught as he was falling and *rip*."

"Nice."

"It got written up."

"I'm sure."

"In 1969 a replant was news."

Billy looks down at his note, uninspired. But he likes Gretchen's number tucked away on the reverse side, like a clue, like somebody might call her with the news and wonder why her phone number was on the note. Was it for love? they might ask. And she might drop the phone, imbued with *no*. Is the number even real? Billy thinks about borrowing a cell phone from one of the doctors but instead decides on uncertainty, not wanting to turn this possibility into a lie. He tears the number free from the note. Gretchen won't live here. No, she'll live tucked beside his wallet-sized map of lower Manhattan, those streets always confusing.

"Hey, you didn't rip the thing apart, did you?" Dr. Marx asks.

"No, just a corner." Billy signs *Billy*. "But what I've written stands. I'm not making any changes."

"Hey, I get it. No edits from the likes of me." Dr. Marx says, his eyes speculating in the rearview mirror. "You're an artist."

The next exit is downtown Albany. The skyline has a random arrangement of five or six good-sized buildings, twenty to thirty stories high. They resemble small-time businessmen determined to treat this town like a city, the government buildings screaming *state capital* a tad too loudly.

"Look at this city," Dr. Marx says. "Not like Miami or New York, both places I worked. Did my fellowship in Detroit in the midseventies. I'll tell you, those nightshifts flew by with the gangs and the drug trade and the sudden advancement in street weaponry. Multiple stab wounds, gunshot wounds, ODs. Fourteen hours lasted as long as five minutes, then they'd tell you to get some sleep. Sleep? How about racquetball. And now I'm here, in Albany. I've given them one of the best Level One trauma centers in the whole country, and what have they given me? Car accidents. The occasional stabbing. Farm accidents. Heart attacks and aneurysms and little boys with little fractures in their little fingers. I tell you, we're ready for war, not Albany. Thank God for my research. Honeysack?"

Honeysack releases himself from his two inches of breeze. "Yeah."

"Have you given Mr. Schine the forms?"

"Oh, crap, yeah." Honeysack opens his briefcase.

"Billy," Dr. Marx says, "these are standard-issue informed consent forms as well as not-so-standard liability forms and what I should—"

"I'll just sign them," Billy says.

"We should probably—"

"I don't want to know anything. I don't want any information. I'm sick of being informed. I'm just going to stay ignorant and do what you guys tell me to do. Let that be it." Billy's voice is no longer cool with concept but trembling with reality.

Honeysack hands over the forms, a bounded tome of no-fault.

In the backseat of the SUV, Billy puts his name in twenty places, every signature a bit different, reflecting a bump or a swerve or a stop as well as the vagaries of penmanship and the quest for the perfectly realized William A. Schine, every signature a small release of air.

The Albany Medical Center Hospital is a collection of additions spreading in every direction from a once impressive original structure of stone and Depression-era stout. The brick, granite, and slate seem on the verge of being eaten by the newer construction. A large glass box hovers behind the old clock tower. Rich couples—Ira and Libbey Flaxon, Jonah and Beatrice Hockner—pronounce themselves in competing wings. The emergency room has its own home, the C. Alan Lipton Trauma Center, which is connected to the main building by a goiterlike atrium.

Dr. Marx pulls into a reserved parking space. He engages the emergency brake for no reason, Billy guesses, other than the satisfaction of gripping the handle and yanking up. He turns around and faces Billy. "Just follow me, the both of you, follow me and don't feel like you have to say anything. It should be pretty quiet in there and anybody who might ask questions won't be there. But if there's a school bus accident or if God has finally decided to strike down state politicians, well then, we'll have to let this opportunity pass and imagine what could've been." Dr. Marx stares right into Billy's eyes, not his nose or his forehead, but in the middle of the middle of the middle of his eyes where the pupil hides when confronted by the brightest light. "Okay, Billy, are you sure you want to do this? You can say no but say no right now and not in twenty minutes."

"I want to do this," Billy says.

Dr. Marx leans in closer. "I have one question for you and that question is why? And please don't say money. What are we giving you? Thirty thousand, right? That might sound like a lot of money, but trust me, it's not a lot of money. If it's just about the money, I'll give you the money. I will. I'll write you a check right now and you can walk away, if it's just about the money. I can't have it be just about the money, not what I'm about to do."

"It's not just about the money," Billy says.

"Then what?"

"I want to do something that will advance human understanding."

"That sounds like bullshit," Dr. Marx says.

"It probably is," Billy admits. "But I want, I really want, something, I guess, something big, you know, something, something . . ." the word sticks in his head, nowhere near the explanation he wants to give, an explanation loaded with truth and beauty, with the dignity this moment deserves. But all he has is something. "I don't know what I'm saying. Why do I want to do this? Because it's something."

Dr. Marx smiles. "Okay," he says and opens his door. "Let's go."

The trauma center perks up with Dr. Marx's arrival, as though the man is carrying a bleeding girl. Everybody rushes up and says hello and nothing else. Small talk is the sole property of Dr. Marx. He stops the head nurse. "Hey Janice, what's up."

"Slow slow slow. A broken kneecap," Janice says.

"Skateboarder?"

"Mountain biker."

"Anything else?"

"Uhm, kiddie stuff, pure PG-thirteen. Oh, Assemblyman Kesler."

"What's it this time?"

"Chest pains."

Dr. Marx turns to Dr. Honeysack and Billy and grandly pronounces, "That's why we're here, gentleman, fifty million dollars for the phantom heart attacks of state officials." Then he slants toward Janice and allows her to publicly ingratiate herself in his presence. "Hey Janice, do me a favor and put a DND on trauma room five until further notice."

"What's up?"

"Nothing to concern you, but we need some privacy."

"Okay."

"If a head so much as peeks in I'll lop it off, swear to God," Dr. Marx says.

Janice eyes Billy like he's a malpractice lawyer investigating some slight, and Billy, uncomfortable with this look, tries smiling though he fears his nerves and how they might work on his mouth, turning innocence into a rat's nest.

Trauma room 5 is like any trauma room as seen on TV except for its temperature, which is cold, and its near silence, which is a protracted hum, and its smell, which is creepily clean, all of which merges into that first sense of winter when everybody notices their breath, if briefly, before moving on, ill-dressed for the change in weather. A clock is mounted on the wall, but this is a space that avoids time; casinolike, Billy thinks, the air similarly ruthless with its oxygen, as if hoping to suffocate the ghosts of losers. "Okay," Dr. Marx says, clapping his hands. "What we're going to do isn't very complicated. The hardest part is keeping the Sal-Gid solution an even temperature, at that essential forty-degree mark. Billy, what I've invented is a refrigerated rapid infuser IV system." Dr. Marx wheels forward a piece of equipment resembling a frozen drink dispenser with tubes where the cups would go. "This is it," he says, "in a nutshell."

"Impressive," Billy says.

"It has over thirteen patents pending," Honeysack tells him.

"Oh."

"The Swedes made it for me," Honeysack says.

"Oh."

"They do good work. The Sal-Gid is totally my own invention."

"Oh."

"The Sal-Gid is the true genius part," Honeysack says.

"Oh."

The three of them stand around awkwardly, like sex is to follow.

"So what's next?" Billy asks.

"You should probably strip down to your underwear," Dr. Marx says.

"Okay."

"Honeysack's doing the anesthesia."

"I have some training in it," Honeysack informs Billy.

"Whatever," Billy says, tossing his shirt and pants into the corner of the room. "I should go on the table?"

Dr. Marx nods.

Billy climbs aboard, stares up at the overhead lights: two round lamps side by side and jauntily cocked as though considering their subject with amusement. Billy alternates betweens arms at his side and arms crossed over his chest. Honeysack hooks him up to an EKG and over his shoulder, on a screen, his vitals sled a course in competing lines of life. IVs are started on his right arm and left ankle. "This isn't my stuff, not yet," Dr. Marx tells him. "This is just to get the catheters in place and push some fluids. We'll do my stuff when you're out."

Billy nods. He's neither nervous nor calm. For thirty minutes, the doctors move about and check and prepare various things, while Billy lies where God knows how many people have died, and lived, were saved and put back together again. Billy senses invisible demons tugging on his shoulder blades and the balls of his feet. Above him, the bright light seems to chuckle. Billy breathes deeply. He starts shivering. His bladder tugs and he wonders if he should bother asking about the bathroom but decides to stay put. Should he mutter a just-in-case prayer? Undeniably, unfortunately, every time he thinks about God he sees the white beard and flowing white hair, the basso profundo voice enfolded in white light. His God is a big cliché. The cold puckers nipples and testicles. Dr. Marx's special blood-freeze machine hums what Billy swears is the opening bass line of "Summer Nights" from *Grease,* a song so easily mocked but damn catchy. Perhaps the Swedes put this into their design, a bit of karaoke for the dying. Ridiculous but Billy hears bleachers and picnic tables. Dr. Marx leans over him. "Okay," he says. "We're ready if you are."

"I'm good to go."

"You can still change your mind."

"I'm fine."

"I'm going to strap you in, okay?"

"Okay."

The straps are good old-fashioned leather.

351

Dr. Marx rests his hand on Billy's head. He's no longer a hummingbird of activity but a great blue heron. "We'll see you soon, okay?"

"Okay."

"Nothing is going to happen to you, I promise."

"Okay."

"Right now, you might as well be my son," he says.

Before Billy can ask what exactly that means, Honeysack has slipped a mask over his mouth and nose and said, "Breathe in deeply and count backwards from twenty."

Dr. Marx rolls his eyes.

"What?" Honeysack asks.

"Just once I'd like to hear a different instruction."

"Like what?"

"Like sing 'Happy Birthday' or something."

"Fine. Don't count, sing 'Happy Birthday,'" Honeysack tells Billy.

The breathed-in gas is a little bit sweet, like in your mouth cotton candy is being spun, and Billy starts singing—*Summer lovin' had me a blast*—along with Dr. Marx's invention, carrying through the tune—*Summer lovin' happened so fast*—Billy picturing the beach and the ocean—*Met a girl crazy for me*—and fun times under that pier as vacation gives you temporary respite—*Met a boy cute as can be*—from who you are back home, even as the lyrics fail you—*Summer fun dance in the sun*—and you try your best to fake your way through—*Until up on those summer nights*—hoping nobody will notice, and if they do, hoping they'll smile at the attempt and maybe join in on the *Wella-wella-wella-umph.*

41

WHITE LIGHT bruises into tender yellow, as if eyes have gripped too tightly and left behind evidence of a struggle. The morphine must've been increased because the pain (before then a sound in the distance, an echo of your loudest harshest scream coming from who knows where) is now a fuzzy whisper relaying the gist of the last day into Billy's ears as he wakes up from a sleep of indeterminate time (five minutes, five hours?), impossibly thirsty. His tongue, his entire oral cavity, seems constructed from an old pink sponge, the sort his mother would never get around to throwing away, sponges having no definite death, only an eternal wake on the side of the sink. His breath must smell the same, addictively nasty. Waking up in this room is a small surprise, with the IV drip, the various life-monitoring devices, the intercom calling out messages for nurses—"Catheter for room two-oh-four"—the ceiling acoustic tile peering down *Go ahead and wail.* Every time Billy wakes up forgetting; every time he wakes up unsure why he's here. Nobody has explained anything. Obviously something has gone wrong with his chest. Every breath hurts, like his sternum is wrapped in barbed wire. And he's nauseous, not throw-up nauseous, but motion-sick nauseous, like a cabdriver is in his head. What does he remember? Bits. He remembers something down his throat. He remembers being wheeled on his back, the overhead lights flashing by like so many movies. He remembers Dr. Marx, garbed in monkish gown, staring over him, the muslin describing a smile. He remembers slipping, the sensation of slipping, of falling through what was once solid. He remembers dull activity, being prodded and pulled, being tended by an array of well-trained hands. He remembers, *You'll be all right* and *He seems to be doing fine* and *Hello, Mr. Schine* from faceless voices. He remembers being expertly lifted as the linens were changed. He remembers moaning. But these are just flashes, as substantial as fever dreams. Nothing is grounded. His bones seem to float beneath the skin, and his eyeballs could be helium-based.

All he knows is he's thirsty.

He remembers the nurse's call button—*If you need anything*—situated on the end of a cord like some self-activating disaster device. But the thing has slipped through the safety bars and dangles between bed and floor, beyond his miserable reach. Luckily the television remote (a comprehensive control that also maneuvers the bed) is resting against his thigh. Yes, he remembers television. He remembers last night's fade of shows, background chatter, like a boy sick while his parents have a party downstairs. Billy pushes on—nope, his head elevates—here, the TV power button and ticks up the volume. The host for *This Old House* begins shouting. "All this wood has to be replaced thanks to decades worth of water damage." Billy would kill for this kind of damage.

"Expensive?"

"Very."

But the TV never really screams. The sound stays within his palm, the loudspeaker cut into the remote for the sake of privacy.

Billy groans.

"You like this show?"

Billy looks over, meaning he crooks his head rather pitifully.

There, in the corner of the room, sits an older man, a newspaper crumpled on his lap. He's in his late sixties, early seventies, gray and saggy, with a particularly urban immigrant face, Billy thinks, a boy of stickball and marbles, cheeks squeezed by grandmothers who lived under the same roof, mothers who sewed for extra cash, fathers who sweated for work wherever they could, brothers and sisters who earned their keep. He is freshly American even after all this time. His eyes have that look of sizing up crowds, a fire-escape gaze, a bearing of bigger things ahead that, my God, have been realized and now retirement burns in the distance. Dressed 1950s informal, in a light charcoal suit without the tie and a pair of brown loafers more comfortable than stylish, his head seems bare

354

without a felt hat. "Because I love this show," he says, his voice sweetly raw, pipe smoke instead of cigarettes. Every word is tamped down and lit with his tongue. He gets up and drags his chair toward Billy. It's obvious walking is not his forte. No, he's a sitter, shoulders hunched, elbows preferring a tabletop or, at a minimum, a set of knees. "I'm lousy with tools," he says, "but I could watch these guys forever."

Nothing about him strikes Billy as familiar, though he carries himself with avuncular ease, like an uncle who rarely visits, an uncle who's willing to unload the family secrets. He has lush crow-black eyebrows, a memory of what was once on top of his head but has now thinned and receded. The hair is still slicked back though, as if balding is no excuse against a good pomade. Up close, the eyes are no bullshit and glint with introduction enough, a sort of *I know you and that's enough.* "I'm always impressed by what they can do," he says.

Billy nods.

"Build things, that's a skill. Renovate. Fix."

Billy frowns thoughtfully.

The man leans forward, pillows his arms over his belly. "So how're you feeling, kid?" He actually says *kid,* says *kid* like this is a world that still says *kid,* like Billy is his boxer who got pummeled in the third round.

"Thirsty," Billy answers.

The man pours a glass of water from the pitcher on the bedside table.

The first sip stings.

"You in any pain?"

"Not too bad."

"Yeah, right. I had a triple bypass, I know what you're going through, so don't be brave with me. Fucking hurts. Treat your chest like a lobster tail. No fun. But trust me, gets better, every day, kid, a little better until finally the food will be the worst thing you suffer from and the fucking nurses waking you up and telling you to get some sleep."

Billy, after another sip, a better sip, asks, "What happened exactly?"

The mystery man, the sayer of *kid,* shakes his head, not with any vigor, just a disgusted faugh. "Assholes cracked open your chest. They were desperate. They got you near dead but you were staying dead, nothing was

355

working, certainly not their fucking little drug, and not anything else in their repertoire, so they cracked you open, a last-ditch effort, they told me, and brought you back. Miraculously, they said. I guess the guy, Dr. Marx, did a helluva job even if he did damn near kill you for no good reason."

"So it didn't work?"

"It failed spectacularly."

Failed. Billy closes his eyes. He tries catching the morphine in his blood, like a surfer with a good swell, but the dosage rolls gently, the waves not nearly as intense as expected, and Billy finds himself riding on calm. Failed.

"But don't you worry, kid," the man says.

That's when Billy asks, "Do I know you?"

The man smiles. It's not a happy smile. His heavy jowls are rueful ballast. "I'm your next of kin," he says. "Clem Ragnar."

Billy wonders if his eyes spell *Oh shit*. "*The* Ragnar?"

"I suppose."

"Of Ragnar & Sons?"

"That was wishful thinking on my part," he says, too sadly for further explanation. "But yes, I'm Ragnar, and please call me Clem."

"I'm a bit out of it, Clem," Billy explains. "But it's nice to meet you after all this time. My head is . . ." The words trail away. His mouth seems disconnected, speaking from a dream where molasses is involved. "I know why you're here and I have some of the money I owe, or will have some of it, half of it, soon enough."

Ragnar raises his hand *please enough*. "I'm going to kill that Polsheck. I read the letter he sent you. Thinks we're the fucking mob, wishes we were the mob. Failed fucking accountant, that's what he is. If he wasn't married to my daughter he'd be gone because the only cash he can collect comes from my wallet. Family, right?"

"So he's not your muscleman?" Billy asks.

Ragnar screws his eyes. "The only thing he beats up is his car. I mean, sure, we all take certain liberties with our letters, whatever works, but he goes all Gotti and wastes too much energy on style. You don't have to worry about Polsheck anymore. I'm personally in charge of your case now.

356

I'm your next of kin. They called my office late Friday and insisted on talking to me, said it was important, so I took the call, and they mentioned your name, which was vaguely familiar from Polsheck's bitching, and they told me you had me as your next of kin and said something had gone very wrong and you were in the hospital and I was needed. Now I was still flummoxed by exactly who the hell you were but I certainly knew Hargrove Anderson Medical—I'm on Calatrix for high blood pressure, two dollars a pill—and after decades of being in the particular field I'm in, I know the sound of panic and money and I knew these people were panicking about everything but money which is a new kind of panic for me. I sensed something like a large cash settlement, the way they talked. So I scratched my Labor Day plans, the wife none to pleased. Send an associate, she said, of course not Polsheck because Polsheck is family and needed for the big barbecue. But they asked for me specifically and if this is what I think it is, I told her I wanted my own hands on this fish. I drove up here to see my next of kin who has been done a mighty wrong. I've been here ever since. I got you this private room in the ICU, which isn't easy."

Billy watches Ragnar, watches him rub his hands together, working his knuckles with his thumb, these old hands, like roots for his arms. "And I tell you," Ragnar continues. "I'm glad I came myself, because the second I rolled up here they whisked me away into a conference room with a bunch of fucking lawyers pretending they weren't lawyers, and they explained the whole situation to me. Said some rogue researchers were to blame, Honeysack and Marx, that they were working without authorization from Hargrove Anderson Medical, that what they did was unacceptable and they've been summarily fired and would never work in research again. Okay, I said. Then they start pushing papers under my nose. They tell me how they've got this watertight informed consent—whatever that is— signed by you and it'll hold up in any court of law. See, they say, he expressly volunteered and even signed a liability release form and under- stood exactly what the risks were. They're like bam bam bam, Sonny Liston. I'm playing dumb, bereaved, telling them you're like a grandson to me, but it's pure rope-a-dope until I know what's going on. They tell me how this non-HAM-sanctioned study paid you on paper thirty thousand,

357

but in light of the circumstances, the outrageous behavior of their researchers, the—quite frankly, they say, which I love, like all the previous talk is far from frank—the bad publicity this might generate would not be good for them. Yeah, no shit. So they're willing to up the ante to an even hundred thousand, all you gotta do is sign a nondisclosure form and the money is yours. You following me?"

Billy nods.

"You look like you're dozing."

"No, no, I'm listening."

"Don't doze." Ragnar stares into Billy, eyes pinning him like hands on shoulders. "Because this is important," he says. "You're not signing anything. You hear me. I don't want you even near a pen. A hundred grand is nothing for these guys, and a million is just a start. What they did to you, look at you, they almost killed you and God knows what kind of permanent damage they did to your heart. No, these guys are going to go higher, much higher, I'm thinking five, six million, maybe more, because if this gets into the newspapers, that's their shit creek. FDA investigation. Massive fines. Right now this is just a small fire and they're willing to go to three alarms to keep it under control. But let me handle the negotiation. Believe me, I'm good at this. Getting money from people, that's my hanging curve. I'll represent you for forty percent of whatever you get and that'll include the money you already owe. A real lawyer would ask for fifty."

"Are you a lawyer?" Billy asks.

"No, but you don't want a real fucking lawyer. Trust me, kid. A lawyer will screw everything up. You bring one lawyer to the table and they'll bring ten. They'll always be able to out-lawyer you. And all of a sudden you're in a fucking trial and fees up the wazoo and you're depending on a jury of cleaning women and truck drivers. Even if you do win, you've got appeals, more appeals, and a judge who can half the reward like that. No, let me handle this. Christ, without me you wouldn't even be here. I'm kind of your partner already. Now they're going to play you against time, tell you the offer is only good for so long and then nothing because they don't want you sitting on this too long, but whatever you do, don't sign anything, don't even talk to them without me around because I know all the tricks. Just sit tight. Ask for more morphine. Tell them the pain is unbearable. Cry mommy. Sleep. Whatever. But don't sign anything. I tell you, the timing could be better. Fucking Labor Day weekend. Because I gotta go, otherwise I'll end up in worse shape than you if my wife has her way. Woman has a hard-on for the last weekend of the summer, like next weekend won't be eighty degrees as well. Personally, I don't get it. Summer officially ends what, September twenty-third, the autumnal equinox, right, so what's the big deal. What are we celebrating anyway, the American worker? Always sounds commie to me. But she has her hard-ons. I'll be back Tuesday afternoon, and by then I'll have drafted some sort of agreement between the two of us, for the up-and-up. After that, we'll go for the jugular and bleed these fuckers. I'll call you tomorrow, maybe even tonight. You understand?"

"Yes," Billy says, exhausted.

"Don't sign anything."

"Right."

Ragnar gets up, groaning. "I'm tempted to break your right hand just to make sure." He gives no indication that this is a joke except a sharp unfunny "Ha" and a barely gentle chuck to Billy's chin. "Now rest up," he says, shuffling toward his nest of newspaper and briefcase. Once again he admires the carpentry on TV. "If it was up to me to build my own shelter, I'd be living in a fucking cave. See ya, kid."

Billy, fading, falling through the mattress, waves, his hand dangling above him as he sinks into sleep, still waving bye, waving, waving, forgetting why he's waving and wondering if somebody will grab him.

42

THE TELETHON is on, the Muscular Dystrophy Association telethon hosted by Jerry Lewis for the last thirty-odd years. Billy stumbles onto the fifth hour—$7,455,635 on the tote—and stays tuned, often fading away with the morphine and sleeping for thousands and thousands of dollars, reawakening with the latest giant cardboard check or minor celebrity or video profile of an unfortunate boy with Duchenne's. Tilted forward in bed, eyes narcotic, Billy is tended by nurses who come in and say, *Oh look, the telethon*, as if this is a forgotten relic, a grandmother's tchotchke perhaps once humored but now viewed as tacky. Billy nods, in on the joke, but when they return and find him still watching, they smile with a certain amount of condescension, like he might actually be interested in this sap. Because who watches the telethon for more than five, ten minutes? Who puts in hours, or God forbid, a whole day? But at this moment it seems, well, necessary to Billy, like a religious made-for-TV event, twenty-four hours of suffering and hope, a fast of dying children. And the morphine helps. Oh yes, the morphine. It's self-administered with a press—*Beep!*—of a trigger that winds its way to the infusion pump and its churning care. "As much as you like, whenever you feel the need," the nurse told him. "There's no danger of overdosing or anything like that," she said. "Most patients give themselves too little." Not this patient. *Beep! Beep! Beep!* Like activating a car alarm except security comes in drips and there's nothing inside of Billy worth stealing. *Beep!* His sternum feels electrified. *Beep!* His chest throbs with painlessness. *Beep!* His joints are as noteworthy as layovers between destinations and his head could be O'Hare. Where am I? Oh, yeah. Here. But temporarily. *Beep!* Ah, morphine. Almost like morpheme, the smallest

360

meaningful unit of speech, which pleases Billy—*Beep!*—this idea—*Beep!*—of pushing the minimum of connection through his veins. The only problem is that sleep never fulfills its promise of rest and is banked in chunks of change, pennies, nickels, dimes that never accumulate like they do for the school children around the country who beam over their pooled check of $51,345.37. Applause from the studio audience. Billy smiles. *Good kids.* The TV remote with its personalized speaker rests near his chin, and the volume is as high as the volume will go. The clapping vibrates the stubble growing on his neck. *Wonderful. These children, these kids, they're our leaders of tomorrow.* This sentiment oozes forth from Mr. Jerry Lewis, who has his arms draped around these wonders, the foot soldiers of his crusade. *Oh, what a lovely future we might have.* Jerry tears or sweats or both, his skin glistening under the lights, his hair obsidian black, as if lava has hardened over Mount Rushmore. It's obvious Jerry's in poor health. His tan is jaundiced. In fact, he almost missed this year's telethon—doctor's orders—but damn the torpedoes, he's here for his kids. He tells the audience only death would keep him away and even then he'd do his darnedest. Laughter builds into ovation. Jerry shticks his left hand *enough* and his right-hand *more.* He nods, taps his chest, worries his hands, blows kisses with obsessive-compulsive affection. Billy smiles. Combined with the *Beep!* of morphine, this is a speedball of instant camp, beautifully American, a triumph of optimism over truth.

$10,436,856.54.

Sunday dinner served and ignored, Billy watches a video profile of Jimmy Rialto, a nine-year-old with Duchenne's who can play baseball like any normal boy. *I ain't letting nothing slow me down,* he narrates with pure gumption, like a latter day Bowery Boy. *So I'm sick, plenty kids sick, some kids worse off than me, healthy kids too, you hear plenty awful things about healthy kids and how they're abused so how can I complain when I'm having all this fun and the Red Sox got a real good chance this year, go Sox.* On camera, his mother glows while his father lowers his head under the weight of ominous emotion. Jimmy sits stiffly in a wheelchair. His atrophied muscles give the impression of rock-hard strength, of a mini-body-builder physique. *Some people say is I got a tough break, but shoot, I say 1986, game six of the World*

Series, now that was a tough break. An impish smile. *Or bounce*. The end. And then *Heeeere's Jimmy*, from Ed McMahon, the cohost, who windmills his arm as Jimmy enters stage right, pushed by Mom with Dad trailing behind with all the enthusiasm of a hitched goat. The audience is on their feet. Jimmy is waving, raising his arms in triumph, which is unfortunate because his dystrophied shoulder blades jut like useless wings. *This, ladies and gentlemen, is a profile in courage,* Jerry thoughtfully pressing his fingers to his lips, *This is the reason I do this, we all do this, year after year until the year we can stay home and just remember the years before, when muscular dystrophy is in the retirement home of diseases playing a game of canasta with polio and smallpox.* Jerry reaches down, kisses Jimmy on both cheeks and has a private word he shares once Jimmy leaves the stage. *I told him, Hey kid, you're my Mickey Mantle who I knew very well.* Ed nods. *Great kid.*

$14,332,509.04.

Celebrities, the stars, from Adrian to Zmed, like Christopher Atkins, Red Buttons, Nell Carter, Tony Danza, Chad Everett, Fabio, Lou Gossett Jr., Buddy Hackett, Julio Iglesias, Arte Johnson, Casey and Jean Kasem, Rich Little, Chuck Mangione, Jim Nabors, Tony Orlando, Markie Post, Mickey Rooney, Kevin Sorbo, Rip Taylor, Leslie Uggams, Ben Vereen, Vanna White, Tina Yothers, Pia Zadora, sing and dance and tell jokes and get seen again, dressed in award show glamour. There's Charo. There's Yanni. There's Norm Crosby who Billy thought was dead. They enter waving, greeting long-lost fame, and they point toward Ed and Jerry and briefly banter and plead for money. *Just a dollar, if everybody gave a dollar, well, we'd have, a lot of dollars,* says Charlene Tilton, bouncing up and down, much to Jerry's *Yoweedoychoomoygaa* delight. They seem to inhale the camera, the lights, like oxygen is a part of these mechanics. Their moment in the sun, however long ago, last month or thirty years, still shines in their eyes when they perform, and though they can be easily ridiculed for being a desperate lot, a laugh riot of sentimental smarm who give their time because time is all they have, for those five minutes onstage they ride the memory of who they once were and hold on tight, faces squeezed, hands fisted, shoulders tensed, like they're never letting go. Billy takes these people, not seriously, no, but not without charity. Even after the applause and the embrace from Jerry, they linger onstage until a nod of *oh, yeah, right*, whereupon they depart, waving long past the curtain.

$20,455,323.23.

Night washes against the window and sweeps, Billy imagines, toward Los Angeles, a tidal wave curling over the Rockies and leveling the land with darkness. The only light in the room is from the TV which glistens with lesser acts—the Famous People Players, Partners-N-Rhyme, the All Night Strut, the High Skating Garcias, Jumpin' Jimes Band, K-9 in Flight, Rock Steady Crew Dancers, the Osmonds Second Generation, Those Darn Accordions—who treat the past-midnight time slots as their biggest opportunity yet. Billy assumes they must be dead by now— *Beep!*—his parents, a full day dead. Who knows if they've been discovered, or if they're still in the bedroom, in bed, nestled together and watching TV like this is their hereafter. "They're dead," Billy says, testing the sentence outloud. They seem to gain substance in death, no longer a collection of various frustrations but an irreducible corpse. "My parents? They've passed away." No more questions, no more ambiguity. He sees them in pajamas, propped up on pillows, holding hands in a world without commercial interruption, while Miss America 1999 sings "America, the Beautiful." Her reign is nearly over and she latches onto the final *sea* with full coloratura, reaching into the air with her left hand and closing her fingers as though gripping a rung and the floor is no longer there and she's hanging on, losing her strength, slipping from the note before finally letting go and bowing into oblivion. Dead, Billy thinks, and now he's a twenty-eight-year-old orphan. He does not begrudge them an afterlife together.

$38,678,932.64.

Breakfast on the tray table, sun in the window, Billy—*Beep!*—daydreams himself floating over Ragnar, Ragnar preparing for the barbecue, getting ice, arranging the booze, and pounding hamburger meat in his palm, or maybe letting his son-in-law do the work so he can sit outside and have a cocktail and take in the Ragnars around him, a small silly event— *Please, Labor Day!*—but his wife was right and how often is that the case, and he's glad he's here and not babysitting in Albany, glad he's noticing his puttering ex-waitress wife as she sashays the tray of plates and silverware, glad he's still married to her, nearing fifty years, glad he maintained this idea of himself as a dedicated, loyal, faithful husband even if he was rarely happy and silently toyed with leaving her for at least ten other woman, no longer bitter but glad, glad he stayed with her for his own sake, for this house, for these children here, all held together by his whim, glad, as the scene washes over his inscrutable face, grandchildren trumpeting blades of grass, the ocean sounding like distant Parkway traffic, glad because God knows how many more good years he has left and his marital poor investment is finally paying off, fifty years of nothing much so he can die feeling loved, Ragnar smiling, brushing sweat from his forehead, figuring he'll give his wife a nice anniversary present, with the millions he stands to collect from the Schine settlement—*Honey?* his wife asks, *You all right?*—and Ragnar nods and strokes her hand knowing the kids love this crap, and thinks, seeing her nasty neck, forty grand should do the trick, that'll buy a decent twenty-four-karat chain from Fortunoff.

$48,001,543.22.

And Billy dreams himself floating over Gretchen Warwick as she walks the streets of New York and flashes her one frame of loveliness per minute, arching her eyebrow as she scopes her reflection in passing dark glasses and pictures those retinas burning with her memory, of Gretchen naked, of Gretchen on all fours, whatever they might remember, Gretchen going down Broadway, Broadway and Chambers, under the old Sun Building where the clock has been broken on 10:17 forever, and Billy imagines himself showering down gold upon her, like Zeus with Danae, by far the strangest of mythological conceptions, the money shot of all money shots, Billy opening up his pockets and letting everything fall, his entire being ground down into dust, hoping her purse will be filled with the man she never kissed and she'll feel on her arm the true weight of worth.

$48,001,664.71.

And Ossap and Dullick handcuffed together and led away, Dullick lifting up his arms in camera-worthy protest, Ossap getting his gravity-straining wrist cut to ribbons, Dullick's arm bandaged because of a dog bite, Ossap's scalp shaved for thirty rhesus-stricken stitches.

$48,002,704.63.

And Chuck Savitch slowly dying, his condition unchanged except for the designation from the church that he is not, as once thought, a victim soul but a sympathetic sufferer, which is a rung lower on the saint ladder—no true miracles would spring from his fingers, only uncanny empathy—which causes the pilgrims to thin, much to the relief of his mother who bends lower and lower over his bed like an unwatered plant, his sister in the kitchen boiling a pot for tea.

$48,003,002.82.

And Honeysack and Marx, and Joy and Rufus, and Sally—Billy is in a reverie of morphine-induced epilogue, seeking meaning in all the people who brought him here, fresh from dead in Albany, like his father who stands in the doorway of his room, a treacly ghost who might be in the wrong place, staring at the room number and a piece of paper in his hand, his haunting unconfirmed by the sight of his tubed-up son. His father? Billy tilts his head toward the doorway. If this is a vision then the vision has aged. A bloodshot nimbus surrounds the man. His hair seems to have been combed by inconsolable tugging, and his clothes are formal yet dispossessed, as if he was forced to flee in the middle of the night and why not take his best suit. But undeniably it is his father in the flesh, if rice-paper thin.

"Abe?" Billy asks.

"So this is your room?"

"Yes."

"They sent me to the wrong room."

"Oh."

"They sent me to the wrong room, to a patient who had his eyes bandaged up, arms and legs tied down, and I thought, I mean, I knew that this wasn't you but I stood there for almost five minutes because it's been a while." Abe's voice is dry and uncomfortable, full of short breaths like his lungs can only respire so many words.

"Did he say anything?" Billy asks.

"Who?"

"That patient."

"No, he was sedated. The nurse talked to me like he was my son. She said he was still a danger to himself, that's what she said until I finally said this isn't my son and they sent me here."

"What time is it?" asks Billy.

"I don't know, a little after eleven."

Billy imagines Do, alone but for the visit of a mistaken father.

Abe stays in the doorway, still uncertain of entry, uncertain of any forward action, his arms wrapped around a manila envelope like a schoolboy fearing a bully. "They called me yesterday," he tells Billy. "They called me and told me you were in the hospital and I should come as soon as possible. They even flew me here on a private airplane and told me what happened."

"Who are they?" Billy asks.

"The people taking care of you."

"Please come in, Abe."

But Abe stays put. "You don't look so good."

"You look better than expected," Billy says, still dazed. "I thought you were dead, you and Mom, I thought Saturday was the day."

Abe's hands crinkle the manila envelope. "She died Thursday night. She stopped breathing in the middle of the night. Just stopped. There were no signs earlier in the day, no sudden turn for the worse, nothing like that. She was the same and then she was dead. And I was right there, right by her side, yes, I was, when she passed."

Thursday night, Billy thinks, his memory brushing aside the curtain and seeing the animals in the courtyard, somewhere in that time, in that evening, asleep or awake, holding Gretchen's hand, hearing the frightening *hush* in the hallway, slipping back into bed after the SHAME vans peeled away, too wired for sleep, head spinning thoughts as if they would crash to the floor if stopped, somewhere in that time his mother died and Billy was none the wiser. Yeats would have the right words, Billy thinks, looking at his father, newly sundered, yes Yeats who Billy mispronounced *Yeets* in high school, like some by-product of Keats, he'd be able to translate the pit in Billy's stomach into proper elegy. *On My Mother, Now Dead.* But death renders a corpse, not a metaphor. And *The Oxford Dictionary of Quotations* is nowhere to be found, stored away somewhere

366

with his personal effects, leaving Billy with his pitiful pit, with his unexpected father standing in the doorway as if an earthquake has struck. "I'm glad you were with her," Billy tries saying without hearing the words and judging them.

"It was the middle of the night but I was there. I was. I begged the nurses to do something, pound her chest, use those machines, but they said they had policies against resuscitation."

"She was sick for a long time," Billy tells him.

"I should've gone to a place where they resuscitated."

"Abe, please come in."

But Abe does not move.

"Maybe it was for the better," Billy says. "She died in her sleep, peacefully." An itch ripens on his scalp and Billy scratches, scratches hard, the scratching creating more itching. Dandruff snows down. His fingernails are crusty with the stuff. "I'm so sorry, Abe."

"We had plans."

"I know."

"I was getting things ready, very busy, all the last details. I didn't have much time to see her on Thursday. I was going to get her home Friday, so we could have a day together in the house."

"It's better this way," Billy says.

"It was going to be perfect. I should've been there but I wasn't. I wasn't with her when she died. I was so busy. I wasn't with her. I said good-bye and the next time I saw her she was at a funeral parlor. They took her away so quickly." Abe glances down as if gazing upon Doris on a refrigerated slab. "And when I saw her she looked fine, all right, considering. I had an outfit for her but I figured why bother, go ahead, cremate her. I didn't tear my shirt and cry over her body. I just looked down at her and felt, well, relieved. That's what I remember feeling. Relief. She's gone and I don't have to go through with the plan. Isn't that awful? That's what I thought. My first thought. Saturday wouldn't be such a headache because I never did hear back from you, and who knows how things would have worked out, if she survived and I died or the other way around, so thank God, I thought."

"It's been a long haul for you," Billy says. "Relief, you know, that's natural. She's finally at peace." The itch on the scalp seems to spread downward, not so much an itch, but something for his hands to do, his fingers insisting themselves on his skin. "Now come in, okay, don't stand out there anymore, just come in."

Abe finally shuffles forward. "I have something for you," he says, stopping in front of the bed. "Something I think is important." He hands over the manila envelope. A will, Billy thinks, her last will and testament done when she first learned she was sick. This is what his mother has left him. Billy feels the outside weight of what's inside. Yes, she always understood, he imagines, she just never had the words. Her eyes, when they glanced away, hinted that she knew and she was sorry but she had no choice but to choose his father over him. Yes, Billy thinks, the envelope has some heft. Maybe she's bequathed him everything, probably not much, but maybe it's more than he thought. Maybe she died so she might give Billy the gift of a father. *Take care of him*, the brass butterfly-clasp suggests.

"I signed it," Abe says.

"Signed what?"

"They told me on the airplane that it was very important that I sign because I was your only relative and you were unable to consent to treatment because of your condition and they needed consent to carry on." Abe seems pleased with his paternal duty.

"When was this?"

"This morning. They were so happy to have found me."

Billy opens the envelope. Inside is a thick and seemingly unbreakable personal damages settlement from HAM. The sum is a quarter million dollars, with the aggrieved party agreeing to a strict nondisclosure clause under penalty of a ten-million-dollar fine. *Abraham Schine* is scrawled throughout the document, directed by red SIGN HERE arrows sticking out of the pages like bloody shark fins.

"They want you to sign as well," Abe tells him.

"I bet." Fresh pain piques the duller ache in Billy's chest and he reaches for the morphine trigger but relents, giving the pain a fingerhold on his sternum. His father rocks slightly and rubs his hands for warmth. He could be the lone survivor in a cornfield, the airplane burning behind him, a man who's found himself alive by mistake. "Do you have a pen?" Billy asks. The slight vibrations in his throat are excruciating. Naked nerve endings beg for *Beep!*

Abe digs inside his jacket—"Uhm, yes"—and hands Billy a ballpoint courtesy of Hargrove Anderson Medical.

"Did you read this?" Billy asks, curious.

"I didn't have time but they gave me the gist, very nice people." Abe, listless, leans against Billy's bed. "Hey, Jerry Lewis," he says, noticing the television and the last minutes of the last hour of the last telethon of this century. Charo is gone. Rich Little is gone. Roy Clark is gone. They're all gone. No more researchers saying how close the cure is. No more executives presenting giant checks. Just Jerry. The camera tightens on his face as he treats his microphone like a flute of overindulged champagne. *Sixty years in this business. Crazy. Little Joseph Levitch from Newark, New Jersey, the trick-monkey Jew who could do impressions.* Above him hangs his official caricature in an almost regal escutcheon: young Jerry bucktoothed and in mid-guffaw. Abe points toward the screen. "In his prime, with Dean Martin, that man pulled in ten grand a weekend and that was 1950s dollars."

Billy nods. Bending his legs, he creates a painful desk with his knees. He starts tackling the signatures, peeling away the *SIGN HERE*'s and sticking them to his thigh. His chest feels stamped upon by small feet, feet playing a children's game, up and down and around and around.

Jerry speaks with a Hollywood lockjaw, an earnest accent of love from the heyday of fabulous. *Good times and bad times, heart attacks and pill addictions, breakdowns and breakups, being number one in the box office to being who the hell is he, but I always had this, this telethon, these kids.* His lips kiss every emotion, his tongue a pink exclamation mark. *All of this.* He queers the air with his hands. *All of you.* He's almost beyond irony, too slippery for sarcasm, so phony he verges on being real. *All of me.* He points into the camera, his fingers splayed flamboyantly, body tired, swaying, chin angled upward, as though bobbing for last breathes. *Just you and me.*

369

The afternoon sun has found the window. The temperature in the room elevates by just enough to raise perspiration on Billy's skin which, thanks to the air-conditioning, brings about a chill. It's an environmental fever. Abe edges up on the bed so he can sit. Billy notices he has a slight hump, and the skin between collar and hair is flaky and red. Billy sticks a SIGN HERE arrow on the back of his father's jacket, an imperative as a small wound.

Jerry presses his fist against his mouth as if suffering from emotional gas. The band is thanked, *best musicians in the world*, the wonderful crew, the cameramen, the cue card boy, the gal who does that thing with the clipboard, and finally his show friends. *Let me tell you about show people. I come from show people, show parents, so I know show people and I know one thing: show people have big hearts. God has blessed show people with talent and energy because show people have such big hearts. Show people care. All these show people, all these great show people here on this show, I called them up and told them about the kids who need their help, about the money needed for research, about how close we are to beating this bastard once and for all, and do you know what every single show person said? When and where? Because that's what show people are all about. Love. Yeah, love. I'll say it.* Jerry taps his hand against his chest, then he laughs, laughs his famous gawky laugh, but he cuts himself short, as if he hears another noise, a more desperate noise, a rattle in his lungs. His once rubbery flesh searches for a different expression.

"He's a born entertainer," Abe says, his back gaining two more SIGN HERE's.

Billy is almost done with the document. His fingers cramp with autograph, sick of putting his signature down. It's starting to resemble a seismograph of something ridiculous; though hundreds of miles away, on the Jersey shore, Ragnar will feel its repercussions. Billy imagines the ice in Ragnar's gin clinking, mistaken for senior tremors and not the rift of pen on paper.

Abe shakes his head. "Younger people don't understand how great he was," he says. "They should give him the benefit of his youth." From his suit pocket, Abe pulls out a Rubik's cube and begins turning the colors, never once checking his progress.

"Is that Mom's?" Billy asks.

"Last few years she no longer cared but I kept it by her bedside just in case."

Billy thinks about asking his father for the old puzzler. Maybe he could give the cube a try and see if he still recognized the pattern and find the solution, see if his hands and brain remember what was once rote. But Abe has a hard grip and what's the point anyway.

The older unwell Jerry dead-reckons on a spot four feet below the camera. *You know what's been my salvation? These kids. These brave kids, they've saved my life. They've shown me more than fame. These kids. All the kids I've known who are buried could probably fill the Hollywood Bowl for three nights.* Though each gesture seems rehearsed, each line scripted, each pause milked, there's something in those uncorked eyes, as if Joseph Levitch is impersonating Jerry Lewis, as if little Joey Levitch, the son of show people, has slipped backstage, lonely and hungry for attention, and peeked onto Mom and Dad onstage. Jerry lowers his head, raises his hand, his index finger, and the band begins to play.

Abe scoots into a more comfortable position. *"Carousel,"* he says rather cryptically, like a minor god's annunciation.

"What?" Billy asks.

"This song, it's from *Carousel*. Rodgers and Hammerstein. 'You'll Never Walk Alone,' it's called."

"Oh, right."

"A wonderful musical. But sad."

Jerry's thin voice cracks—*When you walk through a storm*—trembles—*Hold your head up high*—carries the notes like water in his palms—*And don't be afraid of the dark*. As he sings, the screen dissolves into headshots of boys, a montage of them, with names and dates that end in 1998 or 99: Charlie Sedgwick, 1979–1999, Fred Hanrahan, 1981–1999, Miguel Pettera, 1983–1998. They're the between-telethon dead, tossed in the ditch of a year.

Billy signs his last signature. The document is done.

Abe sag-sag-sags, his head waiting for a soft landing and finding none, snapping back.

"I'm so tired," he says. "I don't think I've slept in weeks."

"Want some water?"

"Please."

With great effort and pain, Billy pours a glass from the pitcher on the tray table.

"Talk about energy," Abe says of Jerry who finds strength in the buildup of tempo. The born entertainer wraps himself around the music and phrases the lyrics with ligament-straining gusto—*And the sweet silver song of the lark*—Jerry—*Walk on through the wind*—practically keening through clenched caps—*Walk on through the rain*—while Abe downs his water. "Could you turn the volume up?"

Billy scoots the portable speaker nearer to his father.

Abe slips off his shoes, releasing an odor of mismatched socks.

Though your dreams be tossed and blown.

Larger feet seem to stamp on Billy's chest, up and down and around and around.

Walk on, walk on.

The intercom above the bed crackles with need.

With hope in your heart.

"Are you hungry?" Billy asks Abe.

"Famished."

Billy reaches for his lunch tray, a full course of easily digestible food. Its slight heft is killing, but Abe accepts it with enthusiasm and tears away the wrapping like a lion ripping through a clear layer of skin. He eats with just about as much delicacy, all the while keeping his attention on the TV.

Jerry is barely holding up—*And you'll never walk alone*—struggling toward the last lyric—*You'll*—girding his entire being—*ne*—for the final—*ver*—push—*walk*—over the top—*ahh*—deep emotional inhale—*loooohhhhh*—as the end note—*ooohhhh*—the final note is extended long past its due—*oooohhh*—Jerry palsied—*oohh*—Jerry melting—*oh*—Jerry near collapse—*nnnnnn*—pointing toward the rig of lights that represents the sky and the heavens above filled with his kids—*naa*—who have marched valiantly with him. Billy leans back onto pillows and tries relaxing his grip on pain. Medical machinery surrounds him, his heart

372

expressed by way of a cuff on his index finger, the beats a mountainscape ever repeating, the nurses in their station conscious of its trace. There seems to be no cause for worry.

Balloons and confetti drift down on Jerry as he keels inside of Ed McMahon's embrace, like a clapper to a bell. The closing tally on the tote is $51,326,832.86. A new record. Jerry wipes his eye with a raised pinky, as if he weeps tea.

The sun through the window illuminates the dust floating in the air, like plankton, Billy thinks, liking the image. The IV drips without sound. The catheter siphons urine into the bag clipped low on the bed. This is me, Billy thinks.

He watches Abe watch Jerry sob. His father is not what this has been all about. No, this has had nothing to do with him. But here he is, a foot away.

Abe sneezes. Snot entangles his fingers.

"You need a tissue?" Billy asks.

"Please."

Billy rips a few tissues from the box on his bedside table.

"I've had a cold forever," Abe says.

Turning once more toward the TV, toward Jerry and his last gasp, Abe gives Billy his back. There are no great pronouncements in that back, only a split seam along the jacket's shoulder and a history of sweat marks under the arms and a cluster of *SIGN HERE* arrows as if ambushed by Apache lawyers. The posture is without incident. The once-tailored suit has become a size too big for these bones. The gray wool must be unbearable in this weather. Around the vicinity of the lungs the fabric seems lighter, as if clothes can wear down from the inside, breath fading like the sun, every fist-shaped heartbeat scraping its knuckles against a bit of surface. Abe moans a small yawn. He's here, Billy thinks, and I'm alive, and maybe that's more than nothing.

"Is the food any good?" Billy asks.

"I'm too hungry to know," Abe answers.

"I know what you mean," Billy says, absorbed with what's in front of him while Jerry blows kisses and shouts rather hopefully, *See you next year.*

ACKNOWLEDGMENTS

Marisa Pagano, Maureen Klier, Ethan Dunn, Greg Villepique, and Sara Mercurio at Bloomsbury. Jessica Craig and Arlo Crawford at Burnes and Clegg. Colin Harrison and Nan Graham at Scribner. Harry Groome and the kind folks at SmithKline Beecham (pre-Glaxo); in particular, the helpful staff at their Philadelphia CPU. Dr. Ed Rabiner. Max and Eliza Gilbert. Parker and Gail Gilbert. Amor Towles. And finally the three people who sat in vigil around this novel these last six years, none of them ever doubting the coma would eventually break: Walter Donahue, Gillian Blake, and Bill Clegg. I survived on your patience and support, on your shouts of Don't go into the light. Thank you, especially Bill.

And, of course, Susie.

A NOTE ON THE AUTHOR

David Gilbert is the author of the short-story
collection *Remote Feed*. His stories have appeared in
the *New Yorker*, *Harper's*, *GQ*, and *Bomb*. He lives
in New York City with his wife and two children.

A NOTE ON THE TYPE

Linotype Garamond Three is based on seventeenth-
century copies of Claude Garamond's types cut by
Jean Jannon. This version was designed for American
Type Founders in 1917 by Morris Fuller Benton
and Thomas Maitland Cleland, and adapted for
mechanical composition by Linotype in 1936.